A
SORCERESS
COMES
TO
CALL

A
SORCERESS
COMES
TO
CALL

T. KINGFISHER

TOR

TOR PUBLISHING GROUP
NEW YORK

A SORCERESS COMES TO CALL

Endpaper art by Ursula Vernon

A Tor Book
Published by Tom Doherty Associates / Tor Publishing Group
120 Broadway
New York, NY 10271

www.torpublishinggroup.com

Tor® is a registered trademark of Macmillan Publishing Group, LLC.

The Library of Congress Cataloging-in-Publication Data is available upon request.

ISBN 978-1-250-24407-9 (hardcover)
ISBN 978-1-250-24405-5 (ebook)

Our books may be purchased in bulk for promotional, educational, or business use. Please contact your local bookseller or the Macmillan Corporate and Premium Sales Department at 1-800-221-7945, extension 5442, or by email at MacmillanSpecialMarkets@macmillan.com.

First Edition: 2024

Printed in the United States of America

0 9 8 7 6 5 4 3 2 1

To Deb

A
SORCERESS
COMES
TO
CALL

CHAPTER 1

There was a fly walking on Cordelia's hand and she was not allowed to flick it away.

She had grown used to the ache of sitting on a hard wooden pew and being unable to shift her weight. It still hurt, but eventually her legs went to sleep and the ache became a dull, all-over redness that was easier to ignore.

Though her senses were dulled in obedience, her sense of touch stayed the strongest. Even when she was so far under that the world had a gray film around the edges, she could still feel her clothing and the touch of her mother's hand. And now the fly's feet itched, which was bad, then tickled, which was worse.

At the front of the church, the preacher was droning on. Cordelia had long since lost the thread. Lust and tithing were his two favorite topics. Probably it was one of those. Her mother took her to church every Sunday and Cordelia was fairly certain that he had been preaching the same half-dozen sermons for the past year.

Her eyes were the only muscles that she could control, so she was not looking at him, but down as far as she could. At the very bottom of her vision, she could see her hands folded in her lap and the fly picking its way delicately across her knuckles.

Her mother glanced at her and must have noticed that she was looking down. Cordelia's chin rose so that she could no longer see her hands. She was forced to study the back of the head of the man in front of her. His hair was thinning toward the back and was compressed down at the sides, as if he wore a hat most days. She did not recognize him, but that was no surprise. Since her days at school had ended, Cordelia only saw the other townsfolk when she went to church.

Cordelia lost the tickling sensation for a moment and dared to hope that the fly was gone, but then the delicate web between her thumb and forefinger began to itch.

Her eyes began to water at the sensation and she blinked them furiously. Crying was not acceptable. That had been one of the first lessons of being made obedient. It would definitely not be acceptable in church, where other people would notice. Cordelia was fourteen and too old to cry for seemingly no reason—because of course she could not tell anyone the reason.

The fly crossed over to her other hand, each foot landing like an infinitesimal pinprick. The stinging, watering sensation in her eyes started to feel like a sneeze coming on.

Sneezing would be terrible. She could not lift her hands or turn her head, so it would hit the back of the man's head, and he would turn around in astonishment and her mother would move her mouth to apologize and everyone would be staring at her for having been so ill-mannered.

Her mother would not be happy. Cordelia would have given a year of her life to be able to wipe her eyes. She sniffed miserably, her lungs filling with the smell of candles and wood polish and other people's bodies. Under it all lay the dry, sharp smell of wormwood.

And then, blessedly, the preacher finished. Everyone said, "Amen," and the congregation rose. No one noticed that Cordelia moved in unison with her mother.

No one ever did.

"I suppose you're mad at me," said her mother as they walked home from church. "I'm sorry. But you might try harder not to be so rebellious! I shouldn't have to keep doing this to you, not when you're fourteen years old!"

Cordelia said nothing. Her tongue did not belong to her. The person that smiled and answered all the greetings after the sermon—"Why Evangeline, don't you look lovely today? And Cordelia! You keep growing like a weed!"—had not been Cordelia at all.

They reached home at last. *Home* was a narrow white house with peeling paint, set just off the road. Evangeline pushed the front door open, walked Cordelia to the couch, and made her sit.

Cordelia felt the obedience let go, all at once. She did not scream.

When Cordelia was young, she had screamed when she came out of obedience, but this gave her mother a reason to hold her and make soothing noises, so she had learned to stay silent as she swam up into consciousness, out of the waking dream.

The memories of what she had done when she was obedient would still be there, though. They lay in the bottom of her skull like stones.

It was never anything that looked terrible from outside. She could not have explained it to anyone without sounding ridiculous. "She makes me eat. She makes me drink. She makes me go to the bathroom and get undressed and go to bed."

And they would have looked at her and said "So?" and Cordelia would not have been able to explain what it was like, half-sunk in stupor, with her body moving around her.

Being made obedient felt like being a corpse. "My body's dead and it doesn't do what I want," Cordelia had whispered once, to her only friend, their horse Falada. "It only does what *she* wants. But I'm still in it."

When she was younger, Cordelia would wet herself frequently when she was obedient. Her mother mostly remembered to have Cordelia relieve herself at regular intervals now, but Cordelia had never forgotten the sensation.

She was made obedient less often as she grew older. She thought perhaps that it was more difficult for her mother to do than it had been when she was small—or perhaps it was only that she had learned to avoid the things that made her mother angry. But this time, Cordelia hadn't avoided it.

As the obedience let go, Cordelia swam up out of the twilight, feeling her senses slot themselves back into place.

Her mother patted her shoulder. "There you are. Now, isn't that better?"

Cordelia nodded, not looking at her.

"I'm sure you'll do better next time."

"Yes," said Cordelia, who could not remember what it was that she had been made obedient for. "I will."

When her legs felt steady enough, she went up the stairs to her bedroom and lay on the bed. She did not close the door.

There were no closed doors in the house she grew up in.

Sometimes, when her mother was gone on an errand, Cordelia would close the door to her bedroom and lean against it, pressing herself flat against the wooden surface, feeling it solid and smooth under her cheek.

The knowledge that she was alone and no one could see her—that she could do anything, say anything, think anything and no one would be the wiser—made her feel fierce and wicked and brave.

She always opened the door again after a minute. Her mother would come home soon and the sight of a closed door would draw her like a lodestone. And then there would be the talk.

If Cordelia's mother was in a good mood, it would be "Silly! You don't have any secrets from me, I'm your mother!"

If she was in a bad mood, it would be the same talk but from the other direction, like a tarot card reversed—"What are you trying to hide?"

Whichever card it was, it always ended the same way: "We don't close doors in *this* house."

When Cordelia was thirteen and had been half-mad with things happening under her skin, she shot back "Then why are there doors in the house at all?"

Her mother had paused, just for an instant. Her long-jawed face had gone blank and she had looked at Cordelia—really *looked*, as if she was actually seeing her—and Cordelia knew that she had crossed a line and would pay for it.

"They came with the house," said her mother. "Silly!" She nodded once or twice, to herself, and then walked away.

Cordelia couldn't remember now how long she had been made obedient as punishment. Two or three days, at least.

Because there were no closed doors, Cordelia had learned to have no secrets that could be found. She did not write her thoughts in her daybook.

She kept a daybook because her mother believed that it was something young girls should do, but the things she wrote were exactly correct and completely meaningless. *I spilled something on my yellow dress today. I have been out riding Falada. The daffodils bloomed today. It is my birthday today.*

She gazed at the pages sometimes, and thought what it would be like to write *I hate my mother* in a fierce scrawl across the pages.

She did not do it. Closing the door when she was home alone was as much rebellion as she dared. If she had written something so terrible, she would have been made obedient for weeks, perhaps a month. She did not think she could stand it for so long.

I'd go mad. Really truly mad. But she wouldn't notice until she let me come back, and I'd have been mad inside for weeks and weeks by then.

Since her mother was home today and unlikely to leave again, Cordelia took a deep breath and sat up, scrubbing at her face. There was no point in dwelling on things she would never do. She changed out of her good dress and went out to the stable behind the house, where Falada was waiting. The stable was old and gloomy, but Falada glowed like moonlight in the darkness of his stall.

When Falada ran, and Cordelia clung to his back, she was safe. It was the only time that she was not thinking, not carefully cropping each thought to be pleasant and polite and unexceptional. There was only sky and hoofbeats and fast-moving earth.

After a mile or so, the horse slowed to a stop, almost as if he sensed what Cordelia needed. She slipped off his back and leaned against him. Falada was quiet, but he was solid and she told him her thoughts, as she always did.

"Sometimes I dream about running," she whispered. "You and me. Until we reach the sea."

She did not know what she would do once they reached the sea. Swim it, perhaps. There was another country over there, the old homeland that adults referred to so casually.

"I know I'm being ridiculous," she told him. "Horses can't swim that far. Not even you."

She had learned not to cry long ago, but she pressed her face to his warm shoulder, and the wash of his mane across her skin felt like tears.

Cordelia was desperately thankful for Falada, and that her mother encouraged her to ride, although of course Evangeline's motives were different from Cordelia's. "You won't get into any trouble with him," her mother would say. "And besides, it's good for a girl to know how to ride. You'll marry a wealthy man some-day, and they like girls who know their way around a horse, not these little town girls that can only ride in a carriage!" Cordelia had nodded. She did not doubt that she would marry a wealthy man one day. Her mother had always stated it as fact.

And, it was true that the girls Cordelia saw when riding seemed to envy her for having Falada to ride. He was the color of snow, with a proud neck. She met them sometimes in the road. The cruel ones made barbed comments about her clothes to hide their envy, and the kind ones gazed at Falada wistfully. That was how Cordelia met Ellen.

"He's very beautiful," Ellen had said one day. "I've never seen a horse like him."

"Thank you," said Cordelia. She still went to school then, and talking to other people had not seemed quite so difficult. "He is a good horse."

"I live just over the hill," the other girl had said shyly. "You could visit sometime, if you like."

"I would like that," Cordelia had replied carefully. And that was true. She would have liked that.

But Cordelia did not go, because her mother would not have liked that. She did not ask. It was hard to tell, sometimes, what would make her mother angry, and it was not worth the risk. Still, for the last three years she had encountered the kind girl regularly. Ellen was the daughter of a wealthy landowner that lived nearby. She rode her pony, Penny, every day, and when she and Cordelia met, they rode together down the road, the pony taking two steps for every one of Falada's.

So it was unsurprising when Cordelia heard the familiar hoof-beats of Ellen's pony approaching. She lifted her head from Falada's neck and looked up as Ellen waved a hello. Cordelia waved back and remounted. Penny shied at their approach, but Ellen reined her in.

Cordelia had never ridden any horse but Falada, so it was from Ellen—and from watching Ellen's pony—that she learned that most horses were not so calm as Falada, nor so safe. When she was very young and the open doors in their house became too much, when she couldn't stand being in that house for one more second, she would creep to Falada's stall and sleep curled up there, with his four white legs like pillars around her. Apparently most people did not do this, for fear the horse would step on them. Cordelia had not known to be afraid of such a thing.

"Oh, Penny! What's gotten into you? It's just Falada." Ellen rolled her eyes at Cordelia, as if they shared a joke, which was one of the reasons that Cordelia liked her.

"Penny's a good pony," Cordelia said. She liked it when Ellen complimented Falada, so perhaps Ellen would like it when she complimented Penny. Cordelia talked to other people so rarely now that she always had to feel her way through these conversations, and she was not always good at them.

"She *is*," said Ellen happily. "She's not brave, but she's sweet."

Ellen carried the conversation mostly by herself, talking freely about her home, her family, the servants, and the other people in town. There was no malice in it, so far as Cordelia could tell. She let it wash over her, and pretended that she had a right to listen and nod as if she knew what was going on.

Cordelia was not sure why Ellen rode out to meet her so often, when she could say so little, but she was glad for the company. Ellen was kind, but more than that, she was ordinary. Talking to her gave Cordelia a window into what was normal and what wasn't. She could ask a question and Ellen would answer it without asking any awkward questions of her own. Most of the time, anyway.

It had occurred to her, some years prior, that not all parents could make their children obedient the same way that her mother made her, but when she tried to ask Ellen about it, to see if she was right, the words came out so wrong and so distressing that she stopped.

Something about today—the memory of the obedience or the fly or maybe just the way the light fell across the leaves and Falada's mane—made her want to ask again.

"Ellen?" she asked abruptly. "Do you close the door to your room?"

Ellen had been patiently holding up both ends of the conversation and looked up, puzzled. "Eh? Yes? I mean, the servants go in and out of my dressing room, but I always lock the door to the water closet when I'm in it, because you don't want servants around for that, do you?"

Cordelia stared at her hands on the reins. They were not wealthy enough to have servants, and there was an outhouse beside the stable, not a water closet. She pressed on.

"Does your family think you're keeping secrets when you do?"

The silence went on long enough that Cordelia looked up, and realized that Ellen was giving her a very penetrating look. She had a pink, pleasant face and a kind manner, and it was unsettling to suddenly remember that *kind* did not mean *stupid* and Ellen had been talking to her for a long time.

"Oh, Cordelia . . ." said Ellen finally.

She reached out to touch Cordelia's arm, but Falada sidled at that moment, and Penny took a step to give him room, so they did not touch after all.

"Sorry," said Cordelia gruffly. She wanted to say *Please don't think I'm strange, that was a strange question, I can tell, please don't stop talking to me,* but she knew that would make it all even worse, so she didn't.

"It's all right," said Ellen. And then "It will be all right," which Cordelia knew wasn't the same thing at all.

CHAPTER 2

A week later, Cordelia's mother went into her large wardrobe and took out one of the dresses in rich, stunning fabrics, nothing at all like the faded gowns that Cordelia normally wore. Evangeline took a scarlet riding habit from among the dresses and it was as if she became another person as soon as the fabric touched her skin, a softer, sweeter one.

"Dear child," she said caressingly, stroking her hand over Cordelia's hair. "I'm off to see my benefactor."

Once or twice a month, she would mount Falada and ride away and be gone overnight, and return with money, or with jewelry that could be sold in the city for money, to pay for bacon and flour and the services of the laundress in the town.

Cordelia knew full well that her mother was visiting a man, and that such things were not considered respectable. But this was how they survived and lived so comfortably. And besides, it was so much easier to be in the house when her mother was gone, as if she could finally draw a breath all the way down to the bottom of her lungs.

She watched from the window as her mother rode away, the scarlet fabric lying across Falada's hide like a splash of blood on snow. Cordelia thought, as she sometimes did, about simply walking away, down the road. She wondered how far she could get, and if her mother would find her again. *Not without Falada, though. I can't just leave him here.*

Instead, she sat in the kitchen and peeled potatoes. There was something very centering about peeling potatoes. She looked forward to having the whole evening to sit and think whatever she wanted and not be interrogated about what she was thinking or why she had any particular expression on her face.

Which was why it was such a shock when, barely an hour after she'd left, Cordelia's mother slammed through the door, breathing hard, with her eyes like shards of broken ice.

Cordelia was so startled that the knife slipped and she gashed her thumb. She shoved it into her mouth, tasting copper and salt on her tongue.

The smell of wormwood swirled around her mother as she stalked into the kitchen. "Can you *believe* this?" she snarled.

Cordelia shook her head hurriedly, even though she had no idea what had happened. It was probably just as well that she had her thumb in her mouth, because otherwise she would have said something, and she was fairly certain that whatever she said would be wrong. As it was, her mother lifted her eyes and said, "Why are you sucking your thumb? You're too old for that."

"I cut it," said Cordelia, hastily yanking it out of her mouth and hiding it in her apron.

"Hmmph." Her mother stared at her broodingly for a moment, then looked away. Almost to herself, she said, "I should have killed him right then."

Cordelia froze. She'd never heard her mother say anything like that before.

"I could have. I could have made him obedient and had him chop his own legs off with an axe. But that woman was there and there were servants and they'd have noticed." Cordelia gulped. "Bah." Her mother stalked toward the stairs, still muttering to herself. "I *should* have made Falada kick the bastard's head in . . . no, they'd want him destroyed, and what a mess *that* would be . . ."

The image of Falada's white legs coated in gore turned Cordelia's stomach. She knew that she should feel much more strongly about the man who would have been killed, but he was a stranger and Falada was her friend. *And if Mother made him kill someone . . . if she made him obedient like she makes me . . . then he'd be a dangerous horse and people would demand he be put down.*

She slipped out to the stable, feeling ill. Falada stood in the dim stall, shining like a beacon in the dark.

"I didn't know she made you obedient too," Cordelia whispered. "I'm sorry. I should have thought."

He swung his head toward her and she wrapped her arms awkwardly around his neck, the way that she had ever since she was a child. "I'm sorry. I didn't know, and you couldn't tell me." She felt very small and selfish.

"I won't let her hurt you," she whispered, even though she knew that she had no power to stop it, and Falada pressed his nose against her shoulder and let out a long sigh.

At dinner that night, her mother was in a strangely merry mood. The best meat was waiting on the counter when Cordelia went down to cook, and her mother even offered to help.

Her mother's good moods had once been more difficult to live with than the bad ones. Cordelia had dared to hope that things would change, that all would be better, that there would be no more obedience, and the weight of her hope had crushed her beneath it. Now she no longer had such illusions. But the respite was welcome, however brief, and perhaps it meant that her earlier mood, and desire for violence, had passed.

As they sat down to dinner, her mother sighed. "There's no hope for it. He'll be useless now."

Cordelia often thought that when her mother talked to her like this, she was really talking to herself. Her job was only to nod at the appropriate places.

"Since I won't be *wasting* my time with my benefactor anymore, and there aren't many rich men here, we'll have to move soon."

"That'll be interesting," said Cordelia, which was a statement almost as neutral as silence.

When she turned back to the table, her mother was looking at her. Staring at her, not merely letting her eyes pass over her, the way she sometimes did. Cordelia felt herself growing still, as if her mother's gaze was a wasp that had landed on her skin and any motion might incite a sting.

"How old are you now?" her mother asked abruptly.

"Fourteen and a half."

"Fourteen and a half . . ." Her mother drummed long fingers on the table. "I had hoped to wait until you were a little older. Men don't like women to come to a marriage with a half-grown brat in tow. Still, it can't be helped. I'm not getting any younger, as my benefactor *so* kindly pointed out."

Cordelia knew better than to agree with a statement like that, and said nothing.

"I can probably still pull in a merchant, though. Not one of the great houses—they all want young blood. But one with money enough to keep us in comfort until you marry a rich man of your own one day . . ." She shook her head. "It's so frustrating, the money one needs to kit oneself out, to get into the right circles."

"Surely rich men would love to marry you, though," said Cordelia. It was a compliment, not a question, and that should be safe, and might prompt more information.

"Oh, certainly they would *want* to," her mother said carelessly. "But their families wouldn't stand for it. Selfish beasts. If I could use magic as I wished, I could have any man in the country. But wedding ceremonies break spells."

"I didn't know that."

"Oh yes." Her mother pursed her lips, clearly annoyed. "Water, salt, and wine, on holy ground. It is *most* inconvenient for sorcerers. That's why I never wasted my time trying to ensorcell a suitably rich husband."

Sorcerer.

Cordelia sat very still, the thought hanging inside her head like a bedsheet on a line. *My mother is a sorcerer.*

She had known that her mother was different from others, that she was capable of things that others were not, but the word *sorcery* had not crossed her mind. The sorcerers she learned about in school were considered low, feeble creatures, charlatans who worked in magical deceptions, and that did not seem to describe her mother at all. A sorcerer might try to pass dried leaves off as coins, say, or make a cow's milk go sour. There were no stories about them making someone obedient.

"It's much easier to get a benefactor," her mother was saying. "But of course if the spell goes awry, or the fool goes off to a wedding, well. They leave you much easier than husbands. Men are faithless." She tapped her finger against her lips. "Perhaps I should marry a country squire with a title and a bit of money . . . yes, I think that might be for the best. Enough money to put you out on the marriage mart as well, like we always planned. And you are seventeen and will soon be married and out of the house. Remember that."

"Yes, Mother," Cordelia said, bowing her head. She wondered if she dared ask Ellen about sorcerers, or if her mother would somehow know, and how terrible the punishment would be if she found out. She went upstairs to bandage her cut, but her mind was full of dead men and gore-caked hooves and she could not close the door against it.

CHAPTER 3

Hester came awake in the night because something had ended.

At first her sleep-fogged brain thought that it might have been a sound. Had there been rain? Had she woken because the drumming on the roof had stopped? *No, there wasn't any rain last night, was there? It was clear as a bell and chilly from it.*

She lay blinking up at the ceiling, the posts of the bed framing her vision like trees. What had stopped?

Fear took her suddenly by the throat, a formless dread with no name, no shape, only a sense that something was wrong, something terrible was coming this way. Hester gasped, reaching for her neck as if to pull off a murderer's hands, but there was only the darkness there.

She was in her own room, in her own bed, in her brother's house that had been her father's house and her grandfather's before him. She knew exactly where she was. If it had been a nightmare, she could have shaken it off, but she was firmly awake now, and the dread was not receding.

Something was coming. It would be here before long. Not tonight, perhaps not even tomorrow, but soon.

Ah, she thought, remaining calm even in her head. *It was my safety that ended. Yes, of course.*

Hester had felt such a nameless fear once before in her life, when she looked into the eyes of a young man that her parents had picked out for her. She had gathered her courage and cried off the wedding. It had cost her dearly but she stood her ground in the face of all opposition. Her parents had raised her to be good and biddable and not cause a fuss and it had shocked both them and Hester herself to learn how much stubbornness she had saved up over the course of those years.

Years later, when the young man's proclivities came to light, she was held to have had a lucky escape. By then, of course, it was much too late. She had been branded a jilt and she was not beautiful enough to tempt any other suitors, nor was there enough money in the family coffers to tempt their pocketbooks. She had been considered firmly "on the shelf" by the time that word came down of what he had done, and the hanging that had followed.

Her father had apologized. Her mother hadn't, but Hester had no longer expected such things.

This had the same taste, the same sense that doom followed and she had only a little time to avert it.

"All right," she rasped aloud. "All right. I hear you. I'm listening."

Acknowledgment seemed to be all that it wanted. The dread released her and Hester gasped in air, feeling sweat oozing from her skin and soaking into the sheets.

She wished suddenly, powerfully, that Richard were there in the bed beside her. They had been lovers a decade earlier, and then he had offered her marriage and she had turned him down, not willing to have him sacrifice his prospects out of pity. He was Lord Evermore to most, with an immense estate and money enough to set half the matchmakers in the city baying at his heels. He needed an heir and a spare and a woman young enough to give him both.

Hester did not exactly regret that choice, but it would be so much easier now to roll over and shake him awake and tell him that she'd had a nightmare. His arms would close around her, and she would lean her forehead against his shoulder and breathe easier. It would have been good to have.

But I don't have it. And whatever is coming, it seems that I will have to deal with it myself.

Hester sighed. She was fifty-one years old now, and her back ached and her knees ached and when the barometer plunged, she found it easier to use a cane. She did not want to be standing in the path of the storm.

And if wishes were horses, then beggars would ride, she thought, and rolled over, and tried to get a little more sleep before something terrible arrived.

In the morning, Cordelia saddled Falada and rode him out of the stable. She took nothing with her, because she had not dared to plan anything in advance. She did not even dare to think about rebellion. She simply rode away, in the opposite direction from her rides with Ellen, staring at the road between Falada's ears.

They went for perhaps three miles, as far as they had ever gone from home, and then Falada stopped.

Cordelia squeezed with her knees, and clucked her tongue. He did not move.

She got off his back and tried to lead him. "It's all right," she said. "Come on." Her voice was shaking for reasons that she didn't dare think about. "Come on, Falada, good horse."

He did not move. She tugged on his halter and he set his feet in the road and did not move.

"It's all right," she told him. "We're going away. You and me. So she won't make you do anything that will get you killed."

He might as well have been carved of quartz.

"We can't stay. She'll make you obedient again, and I can't stop her."

Falada did not stir a hoof.

"We'll go another way," she said, and tried to lead him off the road.

Again, he did not move. Not forward. Not back.

She tried to push him, with her merely human strength. He did not yield.

She actually thought about getting a stick and hitting him,

but no. Not Falada. He was her friend, and you did not do that, not to animals, not ever. Some people used a riding crop, to be sure, but Cordelia would have cut her arm off before she put a mark on that shining hide. *But I have to save him. I have to do something.*

A lump was rising in her throat, and then her mother caught her shoulder and said, "What's going on here?"

Cordelia whirled around, shocked. It took her a moment to say, "Mother? What are you doing here?"

"A very good question," said her mother. "Where were you going?"

"I wasn't—I wasn't going anywhere. I wanted to see what was down this road—I've never gone—but Falada wouldn't move—"

There was no way that her mother could be there by accident. She was miles from home. Her mother was on foot.

"Of course he wouldn't," said her mother, sounding amused. "He knew something was wrong."

She stepped to Falada's head and scratched under his chin with her nails.

Falada stretched out his neck and blinked his eyes and made a soft *hwuff* of pleasure.

"Were you trying to run away?" Evangeline asked.

"No!" said Cordelia. She hoped it sounded like shock. "No! If I was running away, I'd—well, I'd have taken food, wouldn't I? Or water or clothes or something. And I wouldn't! I mean, I love you. I'd never run away."

Her mother laughed. Cordelia dared to hope that her answer had been good enough. *Please, please, let her believe me . . .*

She could not imagine the punishment for trying to run away.

"I know that's not true," said her mother. "He tells me everything, you know. He is my familiar, after all."

It meant nothing. It was monstrous to the point of being meaningless. She did not know what a familiar was, but she knew that Falada could not possibly talk to her mother. She had whispered every secret and every fear into his mane and that would mean that her mother knew them all.

It could not be true, because the world could not be like that.

And then her mother stroked Falada's nose, and he turned a sly eye toward Cordelia and snorted, and Cordelia realized that she was hearing the sound of a horse's mocking laughter.

He thinks that's funny.

He's been telling her everything all along, and he thinks it's funny.

The image came to her of Falada and her mother laughing at her together, and Cordelia thought that she might faint.

"Oh, don't look so stricken," said her mother briskly. "I'm your mother. Do you think I don't know all your little secrets already?" She rolled her eyes and mounted Falada's back, then reached down a hand to Cordelia.

Cordelia took it. She could not seem to breathe. The touch of calico under her arms, when she held her mother's waist, was like sandpaper, and the sharp, woody scent of wormwood closed around her like iron bands.

"So you thought you were saving him, did you?" Her mother shook her head. "Silly child."

"I . . . I . . ." Cordelia could not muster a single defense. Her mind was completely blank.

"I made you," her mother said, looking straight ahead. "I made him and I made you, and you belong to me. Don't forget it."

They rode double back to the house. When they were cresting the final hill, the white outline of the house before them, her mother broke the silence, saying cheerfully, "You know I'd never let anything happen to you. Falada will keep you safe. He'd never let you get lost."

Cordelia nodded. *She's rewriting it in her head already, then. I was getting lost, not running away.*

Relief washed over her and settled in her chest. Her mother did this sometimes, recasting the past into a shape that she found more congenial. This time the changes seemed to benefit Cordelia.

The closeness between them, as she held her mother's waist while Falada carried them toward their front door, gave Cordelia the courage to ask, "Mother? What's a familiar?"

"Like a spirit," said her mother. "Or a tame demon, sometimes. A sorcerer makes one out of magic, or catches one, or binds one. Falada's mine."

My mother is a sorcerer. Falada is her familiar.

She let those facts roll around in her head while they rode up to the stable. Falada's hoofbeats were muffled on the packed earth floor.

"Are familiars all horses, then?" Cordelia asked, when she was finally allowed to dismount. She fought to keep her voice casual, as if it hardly mattered.

Her mother laughed. "No, and wasn't it clever to make him one? So useful to have around. No, most sorcerers are so unimaginative, assuming they've got the power to call one up at all. Always nasty little devils with claws. And witches are worse—cats and dogs, the lot of them, not a drop of imagination between them."

"Are there any others around here?"

Her mother's head snapped up. "Why?"

Oh damn, damn, I shouldn't have asked, I should have stopped at two questions, I shouldn't have tried for a third . . . There was a look in her mother's eyes that she didn't like at all. She cast about wildly for an answer. "There was a dog that barked at Falada a few months ago. I thought maybe it was a familiar."

This seemed to be a good enough answer. "No," said her mother, turning away. "Falada would tell me if he saw one. There're no other sorcerers around here, and the only witch is on the other side of town and she's drunk half the time and senile the other half."

Cordelia nodded politely.

"If you ever see another sorcerer when you aren't with Falada, you must tell me *at once,* do you understand?" Her mother reached out and seized Cordelia's wrist in a bruising grip.

"Y-yes, Mother."

"Don't trust any of them. They'll only want to use you for their own purposes. And don't even *think* about keeping it a secret from me."

"No, Mother." Cordelia had no idea how to tell if someone was a sorcerer, and struggled for a way to ask without making it a question. "I . . . I don't think I've ever seen one. I don't know what one looks like."

Her mother sat back, lips pursed. "Hmm. No, I suppose you wouldn't. I picked a good town to move to. Hopefully that luck will hold. Larger cities mean more sorcerers, and we want to avoid them at all costs."

"Yes, Mother," said Cordelia, who had pushed her luck as far as she dared.

She wondered, as she climbed the stairs to her room, what her mother had meant by "use you for their own purposes." It seemed that there was little enough about her worth using, unless someone needed dishes washed.

A day ago, she would have said it aloud to Falada, turning the words over and trying to puzzle out the meaning. But a day ago the world had been different and Falada had been her friend, and tears slid down her face and dropped, unnoticed, onto the bed.

She tried to remember every secret she had ever whispered in Falada's ear. There were too many, going back all the years of her life. Small ones, like tests failed at school, coins kept to buy a piece of penny candy. Big ones, like riding with Ellen.

How lonely she was. How afraid.

Even one secret was too many.

She felt as if she was coming up from being obedient again, and she swore that she would not scream.

Despite her mother's statements, Cordelia was still surprised two days later when her mother announced that she would be marrying a man in a city near the coast and was going to go see to it. She left Cordelia a few coins and rode off on Falada, her chin high, while her familiar moved like silk beneath her.

Cordelia stood in the doorway and wondered what that meant. Would this man come here? Would she be expected to cook for three? She dreaded the thought. It would be very like her mother to come home with a guest and wonder why there wasn't a steak dinner waiting on the table, and blame Cordelia for the lack.

Worse yet, she might be expected to talk to him. Cordelia dragged out her old primer from school, *The Ladies' Book of Etiquette and Manual of Politeness,* by Miss Florence Hartley, with its yellowing pages and firm, no-nonsense block letters. She read the paragraphs about how to speak to adults until she had committed them to memory. *"Let your demeanor be always marked by modesty and simplicity. Avoid exclamations, they are in exceptionally bad taste and are apt to be vulgar in words. Above all, let your conversation be intellectual, graceful, chaste, discreet, edifying, and profitable."*

"Now, if only I knew how to make my conversation edifying and profitable," she muttered to herself, embarking on a thorough cleaning of the spare bedroom, just in case it was required to hold a potential husband.

In the end, her mother vanished for nearly three days, and Cordelia actually slept with the door closed the second night. The only light came from the moon through the window. Wunderclutter hung in long chains from the upper sill, casting slithery shadows over her bed. It was supposed to drive off evil spirits and dark things that might walk in the night.

Cordelia wished that she could hang it all around the house and keep her mother away.

And Falada. Her stomach roiled with humiliation at the thought. *Falada is worse.*

The day after her mother left, Falada had returned, no rider on his back. Cordelia assumed that wherever her mother was, she had sent Falada back to watch Cordelia. *Spy on me, more like.*

He'd walked calmly from the road and into the stable, and

Cordelia didn't venture down there to check on him. She hadn't ridden him since that day, and the loss felt like liquid filling her lungs, like she could no longer get a deep enough breath. She missed Ellen. She missed riding even more. Before, when it seemed as if the pressure under her skin would cause her to split open, she would have climbed on Falada's back and galloped across the fields. Felt free for a little while, even if the ride always ended back at her house with its eternally open doors.

Now, when she felt that way, Cordelia gripped her temples and made a sound instead. Not a scream, which would have summoned her mother, but a small, shrill noise, like a teakettle whistling. Like the teakettle, it seemed to release some of the pressure.

With her mother gone, Cordelia could have really screamed. She tried it, experimentally, into her pillow, louder and louder, and then the scream broke into a laugh and she rolled over in her bed, feeling giddy and brave and wild.

It would not last, of course. Her mother would return, tomorrow or the next day or the next, possibly with a new husband in tow. But for the moment, the closed door was a balm and Cordelia slept deeply, without dreams.

CHAPTER 4

Three days after her first panic-filled awakening, Doom appeared on Hester's doorstep, in the shape of a woman.

Doom was tall and slender, with the sort of figure that poets described as willowy. She had shining dark chestnut hair and large blue eyes in a fragile, heart-shaped face, and she held the Squire's arm as if she were too delicate to stand unassisted.

Hester noted dispassionately that Doom was beautiful. Hester was not envious, but beauty was a weapon that she did not wield herself, and it was not an insignificant one in the arsenal. Her brother was particularly susceptible to it, and even more susceptible to fragility.

"My sister, Hester," the Squire was saying, gesturing to her. "Hester, love, meet our guest, Miss Evangeline."

"Oh no," said Doom. "It's Lady, I'm afraid." When the Squire tensed, she added artlessly, "Not that there has been a Lord Evangeline for a long time, I fear."

Hester's brother relaxed and patted the hand tucked into his arm. Hester did not roll her eyes, but she considered it.

"Your brother was kind enough to help me," said Lady Evangeline, turning a brilliant smile on Hester. She lost the next few words as the sense of overwhelming dread clutched at her throat. ". . . quite overwhelmed. The city seems so much larger than when I was there last, and I fear I became *quite* turned around."

"Mmm, yes," said Hester noncommittally. *I get it. I see her. You can let go now.* Was her throat working? It seemed to be, although there was a definite rasp to it. "It's grown a great deal in the last few years."

"Exactly. I went looking for the dressmakers that I remembered, and they've quite vanished."

"Asked her to stay for dinner," said the Squire, in jolly tones. Hester suppressed a sigh. Her brother was smitten. This was a common enough occurrence, but generally by normal women, not those with dread and horror spread behind them like wings.

She would have liked to plead a headache and escape dinner, but that would mean leaving her brother alone with Doom, and that was a terrible idea. Hester wasn't certain yet what Lady Evangeline intended, whether she was looking for marriage or money or something more straightforward, like human flesh. Regardless of which it was, her brother would be useless to deal with it. If the woman turned out to be a hag and suddenly ripped her skin off and flung herself, red and bloody, across the table to devour the Squire, the best that Hester could hope for was that one of the footmen might drown her in the soup course while the Squire was still gaping and waving his hands. And of course the footmen could do nothing about marriage at all.

You require a butler for that, thought Hester, and smothered her laugh in a snort.

"Beg pardon, my lady?" asked Doom, a line forming for just an instant between her china-blue eyes.

"Nothing," said Hester. *Steady on, old girl, you'll laugh yourself into an early grave with this creature about.* "Dinner, you say? I'll tell Cook to prepare an extra place."

It was astonishing that she had any appetite at all that night, with Doom seated across from her. Her brother sat at the head of the table, with Evangeline at his left hand and Hester at his right. "Just a cozy family meal," the Squire assured their guest. "No need to stand on ceremony."

Ceremony might have been nice, since it meant that Hester would not be expected to speak across the table at Evangeline. *On the other hand, that means that I won't be able to head Samuel off before he says anything truly dangerous. Not that he's going to propose over the soup course. Probably. He likes beautiful women and he likes flattery, but he's never shown any interest in marriage.*

There had been several quite attractive ladies in her brother's life over the years, including at least one that Hester would not have minded as a sister-in-law, but the Squire had always expressed disdain for "the parson's mousetrap" as he called it. Like many men not overly encumbered by intelligence, he had a great deal of cunning in avoiding personal unpleasantness.

On the other hand, none of those other women had woken such a premonition of dread in Hester's soul.

"So you are in town to visit a dressmaker?" she asked, when she felt that the flirtation going on between her brother and the widow had gone far enough.

"To make an appointment for a fitting, rather," said Evangeline. "My daughter needs an entirely new wardrobe, I fear."

"Your daughter?" This was an interesting new wrinkle.

"Oh yes. You know how it is with children," said Evangeline, smiling at Hester. "They stay the same size for so long, and then they shoot up six inches overnight and positively nothing fits. She is seventeen, old enough to make her coming-out to society and I had planned around that, and then suddenly . . ." She made swooshing gestures with her hands and laughed aloud. "I swear that she looks like a servant now, wearing castoffs, but they are the only things that fit."

"Indeed," said Hester. "Why, I remember when Samuel was young, and my parents despaired of him. He would have a suit fitted, and then by the time he went to pick it up at the store, his ankles and wrists would be hanging out of it. In fact, one time . . ."

It was a timeworn anecdote, and she did not need to turn much of her mind to relating it. Instead she studied Evangeline.

Her manners were perfect, of course. Naturally, Doom would have exquisite manners. The only flaw, if you could even call it that, was that she was clearly not used to servants waiting on her. Occasionally she would catch herself just slightly as a footman replaced a dish, and she had reached out as if to pull out her own chair upon entering the room. But she recovered from these missteps instantly and with a great deal of poise, so much so that Hester was not entirely certain that they were missteps, or part of a carefully woven image of herself as a genteel but impoverished widow.

She could not escape the feeling that there was something very artificial about Evangeline. A physical artificiality, not merely her mannerisms. It had nothing to do with face paint or curling papers, either. Hester considered such things perfectly natural, even if she no longer bothered to use much beyond a little powder herself. No, it was something deeper and more fundamental. Hester could not escape the odd feeling that if she peered closely at the woman's scalp, she would see hundreds of tiny holes where all that chestnut hair had been glued in, like a porcelain doll. She remembered her earlier flippant thought about the woman ripping her skin off during dinner. Suddenly it seemed much less amusing.

"Sister?" said the Squire.

"Eh?" Hester realized that her brother had been speaking. "What was that? You have to speak up, my hearing's not what it was." (This was entirely untrue, but she had found that it was a very good excuse when she had simply been ignoring a dull conversation.)

"I was saying that we must have Evangeline and her daughter down to stay with us, while they are waiting on the dressmakers."

"It's far too kind of you to offer," said Evangeline, looking up through her eyelashes. "I couldn't possibly impose."

"Nonsense," said the Squire. "What do you say, Hester, old girl?"

The old girl in question would have very much preferred to say no, but she did not. She knew that Doom would not be put off so easily. "Of course," she said instead, reaching for her wineglass. "I should very much like to make your daughter's acquaintance."

Cordelia woke because her mother was shaking her awake. It happened often enough, but it seemed early. When she looked groggily out the window, the sky was still dark. "Is it morning?"

"Close enough," said her mother. "Up, up!" She pulled back the blankets covering Cordelia.

"Today is the day we get out of this wretched town," her mother said. Her eyes were shining and her skin was flushed and she looked young. "At last! Small-minded people. I'll be glad to leave. Now pack your things and get in the carriage. We shan't be back here."

Cordelia blinked at her. It had just occurred to her that her bedroom door had been shut and her mother hadn't said a word about it. This was unprecedented in her experience. "We haven't got a carriage," she said, and then softened it so that her mother would not think she was arguing. "Have we?"

"It's a cabriolet," said her mother. "Or perhaps a sulky. I can never remember the name." She laughed carelessly. "Just big enough for two."

"Where are we going?"

"To the coast. To the home of Squire Samuel Chatham, a ridiculous old man who will fall over anything in skirts, but who is old-fashioned enough to offer marriage if he thinks he's thought of it first. I'll be wedding him, and we'll live in rather more comfort than we've managed here."

Cordelia bowed her head. "We're leaving now?" she asked.

"Not next week, silly child! The longer you dawdle, the longer this will take. We must arrive late enough that everyone is overwhelmed with pity for our long journey but not so late that everyone is asleep. Move!"

Cordelia obeyed. Her mother had provided a carpetbag and a bandbox. She packed her three dresses and two hats and her sewing kit and her daybook and pens, and the tiny carved wooden horse that Ellen had given her for her birthday years ago. It seemed unlikely that she would see Ellen again, and she wished there were some way to leave a note for her, but what would it say? Her etiquette primer said that letters of gratitude should be *"simple, but strong, grateful, and graceful. Fancy that you are clasping the hand of the kind friend who has been generous or thoughtful for you, and then write, even as you would speak."* This advice did Cordelia no good at all, because she would have stammered awkwardly and probably said the wrong thing.

Thank you for talking to me and pretending I wasn't strange.

No, you couldn't write a note like that.

When she emerged with her bag, wearing her heavy coat against the cold, she saw the little two-wheeled carriage parked outside, Falada between the traces, and her heart sank. It was a cabriolet and she knew by the crest on the door that it belonged to Ellen's father.

"This is Mr. Parker's," she said, in her most neutral voice.

"It was much too good for him," her mother said. "We'll sell it in the city."

Cordelia swallowed. "Did he . . . did he give it to you?" She wanted to ask *Did you steal it?* but that would be an accusation and her mother did not respond well to accusations.

Her mother's eyes were cold and bright, like fragments of sky reflected in a mirror. "He's given me a great many things over the years. He didn't want to part with the carriage, though, and I may have had to use some force." She laughed and the sound was as cold and bright as her eyes. "Losing his carriage will be the least of his troubles now."

Her benefactor was Ellen's father? Cordelia's mouth was very dry. Ellen had been her only friend, since Falada had proved false. And Evangeline had threatened to have Falada trample him to death, and if she was so pleased with herself, that could only mean that she had done something worse.

Guilt struck Cordelia all over, a cold rush from the soles of her feet up to her hair, and she clutched the carpetbag to her chest and bent over it.

"Don't look so stricken," said her mother sharply. "If not for having him as a benefactor, we'd have starved long ago. The problem is that men get bored so easily. Your father certainly did."

It was all too much, too soon. "I thought my father was dead."

"He is, and he brought it on himself, just as Parker did." Her lips curved in a smile. She snapped her fingers and Cordelia knew that her mother's patience was at an end. She climbed into the carriage with her carpetbag at her feet. Being made obedient would not help Ellen's father, or expiate the sin that had, apparently, been going on for years.

I'm sorry, Ellen. I'm so sorry. Maybe I can write you a letter someday and tell you how sorry I am. She had written many letters in school, practicing her penmanship, though she had never sent one. Her mother had approved. Aristocratic ladies wrote letters to other ladies. It was a good skill to have, and so she had written out dozens of sample letters, thanking imaginary strangers for visits that had never occurred and gifts that did not exist.

None of the schoolbooks had a sample for when your mother had done something terrible to your friend's father. Cordelia bowed her head and stared at her hands in her threadbare gloves. Her mother flicked the reins and Falada set out, pulling the stolen carriage as if it weighed nothing at all.

CHAPTER 5

It was late and the fire had burned down in the grate when the butler announced that their guests had arrived. Hester would normally have gone to bed by now, but her presentiment of Doom was so powerful that she doubted she'd sleep anyway. She had a cup of hot cocoa instead, and sat by the fire, pretending to read a book.

"By Jove, you made it! I was beginning to think you weren't coming." The Squire rose, beaming, and no one could have guessed that he had been snoring gently but a few moments earlier.

"And miss your company? Never!" said Evangeline. "But oh, what a terrible trip we have had. I cannot tell you how glad I am to be here at last." She smiled warmly at the Squire and held out both her hands. He took them, bowing over them, his smile even wider than hers.

"Misfortune on the road?" asked Hester. Her eyes picked out Doom's shadow behind her, a young woman who seemed to be trying to fade into the wallpaper.

"Everything that could go wrong went wrong," said Evangeline. "Our carriage threw a wheel in the rain and went over and half our luggage went flying into a field of mud and cabbages. Dresses everywhere, completely drenched, and the carriage horses panicking and trampling everything. Fortunately a friend happened by and loaned us his cabriolet to continue on, but our coachman had to stay with the carriage to try to soothe the horses." She spread her hands. "And though I am not a poor driver, I am not like you,

Samuel, who can drive to an inch, so we went very slowly all the way here."

During this dramatic recitation, Hester kept her gaze on Doom's daughter. The girl was watching her mother, her eyes wide.

"So I fear that we must throw ourselves on your mercy, dear Samuel, Lady Hester. We have little more than a hatbox or two and what clothes we managed to salvage. Thank heavens we already have an appointment with the dressmaker, or we should look like proper vagabonds indeed."

The Squire began some nonsense about how Evangeline would look stunning even in rags. Hester broke in to say, "I shall have hot baths arranged in your rooms. But who is your young friend here?"

"This is my daughter, Cordelia," said Evangeline, beaming with precisely correct maternal devotion. "Cordelia, make your curtsy to the Squire and his sister. He's been so exceptionally kind, letting us stay with him."

The girl stepped forward and curtsied clumsily to her brother, her eyes on the ground at his feet. Hester was surprised to see that the girl was not a beauty. Her hair was more mouse than chestnut and her eyes more gray than blue. She looked like a badly washed-out copy of her mother, like a handbill that had been left to fade in the sun.

The Squire bowed to Cordelia. "Lady Evangeline, this cannot be your daughter. Your younger sister, surely?"

Good lord, he actually said it. Hester pinched the bridge of her nose. She loved Samuel and had resigned herself to his gallantry, but she did wish that he had more imagination.

All else aside, Evangeline was in her thirties and Cordelia, standing with her hands clasped tightly together, looked twelve. *How old did Doom say she was? Seventeen?*

Cordelia would certainly not be the first girl to look younger than her years, but Hester had her doubts.

Doom was flirting with the Squire again. Hester had missed

the exact exchange, but that hardly mattered. It was unlikely that it would be either enlightening or original. "You must be exhausted after your journey," she broke in. She smiled warmly at Doom's daughter, just to see what would happen. The girl looked at her with wide, startled eyes. A pulse beat in her throat as she swallowed. She looked quickly to her mother, as if she needed guidance in how one responded to even so simple a statement.

"Oh yes," said Evangeline breezily. "After the misadventure we've had, I fear poor Cordelia is quite done in." Cordelia nodded agreement.

Hester wasted no time in ringing for the housekeeper. "Please see our guests to their rooms," she instructed. "And draw a hot bath for each." She smiled at Doom, digging her nails into her palm as she did so. "We won't dream of keeping you up after such an adventure. You must tell us all about it in the morning."

If Evangeline was put out by being deprived of the Squire's presence, she gave no sign. "Dear Lady Hester," she said warmly. Her blue eyes were almost painfully bright. "You are kindness itself."

"The very least I can do," said Hester, and felt intense relief when that blue gaze swept away and its owner went up the stairs after the housekeeper, trailing her daughter like a shadow in her wake.

There were so many closed doors! Cordelia could hardly imagine it. The hallways were lined with doors and every single one of them was closed. *They can't all be closets. No one has that many closets!*

It was an enormous house, bigger than anything in the village, bigger than the Parkers' manor house that Cordelia had glimpsed once or twice when out riding. Presumably such a house *would* have a great many closets, but some of those rooms had to be bedrooms and parlors and studies, and if so, the doors were closed.

For all the good that does me, given that I've managed to humiliate myself as soon as the front door was open.

It wasn't her fault. The door had opened and the man standing there had been so tall and lordly and aloof that he was obviously the Squire, and Cordelia knew her manners and curtsied immediately.

Except that the man had stood looking down at them, and one icy eyebrow had risen slightly in his icily correct face, and her mother had said, "Please inform the Squire we've arrived," and Cordelia realized that she had just curtsied to the butler.

Her mother hadn't seen her. That was the only saving grace in the matter. She would *not* have been pleased. But the footman behind Cordelia had and the butler *definitely* had, and her face went scarlet with embarrassment and then dead white, because what if he said something to Evangeline?

But he did not. Butlers, apparently, did not report such things to their guests. He had ushered them inside and led them, in icily correct fashion, to the sitting room where the Squire and his sister had been waiting.

And really, he looks so much more regal than the Squire does, how was I supposed to know the difference?

She'd been so flustered at that point that her mother had had to tell her to curtsy, a failing for which Cordelia would undoubtedly pay later. And the butler had witnessed all of it, which only added insult to injury.

But still, there were so many closed doors.

"This will be your room, miss," said the housekeeper, pushing one of the doors open. "We'll have a bath and a tray sent up for you. If you need anything else, just tell your maid and I'll see it taken care of directly."

She was a plump, motherly woman, and she smiled down at Cordelia, who gaped at her in astonishment. It had never occurred to her that she would not be sharing a room with her mother, and it was beyond the realm of her most fevered imagination that there would be a maid assigned to her. *There must be some mistake.*

Or does she think that I'm going to be particularly messy? Do I need someone to follow me around to make certain I don't break anything?

That seemed distressingly plausible.

She tried to remember if *The Ladies' Book of Etiquette* had said anything about servants. She thought there was a whole chapter on it, but she'd never paid any attention to it, because there was simply no world in which Cordelia ordered anyone else around. *Servants. Dear god.*

The housekeeper was still smiling at her, although a line was forming between her eyes, and it occurred to Cordelia that she'd been standing there with her mouth hanging open. "Oh. *Oh.* Thank you. That is, I . . . I appreciate . . . thank you . . ."

Her mother nudged her in the back, not gently, and she stopped.

"You're very tired, dear," said her mother.

"Yes," said Cordelia. It was true, and even if it hadn't been, she knew better than to argue with that tone. "Thank you," she said to the housekeeper again, and stepped inside the door.

The room had wallpaper. Cordelia knew of the existence of wallpaper, but she'd only seen it once or twice. It was a soft green damask, and she had a strong urge to run her fingers over it to feel the texture, but she was afraid that she might get it dirty. There was no bed, but there was a little white dressing table with a mirror, several chairs, and another closed door on the other side of the room.

The door clicked behind her. Cordelia jumped, startled, and spun around to see another young woman standing there, who had just closed the door. She was dressed much the same as the housekeeper, with long dark sleeves and a bright white apron. She looked to be a few years older than Cordelia.

"You closed the door," Cordelia blurted.

"Yes, miss." She crossed the space between them and reached out her hand. "I'll take your things, miss."

"My . . . oh." Cordelia looked down at her battered bandbox.

She held it out. It looked very grimy compared to the blinding white of the girl's apron.

"My lady said you've lost your luggage," said the girl. She finally looked up and met Cordelia's eyes, instead of keeping hers downcast. "I've laid out one of my lady's dressing gowns for you, while the housemaid brings the water up for your bath."

"Oh," said Cordelia. "I . . . uh . . . thank you?"

A slight smile crossed the girl's face. "Of course, miss. If you'll follow me?" She pushed open the far door, revealing a vast room with an equally vast bed. Cordelia froze on the threshold, staring. It was bigger than every room in her mother's house put together. The bed alone was almost the size of her bedroom, and it had curtains on it, like a little room all its own. There was a fireplace and a changing screen and a gigantic wardrobe and another small door.

My god, she thought, *how can I possibly keep all this clean? No wonder there are servants, this is a two-person job. Oh dear! How does one wash bedcurtains?*

By this point, the maid had clearly realized that Cordelia was in over her head and took charge of the situation. "The dressing gown is over here, miss," she said, herding Cordelia as efficiently as a hen with a rather slow chick. "If you'll just step behind the screen and take off those wet clothes, I'll see them cleaned and brushed properly."

"Oh," said Cordelia again, and allowed herself to be herded. She stripped off her gown, which was definitely travel-worn and looked absurdly shabby compared to the maid's outfit. She didn't dare think of how it had compared to the briefly glimpsed Lady Hester. Even the dressing gown (which was far too large for her) was magnificent, an enormous royal-blue confection with huge buttons and a lining as fine and silken as Falada's mane. Cordelia ran her fingers over it, wishing that she hadn't thought of Falada, trying not to picture him standing in the stable, a blazing white imposter among the mortal horses.

She sat in the dressing gown, fretfully doing nothing, and the maid, whose name was Alice, pressed a mug of tea into her hands. It was hot and sweet and drinking it seemed to take a great deal of energy. Cordelia thought she could fall asleep right here, but then the door opened and she snapped upright, expecting her mother to demand to know what she was doing.

But it was not her mother. It was two other maids, carrying a copper bathtub between them. They set it in front of the fire and went out again, then returned carrying steaming tins of water. The tub was huge compared to the one back home. "Oh . . ." said Cordelia, realizing how much work it would be, carrying all the water up the stairs. "Oh dear. I don't . . . it's so much trouble . . ."

"Not at all," said Alice firmly. "You're a guest at Chatham House."

"Yes, but . . ." She knew that she should offer to help, but she was so tired and carrying so much water would be exhausting. Perhaps she could convince them to put off the bath until later?

"Here, miss, let me show you the water closet." Alice led her to the small door that she had noticed earlier, opened it, and showed her how the levers worked. This was a revelation, and by the time she was done with the extraordinary novelty of it all, the bath was filled and steam was curling from the surface.

Alice went out again and Cordelia stripped and plunged into the water. She had barely settled in, however, when Alice came back into the room and Cordelia squeaked in alarm, sinking down and hugging her knees.

"Rose or lavender, miss?"

"Wha . . . what?"

"Soap, miss."

Cordelia must have looked panicked, because Alice said, very gently, "May I suggest the lavender, miss?"

"Yes, please," said Cordelia, almost inaudibly.

"I'll wash your hair for you," said Alice, "and you can dry it in front of the fire while you have a bite to eat. How does that sound?"

It sounded overwhelming, frankly, but Cordelia knew that if

she burst into tears, her mother would hear of it and she would have words. She had to have her best manners. This was part of her mother's plan to marry the Squire, and if Cordelia messed that up by being Cordelia, being made obedient was probably the least of the punishments she could look forward to.

She nodded hopelessly and Alice took over. No one had washed her hair in years, and the maid was much gentler than Cordelia's mother had ever been, but the sheer strangeness of the situation kept trying to grab her by the throat. *Calm,* she told herself. *Calm. Stay calm. Don't make a fuss. Do what is expected. Alice already told you what's expected. You'll go sit in front of the fire and eat whatever food they bring you. Calm.*

But the lavender smelled good, and not at all like wormwood. Cordelia slowly let her shoulders relax, despite their desire to hunch up by her ears.

She had a bad moment when Alice held open a towel and said "If you're ready to get out, miss?" and she realized that the maid was going to see her naked. But it wasn't as if her mother didn't barge in whenever she was bathing anyway, and say "Oh, stop, I've seen it hundreds of times before" when Cordelia squawked, so she stared at the ceiling as she rose up out of the water and Alice wrapped the towel around her, and it was all over blessedly quickly.

Her nightdress was laid out on the bed, looking almost embarrassed by its fine surroundings. Cordelia managed to get into it while Alice's back was turned, and then the maid wrapped the dressing gown around her shoulders again and sat her down in front of the fire.

The food was the most delicious that she had ever eaten. There were little rolls and butter and a tiny pot of jam and a sliced pear, as well as a soft cheese that went well with the jam and the pear both. Cordelia ate every scrap.

"There you go, miss," said Alice. Cordelia flushed guiltily—was she supposed to share some with the maid? She hadn't thought—

"Cook'll be pleased to see that you enjoyed it. Now the bed's ready and I've put a warm brick in for your feet."

"Thank you," said Cordelia. She swallowed. *Thank you* seemed inadequate for the food and the soap and the loan of the dressing gown. "Really, I . . . thank you."

"Of course, miss." Alice helped her to the bed. "If you need anything, I'll be sleeping just off the dressing room. Just pull this cord and I'll come at once."

Cordelia looked dutifully at the cord in question, nodded, and vowed that she would not pull it unless the house was on fire.

Alice pulled the curtains closed. Cordelia felt as if she was in a beautiful fabric cocoon. The bed was very soft, but more than that, there were *two* closed doors and the curtains between Cordelia and her mother, and she slept more deeply than she ever remembered doing in her life.

CHAPTER 6

When Cordelia woke, she had a moment of confusion. There were voices . . . but no, there weren't. She'd been dreaming. Perhaps she was still dreaming. The light was sea green and she was surrounded by it on all sides, and everything was soft, very soft, and very comfortable.

Am I dead? Is that why I'm so comfortable? The ground always looks very hard, but perhaps if you're dead and made of bones, it feels soft?

This was an interesting theory, but she lifted one hand and it was made of flesh, not bone, and then she remembered that she was in the curtained bed and there were two closed doors.

In fact, if Mother is in a room like this one, there might be four *closed doors.*

This was a staggering thought. Four doors! Cordelia could think anything and it wouldn't matter if it showed on her face. She could scowl and frown and glare and make terrible faces, *and her mother would never know.*

She attempted to make a terrible face, crossing her eyes and scrunching up her cheeks, whereupon the curtains opened and she yelped.

It was Alice. "I'm sorry to startle you, miss. Would you rather I knock on the door in the mornings?"

"I . . . uh . . ." Could she ask for that? Was that allowed? She took a deep breath. "That would be wonderful."

The maid gave no indication that it was a strange request. "I've brought tea, miss, and there's a tray coming up. It's a bit late for breakfast downstairs, I'm afraid."

"Oh no," said Cordelia, sitting up. "Did I oversleep?"

"Not at all, miss. No one expected you up so soon, after your trip yesterday." Alice smiled at her. "Properly dreadful it sounded, your carriage wheel breaking like that. And breakfast isn't formal, so no one minds if you miss it."

Cordelia relaxed a little. *No one minds* was not the same as *your mother doesn't mind,* but it was close.

The tray had more of the delicious rolls, along with a sliver of ham and a small dish of strawberries. Cordelia found that she was ravenous, but knew better than to agree when Alice asked if she should bring up more. *I must be a good guest. No one must have cause to complain.* She wiped her hands and asked, "What can I do to help clean up?"

The maid paused. "Beg pardon?"

"The room." Cordelia spread her hands. "I can help straighten it, if you tell me the way that you do things here."

Alice was silent for a long moment, and Cordelia began to get the same sinking feeling she had had when she realized that she had mistaken the butler for the lord of the manor. "That is . . ." she stammered, "if . . . if I'm supposed to . . ."

"No, miss," Alice said carefully. "You're a guest, and the Squire wouldn't hear of it. You leave that to us."

"Oh."

The older girl looked into Cordelia's wide, worried eyes and smiled. "I imagine they do things differently in your home. You'll find your feet here soon enough."

Cordelia discovered that she was twisting her dressing gown's belt between nervous fingers and stopped.

"Now I've laid out your gray gown," said Alice cheerfully, herding her into the dressing room.

My gray gown? I don't own a . . . oh. Cordelia eyed the gown in question. She'd always thought of it as blue, but there was no longer even a hint of color left to it. *I suppose it's my gray gown now.*

Alice was acting as if it was perfectly normal for guests to arrive with almost no clothes and what little they had to be threadbare and too short. Cordelia didn't know whether to be grateful or ashamed of the pretense. "Sit down here and I'll do your hair for you, miss."

Cordelia had never had anyone "do her hair" in her life. Was it painful? When her mother brushed it out, her scalp stung and smarted. But even that didn't compare to the fact that someone else was going to far too much trouble over her. Last night, and now this morning too?

"Please, you don't need to bother with me. I'm sure you have much more important things to do."

Alice cocked her head. "You've never been in a great house before, have you, miss?"

Cordelia could feel herself blushing. "I . . . no?"

The maid smiled, not unkindly. She reminded Cordelia of Ellen. "You didn't bring a lady's maid with you," she said, as if lady's maids were something that a normal person might carry around, like a handkerchief. "So when you come here, they'll assign a girl to take care of you. That's me."

"I don't want to be a bother," said Cordelia.

"You're not. I'd far rather be looking after a guest than turning beds or blacking grates. So you're not taking me away from anything. And before you panic," she added, her eyes twinkling, "I'll get a very generous extra wage for being your maid while you're here, miss. The Squire's very good to his people. So please don't feel guilty about it at all."

Cordelia swallowed. "I've never had my hair done," she admitted. She usually just braided it up. When she was young, her mother had braided it. Sometimes she still did, when she was in a certain mood. Cordelia had learned to sit very still while fingers crawled across her scalp like insect feet.

"It will be fine," said Alice soothingly, as if she were the master and Cordelia the servant. "I'll do up your hair so that not even the Archbishop himself could complain."

"Does he often complain about hair?" asked Cordelia weakly.

"Now that I don't know," admitted Alice. She reached her fingers to Cordelia's head and Cordelia tried very hard not to flinch away from the touch. She wanted to squeeze her temples and shriek but that would have looked terribly bizarre, so all she could do was sit and try not to look strange.

"I know the village priest is always talking about maidenly modesty, so I suppose the Archbishop would too, wouldn't he?" Alice said. Cordelia had lost her place in the conversation, but fortunately Alice continued on. "You have to figure that however much a priest is against something, an Archbishop is even *more* against it, don't you?"

She continued in this vein of small talk about nothing in particular for several minutes, while Cordelia slowly relaxed. Alice was very good at combing out hair without tugging and there didn't seem to be any hidden pitfalls in her conversation. She didn't even really seem to need Cordelia's input.

She was just starting to think that perhaps a lady's maid was not the worst thing that could befall one when there was a knock on the door and her mother's voice floated through. "Cordelia? Are you in there?"

Oh god, the door is closed! She nearly leapt to her feet in a panic, but Alice patted her shoulder as if she were a panicked horse and said, "I'll just go answer that, never you fear."

She went to the door with perfect confidence and opened it a crack. "Yes, ma'am?"

"I—oh." Her mother sounded nonplussed. "Is this my daughter's room?"

"Yes, ma'am. She's being dressed now, she won't be long."

"Oh bah, I don't mind about that." Her mother's laugh floated through the crack, pure and delightful and cruel. "I'm her mother, I've seen it all."

"Then you'll want to see her at her best," said Alice pleasantly. "I'll send her to you directly when she's ready."

Oh god, no . . . Cordelia bit down on her knuckle in horror. Alice was defying her mother. She would be punished. She would be made obedient, and she didn't know what was coming. It was like a mouse standing up to a starving wolf.

"I would like to see my daughter," said her mother, sweetness disguising the malice.

"Yes indeed, ma'am. Shall I tell her fifteen minutes? And may I suggest the Blue Drawing Room? It is more suited to a lady's breakfast than the main hall, and I will have the cook send up something delicate and suitable for you." Alice raised her voice just a little. "John Footman? Will you see that the Blue Drawing Room is ready to receive His Lordship's guests in a quarter of an hour?"

Perhaps being reminded that she was a guest in a great house changed her mother's plans. She could not very well destroy a maid on her first morning there, when they were staying on the Squire's charity, particularly not if she had her sights set on marrying the man. *Let her go away,* Cordelia prayed. *Let her rewrite it in her head so that it's all her own idea. Please don't let her do something terrible to Alice.*

She still had her doubts about the existence of God, but apparently someone heard her prayer. Evangeline said, "In a quarter of an hour, then," and Alice murmured an acknowledgment and closed the door.

"Phew," she said, turning back to Cordelia. "I don't know if that's what you wanted, but . . ."

"You sent her away," said Cordelia, in pure awe. "You made her leave. You . . . *how* . . . ?"

"Ah," said Alice. She could not have been more than a year or two older than Cordelia, but she looked suddenly weary and mature beyond her years. "I thought that might be the way of it. When you heard her voice, you looked as if the hounds of hell were at your door." She paused, then added, somewhat belatedly, "Begging your pardon, miss. I don't mean to speak out of turn."

"I've never been able to get her to leave," said Cordelia. Belatedly she realized that she should perhaps have lied, that Alice might talk to someone who could talk to the Squire and fox the whole business of marriage, but she was not a quick thinker and she had never dreamed of anything so incredible as her mother backing down from a lady's maid.

"Some things are easier to have another person do for you." Alice smiled. "Like your hair. Here, let me finish these braids and we'll send you down directly. I suspect she wouldn't take kindly to people being late."

Her dress, Cordelia knew, was a sad shambles, but Alice draped a lovely shawl across her shoulders and she dared to hope that everyone would be too distracted by the shawl to notice. "One of the Squire's sister's," the maid said, "and she won't miss it, and wouldn't begrudge you the loan if she did." Cordelia looked at herself in the mirror, expecting to see the same colorless girl that she always saw, but the shawl was a deep sea green that brought out red highlights in mouse-colored hair and made her faded gray eyes seem to have a shimmer of turquoise.

"Oh!" she said, startled. "Thank you. I look . . . so much better."

"Ah," said Alice. She gave a little curtsy. "Keep me in mind, miss, when you marry and move to a grand house," she said, winking. "Always had an ambition to be a lady's maid, you know."

Cordelia was fairly certain that you weren't supposed to hug the servants—if they didn't like it, they wouldn't be able to run away, after all—so she waved her hands helplessly. "*Thank* you. So much."

"I'll be here this evening to help you take it down, miss," said Alice, "and to help with your bath." She patted Cordelia's shoulder again, a groom sending the nervous horse out of the stable, and then turned and busied herself with tidying.

A footman kindly saw her to the Blue Drawing Room and ushered her in. Cordelia knew that she was early, but her mother would likely be feeling thwarted, so it was best not to do anything to attract her ire. Perhaps she could find a way to deflect it.

The room looked empty at first. It was very grand and full of furniture, including two chairs pulled up close by the fire, and after a moment, Cordelia noticed that someone was sitting in one of those chairs. "Mother?" she asked.

"Probably not," said the woman in the chair. "It seems unlikely, at any rate. I'm old enough, but I do think I'd have remembered."

"Oh! I'm sorry—I was expecting—"

"Someone else," said the woman in the chair cheerfully. "Indeed. I'm Hester, the Squire's sister." She pushed herself to her feet, grabbing for a cane that leaned against the chair. She was middle-aged and round, with heavy hips, and her hair was shot with gray, but her smile was as young as Alice's. "You must be Cordelia. We met last night, but you were so tired, I've no doubt you don't recall."

"Yes, ma'am." Cordelia remembered her manners and curtsied deeply.

"And wearing one of my shawls, too," said Hester, amused. Cordelia turned red and started to pull it off, stammering. "No, no, my dear! I make you a gift of it. It looks far better on you than it ever did on me." She smiled, her eyes crinkling up at the corners. "When you reach a certain age, everyone gives you shawls as a gift. I have closets full of the things. It looks very fine on you. You must always wear that color, I think."

Cordelia swallowed. "You're so kind," she whispered. "Everyone here . . . you've all been so kind . . ." And they were being kind to a viper and her offspring, she knew, and did not dare say to anyone.

"Ah, well." Hester stumped across the room on her cane. "We're bored silly, that's all, and desperate for new faces. I shall leave you to your meeting with your mother. Do come and see me later, if you like. I don't get out as often as I would wish, and it's more fun to do embroidery with someone else to talk to. Or even to read aloud, if you would wish to."

"I . . . yes, I'd be happy to . . ." Cordelia was growing annoyed with herself for stammering so often. *I may not be clever or brave or beautiful, but is it too much to ask that I can form a complete sentence?*

"I'll see you then," Hester said, waving over her shoulder as she left.

"*There* you are," her mother said five minutes later, walking into the room as if she already was the mistress of it. She looked Cordelia over appraisingly. "Where did that shawl come from?"

"Lady Hester gave it to me," murmured Cordelia, wondering if it would be taken away from her, or if her mother would approve. There was no telling for something so far outside her experience.

"Good," said her mother. "She may take a liking to you, and that's useful. The old spinsters are the worst. They don't want to see their brothers married off and you can't distract them with a kiss or a fondle." She tapped her foot. "Yes. Good. See if you can't amuse her."

Cordelia nodded. She had no idea how she was supposed to do that, but Lady Hester had already suggested embroidery. Granted, she had no more idea how to embroider than how to fly. *She did say I could read to her. I do know how to read.*

Her mother was idly stroking the arm of one of the chairs, rubbing the nap of the velvet first one way, then the other. "This is a good house," she said. "Just wealthy enough to be worthwhile, and not so rich that anyone has snapped the old man up already. And he seems an easy enough nut to crack. He wants a mistress, not a wife, but I'll have a ring on my finger in a fortnight."

Cordelia swallowed. It sounded so cold-blooded when she said it. *Does that surprise you? She* is *cold-blooded.*

"You're . . . you're not going to . . ." She couldn't find the words and finally settled on ". . . *do* anything to them, are you?"

"*Do* anything?" said her mother archly. "Like what?"

Cordelia had no idea how to answer. *Make them obedient* was her first thought, but she didn't want to name it for fear of bringing it down on her own head. "I . . . I mean . . ."

Evangeline rolled her eyes. "No, silly, I'm not going to *do* anything. Not really. People notice if you go around tinkering with their heads too much, and if I compelled him to fall in love, it would break at the altar and he'd certainly notice *that*. I shan't risk too much until I'm safely wed."

This was not a great deal of comfort. Cordelia had far too much experience with the sort of things her mother did when she felt safe. She bowed her head and fidgeted with the edge of her sleeve.

A footman arrived with a tray containing more food. Her mother waited until he had set it down, then dismissed him with a grand wave. Cordelia met his eyes, horrified by her mother's high-handedness, but he did not look offended. In fact, he winked at her, and that was sufficiently astonishing that she sat in silence until the door closed behind him.

She waited until her mother had helped herself before picking up another roll and applying butter.

"We'll dine with the family tonight," said her mother. "You must be well-mannered."

"Yes, Mother," murmured Cordelia.

"Use the correct forks and spoons and so forth."

Cordelia froze, the roll halfway to her mouth. "The . . . correct forks?" There was more than one fork? They only had five at home and Cordelia washed them carefully every night for use the next day. How many forks did a person need?

"God," said her mother, putting her hand to her forehead. "I've raised a little barbarian. Yes, silly child. Watch me before you eat, if you can't figure it out."

"Yes, Mother."

"And be charming. To the Squire particularly, and his sister if you can manage it." She paused in her incessant stroking of the velvet. "You *do* know how to be charming, don't you?"

Cordelia's look of panic must have been answer enough. Her mother sighed. "Really, dear, you might at least make an *effort*. This is *important*."

"I . . . I haven't had dinner with many older men before . . ." She had been to the old preacher's house once, before he had died and been replaced by the young one. She did not think she had said more than three words during the entire meal. She racked her brain for advice from her etiquette book, but all she could remember was the line *"The more pure and elevated your sentiments are, and the better cultivated your intellect is, the easier will you find it to converse pleasantly with all."* By those standards, Cordelia was distressingly aware that either her sentiments or her intellect were sadly lacking. Possibly both.

"Well. I suppose that's true." Evangeline tapped a finger against her lips. "Very well. Ask him about himself. Look interested in the answers. Don't contradict him. That sort of thing. You are not trying to attach him yourself, merely to look wholesome and girlish. And above all, don't be moody. It's terribly unattractive in a young woman, and it makes anyone think twice about wanting to live in the same house with them. Do I make myself clear?"

Cordelia had no idea what moodiness might entail, but she nodded anyway. "Yes, Mother."

"Good. Give me a kiss and then go." Her mother smiled. "I am going out riding with the Squire. I think that bodes well, don't you?"

"Yes, Mother," whispered Cordelia again, and slipped away.

CHAPTER 7

Hester sat in her parlor, thinking.

To anyone looking in, she appeared to be embroidering a shawl—or more accurately, to have nearly fallen asleep in the middle of doing so. One of the advantages of age was that you could think a great deal while simply sitting still, and no one would poke you and demand that you go and do something useful.

Doom's daughter had been unexpected. Before their arrival last night, Hester had been half suspecting that the girl would be some great beauty like her mother, perhaps even bait for a trap for the Squire. Middle-aged men had made fools of themselves over young ladies before, and would again before the end of the world.

Certainly she had expected that the daughter would be in on whatever mischief the mother had planned. If there was something not-quite-canny about Lady Evangeline, Hester had expected that to extend to the girl as well.

One look into the frightened-rabbit eyes of the girl had put paid to all those notions. Hester wasn't sure of the whole picture yet, but certainly the girl was terribly nervous, and it did not feel like the nerves of a co-conspirator afraid of being caught.

She looks like a horse that's been beaten so often that it doesn't know what is expected of it any longer. And who doesn't expect that to ever change.

Which was, perhaps, no surprise for Doom's daughter. Hester was quite certain that there was blood and ice behind Evangeline's smile. But then again . . .

What if the girl's bait for a trap set for a softhearted old fool?
Is Evangeline clever enough for that?

She might be. The woman had turned a chance meeting on the street into an indefinite stay at the Squire's home. Not difficult, particularly not in a respectable house with Hester as ostensible chaperone, but Hester suspected that Evangeline had known exactly what she was doing. Had, most likely, set out with this exact goal in mind, if not a precise quarry.

Her woolgathering was interrupted by a hesitant knock on the door. "Eh?" said Hester, not having to fake her befuddlement. "Someone there?" It had been such a light knock that she might have mistaken it. One of the servants would have waited and then entered, but no one did. "Hello?"

Another timid knock. *Heavens, do we have bogles or bogarts or whatever those creatures are that go about rapping on walls? Tommy-knockers? No, those live in mines, I think. Blast.*

"Come in!" called Hester loudly.

The door opened and Doom's daughter poked her head around the jamb. "Hello?" she said. Her voice was very soft.

"Oh, there you are. Come to help an old lady with her embroidery?"

"I'm afraid I don't know how," said the girl, staring at the floor as if she were admitting to some terrible failing.

"It's not fatal," said Hester. Privately she was a bit surprised—most girls with pretensions to gentility learned embroidery, however shoddily, almost as soon as they could walk. "Would you like to learn?"

Cordelia looked up, those frightened-rabbit eyes round and startled. "Could I?" she asked.

"Certainly you can. Very foolish women learn to embroider, and you don't strike me as terribly foolish." She patted the cushion next to her. "Here, take a square of fabric and I'll draw you out a pattern . . ."

It only took a few moments to show the girl a basic stitch.

Hester watched as Cordelia bent over the square of cotton with intense concentration. A line formed between her eyebrows, as if she would make the thread behave through sheer force of will.

"It's a good skill to have," said Hester. "If you've got a dress that's sound but the cuffs are frayed, you turn the cuffs and then embroider over the seams and no one's the wiser." Cordelia flushed a little and Hester saw that the cuffs of her dress had indeed been turned to hide the wear. *Blast. Well, perhaps I can salvage it.* "There's nothing worse than having a gown that suits you perfectly and then ruining a cuff, is there?"

"*You* turn your cuffs?" said Cordelia in clear astonishment.

"Heavens, yes," said Hester. "My gowns are old friends, most of them. I'm not wasting my pin money on a visit to the dressmaker if I can avoid it." She smiled at the girl and after a hesitant moment, Cordelia smiled back. *And if she goes back to her mother to report that the Squire's tightfisted with his money, so much the better.*

It was completely untrue, of course. The Squire was a generous soul to begin with, and Hester had amused herself breeding fancy geese for years, which had brought in a small but substantial income. *And if Doom gets her hooks into my brother, I may have to start up again. Richard's still got the breeding flock I gave him, over at Evermore House, he'll return them if I ask.* Geese were surprisingly easy to work with once you understood the way their tiny minds worked, but they had a reputation for ferocity and for turning bad luck. Also for driving away wicked magic, not that it ever came up. She'd sold quite a number of guard geese over the years. She'd given it up a few years ago, as the birds fell out of fashion, but fashion was fickle and they might well come back in again.

The girl flinched just slightly, barely noticeable. If Hester hadn't been watching her, she would have missed the motion entirely.

"Oh no," said Cordelia, sounding suddenly distraught.

"Did you prick your finger?"

"Yes, but I've bled on your lovely fabric!" She held out the piece of linen, and Hester saw with surprise that her hands were trembling. "I'm so sorry. I'm so clumsy."

"Bah," said Hester. "You're not clumsy. You've only been practicing for fifteen minutes. No one masters a skill in fifteen minutes . . . and frankly, if you did, I should be rather put out, because I have been practicing for over forty years, and I'm not a master yet myself."

She hoped that would win a smile, but Cordelia was a tougher nut to crack than that. Hester examined the small, rust-colored blot on the fabric. "And that's nothing. It'll wash out. If the stain worries you, put a flower over it. Or a butterfly. No one will see it under the floss."

Cordelia blinked at her. "You can do that?"

"Good heavens, yes. I've bled gallons onto hems in my time. Change the pattern a bit, add another touch of embellishment, and no one will ever know that it wasn't supposed to be there all along. Here, let me show you how to draw out a little pattern. A butterfly, do you think? It can be hovering over the flower, and the nice thing about them is that you can make them any color you like, and use up the leftover ends of the thread . . ."

They worked together in companionable silence for several hours. Cordelia tackled the embroidery with fierce determination and improved noticeably while Hester watched. *Interesting. Not a fool, it seems. Determined. Fragile, though, and very young.*

"How old did you say you were, my dear?"

"Four . . . seventeen!" Cordelia's eyes shot up and she stabbed herself again with the needle and yelped.

"Which?" asked Hester gently.

"Seventeen." Cordelia's eyes flicked toward the closed door.

Wanting to bolt, or wanting to make sure no one is listening to hear her slip up? Interesting.

"It's quite all right," said Hester, as Cordelia began to stammer an explanation. She didn't want to make the girl lie to her. For one thing, she wasn't very good at it. "I forget how old I am regularly.

They say it's a sign of senility, but I don't think so. Sometimes it feels like I'm thirty-five again. It was a good age. My mind still feels thirty-five, it's only the rest of me that seems to have kept on going." Which was true, so far as it went, and it moved the conversation along. *Now why has Doom told her daughter that she is to give her age as seventeen? For she doesn't look it at all, and many women would want to claim their child was younger, so that they seem younger themselves.*

She can't be planning on marrying the girl off to my brother. Samuel's a bit of a fool, but he'd have no interest in a little thing right out of the schoolroom. And I would swear that she's trying to hook him for herself, not her daughter.

A bell sounded in the house, and Hester sighed. "Time to dress for dinner," she said, rising. "I'll have another shawl sent up to you, shall I?"

Cordelia blinked at her. "You've already given me so much," she protested.

"Bah. You're doing me a favor by clearing them out. That way Samuel can give me another one for Christmas and I can pretend to be delighted." She smiled down at the girl. "Lend me your arm, will you child? The stairs are a bit more than I like right now."

Cordelia scrambled to help her. She was stronger than she looked, Hester noticed. (She had no actual need of help on the stairs at the moment—the weather was fine and her knees were not giving her more than the usual trouble—but such things were interesting to know.) They parted ways and Hester went to her room, her thoughts as tangled as embroidery threads. *And much like those threads, I need to find a way to assemble them into a pattern that makes sense. Whatever that might be.*

"Damnation," Hester whispered to herself. "Damn it all to hell and beyond." Which was not language fitting for a lady, but this particular lady had a problem far beyond the scope of what she'd originally conceived.

She'd known that she would have to save her brother from

Doom's clutches. That was, if not easy, at least a straightforward enough task. But it was beginning to look as if she was going to have to extract Doom's own daughter as well, and that was a far more complicated proposition.

Hell and damn. I shouldn't . . . but I can't leave her like that. But what if that's what brings the whole thing down?

But what choice do I have?

Hester was no hero, but there was nothing in her that would allow her to turn away from a person who had been dropped on her doorstep. Even if that person had brought Doom along with her.

CHAPTER 8

Dinner was an unmitigated disaster.

The Squire sat at the head of the table, with Cordelia and her mother on either side of him. She nearly panicked when she saw the sheer number of forks and spoons. Dear god. It was a sea of flatware, all glittering in the candlelight. There was even a fork at the top of the plate and another by the spoons. And someone would have to wash them all up afterward?

She meant to watch her mother for cues, she truly did, but the first thing that happened was that an enormous centerpiece was brought in and placed, some kind of absurd folly with a whole lobster in a sea of aspic. Her mother laughed and clapped her hands like a girl. "Now that's something like, isn't it?" said the Squire proudly. Hester rolled her eyes.

Unfortunately the lobster blocked her view of her mother's plate completely, and she had no idea what fork to use. Was there a lobster-in-aspic fork? Were they all for the lobster, and you were supposed to stab at the thing's shell until your cutlery blunted?

A footman set a tiny plate in front of her, with three small bits of bread, topped with some kind of pinkish paste and a small triangle of meat. Cordelia stared at it in numb horror. Which fork? Did you use a fork? At home she would have picked it up with her fingers and stuffed it in her mouth, but clearly you were not provided with this many forks if you weren't supposed to use them. The etiquette primer was no help at all. It had apparently been written by someone who assumed that you already knew which forks to use, and that the worst sin you might commit was passing your plate with a knife or fork on it, or pouring your tea into a saucer to cool it.

The Squire was already eating. Her mother was saying something about the food being delicious, but her voice seemed to emanate from the lobster.

Hester cleared her throat. Cordelia looked over in panic and the older woman tapped the outmost of her forks, almost absently, then picked it up and speared one of the little hors d'oeuvres.

Relief flooded Cordelia so intensely that for a horrible moment, she thought she might faint, followed by an equally intense rush of gratitude. She picked up the outermost fork, which was apparently the small-bits-of-bread-and-pâté fork, and ate.

Next was soup, which used the broad, flat spoon, then asparagus with a mustard sauce, which used another fork and a knife, then a tiny salad, which used yet another fork, and by now even Cordelia was starting to get full and was beginning to understand why Hester kept leaving so much food on her plate. It seemed terribly wasteful.

She remembered belatedly that she was supposed to be charming the Squire. She snuck a look at him but he was deep in conversation with her mother. Cordelia relaxed slightly. Surely she wasn't supposed to interrupt? No, of course not. *The Ladies' Book of Etiquette* said that interrupting was "very ill-bred," which, coming from Miss Florence, was a judgment so savage as to consign the victim immediately to the fires of Perdition.

Two footmen brought in an enormous piece of beef and set it down. It looked as if it weighed nearly as much as a large dog. What in the name of heaven were they doing serving that much meat for four people?

An arm materialized next to her head and she squeaked. It was another footman, or perhaps an underbutler or something similar, taking a slice of beef and setting it on her plate, with a drizzle of dark sauce over it. "Thank you," Cordelia said.

Unfortunately she said it into a gap in the conversation and it rang out much more loudly across the table than she had intended. She shrank in on herself and realized that she had not heard anyone else thank the servants at all.

Her mother's indrawn breath was so loud in her ears that she expected the crystal to rattle. For a moment, she felt like she was back on the doorstep, having just curtsied to the butler.

The Squire turned to her and smiled, his eyes crinkling. Cordelia swallowed and gripped her napkin in white-knuckled fingers. "How are you liking Chatham House?" he asked.

"I ... I ..." Cordelia licked dry lips. "It's very grand, sir," she said, trying not to squeak. "And the maid you lent me is very kind." Wait, no, she was talking about servants again, apparently you didn't do that. She was supposed to ask him about himself. Men liked that. "Ah . . . have you . . . err . . . lived here long?"

The Squire laughed, a great booming laugh that made Cordelia shrink again. "All my life," he said. "The house has been in my family for five generations, since we came across the sea. Though it was not so grand initially. My grandfather had a passion for building and put two extra wings on."

"Fortunately our father was less extravagant," said Lady Hester, her voice dry. "He settled for putting in water closets." She took a sip of wine.

"Water closets are very useful," said Cordelia weakly. She had a feeling that her mother would not consider this charming conversation. She darted a guilty glance at the lobster.

"Mind you," said Hester, "for the amount of walls that had to be knocked out and floors torn up for pipes, I'm not certain that an extra wing would have been less trouble." She smiled politely over the lobster. "I'm sure you know how it is, Lady Evangeline."

"Oh yes," said Cordelia's mother. "Before he passed, rest his soul, my late husband had a passion for starting grand projects that he did not finish. He would read about a new invention and immediately begin thinking of ways to use it about the house. Not one of them worked. I loved him, of course, but it was enough to make a woman long for someone a bit . . . steadier."

Cordelia had never heard so many words about her father in her life. She stared at the beef and the sauce congealing on her plate, wondering if they were true.

When the time came to eat the lobster at last, the plate was removed from the table and then slivers of lobster meat and aspic placed in front of the diners. Even if Cordelia had not been full, she would not have been able to eat. Her mother gave her a sharp glare and jerked her head to the Squire.

"Uh . . . ah . . ." She tried to think of another question. "Do you . . . err . . . like lobster, sir?"

Ridiculous question. He must or they wouldn't serve it, would they? She didn't dare look at her mother.

"Love it," said the Squire happily. "We never had it when I was a lad, you know."

"You didn't?"

"No, my mother wouldn't have it in the house." The Squire spooned up a bit and popped it into his mouth, then dabbed his chin with his napkin. "She was from far up the north coast, you see, where lobster's as common as turnips. Fishermen eat it five meals of the week. Mother said it tasted like poverty and she couldn't abide the smell."

"Where on the north coast?" asked Evangeline, deftly taking control of the conversation. The Squire explained in tediously precise terms, and she clapped her hands in apparent delight.

"I've been there," she said. "Oh, years ago, when I was a girl. With the little white houses with the funny shingles on the roof?"

"Yes, exactly." She and the Squire went back into their conversation, with Evangeline expressing her desire to go back someday— "Such a lovely countryside!"—and the Squire giving her an extensive description of his family's holdings in the region, and every huntable beast that crawled, swam, flew, or ran.

Cordelia sank back into her chair, hoping that she had averted disaster. When she looked over at Hester, the Squire's sister gave her a rueful smile and murmured, "Hunting is always such a spectacle."

It is, Cordelia thought grimly, *and she's going to keep hunting the Squire until she catches him.*

Cordelia woke with a panicky start, remembering dinner the night before. She almost certainly had not been charming enough. She'd used the right forks, at least, but her mother couldn't very well see around the lobster to notice that.

I haven't been in school for years. The most I speak to anyone is after church, or riding with Ellen. Surely she couldn't have expected me to do any better than that.

It was a hopeless thought. Her mother would certainly have expected better. Evangeline was not concerned with such things as shyness or inexperience.

The thought struck her that her mother might come into the room to scold her and that propelled Cordelia out of bed. Her room was such an unexpected oasis that she did not want her mother coming into it if she could help it. It felt safe and Cordelia knew that it would only feel that way so long as Evangeline did not set foot within it.

Alice tapped on the door as soon as Cordelia's feet hit the floor. "Come in," called Cordelia, and despite her dread, the words gave her a tiny thrill, as if she were doing something illicit.

"I've rung for tea," said the maid cheerfully. "Would you like breakfast up here, or would you like to go down?"

Cordelia bit her lip. She would have preferred to see no one, but if she went down to eat breakfast with Hester and the Squire, her mother couldn't do anything terrible to her over breakfast. Would that be better or worse? The longer her mother had to wait, the more likely she was to have rewritten the story of what had happened in her head. That could be good or bad, depending on whether she decided that Cordelia was maliciously stubborn or simply hopelessly ignorant.

In the end, she decided to go down. If the Squire was there, perhaps she could try being charming again and buy herself some goodwill.

As it happened, her mother wasn't there at all yet. "Help yourself, my dear," said the Squire, looking cheerful and avuncular despite the early hour. He waved to the sideboard. "We don't stand on ceremony this early."

Hester was already sitting there with a cup of tea in one hand and a broadsheet in the other. The rest of the newspaper was spread out in the corner between her and the Squire, and they were both picking up pages and reading through it. Cordelia took a plate and set several cold meats and a hard-boiled egg on it. She was not used to quite such an extravagant breakfast.

A servant poured tea for her. "Would miss like chocolate?" he asked.

"Tea is—" Cordelia realized that she was whispering, licked her lips, and tried again. This time her voice came out slightly louder. "Tea is fine, thank you." *Oh damn, I've thanked the servant again.* Her first instinct was to apologize, but if you weren't supposed to thank the servants, you *definitely* weren't supposed to apologize to them. She gave him an agonized look, hoping it would serve as apology without the extra faux pas of being spoken aloud.

He winked at her. Cordelia felt an intense rush of relief and gulped her tea, which was so hot it burned her tongue.

"Good heavens," said the Squire with horrified relish. "How dreadful!"

Cordelia shrank in on herself, thinking that the man had somehow noticed her exchange with the servant, but the Squire was staring at the broadsheet in front of him.

"Eh?" Hester glanced up. "What, did the price of tea go up again?"

The Squire cleared his throat. "'Grisly Scene at Manor House,'" he read aloud. "'Constables were summoned to the estate of the Parker family in the town of Little Haw Tuesday morning, following reports of screams emanating from within the manor. They found there a scene of carnage, as it appears the patriarch of the family, one Edward Parker, fifty-five, had assaulted the other members of his family with an axe.'"

Parker. Cordelia felt the world begin to go gray around the edges. *Parker of Little Haw.* There was a terrible ringing in her ears, but it did not drown out the sound of the Squire's voice, still reading in a litany of fascinated horror.

"'Coroner George Keeling made an examination of eight people and pronounced life extinct, giving his opinion that they had been brutally murdered. The doors were locked and in the opinion of the police constable, no entry had been forced. The deceased include three servants and five members of the Parker clan. Most astonishing is the behavior of Edward Parker himself, who opened the door for the police, stating that "A terrible thing has occurred, gentlemen." He has been taken into custody. Two survivors have suffered grave injury but have stated that it was Parker who attacked them. For his part, he has made no denial of these charges.'" He folded the paper back. "Now what do you say to that, old girl?"

"Monstrous, the things people do these days," said Hester. "That poor family. I wonder if they'll ever know why he did it."

I know why he did it, thought Cordelia, but that was the last coherent thought she had, before the world dissolved into gray and black.

"Really, Samuel," said Hester, annoyed. "You should know better than to read such things at the breakfast table when there's a young girl present." She waved the smelling salts under Cordelia's nose, waiting for her to come out of her swoon.

Swoon was perhaps too mild a term. Hester had seen her share of artful swoons practiced by artful temptresses. They tended to involve the back of the hand pressed against the forehead, an exclamation—"Oh! I feel faint!"—and then a graceful crumpling to the floor, carefully conducted so as to miss any inconvenient furniture.

Cordelia had turned bone white, her eyes had rolled up in her head, and she had slumped over sideways and fallen out of the chair, hitting another one on the way down.

"Didn't even think of it," said the Squire anxiously. "You never balk at any story, old girl. Clean forgot other ladies might not like it. Is the chit alive?"

Cordelia proved that she was alive by coughing and sitting up, pushing away the smelling salts. "What . . . what am I . . . ?" She blinked up at Hester. "Why am I on the floor?"

"You fainted," said Hester, softening the words with a smile. "And no wonder. You'd hardly touched your food yet, and my brother was reading a hair-raiser of a tale over breakfast."

"I'm so sorry," said Cordelia. She scrambled to her feet, started to sway, and Hester caught her arm to steady it before she went over again. "I . . ." She swallowed and Hester saw her pupils suddenly dilate. "Oh," she said, in a much smaller voice, and sat down.

"Don't pay any mind to me," said the Squire earnestly. "So terribly sorry. I'm an old fool, that's all, and forget how to behave around a gently bred young lady. I should never have read such a thing out for your ears."

Cordelia picked up her teacup and wrapped her fingers around it. "It's all right," she whispered. Hester thought she might be fighting back tears. "I'd rather know."

A terrible thought struck Hester. "You didn't know the family, did you?"

The vein in the girl's throat began to pulse. "Little Haw," she stammered. "We're from Little Haw."

The door to the breakfast room opened and Evangeline breezed in, dressed in an extravagant dressing gown that Hester recognized as having come from her own wardrobe about twenty years earlier. Her brother must have offered some of her clothing to replace what Evangeline had lost in the oh-so-convenient carriage accident.

In another situation, Hester would not have minded. She had plenty of clothing that she was never going to wear and she understood genteel poverty and the stories that one might tell to cover the fact that one had only one or two gowns to one's name. But it did strike her as a bit much that Doom had come to her home, and that in addition to making conversation and waiting for the inevitable, she was expected to furnish Doom's wardrobe as well.

"How is everyone this fine morning?" Evangeline trilled. She squeezed Cordelia's shoulder and Hester saw the girl's knuckles go even whiter on the teacup.

"I'm afraid poor Cordelia's taken faint," said the Squire. "All my fault, really. I was reading a regular hair-raiser of a story and I didn't know that you were from that neck of the woods. Damn poor manners of me, and I make my apology to you, young lady."

"It's fine," said Cordelia, as her mother's fingers dug into her shoulder. "I'm sorry for making a fuss." She shot a nervous glance behind her. "I . . . uh . . . I think I should go lie down."

"Probably for the best," said Evangeline, in a glittering voice. The Squire murmured another apology as Cordelia bolted for the door. A footman removed her plate, and Hester made a mental note to send up a tray in a few minutes.

"Please forgive her," Evangeline said. "I think she is still quite fatigued from our journey, and this is the first time she has traveled so far from home."

"No, no." The Squire's mustache quivered with his sincerity. "All my fault, my dear, truly all mine. I forget that most well-bred ladies have nerves. Hester hasn't any at all, you see."

"None whatsoever," said Hester dryly. "Otherwise people might get on them." She turned to Doom. "There was a terrible murder in Little Haw, you see, and your daughter was overset by the thought that she might know the victims."

Was there an imperceptible pause? It was hard to tell. But Evangeline's voice was quite casual. "Little Haw? I can't imagine why she'd think that."

"She said that you were from there," Hester said, genuinely curious as to what the response would be.

The pause lasted a fraction longer this time. "I suppose we're from *near* there," said Evangeline. "I doubt we've gone into the town more than a handful of times. It's not the closest." She smiled at the Squire. "I must beg your pardon for my daughter again, sir. You know how young girls are, giving themselves die-away airs about how close terrible events have come. They think it makes them interesting at that age."

"Think nothing of it," said the Squire. "And it was a terrible tale, I own, so I think no less of her. Sensitive little soul."

"So many girls are at that age," said Evangeline.

"How old is she again?" asked Hester.

"Seventeen."

"She seems so young for it."

Doom's glance was quick and cold. Hester smiled comfortably and adjusted her shawl. "Of course, I'm old enough that everyone looks young to me now. Twelve or twenty, I can hardly tell them apart any longer. And they have so much energy! Goodness. I'm sure I must have been the same, but it's so hard to remember now. Did we really dance all night long back then?"

There you go, she thought, as Evangeline turned away to the sideboard. *Ignore me. Keep thinking that I'm just a silly old woman. It will make it easier for me to do whatever I'm going to do to stop you.*

I just wish I knew what the hell that was going to be.

CHAPTER 9

Dinner that night was horrible.

Hester had been slightly late to supper, and as she took her seat next to Cordelia, the girl turned to smile at her and dread had risen up and grabbed her in a now-familiar embrace.

Cordelia was different. Terribly, dreadfully different, as if fainting had allowed some stranger to sneak in and take over her body. She was smiling and warm and assured. She used the silverware as if she had done so all her life, instead of shooting nervous glances at Hester to make certain that she had picked up the proper spoon. And she *prattled*.

There was really no other word for it. She prattled to the Squire about horses and how beautiful her horse was and did the Squire have a favorite horse and weren't they the most marvelous creatures and surely he had many exciting stories about jumps he had taken on horses and races he had seen? Which he did, of course, and was gratified to tell them all at garrulous length, while Cordelia watched with her lips slightly parted in delight.

Men! thought Hester, disgusted. If she were being honest, though, most of her disgust was for herself. She'd been taken in completely by the terrified-rabbit act, and here Doom's daughter was, clearly cut from the same cloth as Doom herself. *More the fool me, falling for such an act. No, the sooner the pair of them are gone, the better.*

Evangeline made a few comments, but seemed rather quiet this evening. Her daughter was obviously making up for it. Hester ignored everyone else at the table resolutely and had a second glass of wine.

It was not until they had risen from the table and she was about to plead a headache and retire to her rooms that something caught her attention.

Evangeline was making her apologies to the Squire for not joining him for an after-dinner drink, but they were having dress-fitting tomorrow, and she should make an early night of it. She did look a bit weary, her face slightly more drawn than Hester would have expected.

That was not the odd thing. It was when Hester left the room, and found Cordelia standing outside the door. Her face was slack and her arms dangled loosely at her sides. But the eyes that met Hester's were wild with panic, no longer a frightened rabbit, but one in a snare that, in a few more moments, would tighten and end its life.

"And now you're upset with me," said her mother, as Cordelia drew in a great shuddering breath and sat up on the bed. Her body felt like a stranger's and her throat was dry and sore. Her mother had made her eat but had forgotten to have her drink anything. There was a little tea table on the opposite side of the bed that always contained a ewer of water and a glass. Were her legs strong enough to get to it? They were. She got to her feet, swaying, and made her way around the foot of the bed, holding on to the carved footboard for support.

"Really, Cordelia," her mother said, sounding annoyed. "You might at least have made an effort. It's not as if I enjoy doing that, but what else can I do when you sit there like a lump of wood?"

The water struck her throat feeling almost solid, and she choked a little as she swallowed. It hurt, but at least choking gave her an excuse not to answer right away. *She's in my room. She brought me here while Alice wasn't here to keep her out, and now she's in the room. Two doors didn't stop her.*

No amount of doors will ever stop her.

"And if I'm having to talk for you, I can't say much of anything for myself, now can I? Why, the Squire even asked if I was feeling all right!" Evangeline folded her arms and pressed her lips together.

"Yes, Mother," whispered Cordelia, taking another long drink of water.

"You are going to marry a rich man someday quite soon, and to do that, I expect you to be charming. Rich husbands are not exactly thick on the ground, you know, and there are plenty of far more beautiful girls who are going to be competing for the same ones." Evangeline's perfect lips twisted into a frown.

Cordelia's head was pounding and her throat still burned. "We never practiced being charming in school," she said hoarsely. If she phrased it like that, it sounded like she was blaming the school, not her mother. It was the safest way.

Evangeline's frown grew to a scowl. "Worthless teachers," she said. "What is the point of teaching you geometry and not conversation?"

It hadn't been a finishing school. It had just been a little schoolhouse with two teachers, one for older children and one for younger. Cordelia knew that her mother was being unreasonable, because Ellen had told her all about her deportment tutor and how her sisters had been sent to a school for young ladies and how Ellen herself would attend one soon. Learning to be a young lady was a full-time class schedule, according to Ellen.

Oh god, thought Cordelia, staring into the empty water ewer. *Oh god, let Ellen be alive. Let her have gone off riding or gone to the school for young ladies. Let her not be one of the five family members her father killed. Please, god. Let her even be injured, but let her recover.*

Her mother might have kept going, but Alice slipped into the room and curtsied. "Apologies, miss," she said. "I didn't know you'd come up from dinner so soon. Will you be wanting a bath?"

Cordelia shook her head. She wanted to curl into a ball and shake, but she could not do that. She certainly could not ask Alice to stand up to her mother. It was much too dangerous for her and Cordelia both.

"I have a headache," she said instead. "May I have headache powders, please? If it's not too much trouble."

"Of course, miss. And I'll have Cook send up one of her teas. Miraculous, they are."

She stepped out of the room and Evangeline eyed the door with mild dislike. "So many servants," she muttered. "I'd forgotten how many servants you have to deal with in a great pile like this."

Cordelia said nothing.

"At any rate," said her mother, rising, "get some rest. We've the dress fitting tomorrow, and you may not plead headache or fall into a faint at it."

"Yes, Mother."

"I'm doing this all for you, you know."

"Yes, Mother. I know."

She waited until her mother had gone, and until Alice had returned with a cup of something strong and herbal. She drank it dutifully, and let herself be put into the great curtained bed.

When the door had opened and closed again and she no longer heard Alice moving around in the next room, Cordelia slipped out from under the covers, moved the curtains aside, and went to the enormous wardrobe that stood in the corner. Her dresses took up a tiny sliver of the space and the floor was bare.

She climbed into it and curled up into the smallest possible ball on the boards. They smelled of cedar, which was too close to wormwood, but there were lavender sachets tucked into the drawers and that changed the scent to something different. Something safer. She pulled the wardrobe door closed. It was solid wood and it was between Cordelia and the room that her mother had been in. It was not enough but it was something, and eventually, in the cedar-and-lavender-scented darkness, she fell asleep.

Alice had found her in the wardrobe that morning. She had opened the door and reached for a gown and then she had frozen with her hand outstretched, while Cordelia stared up at her in horror.

Their eyes met and held for a long few seconds and what Cordelia read there reminded her of Ellen, the same sadness and pity. She was not proud enough to reject the pity, but she feared it nonetheless, because something terrible had happened to Ellen and she knew that she was not strong enough to keep it from happening to Alice.

The other girl reached down and took her arm and helped her to her feet. Cordelia's back ached from sleeping in such a small space and she made a small sound of pain.

"It'll be all right," said Alice, and Cordelia knew that she wasn't talking about the backache. The maid's hand gripped hers, and it felt almost like a friend's hand, not like someone who was being paid to care for her. "It will."

"It won't," whispered Cordelia. Ellen had said the same thing, and look what had happened to her. "She can do such terrible things and I can't stop her."

Alice squeezed her fingers. "It will come out right in the end," she said firmly. Then she released Cordelia's hand and said, as calmly as if all respectable young ladies slept on the floor of their wardrobe, "Will you be wanting tea or hot chocolate this morning, miss?"

And Cordelia had said, "Tea, please," and had gotten dressed and was ready when her mother came looking for her.

It was a long drive into the city, though not as long as the one to the Squire's house had been. Falada was a bright, treacherous light between the carriage shafts. Cordelia looked out across the cold gray fields and pulled the borrowed shawl more tightly around her shoulders, her face as still and calm as practice could make it. She felt as if everyone should be able to tell that the coach was stolen, and furthermore, what had happened to the rightful owner. It seemed like blood should drip from the seats or the wheels should shriek or something equally dramatic.

But nothing happened. Cordelia watched the landscape go by, the fields turning to houses, the great smudge of the city growing on the horizon, and no one came after them screaming, "Stop, thief!"

They rode in silence for a time, and finally Evangeline sighed and said, "Are you still sulking about last night? Really, Cordelia, you'd think that you were five years old."

"No!" That came out much too explosively. "No, I . . . I'm cold, that's all." That was true enough and not a dangerous observation.

"Oh, is that all? Well, it's chilly out this morning, that's true."

"It is," said Cordelia, determined to speak and shed the accusation of sulking.

"You'll be warmer soon," said her mother cheerfully. "A new coat and muff, I think, lined with fur. You'll like that, won't you?"

"That sounds very nice," said Cordelia. This was also true. It sounded nice. She had not had a new coat in years, and did not particularly expect that to change, but it did sound nice.

Traffic going into the city picked up as they approached. First it was assorted farm carts loaded with produce, then a mail coach, then enclosed carriages that presumably carried passengers. The birdsong of the countryside was replaced with shouting and grumbling and the creak of wheels.

A young man in another cabriolet pulled alongside them and cracked his whip overhead, calling something. Evangeline lifted her chin derisively. Cordelia wondered if he had said something insulting, when suddenly Falada went from a trot to a canter, threading his way between the heavier farm carts with contemptuous ease. Cordelia looked over her shoulder and saw the young man frantically wielding his whip, but his bay horse could not compete with Falada's speed.

"Fool," said Evangeline, pleased. "Thinking he could race me with a mortal horse."

She was not so pleased once they had swung around the outer edge of the city and reached the broad stretch of stableyards that sold carts and carriages and horseflesh. The one that she made toward had an archway over the entrance, with HOWARD's written across it in spiky metal lettering. The yard was already full of people, working on axles and wheels, touching up paint, and Cordelia could hear the sounds of a blacksmith hammering somewhere in the background.

They had barely pulled in when something over the archway flashed with green light and the air suddenly stank of burning hair. Everyone in the stableyard froze and Cordelia could feel dozens of eyes turning toward them. Cordelia's mother cursed softly under her breath.

"Back, back, get back, you gapeseeds," snapped a voice, and a man pushed his way forward. He was short and stocky and his clothing was worn, but he carried himself with absolute authority. *Is this Howard?*

He eyed Falada and snorted loudly, then turned to Evangeline. "I'll not be buying that horse, ma'am."

"Indeed you won't," said Evangeline in crisp tones, "because he's not for sale. I was told you offered a fair price for carriages as well."

Howard gave her a frankly skeptical look. "You were told correctly, but I don't deal in enchantments."

"The carriage is as plain as you are, my good man." Cordelia's mother set the reins aside and stepped down from the seat. The stableman did not offer her his hand.

Cordelia scrambled down on the other side, hoping no one was looking at her. *Oh please, let her not do something horrible in front of all these people.* She didn't know if she was afraid that all the onlookers would be hurt, or simply that they would see it happen and then . . . then . . . well, presumably something would happen.

It struck Cordelia suddenly that she did not know what would happen if someone found out that her mother was a sorceress. Was it illegal? The preacher in church had preached against magic folk, but he didn't say it was a crime, just that it was immoral. *But surely you can't enchant people like Ellen's father and have him murder his family and get away with it, can you? If anyone found out, they'd punish her. That's murder, isn't it? They hang people for murder.*

And I knew about it and I haven't told anyone and we're riding in a stolen coach right now, so I'd be an accomplice.

This thought was so horrifying that she missed most of the negotiations between Howard and her mother. After Falada had been removed from the shafts, another horse went in and drove the cabriolet back and forth under the archway. There was no smell or flash of light, so that must have proved that the carriage was perfectly ordinary. Apparently this was enough to satisfy Howard, because her mother went into a building with him and came out a few minutes later, tucking something into her bag.

"Come, Cordelia," she said, leading the way from the yard. She nodded to Falada, who whickered, turned, and set off at a jog down the road.

One of the stablehands crossed himself as they passed. Cordelia's mother ignored him and swept grandly on, her head held high, walking into the heart of the city.

CHAPTER 10

"Excuse me, ma'am, but I've a problem I could use your advice on," said the servant girl, curtsying.

"Hmm?" Hester set down her embroidery. "Sorry—Alice, isn't it? Or was that your mother? I'm afraid my memory isn't what it was."

"Alice is it," said the girl, smiling. She was a tall, sturdy young woman, and while she looked, to Hester's eyes, impossibly young, she probably wasn't. "My mum was in service here for a few years, but she's called Katherine."

"Katherine, yes. A fine young woman, as I recall. Or not so young now, probably. Married one of the stable lads, didn't she?"

"Yes, ma'am."

"Keeping well, is she?"

"Mostly, ma'am. Her joints pain her something fierce when it's cold."

"Her and me both," said Hester wearily. Her knee was throbbing this morning. "Tell the housekeeper I said to send along some of the balm she mixes up. Perhaps it'll do her some good as well."

"That's very kind of you, ma'am. I'll tell her you asked after her."

"So what seems to be the problem, Alice? One of the lads isn't giving you trouble, are they?"

"Huh!" Alice sniffed. "They wouldn't dare. No, ma'am, it's Miss Cordelia."

Hester raised her eyebrows. It was unheard of for a servant to complain to the lady of the house instead of to the housekeeper, who would then bring it to the lady if she felt it was required. Matters must be dire indeed if Alice was skipping over that worthy's head.

Even if she had been inclined to scold, which she wasn't, this was sufficiently peculiar that Alice claimed her undivided attention.

"Is something wrong? Has she fainted again?"

"Not fainted, ma'am, but . . ." Alice glanced over her shoulder at the closed door. The words came out all in a rush. "Ma'am, somebody's doing something bad to that girl and I'm afraid for her."

Hester sat back, startled. "Something bad?"

Alice nodded. "Don't rightly know what," she admitted. "But she acts like my little cousin did, and it turned out their neighbor was . . . well, never mind that, ma'am."

"Ah," said Hester, a world of understanding packed into that syllable. She and Alice shared a look that for once had nothing to do with rank. "And you think . . . ?"

"Something like, ma'am. When her mother shows up, she flinches like she's expecting the belt. And this morning, I found her asleep in the wardrobe like she were trying to hide."

Hester rubbed her forehead. No wonder Alice had skipped over the usual chain of command. The housekeeper could hardly do anything about Evangeline, and Alice probably knew better than Hester did how quickly gossip spread through the house.

"Have you told anyone else about this?" she asked.

"No, ma'am." Alice shook her head. "It ain't their business and it ain't a thing they need to be talking about." Her lips twisted up. "And it ain't a thing they can fix, either. Nor me. But maybe you can, ma'am."

Hester let out a long sigh. "I don't know," she admitted. "I don't think you're wrong but I don't know what to do yet. I can't just snatch a child away from her mother, even if her mother is . . . ah . . ."

Alice snorted. "Her mother's a fair piece of work, if you'll forgive me speaking so bold, ma'am."

"If anyone asks, I had very harsh words with you about speaking so of your betters and so forth." Hester waved her hand.

"I was quaking in my boots, ma'am."

"Yes, quite. Lord, that woman is dreadful, isn't she? Has she done anything to the staff that I should know about?"

"Given them the rough side of her tongue, but no more that I know of, ma'am. But there's something about the way she looks at you that nobody much likes. Like you're a bit of furniture and she's already deciding whether she'll throw you out."

Hester massaged her temples, thinking that was probably very true. "If you do hear of anything, please come and tell me, Alice. I won't stand for her making trouble with the household. And we won't be letting anyone go on her say-so, in case anyone belowstairs is afraid to speak up because of it."

"Yes, ma'am."

"You did right telling me. I knew that something was wrong, but not how bad it was."

"I think she tries to put a good face on it, ma'am. Afraid to make trouble, maybe, or just afraid that her mother'll hear of it." She scowled. "My little cousin did that too."

"That neighbor was dealt with, I trust?"

Alice nodded solemnly. "Fell down a well. Terrible unlucky, it was."

"Well, accidents do happen." Hester stabbed the cloth with her embroidery needle. "We'll see what we can do for Miss Cordelia. Perhaps there's some useful abandoned wells in the neighborhood. Meanwhile . . . well, she's young and I don't think she's had many friends. I can hardly order you to befriend her, and I know it's awkward because of your position, but if she happens to confide in you . . ."

Alice nodded. "I'll do my best, ma'am. She's no trouble to work for, except that it's hard to get an order out of her sometimes."

Hester nodded. People, regardless of their social class, generally preferred clear directions, she'd found, so that everybody knew where they stood and what was expected of them. It was when people were left to flounder on their own that things started to fall apart.

After Alice had left, she found herself staring out the window again. It was the sort of damp, gray day enjoyed by ducks and frogs and very few humans. Occasionally the fog would solidify into rain, but it would quickly lose interest and go back to being fog again.

"And what the devil am I supposed to do now?" she murmured to the windowpane. "Hiding in the closet, is she?" Hester abandoned the notion that Doom's daughter was a willing co-conspirator, no matter how she'd acted at dinner. That had been a performance, and judging by Alice's report, not one she'd given particularly happily. *The more impressive bit is that she was able to give it at all. I would never have thought she had that in her.*

"I must send for Richard," muttered Hester to herself. "I must." Not that Richard would necessarily know what to do, but at least she would have an ally in the house.

If she was being honest, more than an ally. She felt steadier when Richard was around, more competent, more herself. Maybe she should have married him, dammit. Well, right or wrong, the chance had passed her by. He had moved on, even if he hadn't yet wed. *Not that I expected him to be celibate for the last decade, even so.*

Still, he was her dearest friend. He was also the only one who, if she told him that she had had a premonition of doom, would take her seriously.

And you can do worse for an ally than a lord of the realm. You just have to move before Doom manages to snare the Squire once and for all.

"Be polite," Cordelia's mother ordered, as they approached the dress shop. "Your dressmaker can destroy you with a seam. She can make you look utterly ridiculous and you won't know it until you're at a ball. You will do what she asks and you will not sulk or argue, do I make myself clear?"

I hardly ever argue. And I wasn't sulking at dinner, I just didn't know how I was supposed to make conversation. But she could not say these things, so she only murmured agreement and stuffed the resentment down where it wouldn't color her tone.

Instead she asked, "Do you think the man at the carriageyard will tell people about the magic?"

Evangeline made a scoffing sound. "Assuming he cared, and assuming he found someone who would listen, the very worst they could say was that Falada's got a glamour on him. Which I shan't deny, and shall claim that it was a gift from a friend. No one will care."

"Oh." There were too many people on the sidewalks and Cordelia kept stepping aside, trying not to run into anyone. She found herself falling behind her mother, who walked as if people should get out of her way.

"Do keep up, Cordelia," her mother said, pausing to wait for her. "And don't fret yourself so. No one will suspect a thing. No one suspected anything back home, now did they?" She smiled suddenly, showing a sharp edge of tooth. "And even if they did decide to burn me as a witch, they'd get no joy of it, I assure you."

But what would I do? Cordelia wondered hopelessly. *I'm not a sorcerer, but they'd burn me, too. Assuming anybody burns witches anymore, which I don't think they do?* She couldn't remember hearing of such a thing, but Little Haw was not exactly known for getting news of the wider world.

Oh well. At least if I'm going to be burned at the stake, I'll be well-dressed . . .

The dressmaker was named Mrs. Tan, and she had skin the color of old ivory and thick, shining black hair. She surveyed Cordelia, then turned to her mother. "You said she is seventeen?"

"She is," said her mother.

Mrs. Tan made a noncommittal sound. "She looks young for it."
Cordelia kept her face absolutely still. Her mother shrugged.

"Mmm." Mrs. Tan walked around her, arms folded, tapping
her finger on her forearm. At one point she reached out and tipped
Cordelia's chin up, but did not meet her gaze. She seemed to be
studying the line of her neck.

"Walk," she ordered finally. "To the far wall and back." Cordelia
obeyed, trying not to stumble. She wasn't used to thinking about
how she walked, and suddenly the whole concept of walking
seemed completely absurd. You fell forward and put out a foot to
catch yourself before you sprawled on the ground. And then you
did it again? And this was normal?

*It's like thinking about blinking. The moment you think about it,
you start to worry that you aren't blinking often enough, or too often
and now I'm thinking about blinking, oh dear . . .*

Still, her feet took care of themselves while she was worried
about blinking too much, so that was a small mercy.

An assistant appeared from somewhere, carrying a measur-
ing tape, and circled behind her. Cordelia's gown was in a puddle
around her feet before she realized that the girl had undone the
buttons. She stepped out of it awkwardly, standing in her worn
shift, and the girl whisked the gown away and began applying the
tape to various portions of her anatomy.

"So young looking," said Mrs. Tan again, making clear that it
was not precisely a compliment. "They will wonder, the people,
why she is not in the schoolroom."

"I thought that perhaps you could cut the dress to make her look
older," said Evangeline, with a diffidence that astounded Cordelia.
She was not used to her mother being diffident to anyone. "Lower
the bodice, maybe, so she looks less like a schoolroom miss."

Mrs. Tan was already shaking her head. "No. She will look as
a child playing dress-up, or a worse thing. I will not say it, but you
know the tongues they have in their heads, these people."

"I know," said Evangeline fervently.

"She must be dressed as modestly as any young girl might be," said Mrs. Tan firmly. "But we shall do so in the boldest colors. These pale pinks, these yellows that the misses wear, they only wash her out. Emerald and sapphire, now, these are the colors for such skin as she has." She gestured, apparently to thin air, and another assistant materialized. Mrs. Tan snapped out the names of colors and fabrics and distant ports, and the assistant nodded, vanishing.

"You know best," murmured Evangeline. Cordelia tried not to stare, but she could not shake the feeling that she had fallen into a different world, where a dressmaker wielded more power than a sorceress.

Mrs. Tan's assistant reappeared a few minutes later carrying an armful of vivid fabrics. Then it was Cordelia's job to stand and stand and stand some more, while cloth was draped over her shoulders, rejected, removed, and then re-draped again. *This must be how a mannequin feels.*

It took hours. Cordelia was never asked her opinion, which was fine, because she had no idea what she would say. All she could remember from *The Ladies' Book of Etiquette* was the line *"A lady is never so well dressed as when you cannot remember what she wears"* and somehow, she did not think that Mrs. Tan would agree.

Eventually the fabrics were selected, and then it was time for a plain muslin fabric to mock up the patterns and pins to hold it in place. Cordelia gazed at the wall, wearing the vacant, amiable expression that she had cultivated, while the assistants clipped and pinned and fitted. Her stomach growled embarrassingly. *I should have eaten something at breakfast.*

It should not have been so tiring to stand in one place. She wasn't cooking or cleaning or scrubbing or even riding a horse. Nevertheless, by the time Mrs. Tan and her assistants were done, Cordelia felt as limp as boiled spinach. Her muscles ached from immobility and her feet throbbed.

Even then she was not done. Then there were hats and gloves and stockings to be procured. A man traced the shape of her feet on a sheet of paper and told her mother that it would be five days. Cordelia was surprised that her feet still looked normal. They felt as if they should be glowing angry red, and perhaps snarling audibly at strangers.

"Shoes one must have made," said her mother, "but pre-made gloves are as good as any, I think. Cordelia, are you paying attention?"

"Yes, Mother," lied Cordelia, as she tried on glove after glove, and eventually said that they were comfortable because she no longer had any idea how anything felt. Everything went into packages tied with string—hats, gloves, stockings, a set of undergarments from Mrs. Tan's which had required only a few stitches to fit. "No one will see them," said the dressmaker airily, "until such time as you are married. And if one does see them before then, that there is no lace will be the least part of the scandal."

Alice will see them, Cordelia thought. *I'll see them.* Perhaps neither she nor Alice counted. That seemed unfair. She had never counted for much, but it seemed as if Alice ought to. Anyone who could stand up to Evangeline, even so politely, counted for a great deal.

She was too tired to question why there was a coach waiting outside when they were finished, with the crest of Chatham on the door. The footman was wearing the Squire's livery. He helped her up into the coach and took possession of the packages that Evangeline directed toward him.

Cordelia fell asleep on the coach ride home and woke only as the wheels crunched on the gravel of the stableyard. She climbed out, her knees shaky when she hit the ground, and clutched embarrassingly at the footman for balance. "I'm sorry," she said.

"Not at all, miss," he said. He smiled at her. "Quite a long day, I would imagine."

She nodded gratefully and picked her way inside, up the stairs to her room, hoping that she could collapse for a bit and beg Alice to bring her something to eat at last.

Hester's knee was particularly unhappy this evening, and she decided to go up to her room by the second staircase, which had broader, flatter steps. It took her out of her way and past two extra parlors and a sitting room, but at least she could get up the stairs without puffing and gasping like a horse with its wind broken.

She was just about to put her cane on the first step when she heard a voice from one of the parlors.

"I hope to be out of your hair soon, my lord," said Evangeline. "You've been so kind . . . so unbelievably kind . . . and we have imposed upon your generosity most shamefully."

"Nonsense," said her brother stoutly. "Been a joy to have you. Wish you'd stay longer, in fact."

"Oh Samuel," said Evangeline, in a breathy little voice, "how I wish I could!"

Hester rolled her eyes upward and gazed at the crown molding, wishing for strength.

"So stay a while longer, then. No reason not to, m'dear. Place is livelier with you in it."

"Oh Samuel . . . you're so good . . . and I've become so very fond of you . . ."

There was an ornate vase on a nearby side table. Hester imagined knocking it over with her cane and interrupting the theatrics with a satisfying crashing sound.

"Fond of you too, Evangeline. You must know that."

"But I can't, Samuel. Not respectably. People will talk. They'll say such cruel things."

"Pfaaugh. Don't care a jot for any of that. People have nasty little minds."

"You are so strong, my lord. So determined. But I'm a weak widow alone in the world, and the thought of the gossip—of someone saying I'm throwing myself at you in an unbecoming fashion, when you must know that what I feel—"

Right, that's enough of that. Hester stomped past the doorway, making as much noise as she could with her cane. "Oh!" she said, feigning surprise at seeing the pair inside. "Samuel? Is that you?"

The Squire and Evangeline leapt apart as if they'd been caught doing something illicit. Evangeline flashed a look of unguarded rage at Hester, who pretended to ignore it completely.

"Samuel, I was looking for you. I was thinking since we're already having a bit of a house party with Evangeline and Cordelia here, we might as well make it the real thing. I thought I'd invite Lord and Lady Strauss and their son for a few weeks, and that amusing Green woman, and perhaps Richard."

"Richard, eh?" said the Squire, shooting her a wry look.

And that's what I get for thinking of my brother as a fool all the time. "Well," she said. "You know how tiresome an unbalanced table is. This will give us nicely equal numbers all around. And should you find that you do not wish to ride out after grouse or pheasant or dragons or whatever it is that you hunting gentlemen ride after, Richard and Lord Strauss are old friends as well."

If nothing else, I'll have more warm bodies to throw between the two of you. Imogene Strauss will help me run interference, and Richard will keep me grounded.

And if all else fails, at least I'll have someone to drink myself unconscious with when it all goes to hell.

"There you go, my dear," said the Squire, beaming at Evangeline. "A house party! Completely respectable, and no one could say otherwise."

"Well," said Evangeline, her voice a trifle brittle but otherwise above reproach, "I see that you have thought of everything, Lady Hester. It is too good of you."

"Not at all, not at all." She sank down on a sofa and smiled warmly at Doom. "Are there any particular friends of your daughter's that I might invite?"

"No," said Evangeline, after a scant pause. "No, I don't think so. I can't say that she has ever had any *particular* friends."

And would you have discouraged it if she did? Somehow Hester suspected that she might.

She kept up a stream of deliberately inconsequential chatter about what activities might be best for a house party, until eventually Doom excused herself to go to bed. Hester stifled a sigh of relief as she left and eyed her brother thoughtfully.

Do I warn him? Point out that she may have an eye toward the parson's mousetrap? Or will I risk driving him further into her arms?

She decided not to risk it. Words could always be said, but could rarely be unsaid. And her brother had proved adroit at warding off marriage for many years.

Though I do not think he's faced an opponent like this one before. Hester sought her own chambers and sat down to write invitations. *Come with all haste,* she wrote, wishing that she could say more. She held the envelope in her hands afterward, half hoping that some of her alarm would infuse the paper and carry the message that she could not quite entrust to ink.

CHAPTER 11

The next three days tested Hester's ingenuity to the limit. It seemed like whenever she turned around, Evangeline was giggling in a corner with the Squire. At least once, she was fairly certain that she had averted a kiss by the thinnest of margins.

At wits' end, Hester finally appealed to the highest power that she knew.

"You summoned me, my lady?" asked the butler from the doorway.

"Willard, my old friend, shut the door and come in." Hester gave him a rueful smile. "I'd have come to you, but I fear my knee can't do the steps to your quarters any longer. You'll tell me if they begin to wear on you, won't you?"

Willard's mouth, normally set in a professionally blank expression, relaxed a fraction. "All else may give out, madam, but my knees remain as solid as ever."

"Ah, what must it be like . . ." Hester gestured to a chair opposite her. "Please, sit down. I have a problem, and it strikes me that you're the only one who can help me."

Willard's eyebrows went up infinitesimally at this, but he sat, balancing on the edge of the chair like a youngster about to give a recital.

"How long has it been?" asked Hester, slumping back in her chair. "Since I was a little girl and you fished me out of the duck pond and I clung to your neck like a limpet?"

He smiled, very briefly, which would have stunned many of the younger servants. "Do you really want me to tell you?"

"No, probably not." She sighed. "About our current houseguest, the Lady Evangeline . . ."

"Ah," said the butler, packing a world of understanding into a single syllable.

"Yes. She seems very determined to latch on to my brother."

"If I may be so bold, madam—"

"For the purposes of this conversation, Tom, I'm Hester. You and I share a single opinion on the matter, I think?"

Tom Willard, who had been sixteen when he fished a five-year-old girl out of the duck pond, rubbed his face in his hands. When he spoke, his voice had the smallest trace of accent, the vowels a tiny bit broader, an old man remembering the tones of his youth. "I don't trust her."

"Neither do I. And I suspect that if she gets her feet under the table, she's not going to make either of our lives easy."

He nodded glumly and sat back in the chair himself. "It's not my place to judge your brother's paramours, but she's much too glittering and her daughter is much too frightened."

"Yes. Exactly." Hester paused. "You saw that about her daughter too?"

"Terrified of being any trouble, and no idea how anything works," said Tom shortly. "The maids gossip."

"Does she cause any problems?"

"Mostly the sort you cause by trying not to cause any. She wanted to help them clean the room, if you can imagine, which would make everything take ten times as long. But no, she's very biddable."

"Mmm. Has the mother done anything?"

"Nothing that one could nail down, no. She's on her best behavior with the Squire, I think, and trying to come across as . . . oh, sweet and charming and a trifle naive. No one who's been in service for more than ten minutes buys the act." He stared at his hands, with their long fingers and carefully trimmed nails. "When she isn't bothering to pretend, she's a cold one. I'd be quite interested to speak to anyone who's served belowstairs in her house."

Hester snorted. "I can't even figure out where her house *is*. Somewhere near Little Haw, apparently, but that's a vast amount of ground, all of it out in the country and poor as dirt, I think. Which I wouldn't care about, if she wasn't so cold."

Willard nodded gloomily.

"Right. So, Tom, how are we going to stop her from marrying my brother?"

He raised both eyebrows a proper amount. "I could push her down the stairs, but that seems a trifle drastic."

"We'll take murder off the table for the moment," said Hester, not without a trace of regret. "No, I am more concerned with keeping my brother free of entanglements. Do you know if they have . . . ah . . . ?"

"I don't believe so, no."

The servants would absolutely know, so . . . no. "She can hardly claim to be compromised, given that she's a widow, but it would make things a good deal more difficult." She folded her hands on her cane. "I fear that I interrupted something yesterday. Something that might have turned into, god help us, a prelude to a proposal. We need to keep such things interrupted. Can you help?"

"That I can manage. Your brother will never be so well attended." He paused, then added, "You know that if he actually orders us out of the room, though . . ."

"Yes, I know. If he does, send for me at once." She closed her eyes, grimly anticipating stomping down the stairs at high speed to try to reach the room before her brother did anything foolish, like declare his undying love. Her knee twinged just thinking about it. "If we can get through the next few days, the house party should help provide a buffer. I hope."

Willard nodded, then said, reluctantly, "Or provide witnesses, if we aren't successful."

"I know. I thought of that, too, but . . ." She spread her hands helplessly. "We have to jump in *some* direction. Perhaps with a little more time, we can find some weakness. I'm not above blackmail, you know."

The butler's lips twitched in amusement. "I should be appalled, I'm sure."

"You should be. I don't suppose she's left anything useful lying around? Incriminating letters? Enormous piles of debts?"

Willard shook his head. "Nothing. Well . . . no, nothing."

"What is it?" Hester frowned at him. "Anything might be useful at this point."

"Gossip, though I doubt it's useful. One of the chambermaids is stepping out with a stable lad, and apparently Lady Evangeline's horse is much discussed there."

"Good horseflesh?"

"Let us say, uncanny horseflesh. I am told he has green eyes."

"Unusual, but not unnatural." Hester had done a great deal of reading on livestock breeding when she was working on her geese, and had run across the discussion more than once. "Particularly in a white horse."

"As I said, it's probably nothing." Willard looked uncomfortable. "Stablehands are a superstitious lot. But they do not like her horse. He doesn't act quite right. There's even a rumor that he is enchanted somehow."

"Enchanted!" Hester sat back. "No, I can't believe it. She's as poor as a church mouse. She would hardly pay a sorcerer to cast some glamour on a horse, of all things, and if she were capable of such illusions herself, I doubt we'd know that she only had two or three dresses to her name."

Willard nodded. "I shall keep an ear to the ground for anything more solid, but this, I believe, is not."

"Please do," said Hester. She paused then, and met his eyes. "Tom—I swear to you, I'm not just thinking that I don't wish to lose my place here. It isn't jealousy."

He reached out and took her hand in both of his. "Hester," he said kindly, "I never thought so."

The message said to wait upon her mother an hour before noon. Cordelia went to the Blue Drawing Room with her heart in her throat. She was wearing a gown that she didn't recognize, which she suspected that Lady Hester had had someone alter to fit her. Alice had laid it out in the morning without comment and Cordelia had been too flustered by the message to think too much about it.

A servant came with her, left, and was replaced by another bringing tea. "Would milady like something to eat?" murmured the maid, pouring.

"No, thank you," said Evangeline.

"Cook has prepared some very fine pastries, if—"

"No, thank you."

"May I bring you anything else, milady?"

"*No, thank you,*" her mother said, her smile sliced so thin that Cordelia half expected it to cut her lips. "That will be all."

The maid curtsied and left again, shutting the door behind her. Evangeline waited two breaths, then slumped against the back of her chair. "These servants," she announced, to no one in particular, "are going to drive me quite mad."

Cordelia took her teacup and held it between her hands. "They seem very attentive," she said, which was a neutral enough statement that she didn't think it would get her in trouble.

"Attentive! They are impossible. Every time I turn around, these past few days, there's a maid or a footman or that horrible butler. I can scarcely get five minutes alone with the Squire without one gliding in to interrupt. There is *no* privacy."

The sheer scope of this hypocrisy took Cordelia's breath away, but fortunately her mother was warming to her subject and didn't notice.

"Do you know how difficult it is to seduce a man under these conditions? No, of course you don't." Evangeline reached up as if to clutch at her hair, recalled her elaborately coiffed locks, and began running her nails fiercely over the velvet arm of the chair instead. "The kind of magic I need to do is hard enough without so much interruption."

Dread sank into Cordelia's gut. She was suddenly glad that she hadn't been able to eat anything that morning. "I . . . I thought you said you couldn't use magic to make someone marry you . . ."

"Not to compel him, obviously." Her mother rolled her eyes. "But there's a world of subtle magic available, if you know what you're doing. Just a little touch to make him notice you. A touch to call attention to your lips or your breasts or what have you."

Cordelia gulped her tea, mortified.

"Then once you have his attention, you let the spell fade. It has to be so delicately done that he doesn't notice. Fortunately, men rarely question why they're thinking about a woman's breasts." Her lips curved wickedly. Cordelia stared into her teacup, sure that her ears were turning red.

"Of course, none of that will matter if these wretched servants don't leave us alone long enough for it to work. Gah!" She flung her head back. "It's like juggling smoke, and just when it's starting to take hold, in comes the butler. When I'm lady of this house, I shall see him turned out without a reference."

"Without a reference?" squeaked Cordelia, who knew, from listening to Alice, that this was a savage blow to any servant. "Isn't that harsh?"

"He'll be lucky if I don't turn him out without his *feet,*" her mother snapped.

As if on cue, the door opened. The maid bobbed her head and said, "Just brought you a little warm-up on the tea, milady."

"How *kind,*" said Evangeline, through her teeth. Cordelia smiled helplessly at the maid, trying to warn her off with her eyes.

As soon as the door closed, Cordelia's mother leaned back in her chair, pinching the bridge of her nose. The cups began to rattle on the tray and Cordelia grabbed for hers, burning her hand as the tea slopped over the side. The tongs vibrated against the rim of the sugar bowl.

Evangeline exhaled, slowly, and the vibrations stopped. Cordelia swallowed. She could not remember the last time her mother had displayed so much frustration.

It's because she can't take it out on anyone. She always gets angry and does something, but she's not allowed to do anything here, not yet, because it might draw attention.

Cordelia stayed very still, hoping that her mother would not realize that she had a potential victim sitting in front of her.

"About this house party," Evangeline said abruptly. "The old lady's mentioned it to you?"

"Yes, Mother." The thought of interacting with so many new people made Cordelia feel a little ill, but she had tried to express polite enthusiasm. She didn't think Hester had been fooled.

"Lord and Lady Strauss have a son," her mother said. "A little older than you, I think. You will be expected to associate with him and be friendly, but it is imperative that you *not* be caught in a compromising position with him, do you understand?"

Cordelia blinked at her mother, wondering what a compromising position was. Before she could find a way to word the question, Evangeline had continued. "The Strauss fortune is adequate, but I will not waste you on a youth who will linger on an allowance for thirty years, waiting for his father to die."

"Yes, Mother," said Cordelia.

Her mother narrowed her eyes. "You will *not* fall in love with this youth," she said. "Do I make myself clear?"

Cordelia had not even considered such a thing. Her mouth fell open and she knew that she was gaping like a goldfish flipped out of a pond.

"It's fine if he falls in love with you. Useful, even." Evangeline raised a warning finger. "But *you* will not fall in love. You go about falling in love and you start keeping secrets. At worst you'll catch pregnant and waste all my hard work. Do you want that?"

"No, Mother."

"You may think that he'll marry you once there's a baby, but they never do, do you hear me?"

"Yes, Moth—"

The sugar bowl turned over, spilling cubes everywhere. Cordelia yelped, then hurriedly began trying to gather them up. When she grabbed one, it vibrated in her hand like a trapped insect.

"I already made that mistake once," Evangeline said. "I thought your father would have to marry me. But he didn't, and so I had to take steps."

Cordelia stopped trying to corral the sugar cubes. Her mother was staring at the ceiling, but Cordelia could hear the soft hiss of water suddenly boiling inside the teapot. "I didn't know that," she said.

Evangeline made a short, sharp gesture with one hand. The hissing stopped, and the sugar cubes fell inert on the floor. "He doesn't matter now. *I* made you. You belong to me, and you're not going to ruin my plans with some young puppy."

"Yes, Mother."

"If I suspect such a thing, I will have to *deal* with him, do you understand?"

"I won't, I swear," said Cordelia frantically, feeling horribly guilty even though she'd never met the young man. *Dealing with him* sounded so dreadfully final. *The blood of Ellen's family is already on my hands, I can't let anything happen to anyone else if I can stop her.*

"Mmm." Evangeline studied her face broodingly. "You don't know what young love is like," she said. "Comes over you like a fever. You'll tell yourself that no one else in the history of the world has ever felt this way before."

What do I say to that? Is there a right answer? "I'll be careful," promised Cordelia. "If I start to feel anything like that, I'll tell you."

Her mother nodded. "Good child. Now make yourself scarce. Go distract the Squire's sister, if she'll have you."

"Yes, Mother," said Cordelia, and fled, leaving scattered lumps of sugar behind her.

"Lady Hester?"

"Hmm?"

"What's a compromising position?"

Hester's hand jerked and she spilled tea into her lap. "*What?*"

"I'm sorry! I didn't mean to—"

It took a few minutes to clean up both the spill and the apologies, but eventually Hester had dealt with both. "Now then," she said, fixing her gaze on Cordelia. "Why are you asking about compromising positions?"

Cordelia swallowed. "My m-mother told me to avoid them. But they never taught us in school what one was, and she was in a mood where I didn't want to ask."

"Yes, of course." Hester rubbed her forehead, wondering again how much she dared to say to Doom's daughter. "A compromising position is when you're . . . ah . . ." She looked at Cordelia's small, guileless face and tried to figure out how to phrase it. "When you're alone with a man that you aren't related to, with no witnesses, and something might happen."

"Like what?"

"That your . . . ah . . . virtue might be compromised."

Cordelia looked blank. Hester stared briefly at the ceiling and was intensely glad that she'd never had children. "Fornication, child. If you're alone with a man long enough that people think he's had a chance to bed you."

A squeak of horror was enough to tell her that she'd finally gotten through. Hester massaged her temples. She didn't have a headache but it felt as if she ought to.

"What would happen?" breathed Cordelia in fascinated horror.

"Well, if he's an honorable man, he marries you."

"What if he isn't?"

"Then if you're unlucky, he marries you anyway. Otherwise he gets away scot-free and you're ruined for polite society."

"But that's not fair!"

"Not remotely," Hester agreed. Privately she was rather pleased to see Cordelia flush with outrage. *Fight back a little, child. Even a rabbit in a trap can bite.* "Even worse, you don't have to have done a damn thing. Just being alone with a man for long enough without a chaperone is enough to condemn a woman in some people's eyes, even if all they did was sit and read the Bible together."

Cordelia's eyes were round with horror. "*What?*"

"I know. It's utterly ridiculous. It would almost be funny if so many girls didn't suffer for it."

"But *why?*"

Hester lifted her shoulders in a vast shrug. "Men are terrified of being cuckolded."

"Of what?"

Hester gazed at the girl for a long moment, then reached into her housecoat's inner pocket and removed a flask. She tipped the contents into her tea, took a long sip, and felt it burn all the way down. *For medicinal purposes only, but I believe this counts. How on earth did Doom send this girl out so completely unprepared?*

In her heart, though, she knew. Evangeline thought of her daughter simply as an extension of herself. *Not the first mother to do so, nor the last, I imagine, though she's taken it to an extraordinary degree.* Since Evangeline knew all the intricacies of proper societal behavior, she simply assumed that her daughter must as well.

How did someone that utterly self-centered manage to raise a child at all? She must have had a nursemaid, but clearly not a tutor. Although the girl's never mentioned a nurse . . . Not that you've ever really asked.

But how else would Doom have managed to keep a child alive—magic? Hester snorted at her own thoughts.

"All right," she said, putting the flask away. "Let's start at the beginning . . ."

Cordelia lay on the bed, staring at nothing in particular. Her head felt unpleasantly full.

I thought your father would have to marry me. But he didn't, and so I had to take steps.

The words might as well have been printed on the back of her eyelids. She couldn't stop thinking them.

Was my father her benefactor, the way Mr. Parker was? And Mother got pregnant with me, and my father refused to marry her?

She'd known how babies were made, of course. There was whispering and snickering about it at school, and a girl named Marion had told everyone in gleeful detail one morning before class. But Cordelia had never quite connected that with parentage and legitimate heirs and legal inheritance of property, which Hester had walked her through with great patience.

"But if they think that a girl might be pregnant because she was compromised, why not just wait a few months and see?" Cordelia had asked, baffled. "Then you'd know for certain and everything could go back to normal."

Hester had groaned. "Because it's not logical." She took another slug of her tea. "Believe me, if I ruled the world, we'd see a lot of things set right." She frowned. "On second thought, never mind. It seems like too much work, ruling the world."

The thought came to Cordelia that her mother would have been perfectly happy ruling the world, but she wouldn't have bothered doing the work. She would just have told Cordelia to do it. Or possibly Falada, for the bits that Cordelia couldn't be trusted with.

It occurred to her to wonder, suddenly, if Falada resented Evangeline as much as Cordelia did. Did he feel like a pawn in a game, too? Did he have any privacy, in his head or in his stall? Did he care?

Then she thought of that sly look, and the way that he had snorted with laughter when she had finally realized that he told her mother everything. No. No, he didn't care. Or he thought it was funny. Perhaps familiars were different that way. Anyway, it didn't matter, did it? Not compared to what she'd learned about her father.

. . . he didn't, and so I had to take steps . . .

Had Evangeline taken steps the way that she had with Mr. Parker?

Cordelia turned the thought over and over. She could no longer doubt that her mother was capable of something terrible, but surely not . . . surely not to the father of her child?

How would I even find out? Look for a newspaper from fourteen and a half years ago? I don't even know my father's name.

Cordelia closed her eyes and told herself, very firmly, that she was letting go of the thoughts. *There's nothing I can do right now. I just have to make sure that she doesn't think I've been compromised.*

She thought about getting into the wardrobe again, but the bed-curtains were closed, and they were almost as good as a door. If she pulled the blankets over her head, that was two doors and two layers of fabric between her and her mother, and that was almost enough to pretend that she felt safe.

It's not that she can't come in, it's that there will be a little bit of warning. That's all I need. Just a little bit of warning before I have to face her. That's all.

CHAPTER 12

Lady Hester's houseguests began to arrive the next day, and Cordelia had no idea what to think of them. Lord and Lady Strauss did indeed bring their son, although he did not look like the sort who would inspire the world-shaking passion her mother had warned her about. He was tall and skinny, with an Adam's apple so prominent that it made his neck look kinked, and he wanted to talk about horses at remarkable length.

Lord and Lady Strauss were rather more interesting. Lord Strauss was also tall, but much wider than his son, with black skin and tightly curled hair. He had a deep voice and kind eyes, and when he laughed, the sound filled the room. Cordelia noticed this while trying not to appear to do so. *"None but an excessively ill-bred person will allow her attention to wander from the person with whom she is conversing,"* according to *The Ladies' Book of Etiquette,* though it did not provide any advice on what to do if your conversational partner assumed that you knew ten times as much about horses as you actually did.

Lady Strauss eventually shooed her offspring away and smiled apologetically at Cordelia. She had white skin and green eyes as sharp as peridots. "Do forgive him, my dear," she said. "He has not yet learned the art of making his passions interesting to other people. You are kind to put up with him as long as you have."

"Oh . . . no . . ." Cordelia swallowed. "I . . . err . . ." *Stop stammering, this isn't an inquisition. Pretend you're talking to Lady Hester.* "I appreciate it, really," she said carefully. "I'm not very good at conversation, myself."

"You're too kind," said Lady Strauss. "I love him dearly, but I know what he's like. Men are like that, my dear. It's a rare one that settles down enough to talk to before they're thirty."

Cordelia didn't know whether to laugh or not. Fortunately dinner was served before she had to decide. She was seated next to Master Strauss, but she was reasonably confident of her ability to handle utensils by now, and anyway, it didn't seem like he would notice if she used the wrong fork. Best of all, her mother was down the table, near the Squire, and couldn't see her. All she had to do was nod alertly and not spill anything and she could escape. *In fact,* she reasoned, *it might be better not to talk to him too much. That way no one will think I'm in danger of being compromised.*

Not that I could really be compromised at the dinner table. I don't think.

Not talking proved easy enough, because young Master Strauss began immediately telling her about phaetons and racing carriages and high-perch and driving unicorn and a great many other phrases that had very little meaning to her. She let it wash over her and simply waited until he stopped to take a breath before interjecting, "Oh," or "Hmm," or "My goodness."

Apparently this was acceptable, because after dinner, she pled headache and went up to bed and her mother patted her hand in a distracted way and didn't look angry or as if she cared at all.

"So you've decided to have a house party, hmmm?" said Lady Strauss. She had brought a bag of knitting to the solar, but Hester knew from long acquaintance that Imogene Strauss had been working on the same scarf for the last decade and carried it purely for protective coloration.

And indeed, as soon as tea had been poured and the door had closed, Imogene reached into the knitting bag and fished out a deck of cards and a flask. "I don't suppose I could interest you in a game, Hester?"

"Not on your life, you old cardsharp. But you can pour a little of that rum into my tea."

She obliged, and topped hers off as well, before shuffling the cards with hand-blurring skill and dealing out a solitaire spread on the table. Her hands were old and gnarled and the lace at her cuffs did not quite cover the thick blue veins, but she flipped cards as cleanly as any riverboat gambler. "I gathered by the way you worded the invitation that you've an ulterior motive for this little get-together?"

"Whatever makes you say that?"

"You underlined the *please* in *please attend* three times. You've never been an underliner, Hester, not even when we were at school."

"Yes, well. It seemed the easiest way to handle things. And I am very, very grateful to you for coming, you know."

Imogene put the ace of spades on the top row and followed it with a two. "The easiest way to handle this ever-so-charming woman staying with you, I take it?"

Hester grunted. She was not about to confide her premonition of doom, not even to Imogene, but the truth of the situation was damning enough. "She's setting her claws into Sam. He's fended off fortune hunters before, but she's a good deal sharper."

The ace of diamonds made an appearance and was duly placed in the top row. "Hmm," said Imogene noncommittally.

"You met her at dinner last night."

Imogene did not take her eyes off the cards. "Yes. It was plain within the first five minutes that the woman is out for marriage, and I suspect it's not the first time. Do you know anything about her?"

"Not a damn thing. Everything she lets slip sounds perfectly reasonable and I haven't been able to verify any of it. Her daughter's dropped a few hints, but not intentionally."

"Nervous little thing, isn't she?"

"Very. Clever enough, but ignorant as a newborn chick and knows it." Hester thought about mentioning Cordelia's behavior at that very strange dinner, but decided against it. There had not been a repeat, and all of Hester's suspicions were too vague and too bizarre to say out loud. "She'd do well enough if she was out from under her mother, I think."

"Hmm." Imogene studied her cards. "Perhaps. Do you want to know what I think?"

"No," said Hester. "I invited you to a house party and began discussing the alarming woman currently pursuing my brother simply so I could watch you cheat at solitaire."

Her old friend snorted. "Is that why you invited Lord Evermore? To try and persuade her to turn her attentions elsewhere?"

Hester froze with the teacup halfway to her lips.

Evangeline and . . . Richard?

Sharp green eyes searched her face. "Ah. Not your plan after all, I see." Imogene swept up the cards and began to shuffle them. "Pity, it would have been quite a clever one. Evermore is wealthy and unattached."

"Yes," said Hester faintly. Unattached. Yes. He was *unattached.* She could have attached him years earlier and had not, for reasons that seemed increasingly foolish now. *Because a woman with her own inheritance has a little power, a wife has none at all. Because I made my own life after my betrothal ended in disaster, and I was too proud of that to give it up.*

Because I could not bear to become old where he could see me.

She did not say any of these things to Imogene, because her friend would have cut them apart as neatly as she cut a deck of cards.

"It's not too late, you know," Lady Strauss said quietly.

"I'm old," said Hester.

"So's he."

"Yes, but fifty-year-old men still marry debutantes, not fifty-

year-old women with bad knees." She gestured self-deprecatingly
to herself.

"I think you do him a disservice," said Imogene. "And yourself
as well. Still. Who else is coming?"

"The Green woman."

"Oh, *her*."

Hester raised her eyebrows. "Do you dislike her so much?"

"I adore her, as you very well know. It's impossible not to. The
problem is that she will throw all the rest of us in the shade. No
one so plain should be so gorgeous. It sets a bad example for the
rest of us plain people."

Hester snorted. "I thought it would be interesting to see what
Evangeline would do."

"*Interesting.*" Imogene turned over a single card and studied it
thoughtfully. "Yes, I suppose. Adding a tiger to another tiger's en-
closure is also interesting, I'm told."

"She was Samuel's mistress at one time. I am hoping he might
be reminded of why."

"Or hoping that his new flame will show herself badly by example? Mmm." Imogene held up the card she had drawn. It was the
queen of spades. "Be careful, Hester. You may drive her to move
more quickly on your brother than you want."

Hester grunted. "I know. I just hope that between you and I
and Richard and Willard, we can find some way to stop her."

"Oh, well, if Willard's involved, what chance does she have?"
Imogene rose to her feet. "Perhaps I'll go play cards with this
houseguest of yours. It might prove very interesting for all involved."

Master Strauss cornered Cordelia at breakfast, and was talking
about horse breeding. Again.

". . . but the hunting lines out of Stanville's stables! Gad, but if
you could see them! Incredible necks, the lot of them . . ."

"Mm-hmm," said Cordelia. She knew that she was supposed to make eye contact when someone was speaking to her, but young Strauss had a pimple at the corner of his mouth that had become huge and white-headed and her gaze kept drifting back down to it involuntarily.

". . . and hindquarters. Bunchy, you know, which was out of fashion for years, but that's where the power comes from in your hunters, but of course Stanville knew that, so he bought some of the finest studs in the country for a song . . ."

Everyone got pimples, of course, she didn't think any less of him for it, but it still drew the eye like a magnet. Cordelia glanced away to find her tea and took too large a swallow, nearly choking. She dabbed at her mouth with a napkin.

". . . fifteen years later everyone is scrambling . . ."

Was there any way to tell him? No, there couldn't be. *The Ladies' Book* was very clear: "*Avoid carefully any allusion to the personal defects of your companion.*"

Her mother came in, which was either a reprieve or a dreadful escalation. *Out of the frying pan and into the fire, more likely.*

"Mrs. Green will be here later this afternoon," said Hester. "And Lord Evermore. Then our party shall be rounded out nicely!" She beamed at the room in general.

"I have not had the pleasure of Lord Evermore's acquaintance," said Evangeline.

"Oh, a fine fellow," said the Squire. "Wealthy as you like, but not high in the instep. He sets a good table, but he's not one of these frippery fellows you see about town, with their collar so starched that they can't turn their heads."

"And Mrs. Green is a delight," said Mrs. Strauss. "I always enjoy her company. Such a fine idea to invite her, Hester."

"Oh, she will put us all in the shade," said Hester, turning the newspaper. "She dresses so elegantly. I'd resent her terribly if she wasn't so charming."

"Good old Penelope," said the Squire. "Always livens up a room, doesn't she?"

Cordelia slipped a quick glance at her mother. Evangeline was buttering her toast with every impression of enjoyment, but her eyes flashed.

It occurred to Cordelia that this Mrs. Green might be considered a rival for the Squire's affections. Her heart sank. Her mother did not like to be thwarted. *Has she ever had a rival? What will she do?*

Apparently what she would do was catch Cordelia looking at her. Evangeline's eyes narrowed just slightly, and Cordelia quickly wrenched her head away, back to Master Strauss, who was still telling her breathlessly about Lord Stanville's stables. Cordelia wondered if she was supposed to know who Lord Stanville was. Was that something that everybody knew? Maybe he was famous and it would be strange that she didn't know. Better to simply smile and nod.

She found herself staring at the pimple again and dropped her gaze hurriedly.

"Oh, look at this," Lady Strauss said, reading aloud from the paper. "What a marvelous scandal! 'At the wedding of Lord M——, when the service was performed, this paper is informed that the bride's hair, previously blond, transformed to mouse brown on the spot. Could magic have been used to change her hair color? This paper makes no judgment, but is unaware of alternate explanations. Lord M——, as readers will doubtless be aware, has been heard to express decided partiality for blondes . . .'" She folded down the edge of the paper and grinned over the top of it at her husband. "Now aren't you glad that *you* didn't prefer blondes?"

Her husband laughed. "Silly chit," said the Squire, shaking his head. "Thinking that a spell would hold up through a church wedding. What was she thinking?"

"Water, wine, and salt," murmured Evangeline, bringing a dainty bite to her lips and then patting them with the napkin.

"P'raps the fellow who sold her the spell said it would hold up," said Hester.

"Two-bit conjurers always promise things they can't deliver," said Evangeline, with an artful roll of her eyes. "A real sorcerer would have known better."

"Not many of those around though, are there?" said the Squire. "Not for a hundred years or so, if they ever existed at all. Now they just go around magicking up horses so they don't look lame when the buyer's there, or charming away warts. Or changing the hair color on silly girls."

Cordelia sat very still, not looking at her mother.

"Perhaps it was an alchemist," said Hester. "Sold her a hair dye and said it wasn't magic."

"Oh, *alchemists,*" her brother said, snorting. "Loons, the lot of them, trying to turn lead into gold and blowing themselves up half the time in the process. I shouldn't think there's many of them left either."

Cordelia was almost relieved when Master Strauss embarked on a long, meandering tale about a horse that had been dyed black and how the dye had run in the rain so that it became a purple-streaked horse. She laughed at that, possibly a little too loudly, and Master Strauss, encouraged, began recounting the pedigree of the horse in question unto the seventh generation.

"Cordelia, dear," said her mother, when she rose from the table, "will you join me in the Blue Drawing Room?"

Cordelia's heart sank, but she murmured, "Yes, Mother," and was not entirely glad to escape the discussion of carriages and horseflesh after all.

CHAPTER 13

"I have told you not to fall in love with Master Strauss, have I not?" snapped her mother, as soon as the door was closed.

Cordelia gaped at her. "I—but I wasn't—I haven't—I didn't even—"

"You appeared to be hanging on his every word," said Evangeline, in a deceptively pleasant voice. "And batting your eyelashes, no less. Has young Master Strauss charmed you after all?"

"No!" said Cordelia a bit desperately, wondering how she had been batting her eyelashes, maybe she'd just been blinking, oh god, she was blinking wrong, she knew it, she'd been worrying about it ever since visiting the dressmaker. "He—uh—" She closed her eyes, feeling a blush climbing her face. "He had a pimple," she said, to the backs of her eyelids. "I was trying not to stare at it, but it was . . . he kept talking and it was wobbling . . ."

She steeled herself for a lecture on ladylike behavior.

A snort broke the silence. Cordelia's eyes flew open to see that her mother had a hand over her mouth and her shoulders were shaking with laughter.

Oh. Well. That's . . . good? I guess? She was never certain what to do when Evangeline was in a good mood. Bad moods were at least predictable.

"Oh, Cordelia," her mother said finally, wiping at her eyes. "Oh my. I should have known that no daughter of mine would be fool enough to fall for such a wretched boy." She stood up and held out her arms. "Come here."

Cordelia's heart sank, but she knew better than to let her dread show on her face. She shuffled forward and let her mother embrace her. Wormwood tickled her nose, chokingly familiar.

"Everything is going so well," Evangeline crooned against her hair. "The Squire just needs the slightest little push. Then we'll have enough money to find you your rich husband, and we'll be *really* wealthy. Then life will all be easy, you'll see. Like it should have been all along, if your father had done the honorable thing."

Cordelia stood quietly in her mother's arms. Her skin crawled and she wanted to pull away, but she knew better. And part of her—a tiny part that she had never quite lost—wanted to be there and wanted it all to be true so that her mother would love her and maybe things would change. Maybe she would do everything right and she would never be made obedient again.

She watched that part of herself dispassionately, as if it belonged to someone else. She knew better.

Most of her knew better.

She wished that she could find that tiny part and drag it out and stomp it into the dirt. But she couldn't, so she waited until her mother released her.

"This Lord Evermore may be promising," said Evangeline. "He's wealthy, by the sound of it. Charm him. It will be good practice, if nothing else. And who knows? Perhaps he'll come up to scratch. If you don't need to compete against other debutantes, so much the better. And he's as old as the Squire, so we may both be widows before we know it!"

"Yes, Mother," said Cordelia, despairing. *Charm him? I don't know how to charm anyone.* But if she said so, she would practically be asking to be made obedient so that her mother could charm the lord instead.

"I promised to help Lady Hester with embroidery," she said, keeping her eyes on the floor. If she didn't look up, no one could read the hate in her eyes, for her mother, for herself, for the whole world that had conspired to put her in this position.

"Good," said her mother. "Keep her distracted."

As she climbed the stairs to the solar where Hester spent most afternoon, Cordelia thought to herself—*That's not why I'm doing it. At least, I don't think it is, is it?*

The thought nagged at her that by talking to Lady Hester, she was serving her mother's purpose, even if she didn't want to.

Would it really be so bad if her mother married the Squire, though? Hester was kind to her and answered all her questions like Ellen had, without making her feel like she was strange for asking. Alice was more than kind. *And I could live in this house and not eat potatoes at every meal and not have to wash the dishes between meals because there's so few of them. And even the Squire is nice, in a distracted sort of way. Would it be that bad?*

Maybe it wouldn't be.

But I also don't want Mother to hurt any of these people. I don't want her to turn the butler off without a reference, even if he scares me. And Alice stood up to her once, what if she remembers that? Cordelia shuddered at the potential ramifications.

I could tell Hester what Mother is. I could warn her. I could say . . .
What exactly would she say?

My mother's a sorceress and she controls people's minds sometimes— but she hasn't controlled your brother, because she wants to marry him—but I think she drove my friend's father to kill his family with an axe—and she's dangerous and her familiar is a horse and she won't let anyone close doors—

Did that sound ridiculous? Cordelia couldn't tell. She was afraid that it might be. People didn't seem to believe in magic the way that she understood it. The man at the carriageyard had been annoyed but not frightened. He'd thought that Evangeline was trying to cheat him, not that she might be dangerous.

You could just ask Lady Hester about magic. If you ask, then you'll know what she thinks, and you'll know where to go from there.

Even asking seemed horribly difficult. If her mother found out, surely she'd know why Cordelia was asking. It would be safer not to say anything.

And what if what happened to Ellen happens again, because you didn't say anything?

The thought sank in like a needle into her finger, a bright stab of pain that made her flinch.

No. I have to say something. Somehow.

Cordelia glanced around in the hallway, but saw no one. She set down her basket of embroidery, pressed on her temples, and made a tiny sound, just one, to let the pressure out. Immediately she felt better, or at least as if the ratcheting tension wasn't getting any worse.

Afterward, she sat for a moment, hugging her knees. The carpet runner was a little worn here, and there was a ridge in the wallpaper where it had bubbled and been pushed back down. A week ago, Cordelia would have wondered if the Squire lacked the money to fix it. With seven days of hard-won wisdom, she had realized that the Squire was so wealthy that he simply didn't need to care. No one was going to look at Chatham House and think that the inhabitants were poor, so why bother rehanging perfectly good wallpaper because of a minor imperfection?

It was a strange reflection that, like Hester turning the cuffs on her gowns, you were somehow allowed to be poorer if you were rich than if you were actually poor.

She reached the door of Lady Hester's solar. *Just ask about sorcerers. It's not that hard.* She slipped inside and saw that Lady Strauss was in the room as well. "Oh," she said, uncertain whether Hester wanted to be interrupted. "I . . . err . . ." She held up her embroidery. "I can come back later if you'd rather?"

"Sit, sit," said Hester. "The more the merrier. Just don't play cards with Imogene here."

Lady Strauss made a tsking sound. "For shame, Hester. You make me sound like a swindler."

"If you ever run out of money, you could go to any gambling hall in the city and break the bank."

"She exaggerates," said Lady Strauss to Cordelia. "It makes her feel better about losing to me. Now tell me, child, where are you from?"

"Little Haw, my lady." Cordelia drew out her embroidery. She had made some progress on the flowers and butterflies, and showed it shyly to Hester.

"Oh, very nice! You're getting the hang of this nicely. Here, let me show you a cranefly knot. Very handy for some things." She demonstrated twice, then handed the square back. Cordelia bent her head over it.

"Little Haw . . ." murmured Lady Strauss. "No, I can't say I know that one."

"It's very small," said Cordelia.

"Yes, of course. And Hester tells me that you came into town to buy dresses?"

Cordelia nodded distractedly, focusing on the knot. She thought that they were probably waiting for her to answer, so she added, "For my coming out. Mother says I'm to marry a rich man."

She did not see the looks exchanged over her head. "Every girl's dream, of course," said Lady Strauss, with a gentle bite of irony. "Any particular rich man?"

Cordelia shook her head. Evangeline had never suggested that there was a difference between them. They were all the same so far as she knew, a faceless class of humanity that existed somewhere off in the distance, like the old country across the water.

"Have some tea," suggested Hester. She leaned forward and poured, then handed the teacup to Cordelia.

"Have you met many rich men yet?" asked Lady Strauss, as Cordelia dropped a lump of sugar in her cup.

Cordelia shook her head again. "No. Not yet."

"That's probably for the best," said a voice from the doorway. "If they didn't earn it themselves, they're usually wastrels, and if they did earn it, they're usually so focused on earning more that they've no conversation at all."

"Penelope!" Lady Strauss leapt to her feet. Hester didn't, but she banged her cane on the floor and laughed in clear delight.

Cordelia tried to turn her head all the way around like an owl, failed, jumped to her feet, and managed to upset the sugar bowl. Lumps bounced across the table. She turned scarlet and began attempting to corral the wayward sugar.

"Oh dear," said the newcomer, kneeling beside her to help. "It's my fault for popping up behind you like a jack-in-the-box. Here, there's one by your embroidery—there. At least it's only the sugar!" She sat back, grinning at Cordelia. "Imagine the mess if you'd overset the bowl of live mice!"

Mice . . . ? Cordelia blinked at her, astonished. Hester snorted. "We stopped serving live mice with tea ages ago, Penelope."

"Strictly for formal occasions now, is it?" She put the back of her wrist to her forehead. "And when I think of the extraordinary rodent teas I've had over the years . . . oh, the heart bleeds, so it does."

Rodent teas? *What?*

Lady Strauss shook her head. "Your humor is still as peculiar as ever, Penelope. Best introduce yourself before our young friend here thinks you've escaped from an asylum."

The woman made an abbreviated curtsy, given her position on the floor. "Penelope Green, at your service."

Penelope Green was tall and beautiful, except that she wasn't. Cordelia's brain insisted that she must be, but her eyes were reporting that she was actually no taller than Cordelia, that her cheeks were heavily scarred with the cobblestone marks of smallpox, and that she was wearing a silk gown in a staggeringly vivid shade of green that should have made her look bilious.

And yet.

Cordelia's brain told her eyes to look again, because when Mrs. Green stood up, even though she wasn't tall, she was still the most important thing in the room. It was like she stood in a personal sunbeam, even though it was overcast and the sky outside the windows was quite gray.

It occurred to Cordelia that she had been staring at Mrs. Green while still half bent over, holding the sugar tongs, and immediately flushed. "I'm . . . er . . . Cordelia." She hastily returned the tongs to the bowl.

"Cordelia and her mother are my brother's guests," said Hester, "and Cordelia's been kind enough to keep an old lady company up here."

"How good of her. Who's the old lady, then? I don't see her."

Hester made a rude noise. "I'm fifty, you know."

"Yes, and if you were a man, you'd be considered barely old enough for politics. People would call you 'that young Hester lad.'"

"Look at you," said Lady Strauss, taking both the newcomer's hands. "You look spectacular, as always. It's infuriating, you know."

Mrs. Green laughed. "You look beautiful yourself, Imogene, and you know it. And you, Hester . . ." She settled herself on the arm of Hester's chair with as much grace as a queen taking a throne. "Hester, love, you have been sleeping badly and worrying too much, haven't you? Is your knee bothering you?"

"Oh, partly, partly." Hester shook her head. "We can discuss all that later, I imagine."

Cordelia wondered if *later* meant *when there isn't a stranger present*. She swallowed a too-hot gulp of tea, then pressed her tongue against the roof of her mouth, feeling the pebbly texture of a burn starting. *This probably isn't the best time to ask about sorcery. Not when they're all getting caught up. It would look odd, wouldn't it?*

She put her head down and focused on her embroidery while the three women talked over her head about places she had never been and people she had never met. Almost she thought that she had succeeded in becoming invisible, but then Mrs. Green nudged her. "Now then, we are being frightfully tedious, aren't we, Cordelia?"

"No, no, of course . . ." Cordelia hoped that her lack of interest had not been obvious, but feared that it was. "That is, I didn't mind, really I didn't."

"Bah. There is nothing more boring than listening to people talk about total strangers. At least unless the strangers are doing something scandalous. Imogene, tell us something scandalous to entertain our young friend here."

Lady Strauss rolled her eyes. "I have no illusions about who I'm actually entertaining, Penelope. Oh, very well. Let me think. Do you know that Lord Ryhope's wife was caught with one of the footmen?"

"Scandalous, but hardly unexpected," said Penelope. "Ryhope's, what, two or three hundred years old? At least? He's keeping a sorcerer in the cupboard to keep him from turning to dust."

"He's seventy-two," said Hester, with some asperity.

"Never say it." Penelope stirred her tea, shaking her head. "That sorcerer is doing a terrible job, then."

Cordelia could not imagine a better opening. She licked her lips. *Just ask. It's not that hard. It's just gossip. They've been doing it all afternoon. Try to phrase it like you're curious, that's all.*

"Do people really keep sorcerers for that?" She ducked her head immediately, in case they were staring at her, and became very interested in her tea.

"No, no," Hester assured her. "They can't do that. Penelope's making one of her jokes again."

"They can't keep you young, anyway," said Penelope thoughtfully. "I imagine they could make you look younger, though, at least for a little while."

"They can?" Cordelia's eyes went wide.

"If they can make a broken-down horse look like a champion long enough for money to change hands, they ought to be able to make us all look twenty again." Mrs. Green glanced at Cordelia, then grinned ruefully. "No, I'm not really serious. Illusions are all that most of them can manage. If you're looking for a sorcerer to change your hair or your horse's coat, I'd advise against it, though.

A rinse with lemon water is more effective on your hair, and you're better off buying a new horse."

"Not to mention that such things always fail at the wrong time," said Lady Strauss. "Like that silly girl last week who had one turn her hair blond, and then of course it failed in the middle of the wedding."

"Water, wine, and salt to break the spells," said Cordelia, repeating what her mother had said about weddings.

"Yes, exactly."

"Hmm." Hester tapped her fingernail against her teeth. "Was a fellow came through the village a while back, as I recall. Sold a load of ewes to one of our shepherds, and then as soon as he was out of town, most of them suddenly grew b—"

"*Hester,*" said Lady Strauss.

Hester coughed. "Sorry. I forget that not everyone follows animal husbandry as I do. At any rate, they were, uh, boy-sheep. Culls, by the look of them. Not fit for anything but mutton. He was furious, but of course the fellow was long gone."

Cordelia's heart sank. Illusions, making a shepherd think rams were ewes . . . was that really the only kind of sorcery people believed in? "Is that all that sorcerers do, then?"

"Pretty much," said Lady Strauss, laying down a line of cards. "I've gambled with a couple of them. One was pretty good at muddling the cards, but he still wasn't a great player." She pulled a face. "One, though . . . he walked away with the whole table's money. I had an inkling that he must be cheating somehow, though I couldn't catch him. I wasn't in deep, thank god. Two days later I hear that he tried it with a fellow from the southwest, where they still take these things seriously. This man had been wearing a ward and it went off when the first fellow went to lay down his first hand."

Cordelia stared at her embroidery and wondered if it had flashed green and smelled like burning hair.

"Anyway, the fellow with the ward took offense and pinned the sorcerer's hand to the table with a knife." Lady Strauss's lips curled in a feral smile of satisfaction. "And that's why if you're going to cheat, you had best be smart enough not to get caught."

"I'm surprised there aren't wards like that in every gambling club," remarked Hester.

"Too hard to come by," said Lady Strauss. "I looked into getting one myself after that, but they want a fortune for the things. High-end horse traders keep them, and racetracks, but other than that, how often does it really come up?"

"Can't they just use water, wine, and salt in the gambling club?" asked Cordelia. "If it works at weddings, wouldn't it work somewhere else?"

"Only on holy ground," said Lady Strauss with clear regret. "That's the fourth part."

"Well, then Cordelia's come up with a brilliant solution!" Mrs. Green ducked her shoulder and nudged it into Cordelia's arm, almost as if they were friends. "Imogene, when you build your gambling hall, you simply must do it on holy ground, that's all."

"I'm sure the Archbishop would love that," said Lady Strauss dryly.

"Why not? He's always complaining that not enough people go to church."

Cordelia let out a shocked giggle at that, and Mrs. Green laughed herself, winking at Cordelia.

"What makes something holy ground?" Cordelia asked, when the room had fallen quiet again.

Lady Strauss played another line of cards and scowled down at them. "The Archbishop would say that the Church consecrating a patch of ground makes it holy."

Mrs. Green arched an eyebrow. "You say that like you disagree, Imogene."

"Not in public I don't. But I do think . . . oh, I don't know what I think. Not really." For the first time since Cordelia had met her, Lady Strauss seemed indecisive. "The Church isn't so old, you

know. Not compared to some places I've seen. In the old country, there were ruins from a thousand years before anyone like the
Archbishop was around to bless them. But I still felt that those
ruins were on holy ground."

"Because the people who had lived there had consecrated the
ground?" asked Hester.

Lady Strauss shrugged helplessly. "Maybe. Maybe what we call
holy ground is only holy because I believe it and you believe it and
hundreds of other people have believed it, and all that belief builds
up like snow on a patch of ground and *makes* it holy." She looked
back down at her game. "Don't ask me. I don't know how the
world works, just how cards work."

It was an interesting idea. It tugged at Cordelia's brain and
made her think about things she didn't usually think about. The
needle moved over and under her piece of fabric, and her thoughts
moved over and under each other, and for a minute or two, Cordelia almost forgot that her mother was somewhere in the house,
only a few closed doors away.

CHAPTER 14

Cordelia first saw Lord Evermore as the party assembled before dinner. He was a tall dark-haired man, so thin that it made him look taller still, with bony wrists and deep-set brown eyes. He stood beside Lady Hester's chair, his head bent as he listened.

What struck her most strongly, however, was that he was *old*. There was silver at his temples and threading his hair. Fine lines had etched the skin around his eyes and bracketed his mouth.

He's as old as the Squire or Lady Hester! Surely Mother can't expect me to marry someone like that?

She knew the thought was foolish as soon as she had it, and felt a flush of embarrassment, even though she hadn't said it out loud. Of course her mother would expect that. *A rich man,* she'd always said. Not *a young man.*

"Lord Evermore," her mother said warmly, taking Cordelia's hand and drawing her across the room. "Let me introduce my daughter Cordelia. Cordelia, this is Lord Richard Evermore."

"A pleasure to meet you, Cordelia," said Evermore, bowing over her hand. He had a low, pleasant voice—or at least Cordelia might have thought it was pleasant if she had not been instructed to charm the man.

Evangeline pinched her arm sharply before releasing it. Cordelia, jolted, curtsied more deeply than she probably should have. Lord Evermore's eyebrows went up. Cordelia felt her face growing hot. She took a deep breath and said, "It is very nice to meet you, sir."

That came out all right. I think. Her flush cooled. She wanted to hide in a corner, but with her mother standing right there, she didn't dare. *Charming. I am supposed to be charming.* "Did you have a pleasant . . . er . . ." Too late she remembered that it had rained all day. "A long journey?"

"Neither one, I fear," said Evermore easily. "Only a few hours, but it rained the whole way. Though I have hopes that it will dry out tomorrow."

"I hope so, too," said Evangeline. "I do so love to ride, and staying in these last few days has been dreary."

"I don't mind a few drops, but there's not much point if it's mud halfway to the horse's knees," said the Squire, joining them. "Though the hunting's always good, that first fine day after a spell of rain."

"And now they'll be off on hunting talk," said Hester, casting an amused look at Cordelia, "and we'll get nothing more out of them for the rest of the evening."

Lord Evermore looked over at Hester fondly, almost the way that Lord Strauss looked at Lady Strauss. "I suppose we could talk about breeding geese instead," he said. "Then we'll get nothing more out of you for the evening either."

Hester poked him in the shin with her cane. "How is my flock doing, anyway?"

"Healthy and belligerent."

"Any sign of arthritis in the younger ones?"

Evermore smiled wryly at the others and mouthed, *I told you so.* The Squire laughed. Cordelia giggled, because giggles were supposed to be charming, and hoped that it didn't come out sounding too strained.

"I had no idea that you were so fond of . . . fowl," said Evangeline.

"Oh, Hester's a genius when it comes to geese," said the Squire proudly. "Back when they were all the rage, we had people coming and going at all hours, trying to get a pair of her birds for themselves."

"My goodness." Evangeline turned a dazzling smile on Hester and Lord Evermore. "I had no idea you were so accomplished, Lady Hester."

"The geese did most of the work." Hester's tone was dry as snakeskin. "I just made sure we ate the ones who weren't up to snuff."

"How *ruthless*." Evangeline put a hand to her mouth.

"Got to be," said the Squire. "Same way with horses. You let one bad sire in and it takes generations to clear up."

"Fortunately goose generations are much shorter than horses'," Evermore said.

"Easier to eat, t-too," said Cordelia, greatly daring. *Was that funny? Will anyone laugh or will Mother apologize for me or—*

The Squire threw back his head and guffawed. Hester and Evermore both chuckled. Her mother cast her an approving look and Cordelia felt weak-kneed with relief.

Her relief carried her almost through to dinner. Then things took an unpleasant turn, although Cordelia knew that she couldn't possibly be blamed for it.

No, the problem was Mrs. Penelope Green. She swept into the parlor fashionably late and every eye turned toward her. The Squire left Evangeline's side to greet the newcomer, and stayed there, chatting with her.

"Ah, you've invited Mrs. Green," said Evermore. "An excellent choice."

"Such a lovely woman," said Hester. "She livens up any gathering, I've found."

"She certainly seems to be an original," said Evangeline, showing her teeth. "Why, I haven't seen a gown like that since I was a little girl!"

"Oh, indeed," said Hester. "If any of us tried to pull that off, we'd look hopelessly dowdy. But Penelope walks into a gathering and leaves a new fashion behind her." She beamed up at Evermore. "Do you remember, Richard, when she took snuff off Lord

Stanville's wrist at the opera? They had to carry his mother off in strong hysterics."

"I remember it well," Evermore said. "The lady's shriek shook dust from the rafters. The soprano was positively anticlimactic afterward."

"Two days later, half the women in the city were carrying a snuffbox," Hester said, shaking her head.

"I've always found snuff to be a filthy habit," said Evangeline coolly.

"Oh, absolutely vile," Hester agreed. "The one time I did it, I had *such* a sneezing fit. And Richard here had the gall to *laugh* at me." She thumped his shin with her cane again.

"You sounded like a tree frog," said Richard. "*Eh-chee! Eh-chee! Eh-chee!* All high-pitched and run together. It was adorable. Well, it would have been, if you weren't turning as green as a tree frog, too."

"Hmmph!" Hester nodded to Cordelia. "Let that be a lesson to you, my young friend. If you are going to take snuff, never do it in front of a man. At least not the first time."

"Applies to cigars as well," said Evermore.

"Cordelia," said her mother blightingly, "would never do anything so unladylike."

Cordelia had only the vaguest idea what was in snuff anyway, but couldn't imagine snorting something that looked so much like finely ground horse droppings. "No, Mother," she murmured.

"I am surprised that so many mothers allowed their daughters to even *carry* snuffboxes."

"Oh, well, it was all in good fun," said Hester. "I doubt many of them had the faintest idea how to take the stuff. But for a month or two, you positively had to be seen with one. Fashion, you know."

Evangeline's mouth curved down, and then, to Cordelia's intense relief, the bell rang calling them in to dinner.

Unfortunately dinner itself proved no relief. "Is there a Mr. Green?" Evangeline asked Penelope pleasantly. The women were seated on either side of the Squire. Cordelia wondered if anyone else could see how hard her mother's eyes were when she said it, like cold blue glass.

"Sadly no," said Penelope, shaking her head. She put a hand to her heart. Cordelia saw the Squire's eyes travel along her arm to her cleavage, accented in a square bodice that Mrs. Tan would definitely have said was not in fashion. "Poor man. He was a great friend of Samuel's."

"Eh? Oh, yes," said the Squire. "A great gun, old Silas was. Terrible loss."

"You understand, of course," said Penelope, smiling sadly at Evangeline.

Evangeline inclined her head. "It was so long ago," she said. "I remember him fondly, but truly it seems as if it belonged to another life."

"That's lovely to hear. We widows so often find ourselves in such a precarious state."

"Oh yes. Though *my* lord was good enough to provide for his family."

Cordelia wondered if that had been an insult. It had felt like one, somehow. But Penelope Green only laughed and said, "Poor old Silas was never much good at such things. The most charming man you'd ever meet, but he never thought ahead. Do you remember, Samuel, that time on the hunt that he jumped the hedge when you yelled at him not to?"

"The damn fool," said the Squire, with clear affection. "Swore his horse could clear it. And it did, too, just barely."

"I'm sure the bull in the field was very impressed," said Penelope, with a bubbling laugh. "I know that horse came back over the hedge like his tail was on fire. Now *that* was a clean jump." The two of them joined in laughing, and Cordelia stared at her napkin so that she didn't have to watch her mother's eyes get colder still.

*   *   *

Hester stood out on the balcony in the late evening, listening to the breeze sigh through the old chestnut trees below.

She was not quite ready to retire for the evening, but she also did not wish to climb the flight of steps down to the library. *If only my illustrious ancestors had designed a home with everything on the ground floor. I wonder if any of them eventually regretted it, once their knees started to go?*

Her compromise at such times was the balcony off the dining room. Dinner had been cleared away, and all the guests had retired to their own amusements. Hester had done her proper duty as a hostess, and now she could stand on the balcony and stare out over the trees while the stars came out, one by one.

She had just performed the mental calculation of whether sitting down would be worth getting up again, and decided that it was too cold to linger for long, when arms went around her. Her mind tried to be startled, but her body knew exactly who it was. She leaned back against him despite herself. "Richard."

He kissed the top of her head. Hester was perfectly aware that hair didn't have any nerves, and anyway there was a little lace cap between his lips and the hair in question, and she still felt it all the way down to her bones. She sighed again.

Her body wanted to relax, to melt against him like warm butter. Her body was an idiot. She told it sternly that there would be absolutely no melting.

"I've missed you," he said.

"Bah. You can't have. An eligible bachelor with a fortune? You must be knee-deep in marriageable young ladies."

"It's true," he agreed mournfully. "I had to hire an ex-pugilist to sweep them out of my way when I go out. And two footmen to follow after and collect the poor things, give them a little brandy, and release them back into the wild."

Damn him, he could always make her laugh. She smothered it with a cough and pulled away. He released her immediately but didn't step back. She could feel the warmth radiating off him and somehow she didn't seem to be moving away either.

"You look very well," she said, which was an understatement. Age had only improved him. He had always had a boyish face, and the silver in his hair tempered that. How he was not considered one of the most handsome men in society baffled her utterly. True, he was slim and wiry rather than solid, and he didn't bother padding his coats to broaden his shoulders, and no, he'd never fought a duel and you couldn't consider him dashing, exactly, but surely society wasn't *that* blind, was it? When his eyes were always good-humored and his lower lip curved just *so* . . .

"Something's weighing on you," he said, looking down at her. "What can I do?"

Hester rubbed her hand over her face. "You're here," she said. "That helps more than I can say."

"Will you tell me about it?"

She glanced around the balcony. No one was listening here. It would have been ideal, if not so cold.

Richard took off his coat and draped it around her shoulders without a word. The fabric smelled like him, like aftershave and soap and skin. She would have recognized the scent if she were a hundred years old and a continent away.

She hesitated, then shoved her reluctance away, annoyed. *Why even invite him if you're not going to talk to him? He's your friend, not your security blanket. If you sound like an old woman afraid of her life changing . . . well, that's the risk you run.*

So they sat down and she told him. She told him everything, even what Alice had said about Cordelia, even the fearful look in her eyes after that very strange dinner.

She told him even of her feeling of doom, though she tried to make light of it, and she didn't say that it had come over her before Evangeline had even arrived. That was too much, even for Richard. She hedged instead. "I had a terrible feeling when I saw her. You know how people talk about love at first sight? This was like . . . fear at first sight." She forced a laugh. "I know that sounds like I'm being histrionic."

"You are never histrionic," said Richard. "I once held a goose while you cut out an abscess on its foot with a penknife. Then you took off your apron, washed your hands, and went to the ball that we were supposed to be attending."

"The goose recovered, I'll have you know. Lady Mercer gave me updates on him for years, until he finally perished at advanced old age. He was a good sire, too. One of my best lines."

He shook his head and reached out to take both her hands in his. His hands were very warm and hers were cold. Hester stared at the shape they made together, his larger and darker, with a faint smear of ink on the side of his thumb.

"And so you brought Mrs. Green so that Evangeline would not show herself to advantage. Clever Hester."

"It sounds quite calculating, when you say it like that."

"Perhaps. But it's not as if you forced the lady to be so obviously put out by competition." He absently rubbed his thumbs across her palms, and she tried to sit still and not to feel the motion like a burning brand against her skin. "If I invited you to a house party and you did not like someone there, you would hardly glare daggers at her over dinner."

"It's true," said Hester. "I'd be very polite over dinner. I'd simply push her down the stairs later."

"Exactly. This Lady Evangeline is not a subtle creature."

"Is pushing someone down the stairs subtle?"

"I have every confidence that you would do so discreetly." His smile was quick, just for the two of them, there and then gone. Lord, she'd missed that smile. "At any rate," he continued, "I don't know what I can do in this case, but I will try. Would you like me to tell Samuel stories of matchmaking mothers intruding on my pleasant bachelor life? Or about how my cousin wed an utter shrew in his later years and she has made his life a torment?"

"*Did* your cousin marry an utter shrew?"

"No, he married a rather nice woman from Virginfort, and I'm told they regularly wander through small villages together, looking for interesting cheeses. But I'm sure I could come up with something. Perhaps I'll give her dozens of grasping relatives that descended upon him as soon as the wedding wine had been drunk."

"I don't think Evangeline's got any relatives, except Cordelia."

"The daughter? Yes. She seems very shy, but if what Alice says is true, there's little wonder."

"I'm not sure if *shy* is the right word, exactly. Scared witless and watching everything she says so that she doesn't contradict her mother, definitely. But she seems to like being around me, and she was definitely charmed by Penelope earlier . . . but then again, who isn't?"

"Some of us are charmed by other sorts."

Hester knew perfectly well what he meant and went back to staring at their hands. "I worry for her," she admitted. "I want Evangeline gone, but I can't just turn away from the poor girl."

"You can't save everyone, you know."

"I'm not trying to. But if someone who needs help falls in your lap, you help them. It's what you *do*."

Richard chuckled softly. "You haven't changed."

"I'm older and fatter and my knee hurts," she said tartly, pulling her hands away. "And I have less patience for fools."

"You look magnificent," he said with absolute conviction, and tore her heart in half without even trying. "And you have never had the slightest bit of patience for fools. I'm sorry about your knee, though. None of the doctors can do anything?"

"It's all laudanum, and it makes me fuzzy-headed. And I need all my wits about me right now." She scowled, pulling her shawl tighter around herself. The sleeve of Richard's borrowed coat slid down her shoulder, and he reached out to straighten it without comment. "And it's cold out here, and I should probably go inside, or my knee really will hurt."

He nodded and rose to his feet, pulling her up without effort. She handed him back his jacket and stood, leaning on her cane, while he put it back on.

"I do appreciate you coming," she said. "I know I'm not always . . . I know that . . . well. Thank you."

"Always," he said. "You know that."

"Yes. But I shouldn't rely on that."

He ran his hand through his hair. A stray lock fell across his forehead and Hester's fingers itched to straighten it. She gripped her cane more tightly.

"Hester," he said finally, "you know that if Samuel marries again—if you can't stay here—you know that you'll always have a place with me."

She nodded once, jerkily. She could not meet his eyes. If she did, she would be lost. If he touched her again, she would dissolve completely.

But he did not. He opened the door for her and let her go through first. She made her way up the stairs, holding the rail in one hand, hoping that he was not watching. She did not want him to see how badly her knee pained her. She hated pity from anyone. From Richard, it would be unbearable.

Once she was in her room, in her own bed, she sagged against the pillows. Was she going to cry? No, she wasn't. Damn. Tears might have helped.

He hadn't asked her to marry him again. He hadn't needed to. The offer still hung in the air between them, almost visible, like thunder.

What could she say? *I can't marry you, because I look like this, and you look like that. And I will grow older and fatter and frizzier, and eventually I will need a carry-chair instead of a cane. And meanwhile, you will be tall and distinguished and your hair will go to silver gilt and everywhere we go, people will look at us and think, "What is he doing, married to* her?"

She'd told him as much, the first time. He denied it, but he was still a man, even if she loved him, and he did not quite understand. She'd let him believe that she was unwilling to see that question in so many people's eyes.

She had never had the courage, or the cruelty, to tell him the real truth. *I don't care about other people. Society can go hang. But if I ever looked in your eyes and saw that question, it would destroy me utterly. I could never pick up the pieces after that. There would be nothing left.*

So she did not. Hester could be an eccentric old woman who raised geese and wore peacock feathers in her hat and was happy enough. Better to keep that happiness close. *I love you, and I trust you, and there is no one I would rather have at my back. But I cannot expect you to ignore the world forever for my sake. Sooner or later, you will find someone who will not embarrass you in your old age.*

Thinking of that other woman, whoever she was, Hester felt a red flash of hatred, and bared her teeth against the dark.

CHAPTER 15

"That scarred *hussy,*" Evangeline growled, stalking back and forth across the parlor like a panther wearing muslin. "I hate her, I hate her, *I hate her.*"

Cordelia huddled in a chair, wishing that she could crawl into her shawl like a limpet. She had never seen her mother so furious before. Angry, yes. Frustrated, certainly. But usually she was bemoaning the stupidity of other people, and how obnoxious it was to always be working around them. Cordelia had never seen her in such a thwarted rage. Her only hope was to stay absolutely still and pray that her mother forgot she even had a daughter.

Evangeline's flawless skin was mottled with red, like a hothouse orchid. "I hate her!"

Cordelia was quite certain that her mother had never admitted to hating anyone before. To hate someone would be to give them too much respect. Yet somehow Penelope Green had merited this simply by existing.

It had been two days. Two days of watching her mother fray at the edges, of the Squire sandwiched between Penelope Green and her mother at dinner, in a cloud of conversation that glittered like knives. Two *very long* days.

Evangeline would throw out a statement like a blade and Penelope would deflect it, often with some self-deprecating comment. And then, instead of returning the attack, she would usually find a way to make the Squire laugh, which only made her mother colder and angrier and more determined to strike again.

Cordelia was astonished to find that she was actually embarrassed by her mother's showing in those conversations. *I wish Mother wasn't doing it. I wish she didn't look so petty when she does it. Except I don't know if anyone else thinks that she looks petty. Maybe this is how people talk all the time. I don't know.*

She should have been glad that none of the delicate barbs that Evangeline threw ever seemed to lodge in Mrs. Green's flesh. She *liked* Penelope Green. But it was still embarrassing to watch and whenever the Squire turned toward Penelope instead of her mother, Cordelia felt her heart sink.

They had all gone riding yesterday. Cordelia still wasn't certain how it had happened. There had been another barbed conversation at dinner and one thing had led to another.

"Do you ride, then?" Evangeline had asked.

"Badly," Penelope answered, with disarming frankness. "I can just about stay on the horse if the horse decides to let me."

"Samuel and I were talking of going on a ride tomorrow, but of course, if you don't enjoy it . . ."

Mrs. Green's eyes crinkled up as she smiled. "Oh, I might manage something. The weather looks to be glorious. Samuel, do you still have Dancer in the stable?"

"Good heavens, Penelope, that gelding is as old as I am!"

"Yes, and we understand each other very well."

Cordelia had been twisting her napkin under the table and hoping that her mother wouldn't swoop in with some other jab, when suddenly Mrs. Green had turned and looked across the table. "Cordelia, my dear, do you ride?"

"I . . . uh . . ."

"She does," said Evangeline coolly.

"Wonderful. Then please, I beg you, come with us." She waved her hand at the Squire and Cordelia's mother. "That way when these two gallop off like proper equestrians, flying over fences, we can amble happily along."

Cordelia had wanted to protest that she had never ridden any horse but Falada, but of course she couldn't. No one knew that Falada wasn't an ordinary horse. And she could remember, at that awful obedient dinner, all the chatter with the Squire about horses and riding horses, so what choice did she have?

"Yes," she said. "Yes, of course. Thank you for inviting me."

The shocking thing was that it hadn't been bad. The groom had brought her a pony named Minnow, who was round and placid and good-natured. Cordelia had mounted and immediately learned that she had no idea how to control a regular horse. Fortunately Minnow followed Dancer, who was just as good-natured, and Mrs. Green chatted gaily about the weather and the scenery while Cordelia tried to sort out what to do with the reins and how hard to squeeze with her knees.

A snort had shaken her from her concentration, and she'd looked up. Falada walked beside her, lifting his head high so that he looked down at her on Minnow's back. Cordelia looked up into Falada's eye, light green framed with dark pink skin that stood out against the shining whiteness of his coat. The paleness of his eyes made it easy to see what most people forgot—that a horse's pupils are slotted like a goat's, and Falada's held sly mockery that would have put any goat to shame.

He gazed down at her, her mother's familiar, so much taller than Minnow, and then very deliberately, he winked.

A spasm of fury had clenched like a fist around Cordelia's heart. All the old betrayal washed over her. She'd dropped her eyes and stared at Minnow's mane, the long black hairs trailing over her riding gloves, and thought *I loved you.*

She could not remember ever thinking that about her mother.

Luckily, Evangeline had then announced that she wanted a good gallop, "to shake the fidgets out," and the Squire said "Capital!" and the two raced off across the field. Cordelia reached out and patted Minnow's neck, which was warm and solid and ordinary, and felt the fist at her heart unclench a little.

Penelope had looked over at Lord Evermore, who was looking

after the riders wistfully. "Well, go on! Don't sit here when you really want a good run."

"And leave you lovely ladies unattended?"

Penelope made a rude noise. "Samuel's estate may not be so well run as yours, but there aren't brigands lying in wait twenty yards from the house. Go on."

"Well . . . if you insist . . ." He had grinned at them both, looking briefly much younger, then galloped off after the other two.

"Just as I suspected," Penelope said cheerfully. "Richard is a lovely man, and occasionally gallant to the point of obnoxiousness."

"Mother wants me to flirt with him," Cordelia confessed. "But I don't know how."

The older woman looked over, startled. "There's not much point to it. He's hopelessly in love with Hester."

Cordelia blinked. "Really?"

"Really. Now listen to that bird singing in the trees. I've absolutely no idea what it is. Do you?"

Cordelia shook her head.

"Then it is probably a new species, and we shall name it for science. Does it sound like a crested mouse-warbler to you?"

Cordelia was beginning to understand Penelope's sense of humor by now. "I think it's a white-throated babbler," she said solemnly.

"My goodness! At this time of year? Well, you may be right." Mrs. Green adjusted her riding habit. "*That,* however, was definitely a willowy frog-warbler, don't you think?"

The sun was warm on their faces. They meandered across the field, inventing increasingly outrageous names for birds that probably didn't deserve them. Minnow grabbed mouthfuls of grass and Cordelia was absolutely at a loss for how to stop her—did she haul on the reins? really? she'd never even considered doing that with Falada—but Penelope didn't seem troubled by it at all.

"Not much of a ride, was it?" asked the stablemaster, when Dancer and Minnow strolled back into the stableyard an hour later.

"It was exactly the sort I prefer," said Penelope firmly. "A lovely day on a very peaceful horse. And Cordelia's good company." She grinned over at Cordelia. "Let me know if you'd like to amble around another day."

Cordelia must have said something appropriate, but what she was thinking, in pure amazement, was *Good company? Me?*

No one had ever said such a thing before. It was such a small bit of praise, but it stood in splendid isolation inside her skull. *Good company.*

Another person wanted to be around her. She was not imposing on someone's time. It was staggering. Her friends at school had been temporary alliances, and even then she was on the outside looking in. Ellen had ridden with her out of courtesy and habit and . . . well, probably pity, if she was being honest. Hester was a kind hostess and a generally good-natured person.

Cordelia was aware of how pathetic it was to be so warmed by such a minor statement, and yet it wrapped around her anyway, a bit of praise that she had won for herself, by herself.

"I *hate* her," Evangeline growled again, wrenching Cordelia's attention back to the present. "I've got to get her out of here. The Squire likes her entirely too much, God knows why, and he's known her for years. Nostalgia for their lost youth is like an aphrodisiac for middle-aged men." She scowled, then caught a glimpse of herself in the mirror over the mantel and spent a moment smoothing out the lines in her face. "Cordelia!"

Cordelia jerked, startled. "Yes, Mother?"

"You've spent time with her. Has she let anything useful drop?"

"Useful?" All she could think was *good company,* and surely that was of no use to anyone else.

"Something I can use against her, stupid girl! Something damning!"

Cordelia didn't have the faintest idea what such a thing would look like. "I . . . I don't know . . . like what?"

Evangeline hurled herself into a chair. "Something scandalous.

Something that paints her in a bad light. Gambling debts or affairs with married men or secret Catholicism. *Something.*"

Cordelia tried to think of anything that might count, then realized that if she *did* know anything, she would never tell her mother. *I have to tell her something, though. She could make me obedient and send me to spy on Hester and Penelope and Imogene if she doesn't think I'd do a good enough job.* "I think she uses a lemon-water rinse on her hair?" she said cautiously.

"Not enough. Other women might care, but the Squire certainly wouldn't." She raked her nails down the arm of the chair. "I will not be outdone by a mere dabbler!"

"Dabbler . . . ?"

Evangeline's laugh held no humor. "You didn't notice? No, of course not. She's a sorcerer. Oh, not a *trained* one." She laughed again, probably at Cordelia's expression. "Wouldn't make even half a hedge-witch. I doubt she knows she's doing anything. Why do you think all these fools adore her?"

Because she's funny and kind to people? But maybe she wasn't. Maybe it was magic after all.

But no, *good company* had been real. And they really had made up silly bird names together. Maybe the sorcery made people more inclined to like Mrs. Green, or maybe that was why she seemed taller, but she was . . . well . . . *nice.* And Evangeline had a lot more sorcery, and no one thought she was nice, unless the Squire did.

Cordelia licked her lips nervously. "I'll keep listening for something useful," she promised. "I really haven't talked to her that much, but I'll keep listening."

"Do that," said Evangeline broodingly. "Otherwise I might have to take desperate measures."

Cordelia shuddered at the thought.

When Cordelia arrived in the solar, Lady Strauss and Mrs. Green were already there. She thought of leaving again, but Mrs. Green immediately patted the divan beside herself. "Come, sit, my dear Cordelia! You must save me."

Cordelia sat. She tried to study Mrs. Green covertly, wondering if she could feel some kind of sorcery radiating off her skin. "Save you?"

"Yes. Imogene is trying to persuade me to play cards. If you join in, she'll at least be reasonable and play for sugar lumps instead of trying to wring my life savings from my poor tender flesh."

Lady Strauss rolled her eyes. "Oh, very well. If you insist." She began to deal the cards out. The pack was worn, the edges showing little nicks of white. They matched the teapot on the tray, which had faint white marks around the rim where the painted design had begun to wear away.

"I don't know how to play," Cordelia protested.

"Oh, we're for it now," said Mrs. Green. "Look at the unholy light in her eyes! Imogene, be gentle. She is young and I am poor."

"You are not poor," said Lady Strauss. "I refuse to believe it. No one who wears gowns like yours could be poor."

Mrs. Green scoffed. "Do not mistake genius for price, dear Imogene. I know precisely what suits me and I refuse to chase the latest fashions. There is nothing like fashion to make one look terribly dated." She swept her hand down the length of her dress, a sleek wrap in glowing saffron silk. "Last year's fashions were all lace and ruffles. I refused to add a single ruffle, which means that I may continue wearing this gown in style *and* that I did not spend last year looking like a birthday cake. An enormous savings in both money and dignity." She caught Cordelia looking at her and added, "Beautiful women have an easier time of it, at least while they're young and beautiful. The rest of us must develop style. It's not so easy as beauty, but it lasts longer, and it's less brittle."

"Brittle?" asked Cordelia, puzzled.

"Oh lord, here she goes," muttered Imogene.

"Brittle," said Penelope, nodding. "Physical beauty is fragile, my dear Cordelia. Say that you are a great beauty, a diamond of the first water, beloved and admired by all."

Cordelia tried to imagine such a thing and found it vaguely horrifying. "Wouldn't people be staring at you *all the time?*"

"Yes, and that's exhausting, too. You can never scratch an itch or blow your nose or do any of the indelicate deeds that come of mortal flesh. God forbid you get the hiccups." She sat up very straight, sweeping her hands as if she was lecturing from a podium. Imogene rolled her eyes and rescued the deck of cards before she knocked it on the floor.

"Now," Penelope went on, "say that you, our diamond, are at an assembly. There is dancing, there are refreshments, and some fellow bumps into another one and both are drunk and they launch themselves at each other in a bout of impassioned male fisticuffs. Right! Left! Parry! Jab!"

"Careful!" Hester had to duck the jab. "This isn't a boxing ring."

"Neither is the assembly. In fact, they are battling by the refreshment table. An immense ice sculpture stands atop it, crowned by a frozen representation of a herring—"

"Why a herring?"

"It's the Herring Ball, obviously. Don't try to distract me with trivia, Imogene. At any rate, a careless blow strikes the sculpted herring's tail! It flies off the table and you, our diamond, are in its path! The sharp ice slashes across your flawless cheek, blood goes everywhere, ladies faint in the aisles, the two gentlemen immediately challenge one another to a duel for having injured you, and you are carried away to the doctor."

Cordelia's eyes were very round. Imogene nudged her and said, "This is one of her better ones. Last time she gave this speech, it was a fall from a horse spooked by a rare butterfly released by a rogue lepidopterist."

"The doctor does his best," Penelope continued, pretending not to hear. She clasped her hands to her bosom. "But alas! The stitches, no matter how perfectly aligned, are stitches still. The side of your face has an immense scar, from eye to chin, and your beauty is forever marred in the eyes of the world." She turned on Cordelia. "Now! *What do you wear?*"

"I ... uh ... I ..." Cordelia had no idea how to answer. "A veil?"

"The most practical answer, yes, but it dooms you to live forever behind a veil, lest you expose your fractured beauty to the assembly. Such is the problem of beauty. Once it is imperfect, the admiration it has won you is at an end. Whereas if you have invested your time into cultivating *style*—" She swept her hand down the length of her gown again. "—you simply do what you can with face powder, put on a particularly daring hat, and go out to the next assembly. People will think you are terribly brave and fall all over themselves to compliment your hat." She lifted her chin and winked at Cordelia. "So ends the lecture."

"I f-feel like I should applaud," Cordelia said. *Was that sorcery? She said all that, and it really seemed like it meant something, but maybe the sorcery made me feel like it meant more?*

"Oh, *don't*. It only encourages her." Imogene looked over the top of her cards. "Also, it's your turn."

"Bah. And here I hoped to distract you so that you will not take all of my meager savings."

"Surely you must have some gentleman who is even now showering you with expensive gifts?" said Hester.

"Alas," said Mrs. Green mournfully. "My last benefactor fell in love, if you can imagine it. I begrudge nothing for love, you understand, and I would dance at their wedding if it were not totally inappropriate to invite one's former mistress to your wedding, but it has left me in a sad state of affairs."

Wait . . . is she saying that she was someone's mistress? And everyone knows about it?

The thought was far more shocking than mere sorcery. Cordelia thought she must certainly be mistaken. Except that Lady Strauss, dealing out cards to all three players, said, "And here I would swear that I heard you were passing the time with young Baronet Vann."

Mrs. Green curled her lip. "That puppy. Oh, he fancies he's in love with me, but I am not so desperate as to take a child's allowance, even if he could afford me, which he can't. That is part of why I came out here, dear Hester, not merely for your company. I am hoping that he will find someone else to trail after. The boy makes me feel positively *maternal*."

It occurred to Cordelia that this was the sort of thing that her mother might like to know. Being a mistress wasn't respectable. *Would she try to use it against Mrs. Green, even having been one herself?*

Silly question. Of course she would. Cordelia looked up at the side of Mrs. Green's face, with its network of smallpox scars that had left the skin there sunken and cobbled. Not so far-fetched as a herring ice sculpture, but still, Cordelia suspected that she understood why Penelope set such a premium on style.

She wrenched her gaze back down to her cards. Hester leaned forward and tapped one. "Play that," she said, "it'll take the trick."

"No helping," said Lady Strauss.

"You didn't bother to explain the rules," said Hester, "so it's the least I can do. Play the three next, Cordelia."

"Pah." Lady Strauss tossed her hand down in defeat and dealt out another round. She glanced over at Penelope. "You could do worse, you know. Vann's father will leave him a fortune."

Mrs. Green snorted. "If I thought it had a chance of giving the old tyrant apoplexy, I might take up with the boy after all, simply to rid the world of a dreadful wretch. But you can never count on people to die just because it would make your life easier."

Don't listen, Cordelia told herself, concentrating on the cards in front of her. *What you don't hear can't be used against them.* She bit her lower lip, but it was impossible to close her ears completely.

". . . heard Vann's sister ran off with a schoolteacher . . ."

". . . good for her if she did . . ."

". . . not something I can fix . . ."

". . . Cordelia . . ."

She caught her name and looked up, surprised. "Sorry?"

"It's your turn, dear," said Lady Strauss gently, and Cordelia played a card completely at random and ended up winning the hand, entirely by accident.

CHAPTER 16

Mrs. Green was late to breakfast the next morning, and came in heavy-eyed, moving more slowly than usual. Cordelia saw dark circles under her eyes and hastily surrendered the teapot to her.

Hester frowned, looking across the table. "Penelope, are you well?"

Mrs. Green laughed, but it was not quite up to her usual exuberance. "I fear I didn't sleep well last night. The storm kept me awake, that's all."

Lady Strauss and Hester exchanged puzzled looks, but it was the Squire who said, "Storm? Was clear as a bell all night, m'dear."

"What?" Penelope looked genuinely startled. "There was a terrible wind. It blew my balcony doors clear open and rattled the windows like anything."

More looks were exchanged. Lady Strauss said, cautiously, "Penelope, dear, we're on the same side of the house and there wasn't a breath of wind. I'd swear to it."

A sudden suspicion gripped Cordelia and she looked over at her mother. Evangeline was nibbling daintily at her toast with a small smile on her face.

She couldn't have done something, could she?

No, surely not. She twists up people's minds, she doesn't control the weather. This must be something else. Surely.

"No wind? None at all?" Penelope sat back in her chair, and then suddenly she laughed aloud, much more like her old self, and said, "Well! You've relieved my mind enormously, then. I must have been dreaming. And in that case, it was *all* a dream, and I'm not going out of my head." She grinned at the others around the table. "And now I shall be that terribly boring person and tell you about my dream, while you all secretly wish you were elsewhere. But I promise you that this was a regular whale of a dream."

"Do tell," said Lady Strauss, leaning forward. "I've always thought that you could tell so much about a person from their dreams."

"Well, if you find out all my secrets, please don't share them." Mrs. Green folded her hands. "In my dream, there was this terrible wind, you see, rattling the balcony doors. Such a wind! I almost thought I heard voices in it, and as you all know, I am not the sort of person who imagines such things. I've absolutely no nerves at all, I fear. Put me in a haunted house and I will sleep like a baby." She gave a self-deprecating shrug. "Still, this wind was something quite different. I kept listening, wondering if someone was outside, calling to be let in. It had that quality of speech to it, you know?"

Lady Strauss nodded. The Squire folded back the corner of his newspaper. "Lot of nonsense," he muttered.

"I don't know," said Lord Evermore mildly, "do you remember that blizzard that struck old Hollowell's hunting box? We were stuck for two days with the wind howling, and when it blew just right under the eaves, it sounded like a horse screaming. We slogged out to the stables three times checking on them."

"Mmm. Forgot about that." The Squire jerked his chin in agreement. "Fair enough."

"It was all a dream anyway," said Mrs. Green. "I wouldn't make any claims for winds that happen in other people's heads. I thought for a moment I heard—well, never mind. But at any rate, I got out of bed, and the balcony doors were rattling like anything. Then they flew open and banged so hard against the wall that I was afraid the glass would shatter. I went to close them—which now that I think of it was *not* sensible, since if they banged open again, they very well might break, but of course we're not always sensible in dreams, are we? But when I reached the balcony, the wind died down. I stepped outside, wondering if the storm was passing. But then . . ." She gave a little laugh. "Have you ever had the sense that someone was watching you? Because I had the strongest feeling of eyes on me."

"Something dangerous?" asked Lord Strauss.

"Oh, I shouldn't say that, no. It was more like being at an assembly, you know, and then you turn around and someone is glaring daggers at you from across the room." Penelope shook her head. "I would have gone back in at once, you know—I was in my night rail, and it would be a trifle scandalous if someone was watching me—but I looked over the balcony and do you know, I saw the oddest thing?"

She paused then, and looked around the group. Even the Squire had put down his newspaper and was listening raptly.

"What was it?" breathed Lady Strauss.

"A glow," said Mrs. Green. "Like foxfire. Some glowing shape just past the little line of trees. I couldn't see it all, just bits and pieces between the trunks. I watched it moving and I had the oddest feeling that it was watching me back."

"A person?" Hester asked.

"No, that's the oddest thing. It was much larger than that. The size of a horse or a cow, I'd say. And it kept moving back and forth, but it always kept the trees between us. Like it knew that I was there, and didn't want me to see it."

"What happened next?" asked Lady Strauss.

Mrs. Green spread her hands helplessly. "I went back to bed. Although apparently I never left it at all, since I dreamed the storm on top of everything else. And here I'd been thinking that the wind was real and half wondering if the glowing beast might be as well." She sat back. "Good thing that it was a dream, because think what a mooncalf I should sound like, insisting that I'd seen a great glowing creature stomping around the grounds!"

"I expect Samuel would set out to hunt it," said Hester dryly. "He's gone out on the strength of flimsier tales."

The Squire snorted from behind his newspaper. Mrs. Green laughed. "When they tell you to chase your dreams, I suspect they mean something else entirely. Though I do wish my dream had given me just a glimpse of whatever it was. A white stag, like in the old stories, do you think? A Questing Beast?"

"Perhaps it was a unicorn," said Master Strauss, who had been picking at his eggs and pretending he wasn't fascinated. "They're supposed to glow, aren't they?"

"I fear," said Penelope archly, "that it's been many years since a unicorn would gladly suffer *my* presence."

There was a half beat of silence and then everyone burst out laughing, except for Master Strauss, who turned beet red. Penelope leaned over and patted his hand, murmuring something that Cordelia couldn't hear, and he smiled at her, but his blush did not recede.

A glowing creature the size of a horse. A creature that watched her through the trees. Could it have been Falada?

No. It was a dream. She said it was a dream. Everyone else would have noticed if there was wind.

But she remembered suddenly the trip home from the church, her mother waving her hand, and the wind that came from nowhere, making the branches of the hedgerow bend down before her.

Cordelia's eyes flicked briefly to her mother. Evangeline's eyebrows had drawn down and she was no longer smiling.

"I hope you wanted to see me for more than gossip," said Hester, letting herself into Lady Strauss's suite the next evening. "Otherwise my knee will have words with you." The walk to the guest wing involved two flights of stairs, one up, one down, and she could tell by the ache that the barometer was dropping.

"Gossip, yes, but also brandy." Imogene lifted a bottle. "Danielle, love, will you leave word we're not to be disturbed? Hester and I are going to get blindingly drunk, I think."

"Are we?" Hester exchanged a wry look with Imogene's lady's maid. "Well, in that case, tell the housekeeper to have a footman or two on hand to help me back to my chambers, if you would."

Danielle shook her head. "I suppose there is no point trying to talk you out of it, madam?"

"Is there ever?" asked Hester. Lady Strauss made a rude noise. Danielle dropped a perfunctory curtsy and left, shutting the door behind her.

Hester dropped onto a chair and sighed with relief. As pleased as she was to see Richard, the effort of pretending not to be in pain around him could be exhausting. *Not that he would think less of me, but it pains him to see it, and I would rather not be the object of pity.*

And yet . . . and yet . . .

Last night, after dinner, they had both retired to one of the sitting rooms. She'd embroidered and Richard had read a book—some stultifyingly dull volume on novel irrigation methods. They hadn't spoken for more than an hour, just sat in their chairs, not too far from one another, in a silence so companionable that Hester wanted to drink it down like wine.

Imogene moved the tea tray closer and poured a spot of brandy into each cup. "I played cards with her."

"Oh? And?"

"And I think you'll have a sister-in-law by month's end, unless you do something drastic."

Hester's eyebrows shot up. "All that from a game of cards?"

"I know you don't think much of it, but you can tell more about a person in the way they play games than from hours of conversation. I threw the first few hands, just to see what would happen. She wasn't taking me seriously until she lost the next four or five, and then she became annoyed."

"And?"

"And she became polite. Very, very polite. If she could have politely cut my throat in the parlor, she'd have done it. There is a woman who does not wish to be crossed."

"Who won?"

"She did. She decided that she was going to win and I decided that I liked living." Imogene gestured with the flask. "But she was good, too. Didn't miss a single opening, didn't dither. Once she decided that it mattered, she was savage."

Hester groaned. "That's what I'm afraid of. She's decided that marrying my brother matters."

Lady Strauss set the flask down and stared at her hands. "Have you got any plans?"

"I've spoken to Richard. I'm hoping he'll be able to think of something."

"I still say that he might prove a more appealing target, if you're wanting to distract her from your brother."

"Perhaps," said Hester. "I also thought, perhaps, that Samuel might rekindle something with Penelope . . ." She trailed off.

Imogene looked at her teacup, looked at her flask, and then pushed the tea aside and simply swigged it.

"No?"

"If I were Penelope, I'd think twice. That is a great deal of ruthlessness to put oneself in the path of—"

Someone screamed.

It was a woman's scream, full-throated and bloodcurdling, a scream of agony or terror or both together. It rang out shockingly close, barely muffled by doors and walls.

"Dear god!" Hester shot to her feet, heedless of the pain in her knee. Imogene lunged for the door and flung it open before the echoes had even died away.

Two footmen pounded past. Doors opened all along the wing. Hester heard Richard's voice shout a question.

Another scream, scarcely softer than the last, ripped through the house.

Richard and the footmen flung themselves at a particular door. Hester hobbled toward them as the hallway filled with servants. "It's Penelope's room!"

"Mrs. Green!" Richard slammed his shoulder into the door. "Mrs. Green, what's wrong? Are you hurt?"

The door refused to yield. Hester grabbed one of the maids. "Get the housekeeper! She's got the keys!"

"No time," said Richard grimly. He nodded to the footmen and all three put their shoulders to the door. "On three . . ."

The door was old oak, elegantly carved. It held. The latch did not. The door slammed against the wall with a boom that echoed through the house like cannonfire.

"What the devil . . . ?" Samuel and Lord Strauss crested the stairs. "What's going on?"

Richard cursed softly, but with astonishing venom. Hester could not remember the last time she'd heard him swear like that. He stepped into the room and Hester heard him say, "Penelope, what's going on?"

"Out of my way," Hester told a footman. He tore his eyes away from the scene inside the room and blinked down at Hester.

"Ma'am—begging your pardon—this is no sight for a lady's eyes."

Not the sort of phrase you want to hear when your friend may be injured. Hester gritted her teeth, wedged her cane between the doorframe and the footman, and let him decide whether he wanted to use force to stop her.

He did not. She got her head around the edge of the frame and her mouth sagged open.

Penelope Green stood in the center of the room. She was holding a long knife and blood had spattered her dressing gown in lurid scarlet. Her eyes were huge and her mouth worked but no sound came out.

Hester's first wild thought was that Penelope had somehow nicked herself opening a letter.

Her second was that people did not bleed like that from nicks. Her eyes followed the line of blood down, to a heap of black and white cloth lying against the wall. Black and white, dyed dramatically red, with an outflung hand as white and waxy as a lily.

My god, it's her maid.

"Penelope," said Richard, in a very calm voice, "it's all right. Everything will be all right." He took a step forward, his hands held up in front of him. "I don't know what's wrong, but we can fix it."

"No," whispered a small voice. "No, no, no . . ."

Hester's gaze jerked sideways. Evangeline was huddled on the far side of Penelope and the maid, near the door to the balcony. Her gown did not appear bloodied, but her hair had fallen from its coiffure and hung over her face.

The door was open and a breeze from it sent Penelope's dressing gown shifting around her legs, where it was not slicked down with blood.

"Penelope," said Richard again. "If you just give me the knife, we'll sort this out." He took another step forward.

Penelope's throat worked. The knife blade shook in her hand. "Did . . ." she choked out. "Did . . . nnn . . ."

"I know," said Richard soothingly. "It will be all right. Just give me the knife."

"Hester, old girl," said her brother, practically in her ear, "what the devil is going on here?"

"She killed her!" screamed Evangeline, shockingly loud in the taut silence of the room. "She took a knife and killed her!"

Samuel swore and pushed past Hester. "Best let us handle this," he said over his shoulder, which Hester ignored completely.

"Everyone stay calm," said Richard. "Samuel, stay back, if you please."

"Dammit, Evermore—"

"Samuel."

Her brother subsided fretfully. Hester saw the spark of cold blue eyes between the dark curtains of Evangeline's hair, watching.

"Now, Penelope," Richard began, "I know this is all very upset-
ting, but if you just—"

Penelope's wide eyes grew even wider, darting from side to
side. "Did . . . nnnnnn . . ." For a moment they caught Hester's,
and she was struck by how much Penelope's gaze resembled Cordelia's, the same look of a beast in a trap, though Penelope's was
all horrified rage and despair.

And then she turned and strode jerkily toward Evangeline, still
holding the knife aloft.

"Penelope!"

"Evangeline!"

Time slowed to a crawl. Richard lunged for Penelope. Samuel
lunged for Evangeline. The two men nearly collided, and as Hester watched, Penelope Green staggered past the other woman and
out the balcony door. She leaned far back, like a drunk trying to
keep her balance, but she kept moving forward, and suddenly
Hester knew.

There was no world where she could reach her friend in time,
but she tried anyway. It didn't matter that her knee tore itself to
pieces. She stabbed her cane down into the carpet, trying to run,
but it was too late.

Richard was closer, but even he was too late. His hand, reaching
out, just brushed her hair.

Penelope Green, knife still in hand, threw herself over the balcony and was gone.

CHAPTER 17

"She'd already stabbed the maid when I got there," said Evangeline, in a high, trembling voice. "I'd just walked in and I saw her and at first I didn't know what had happened. Then I saw that poor girl and there was so much blood . . ." She covered her face with her hands.

"There, there," said the Squire, patting her shoulder. "There, there. It's not to be wondered at. You don't expect to walk into such a thing."

They had all moved back to Lady Strauss's suite and Willard had brought tea and brandy. The room was a mirror of the one that Mrs. Green had been staying in, and everyone kept looking toward the balcony door, despite the heavy curtains covering it.

There was blood on Evangeline's fingers, Hester noted. She looked over at Richard, who nodded to her, almost imperceptibly.

"Forgive me, madam," he said. "Did you go to the maid, then?"

"What?" Evangeline took her hands away from her face. "Did I?"

"You must have," said Hester, "since you've got blood all over you."

The flash of anger was so swift that no one would have noticed if they weren't already looking for it. Evangeline looked down at her hands and began to tremble. "I must have. Yes. Oh god . . ." She wiped frantically at them with a napkin from the tea tray. Everyone watched in silence until Samuel mumbled something and pulled out his handkerchief to offer her.

"Why were you in Penelope's room to begin with?" asked Lady Strauss.

"She'd asked me to come. Said something about a brooch to loan me, that she thought would go well with my hair." Evangeline shook her head.

Imogene nodded, as if this were perfectly understandable. Perhaps if you didn't know Penelope, it was.

"I thought she was going to stab me next," said Evangeline. Her eyelids fluttered. "I was so frightened . . ."

"Yes, of course," said Samuel gruffly. "Understandable. Anyone would be."

"It was like she was possessed." The words began to dissolve into tears at the edges. Hester stared into her teacup and thought uncharitable thoughts.

Even Doom might be upset, having someone brandish a knife at her.

Penelope Green would no more stab someone than she would fly to the moon.

Penelope Green is dead.

It was impossible. She couldn't believe it. She'd watched her friend go over the railing and she didn't doubt for a minute that Richard had been right when he said that she died instantly, but still . . . *dead?* How was that possible? Surely she would walk through the door in just a moment, scarred and ravishing, and everyone would turn toward her, like flowers toward the sun. Surely that bright, hilarious light had not been snuffed out.

It's perfectly normal, Hester told herself. *Anything so fast and so irrevocable feels impossible. Of course you don't believe it. It'll hit soon, and you'd best be tucked up in bed when it does, so that you can cry your eyes out in peace.*

She closed her eyes for a moment and pictured a goose. A perfect goose, the sort that she had bred a few times, a tall, plump bird with dove-gray feathers and a deep orange bill. The rump would be white, the chest smooth, without an obvious keel. Like that. Yes. She took a deep breath and felt a fraction calmer.

"Did she say anything?" asked Richard. "Any hint why she might have done something?"

Lady Evangeline bit her lower lip and looked at Samuel. Hester saw without surprise that she could cry without her nose turning red or her eyes going puffy. *If I didn't already loathe the woman, I certainly would now. Nature is so unkind.*

"She said . . . she said . . ." She put her face in her hands. Imogene looked at Hester and Hester schooled her face to be carefully blank.

"Anything you can tell us may be helpful," Richard said.

"Yes, go on, pet, it's all right. Nobody will be angry at you," said the Squire, patting her shoulder. "I've got your hand right here and you just squeeze as tight as you need to."

Evangeline gave a watery sniffle. "Yes, I just . . . it's so . . ." She swallowed. "She said that once I was out of the way, *he'd* be all hers again."

"Eh?" The Squire's eyes bulged. "The old girl said what? But that was over years ago and she was the one who—"

He cut himself off, rather too late for propriety. Lord Strauss coughed. Richard rubbed his temples.

"She looked so odd," he murmured, almost to himself. "Like a wind was blowing her over the railing. I've never seen anything like it."

"Yes," said Hester, sitting bolt upright. "Like a strong wind." Trust Richard to put his finger on it, as Hester recalled the dream Penelope had shared with them just that morning. The one with the wind that blew open the balcony doors. "And she was fighting against it."

"There wasn't any, though," said the Squire. "I was right there. So were you, Evermore."

"No. No, of course not." Richard shook his head. "Forgive me. It's been a terrible evening, and I'm getting fanciful. Perhaps—"

Whatever he was going to say next was eclipsed, however, as Evangeline dissolved into tears and flung herself in the Squire's arms. "There, there," he said, patting her back and looking at the others as if daring them to say something. "It's all right, pet, it's over now."

"Yes," said Hester, pushing herself to her feet. Her knee felt as if there was a live coal under the cap. "Yes, it's been a terrible evening. In the morning, I suppose we'll have to tell the constables."

"Already sent Jack out with a note," said the Squire. "They'll be around first thing tomorrow."

Hester nodded. "Then I suggest we all go to bed," she said wearily. "Everything will be easier in the morning."

The others murmured assent. Hester left the room before she could see what the Squire did with Evangeline. She knew that Doom had won this round, and she didn't have the heart to see it play out. *And there's not a damn thing I can say that won't look like I'm bullying a frightened woman.*

Hell, maybe I would be.

Richard followed her, taking her arm and she leaned on him rather more than she wanted to. "Your knee's bothering you," he murmured, as they slowly tackled the stairs.

"I could have called one of those sturdy young footmen to carry me instead."

"And deprive me of the chance? How often do I have a beautiful woman pressed up against me without anyone thinking twice about the proprieties?"

Hester told him where he could put the proprieties.

"I see that sailor's mouth of yours hasn't changed."

"You could hardly have expected it to. Particularly since you taught me a few of the words."

"The student has, I think, outshone the master."

"Bollocks. Don't tell me that men don't have words they use when no ladies are around."

"We do, but I expect ladies have words they use when no gentlemen are around, so I'm not sure that counts."

Hester sniffed haughtily. As Richard no doubt intended, the

conversation had been a welcome distraction from the pain. They reached the hallway to her chambers.

"Is it very much worse than it was?" he asked in an undertone, as they approached her door.

"No," she lied. "I was just a fool and tried to run on it, because Penelope . . ." She swallowed the rest of the words, feeling tears starting in her throat.

Richard moved to embrace her and she put her hand on his chest. "Don't," she said hoarsely. "Don't be kind to me. I'll start bawling if you do."

"I think I'd survive."

Hester closed her eyes and imagined, just for a moment, being weak. Laying her head on Richard's shoulder and letting him be strong for her. Letting herself pretend that the gulf between them was something that could be bridged with love and care and tears.

"I'm not sure I would," she told him, and walked blindly through the door before her grief could overwhelm her at last.

The next morning passed in a haze of misery. Mary, Hester's maid, rubbed goose grease on her swollen knee and wrapped it tightly while Hester cursed through gritted teeth.

"If you'd let me send for the doctor, this'd be easier," Mary told her crossly.

"He'll give me laudanum, and what's the good of that?"

"The good is that it'll hurt less," Mary said, helping her into her dressing gown.

"Fat lot of good it'll do if it puts me to sleep in the process."

Mary gave her a wry look. She'd been in Hester's employ for over a decade and took no nonsense. "Any particular reason you want to be awake for the pain?"

Hester sighed. "I have to keep my wits about me. That woman's got Samuel eating out of her hand now."

Mary's lips thinned, but she didn't argue the point. She helped

Hester into the sitting room and set her in a chair, draping a lap quilt over her legs and sending for tea to fortify her against the trials to come.

Her first visitor was her brother, come to see how she was doing. "Nasty shock." The ends of his mustache looked ragged, as if he'd been chewing on them. "Terrible business. But who knew the old girl had it in her?"

"I would swear she didn't," Hester said.

"Just goes to show you can't ever tell." He ran his hand over his thinning hair. "Back when she and I . . . when we . . ." He cleared his throat.

"Had an understanding," Hester offered, bemused. *The woman killed herself in front of us and you're still hung up on the dignity of her having been your mistress years ago.*

"Right, yes." The Squire coughed. "Never showed any sign of that. Never a wild one. Never would have thought it."

"No, she never was." Hester stared into her teacup. "I'm sorry I invited her," she said. "That is, I feel if I hadn't, she'd still be alive." The teacup shook in her hand and she glared at it as if it belonged to someone else.

"No, no," said Samuel hastily. "Nothing like that, old girl. Brace up. If someone's a bad 'un, it comes out eventually. Blame's all on her. Stabbing someone at your friend's house party! Shockingly bad form, what?"

Hester stared into her brother's earnest face and didn't know whether to laugh hysterically or dissolve into tears. She drained her teacup instead.

"Just what I told Evangeline," Samuel continued. "Not her fault at all. Poor thing was trembling like a kitten."

I'm sure she was, thought Hester grimly. *And telling you that you were the only thing that made her feel safe, I'll bet.* She murmured reassurances to her brother and then Mary chased him out of the room and poured her more tea.

The next visitors were two constables, who wanted her statement

on what had occurred. One was short, with a shock of red hair, and one was tall, with a long neck and a narrow, angular face that reminded her of a gander she'd owned once. He'd been a good goose. She'd gotten a fair few chicks out of him.

"Terrible business," Red said, sitting down. "We won't trouble Your Ladyship for long." Gander leaned against the back of a wingback chair and said nothing.

"Terrible, yes," said Hester. She took a fortifying gulp of tea and wondered what Richard had told them. "Ask your questions."

"Can you tell us what you saw, precisely?" asked Red.

Hester ran down the list of events from the time she'd heard the scream. It made her realize just how quickly everything had occurred. Strange that something so huge and irrevocable could happen in so little time.

"Did you recognize the knife?" Gander interrupted, speaking for the first time.

Hester paused. "You know, I didn't think about it at the time, but it may have been the one from the library. My grandfather collected all manner of objects. He couldn't travel, you see, so he lived vicariously by buying things from the old country." She nibbled on her lower lip. "You'd have to check. Willard can help you there."

Gander nodded to Red, who quickly scrawled a note on his pad.

"That means she didn't plan it, doesn't it?" said Hester. "If she used a knife from here?"

Red shot a look at Gander, clearly deferring to him. Gander shrugged. "That's one possibility. We are merely collecting facts."

"Penelope Green would never have stabbed anyone," said Hester. "I want you to know that." She stopped, pinching the bridge of her nose. "At least, I would have sworn . . ." She hated how her voice sounded, how weak and querulous and old, so she stopped. *Obviously she* did *stab someone. These men wouldn't be here if she hadn't.*

"Your Ladyship—" Red began, and his voice was so obviously that of a man being kind to a flustered older lady that Hester wanted to curse him out roundly. *Which will not help at all. Get control of yourself.*

Mary stepped in and fussed with Hester's shawl, keeping a sharp eye on the two constables. Hester took a deep breath. "Forgive me," she said. "I know what happened. But I would have sworn that Penelope would never have hurt a fly. Given the fly the cut direct, perhaps."

A muscle in Gander's cheek twitched, not quite a smile but close. Red said, "I understand, Your Ladyship. Please continue."

"There's not much more to tell. Richard asked her to give him the knife. Evangeline shouted something, and then Penelope turned around and went for the balcony." Hester grimaced. "She looked like she was trying to fight a strong wind. I would have said she didn't want to jump."

Gander put up an eyebrow. Red put up both of them. "Well," Red said, after a moment, "it's hard for some people to . . . err . . . nerve themselves up for things. You know. Is there anything else you can tell us?"

Hester stared at the ceiling. *And what could I tell them? That I don't actually believe that Penelope would kill herself?*

But she did. I watched it happen. And she stabbed Ruth, and . . .

No, wait. No one saw her stab Ruth.

"No one saw her stab Ruth," she said out loud.

Red flipped through his notebook. "Ruth Svensdottir, her lady's maid, correct?"

"Yes. I didn't know her last name, but yes, that's who I mean. Penelope never had anything bad to say about her, though. And why would she stab her maid, anyway? To hear Doo—Evangeline talk, Penelope had planned to kill her all along. What would stabbing Ruth accomplish?"

Gander and Red exchanged looks again. "Perhaps she was an inconvenient witness," Red said.

Hester suspected that Ruth would have been more likely to grab Doom by the ankles and help her mistress carry the woman to a shallow grave, but it didn't seem like something she ought to say to the constables. "Evangeline said that Ruth was dead when she entered the room." Hester spread her hands. "I'm sorry, gentlemen. I know this sounds like I'm grasping at straws, but it just doesn't make sense. Penelope had to know she'd never get away with it. She wasn't a foolish woman."

Gander tapped the back of the chair. Red looked to him, like a sheepdog receiving a herding command, and nodded. "People can become unbalanced," Red said gently, closing his notebook. "It happens more often than you'd think. Oftentimes the friends and family are the most shocked. Thank you for your time, Your Ladyship."

He rose. Hester sank back in her chair. *I haven't convinced them that anything strange is happening. I don't know if I've even convinced myself.*

All I know is that if I hadn't invited her here, she'd probably still be alive. Her and Ruth both.

Guilt rose up in her like bile, swamping her senses. Hester closed her eyes, forcing herself to picture geese again, a flock on them on the water, their heavy bodies suddenly as graceful as swans. From a great distance, she could hear Mary scolding the constables about "bothering a sick old lady" and thought, *Am I an old lady, then? Already? But I haven't figured out how to age gracefully yet.*

Penelope would have known how. She was doing it. What changed?

She sighed and let Mary fuss over her, bringing a fresh cup of tea. "No, I don't want to go back to bed," she said, in response to the fussing. "Getting out of it was too much work."

"I can bring you a tray in bed, you know."

"Yes, and I'll spend the night with crumbs if you do. You might bring me my embroidery here."

There was a hesitant tap on the door. Mary glared at it. "That had better not be those policemen again," she muttered, but opened it anyway.

Cordelia stood there. The young woman's lips were pale and

bloodless, but her face was composed. She bowed her head too deeply to Mary. "May I come in, please?"

"Lady Hester's not feeling quite the thing—"

"Let her in, Mary." *Perhaps she'll have another question, like the one about being compromised. God knows, I could use something to distract me completely, or I'll sit here brooding until nightfall.* "What brings you here, child?"

"Are you all right?" Cordelia asked. "You weren't hurt?"

"No, I'm fine. You're kind to ask, though."

The girl bit her lower lip, bringing a brief flush of red to it. "I ... that is ... I wanted to say ..." Her eyes sought out Mary, who was bustling determinedly over the tea service.

"Mary," said Hester, "I think I could eat a little after all. Will you go down to Cook and ask if she has anything very light? A thimbleful of broth, perhaps?"

Mary gave her a long, level look that said that Hester was not fooling anyone, but said, "Very well." She swept out the door with more dignity than Hester had ever managed at any point in her life. Cordelia's gaze tracked her departure.

"Now," said Hester, "what is it that you wished to say in private?"

Cordelia squared her shoulders and met Hester's gaze with great calm.

"You probably won't believe what I'm going to say," she said. "I know that. But I have to tell you anyway. It's the only thing I can think of to do. Maybe you'll have some way to fix it."

Hester stared at her, completely at sea.

Cordelia lifted her chin. "I think my mother killed Mrs. Green."

CHAPTER 18

Cordelia was calm.

She had been washing her face when Alice burst in and told her the dreadful news. She was still holding the damp washcloth as she sank down in her chair, while the guilt and horror grew inside her head with every word. *You failed. All your hand-wringing and hoping and dithering didn't change anything. Mrs. Green died like Ellen died and you did nothing to stop it.*

You heard what they think of sorcerers! No one would have believed me if I'd tried to warn them! And if Mother had found out what I said, she would have . . . would have . . .

The voice in her head whispered, *But you didn't even try.* She wrung the washcloth between her fingers, feeling tepid water drip down her wrists.

"It's awful," said Alice, in unconscious echo of her thoughts. "No one can believe it."

Cordelia could believe it. *Mother could make* me *obedient. Mother could make me stab* you *while I was obedient, and afterward everyone would say they didn't believe it. And there is nothing that I could do to stop her.*

There is nothing that I can do to stop my mother from killing anyone who gets in her way.

Something inside her snapped. She could feel it like a physical blow, like a bone breaking. The weight of dread on her chest crashed down and the scaffolding that had held it up was crushed underneath.

And suddenly she was calm.

It was the calm of a burned-out house or a ravaged field, the calm that comes where there is no longer anything to lose. It was almost like being invincible. The endless frantic fluttering of her thoughts had stilled. She knew what she needed to do.

If Mother finds out . . .

Cordelia ignored the fearful whisper. If her mother found out, she would do something terrible. If she didn't find out, she would still eventually do something terrible. There would be no difference at all, except that perhaps no one else would die like Penelope and Ellen's family.

"I need to speak to Lady Hester at once," she said, standing up and tossing the cloth aside. Her hands did not tremble and she did not stammer when she spoke.

"She—she may still be with the constables—" said Alice, startled.

"Then I will speak to them, too."

She pulled the blue shawl around her shoulders and went out.

Cordelia knew, even now, that the calm would not last. It would crack and fall apart and all the horror would come rushing back in. Certainly it would not survive an encounter with her mother. So she walked to the family wing of the house as quickly as she could, praying that no one would see her.

Luck was on her side. A surprised maid pointed out Hester's door, but other than that, she saw no one on the way. She tapped on the door and went in.

When she announced that her mother had killed Mrs. Green, Hester's mouth fell open, but she recovered quickly enough.

"My dear, I was there," the older woman said. "I saw Penelope . . ." She stopped and put her hand to her mouth. Cordelia watched it all from a little distance, unsurprised.

"I know how it sounds," she said. "Let me explain. My mother is a sorceress, and she can make people obedient."

She expected disbelief or lack of comprehension, but Hester sat up straighter, her eyes narrowing. "Wait. What do you mean by that?"

Cordelia told her. When she described what it felt like, a sliver of panic tried to lodge itself in her chest. She examined it dispassionately and set it aside. *Later. When I have done what I need to do. Then I can panic.* It was no different than learning not to scream when she came up out of being obedient.

"And you think . . ." Hester swallowed hard. "You think that your mother may have done this to Penelope?"

Cordelia nodded.

"This is mad," said Hester. She tried to pour herself some tea, but her hands shook too badly. Cordelia took the teapot away and poured, then pressed the cup into Hester's hands. "This is utterly mad. It can't be possible. Sorcerers can't *do* things like that. They— you heard Imogene—they cheat at cards. They make old horses look young. It's all just—just flimflam and trickery!"

"Hers isn't. She did it to Ellen's father, too. Mr. Parker, I mean. He killed his entire family with an axe. The article in the paper that the Squire read that morning, when I fainted. That's why. I knew her. She was my friend." She almost added that her father had probably died the same way, but she didn't know for certain, and it seemed like too much all at once.

Hester took a gulp of tea. Her eyes were fixed forward, but not on anything that Cordelia could see. "Penelope didn't look right," she said softly. "I knew she didn't look right. It was her eyes. She looked like she was fighting something. And when she went over, Richard said it looked like she was walking against the wind. She did. She did look like that." Her cup clattered in the saucer and she cursed softly and dropped it back on the table.

"She must have been very strong, to fight it," said Cordelia. "I never could."

Hester's eyes snapped to her. "Why are you telling me all this now? Why didn't you tell me before?"

"You wouldn't have believed me."

"I don't believe you now!" Hester clutched her head. "This—no, this isn't possible. I want to believe it because I love Penelope and I hate your mother—I'm sorry, but I do—"

"So do I," said Cordelia, and the calm rippled a little, as if something massive had shifted beneath the surface.

"But I shouldn't believe it just because I want to believe it. I shouldn't. I . . ." Hester took a deep breath. "Why *are* you telling me this?"

"Because she won't stop. It doesn't matter if I do what she wants. It doesn't matter who I marry or if I learn to be charming." Cordelia felt as if she were gazing down a long, long tunnel, into the future. "She'll never stop, and I will never be free."

Hester felt as if her mind were coming undone. She did not believe the story that Cordelia had just poured out. It was unbelievable. Sorcerers simply didn't have that kind of power. They swindled the unsuspecting and cheated at cards, and even then, it was generally felt that the victims should have known better. A sorcerer with the power to actually take over someone's body was simply absurd.

There were *stories,* of course. But they were old stories, all mixed up with fairy tales and giants and the Devil holding court at the crossroads. If anyone had ever had that power, they were comfortably dead.

It couldn't be true, and that was all there was to it. This was no more than a panicked young girl trying to make sense of a heinous act. That was all.

Except.

Except that she had looked into Penelope's eyes.

Didn't it remind you, even then, of Cordelia after that dinner? The one where she says she was made *obedient? Eyes like an animal in a trap?*

Penelope Green had not been a frightened rabbit but a wily old fox, and yet . . . and yet . . .

Cordelia's absolute calm reminded Hester of a rabbit, still—one in shock, who sits and watches the predator's approach. It should have been heartbreaking, but Hester was forced to be glad of it. She could not handle wailing and tears right now. She was too close to the edge herself.

But if she was wailing and babbling about sorcery, you could just dismiss her out of hand. Tell her that she was overwrought. Instead you're listening, even though you know *it's completely mad.*

Evangeline, a sorceress?

It was too easy. It tied everything up so elegantly and put the blame on a hated villain, not on her dead friend. Hester was suspicious of easy answers.

Her first thought was to send for Richard and have Cordelia tell him her story. Get a second opinion, one that she knew would be rational and fair. But she dismissed it almost at once. *He* will *be fair, and he'll tell me that it's absurd. Because it* is *absurd. Sorcerers don't do things like that. You know that.*

But if it is *true . . .*

On some level, she wanted it to be true. If it was true, then Penelope was still the woman that Hester had believed her to be, her friend who told ridiculous stories and made stirring speeches about the importance of style. She had not stabbed someone and then taken her own life. She had been a victim of a terrible spell and she had fought it, valiant to the end.

If it was true, then Hester's sense of doom had a cause, not merely the panic of an old lady seeing her comfortable life slip away.

"Proof," she muttered aloud. "I need proof. This is too much." She gripped the head of her cane, anchoring herself in the smooth polish of the handle, the solidity of the wood.

Cordelia frowned. She was perched on the edge of the old gold velvet sofa, sitting up very straight. Her gown was a deep, exquisite sapphire that brought out the color of her faded blue eyes. Faded blue eyes, faded brown hair, a washed-out copy of her mother. "I don't know how to prove something like that. The horse trader in town, he'll remember, maybe? The way the ward went off when Falada walked through?"

"Which would only prove that there was a glamour on the horse," said Hester, trying to assemble her thoughts. "Which is a far cry from this obedience."

"If I knew anyone else who had been obedient, you could ask them," said Cordelia slowly, "but . . ." She trailed off, suddenly thoughtful.

"What?"

"Mr. Parker," she said slowly. "At the manor house in Little Haw. I don't know what Mother did to him. Something like that, I think. She made him do it. If you talked to him . . ." She frowned. "I don't know. I don't know if there's anything left of him. She said she broke him."

Hester seized on the suggestion like a lifeline. "Nor do I, but I know who can find out." She leaned over and yanked on the bellpull. "We'll send Richard."

CHAPTER 19

It was a grim party that assembled for dinner. Cordelia almost didn't attend, in case her mother was there, but then it struck her that if her mother had gone so far as to make someone obedient, she might do it to someone else, and perhaps Cordelia could spot the signs.

And what would you do if you did? You don't know how to break the spell or you'd have done it for yourself already.

She didn't have an answer, but she dressed for dinner anyway. Alice did up the tiny buttons at her sleeve and watched her with a faint, concerned frown, completely devoid of her usual chatter. Cordelia wanted to reassure her, but she had no real idea what to say. "It's all right," she said finally. "I'm all right." And then, realizing that a servant probably wasn't particularly worried about the person they were waiting on, except as it pertained to them, "Are *you* all right?"

Alice's eyebrows shot up. "Yes," she said. "Everything's in a muddle, since what happened to poor Mrs. Green, and the gossip belowstairs would curl your hair, but it's nothing that won't pass."

"I'm sorry it's such a muddle," said Cordelia, and went down to dinner, still clinging to her strange, hopeless calm.

Neither Evangeline nor Lord Evermore attended, and though the former's absence was unremarkable under the circumstances, everyone seemed surprised by the latter.

"Saw him riding out at noon," said Master Strauss. "On that big bay hunter with the white socks. Going hell for leath—"

"Jacob."

Master Strauss flushed. "Begging your pardon," he mumbled. "I didn't mean to swear in front of ladies."

Hester let out a long sigh. "And at this point, Penelope would say something bright and obscene to break the tension." She took a gulp of wine. A gloomy silence fell over the table.

"Did Evermore say where he was going?" asked Lord Strauss, one big hand covering his wife's.

Everyone looked at Hester, which didn't seem to surprise her. "He had something urgent to attend to," she said. "He promised he'd be back in a day or so." She looked over at Lady Strauss. "I realize that this house party has become rather more dreadful than anyone expected. If you wish to return home, no one could blame you."

"Don't be absurd," said Lady Strauss. "I'd hardly leave you at a time like this. What kind of friend would I be? I'm shocked at Richard, frankly."

"No, no," said Hester hastily, "don't be. It really was urgent. He didn't want to go."

That was something of an understatement. Cordelia had been present as Hester practically begged Richard to track down Mr. Parker. "It has to be you," she said. "You're the only one with enough clout to walk into a prison and have someone listen to you."

"It seems like a wild-goose chase," Lord Evermore said, glancing at Cordelia. "Interrogating a murderer because of . . . what, exactly?"

"I hardly know myself," said Hester. "Just ask if he knows Lady Evangeline."

It had occurred to Cordelia that the magic that had been laid on Ellen's father might have included something to cover her mother's tracks. *She wouldn't just leave him able to blame her, would she? Even if no one believes in real sorcery anymore, she wouldn't want someone listening to him and asking questions. But how far would that go?*

"You might ask him about his cabriolet," she said. "If he doesn't seem to know m-my mother. I think he might remember that."

Evermore's eyes were full of questions, but he bowed over Hester's hand. "If this is truly important . . ."

"It is," Hester said firmly. "I promise I'll explain everything when you get back."

"I hate to leave you," muttered Evermore. "Particularly at a time like this."

"I hate for you to go. But I need this question answered. After that we'll figure out what to do." Her gaze had strayed to Cordelia and Cordelia had nodded, hoping that this, too, was a problem that Hester could solve.

Someone touched her hand and Cordelia jumped and let out a squeak. "Oh!" she said, immediately apologetic, "I didn't mean to—I'm sorry, I was—"

"Don't fret, my dear," said the Squire, who had rather clumsily patted her hand. "You were miles away, and who can blame you? Worried about your mother, I expect."

Cordelia dropped her eyes, hoping that would be taken as answer enough. Through her lashes, she could see the Squire nod. "Don't fret," he repeated. "She'll be right as rain in a few days. Just the shock, you understand, and who can blame her? Not the sort of thing a gently bred lady expects to have happen."

"Unlike gently bred men," said Hester, in dulcet tones, "who have assassins leaping out of every bush."

Lord Strauss had a sudden coughing fit. The Squire sputtered something and Hester shook her head, lifting a hand. "Forgive me, Samuel. That was in poor taste. It's just . . ."

He took his sister's hand and squeezed it. "We're none of us doing so well," he said.

"It's not as if any of us have much experience with this," said Lady Strauss. She waved off a footman who was attempting to replace her sliver of meat and sauce with a second, slightly different sliver. "All those classes on proper etiquette for hostesses and they never mentioned what one is supposed to do after a murder."

Cordelia wrung the edge of the tablecloth between her hands. *Two murders. It was two.* She looked up and found Hester watching her. The older woman gave an almost imperceptible nod, and lifted her wineglass, and the pressure in Cordelia's chest eased a little. Hester understood. Hester might even believe her.

She wasn't completely alone.

The footman took her plate away and put another one in front of her. Some kind of braised greens. Cordelia managed to eat several bites, and it was not until the meal was over and the dishes removed that she realized that she had not once worried about which fork to use.

"I'm sure your mother would be glad of a visit from you," said the Squire, as they stood. He patted the air near her shoulder, perhaps not wanting to touch her, for fear that she would jump and squeak again.

Cordelia's heart sank. Her calm felt like a sheet of ice and she could already feel cracks forming in it. *She'll be able to tell. She'll take one look at my face and know that I told Hester that she was a sorcerer. I know she will.*

But of course if her mother was upset, she should visit. That was what a normal mother would want, and what a normal daughter would do. Not visiting would look suspicious.

"I was . . . I didn't want to bother her. If she was resting."

Lady Strauss came up on her other side and gave her a quick squeeze with one arm. "It'll do her good to see you," she said. "If I'd been through something frightening, I'd want to see that my children were alive and well. Even if I knew they were fine, there's nothing quite like seeing. And mothers aren't quite rational about these things, you know."

Cordelia bit back a hysterical laugh. *No. Not quite rational.* Lady Strauss meant well. Likely she still thought of Evangeline as a rather obnoxious fellow guest. Hester wouldn't have told her, not without some sort of proof.

Please, god, let Lord Evermore find Mr. Parker and find out something. They need to believe me.

"I'll go and see her," she murmured, and fled the parlor, feeling the ice cracking beneath her feet.

A stone-faced maid let her into her mother's suite. She was a good deal older than Alice, her eyes downcast. Cordelia wondered what she had suffered in her mother's employ. *Not that Mother will do anything that you could complain about, not really. But I doubt it's easy either.*

She certainly had enough to say about my cleaning back home.

A pang of longing swept her at the thought, for the little room in the ramshackle house, the windows barred with wunderclutter, the two boards that squeaked when you stepped on them, but in different notes, so that you could stand with your feet apart and bounce and draw a creaky call-and-response from the bones of the house.

She had not been happy there, but she had only had herself to worry about. Worrying about other people was becoming exhausting.

The suite was a mirror of Cordelia's, in rich greens instead of blues. "Who's there?" her mother called from the bedroom, in a trembling voice that still carried remarkably well.

"It's only me." She went to the doorway and looked in.

Evangeline lay propped up in the bed, pale and wan, her hair artfully disheveled around her face. She wore a dressing gown that looked too big for her, making her look small and fragile in the vast expanse of dark green damask coverlet.

She tilted her head to look at Cordelia and didn't bother to hide her disappointment. "Ah." Her gaze went past her, to the maid, and then she stretched out a hand. "Come here, my darling. Mildred, will you fetch us a fresh pot of tea?"

The maid, presumably Mildred, dipped her head and turned away. Evangeline waited until the outer door had clicked shut, then sat up, scowling. "Close the door," she said, "and lock it. I still don't trust these servants. They all answer to that dreadful butler."

Cordelia closed the door and stared at the lock. It was the simplest kind of lock, a little bent hook that dropped into a metal eye. She had never locked a door before. She had never been allowed to lock one. There were no locks on the doors at home.

"Hurry up," said her mother, voice no longer trembling. "The Squire's promised to come by later, and I don't want him to be standing around waiting."

She lifted the little hook. She could not shake the feeling that it should have been enormous, a weight that she could barely lift with both hands, instead of a little piece of iron that she could pinch between her thumb and forefinger. She fed the hook into the round metal mouth and it made the softest *clink*, barely heard over the sound of the ice breaking inside her, cracks running in every direction, ready to split apart at the slightest pressure and cast her into an icy sea.

She schooled her face to dull amiability before she turned back. *Mother can't read my mind. She can't.* Even though it felt as if her guilt must surely be emblazoned on her forehead in foot-high letters, if she kept her expression quiet and didn't run off and tell Falada, there was no way that her mother could know that she had confessed everything to Hester.

"Well?" said her mother, carefully tugging the neck of the dressing gown aside to reveal the slender length of her neck. Her skin was as pale as her familiar's, her ice-blue eyes picking up the green of the bedclothes. "How do I look?"

False. Wicked. Sly. "Like Falada," Cordelia blurted.

Evangeline sat up, dressing gown forgotten. "Like a *horse*?"

"No! I didn't mean . . ." She swallowed, trying to fumble forward.

"Pale. And graceful. And beautiful. Like him. And your eyes look green because the fabric . . ."

"Oh, I see. Hmm." Evangeline sat back, carefully re-mussing her hair. "I am *trying* to look waiflike. It's not easy when you're over thirty-five."

Cordelia relaxed infinitesimally. "The Squire sent me to see you," she said cautiously. "He seemed worried about you."

"That's good. That's very good. Mind you, you *should* have come on your own." Her eyes narrowed.

"I didn't know if that's what you would want."

"Mmm." That was a worrisome sound. It meant that judgment had been deferred, not forgotten. "What is happening out there?"

"Errr . . . well . . . everyone is very upset, of course . . ."

Her mother's eyes speared her. "Upset that I was nearly killed, or upset *that woman* is dead?"

"A little of both, I think," said Cordelia, wondering how much she could express without putting someone in danger. "They aren't saying which out loud. And the Squire keeps saying what a shock you've had." *There, that ought to be safe.*

"He's the one that matters." Her mother took a small hand mirror from the bedside table and checked her appearance in it. "What about that dreadful sister of his?"

"I think she's just generally upset," Cordelia said carefully. "She kept saying that she couldn't believe Mrs. Green would *do* that."

"Not without a great deal of work, she didn't." Evangeline set the mirror back on the table. "Miserable creature. She couldn't even die politely."

Blood roared in Cordelia's ears. She missed the next few words. *She just admitted it. I didn't think she would just* admit *it.*

Why not? She admitted what she'd done to Mr. Parker. She's proud of it and you're her audience. Who else does she have to brag to? Falada?

Her calm failed her. The ice had broken apart at last and her chest was full of shards. Penelope had died and the maid she'd never met had died and Ellen's family had died and her mother had done all of it and nothing Cordelia did, not now, not ever, would bring any one of them back.

". . . look so stricken," her mother was saying. "I would have been perfectly happy if she just left, but you saw how that worked. I try to upset her, have Falada lurk where she can see him, and she makes a damnable *story* over breakfast of it! And *you* couldn't find any information worth having on her. No, it was obvious that I had to take matters into my own hands."

Cordelia swallowed. "You . . . you could have tried again. With Falada. Couldn't you?"

Evangeline rolled her eyes. "And she'd find a way to become the center of attention again if I did. The Squire kept mentioning her as it was." Her face softened suddenly and Cordelia braced herself. "Perhaps you're too young to know. I suppose it's the sort of thing you only learn with time. If a man keeps bringing up another woman's name, be on your guard. He'll tell you that they're friends or that it's over between them, but if her name's on his tongue, it means she's in his thoughts. Remember that, won't you?"

"Yes, Mother," whispered Cordelia, thinking, *Who the hell cares what some hypothetical man is thinking about, you murdered a woman last night!*

She wanted to be the sort of person who said it out loud. Penelope Green would have. But if she did, her mother would just wave her hand and make her obedient and it wouldn't help anyone.

Cordelia had no idea what she could do that *would* help anyone. She'd told Hester everything. What else was there? She lifted her eyes to her mother, who was inspecting her nails with a slight frown.

I could try to kill her myself.

The thought arrived, seemingly from nowhere, and squatted on her heart like a toad. She could not look at it. She could not look away from it. It was huge and impossible and fascinating.

She can't read my mind. If she could, she would have known right

*away what I told Hester. I could get a knife from the kitchen and stab
her from behind.*

She pictured it vividly, the knife going in, her mother falling to
her knees, blood pouring down the pale fabric. Then she almost
snorted at her own thoughts. *You've never stabbed anything, except
potatoes. The neighbor lady kills the chickens, and even cleans them
for you. You cannot simply stab your mother like she's a potato. Do you
think a knife just goes into somebody's back like that? With all those
ribs in the way? You'd end up cutting her, maybe, and then she'd turn
around and see you with the knife and make you obedient for the rest
of your* life.

The outer door opened, startling Cordelia so badly that she
jumped. "That will be the tea, I expect," her mother said. "Don't
just stand there staring. Open the door!"

Cordelia fumbled with the latch. In the outer room, she heard
the maid's voice, and then another, deeper one. Her mother's
breath hissed in with excitement. "The Squire!" she whispered,
and fell back against the pillows, arranging her hair with a few
swift motions. "Open it, quick!"

"I—oh, hello, m'dear." The Squire smiled at her. "Is your mama
awake? Just wanted to check in on her."

"Samuel?" Her mother's voice was tremulous again. "Is that
you?"

"Large as life." The Squire gave Cordelia an apologetic look as
he slipped past her. "Didn't mean to interrupt. Just came to see if
you're feeling any better."

"Samuel," her mother said, in a soft, tremulous voice. "I'm so
glad you're here. I know you're terribly busy with all that's gone
on—with more important things—"

"Nonsense! Nothing more important than your recovery,
m'dear."

She reached out a hand and laid it on his arm, her eyes shining.
"It means so much to me. I can't tell you . . . somehow I only feel
safe when you're here . . ."

Cordelia quietly let herself out. When she went back to her room, she looked out the window and saw a white shape moving in the distant trees. Even from this distance, she recognized Falada.

He passed out of sight, moving from right to left. She waited there, holding her cup of tea while it cooled. She could hear Alice moving in the next room, laying out the next day's clothes, and wondered if the maid could see him too.

A little while later, she saw him again, still moving at an easy trot, circling the Squire's house like a carrion-eater waiting for someone else to die.

CHAPTER 20

Another day passed, and another dinner. Conversation, already stilted, became nearly impossible. Hester was forced to be grateful to Imogene's son, Jacob, who embarked on a treatise about horse training that would normally make her want to run screaming into the night, but which was significantly better than silence.

She wondered where Richard was, and how he was faring. Maybe it was a fool's errand. Probably it was. She wavered back and forth between believing Cordelia's story and doubting it, often several times an hour.

After dinner, the party retired to the parlor. Samuel excused himself to go check on Evangeline, and the rest of them sat around the room, looking at each other with dull eyes. Even Master Strauss's well of horse-related information eventually ran dry.

"Cards?" asked Imogene, waving a deck in the air. "Anyone?"

No one said anything.

"We needn't play for money."

Still no one said anything.

"Come on, I'll spot you an ace. Cordelia? Hester?"

Hester groaned. "This is dreadful," she said. "Not you, Imogene. I'm glad you're here. I just can't imagine that we're terribly good company at the moment." She looked around helplessly. "Perhaps it *would* be better if everyone just went home."

"Not before congratulating me, I hope," said the Squire from the doorway. "You see, Evangeline has just consented to be my wife."

* * *

The words hung suspended in the air of the parlor for so long that Hester started to question whether they had ever been spoken at all. Surely she'd imagined it. Surely her brother had not just said that he was engaged to Evangeline. Surely Doom had not won.

But Evangeline was standing behind the Squire, her hand clasped firmly in his, and the look in her eyes was unadulterated triumph.

"My goodness!" said Lady Strauss, into the horribly awkward silence. "What a surprise!" She shot Hester a warning look and all at once the words landed and became something real, something that was happening *right now,* like the ground coming at you after the horse had thrown you off.

It's too soon! Hester wanted to cry out. *It can't have happened so fast!*

The sense of impending catastrophe had been with her for so long now that it had almost faded to background noise, but suddenly it all came roaring back, clutching at her throat like a strangler. *Doomed, you are doomed, the worst has come, the worst is* here, *you have failed and all will be ashes . . .*

But it can't be! It's too fast! I'm not ready . . . and Richard's not back yet . . .

It was a tiny, hopeless thought, in a tiny hopeless voice, but it stiffened her spine. She was not a maiden in a tower, waiting for her faithful knight to save her. She was a grown woman, goddammit, and even if an aged spinster was among the most socially powerless of creatures, she would not concede to Doom without a fight.

But now was not the moment. Evangeline had moved, swift and sure, while Hester was still fumbling about, trusting to her brother's instinct for self-preservation. If she was going to extract Samuel from Doom's possibly sorcerous clutches, the last thing she wanted to do was show her hand too soon.

Bless Imogene for filling the gap. She roused herself from her horror and plastered a smile on her face. "How delightful! Samuel, you dog! You never so much as hinted to me!" She stretched out her hands toward the couple. "Why, you could knock me over with a feather!"

"Had to be a gentleman, of course," said the Squire gruffly. "Couldn't go talking until I knew my feelings were returned, don't you know."

"Yes, of course. Quite right," said Lord Strauss, nodding approval.

Evangeline leaned in closer to the Squire, her cheek against his shoulder, and then suddenly Cordelia leapt up and clapped her hands together.

"Oh, how wonderful!" the girl cried. "We shall be a family now!" She practically danced up to the Squire. "Shall I call you Papa, sir?"

What, Hester thought, *the absolute bloody blistering hell?*

Then Cordelia giggled.

She had laughed often enough these last few days. Penelope Green could have pulled a chuckle from an anchorite. But Hester *knew* Cordelia's laugh, a tiny, timid tapping, like a scattering of seeds across stone. It was certainly not a giggle, and it had never been accompanied by a girlish toss of her head.

Except for that one, terrible dinner. She'd giggled then, hadn't she?

It's happening right now. This minute. She's being—what did she call it—being made obedient. *Evangeline is working her body like a puppet.*

Hester half rose out of her chair, heedless of the scream in her knee and the stab of sympathetic pain in her opposite hip. She had to stop this. She had to do—had to—

Do *what?*

Cordelia turned toward her, almost prancing across the intervening distance. Hester stared as she came closer, her mouth turned up in a broad smile. Her hands settled on Hester's left arm.

Her eyes showed white all around the edges, like a frightened horse's, and the horror and helplessness in them struck Hester like a blow.

I don't know how to stop this. I don't have the faintest idea. I send Richard off for proof, like an absolute mooncalf, when I should have been trying to find everything ever written about sorcery and how to stop it. She felt as if she was watching someone mortally wounded bleed out on the floor in front of her, with no idea how to staunch the flow.

"You shall be my aunt now," said Cordelia's mouth, while Cordelia's eyes screamed.

Don't give it away. Don't let Doom know that you know. "Yes," said Hester. "Yes, of course. How lovely that will be." She patted the girl's hand, feeling her skin crawl at the touch. Cordelia's skin was ice cold and clammy with sweat.

Her eyes went over Cordelia's shoulder, to where Doom stood, still clinging to the Squire's hand. The woman's gaze was slightly unfocused, her face arranged in a pleasantly neutral smile. Perhaps it was difficult to work two bodies at once. That seemed likely. Hester remembered how Cordelia had stood, blank-faced, in the corridor while her mother spoke to the Squire, not even acknowledging Hester's existence.

"You must have so much planning to do!" said Imogene, once again coming to the rescue. Hester would send word to the Church requesting that she be canonized as a saint at once. "How soon will you be wed?"

"Oh, as soon as possible," said the Squire carelessly. "I'll send for a special license. No need for a big church wedding, you know, was never one for all that frippery!"

"A small service in a small chapel will be more than enough for me," purred Evangeline, looking up at the Squire with a look that might have been adoring if not for the hardness of her eyes.

"My goodness," said Hester. She pushed herself to her feet. Cordelia almost didn't move out of the way in time, and Hester saw a line form between Doom's eyebrows. "My goodness," she said again. "We have so much planning to do. Why, the thought makes me quite faint! But a good faint, a good one, not a bad one, not like when I haven't eaten breakfast, you understand . . ." She let her mouth witter on, hoping that her brain would come up with something brilliant in the interim. It declined to do so.

Imogene took one of her arms with a wry smile. *I know what you're doing,* that smile said. "Let me help you upstairs," she suggested. "And we'll plan the guest list, shall we?"

"Not too many people, mind," the Squire huffed. "I said a small wedding, and I meant it!"

"No, no, of course not. We shan't invite any of the cousins, which is probably for the best, because we have so many cousins, you know, and I've always thought that Cousin Celia's children were dreadfully ill-behaved, although maybe they've improved, it's been years, and I do think that children are likely to improve, don't you? Particularly when the problem was that they would jump on the furniture and filch pastries from the tea trays, and of course you don't expect anyone to do that once they're past thirty, do you?"

Samuel and Lord Strauss had a slightly glazed expression after this recitation. So did Doom, although Hester doubted that she was listening.

"I'll help you upstairs, Auntie," said Cordelia, clapping her hands. "May I call you Auntie now? Oh, do say yes! I would like it best of all things."

How in the name of God did I not realize what was going on before? This doesn't even sound like Cordelia. She talks like girls did when I was a child. Mostly girls we didn't like. The sort of girl who runs to tattle to an adult at any opportunity.

Cordelia's ice-cold fingers closed on her other arm like a vise. The girl's mouth was still stretched in that terrible smile, showing all her little white teeth. If she had suddenly turned her head and sunk those teeth into Hester's cheek, it would have been a shock, but not really a surprise. *The rabbit in a trap again, biting anything that gets too close. And this has been going on her entire life? How has she not broken completely?*

Perhaps she had. As Hester had learned from her engagement, long ago, sometimes it didn't matter if you broke. You kept going. You weren't given a choice.

"Well," said Imogene, once they were out of the room and partway up the steps. "I told you, didn't I?"

Shit. Doom could hear every word through Cordelia's ears, couldn't she? "I never would have thought it, at Samuel's age," Hester said hurriedly, giving her friend's arm a warning squeeze.

Imogene gave her a puzzled look. Hester widened her eyes. Imogene's gaze flicked suspiciously to Cordelia. *I am going to have to explain later,* Hester thought wearily, and then, *How the hell do I explain this? I still don't have proof.*

Her lack of proof seemed increasingly trivial at this point. Surely anyone who so much as looked at Cordelia's face would know that something was happening. Surely.

"Do you not approve?" the girl asked mournfully, her face rearranging into something that resembled a pout. Imogene's eyebrows drew down sharply. *And now she is thinking that Cordelia has been an extraordinary actress all this time, and trying to remember what she has said . . .*

"Of course I approve," said Hester, stomping up the steps. Cordelia was providing no physical support at all, which gave her an excuse to brush the frozen fingers from her sleeve. "Careful, my dear, that's my cane arm. Let me lean on Imogene for a bit. Will you run up to my room and ask the maid to bespeak me a hot compress for my knee? It's paining me something awful tonight."

Cordelia's face went briefly blank, then she dipped her head and hurried up the steps in front of them.

"What the hell is going on?" murmured Imogene in Hester's ear.

"I'll explain later. It's very complicated."

"It would almost have to be. Is the girl her mother's creature, then?"

"No," said Hester, sighing, "not the way you're thinking. That's the problem." She paused on the landing and rubbed her temples. "I promise I'll tell you everything as soon as I can."

Her friend's eyes were bright with curiosity, but Imogene was too good a card player to let it show. "I'll look forward to that," she said quietly, and helped Hester up the last flight of steps to her room.

Cordelia fell heavily across the bed and a moment later, the obedience lapsed. She lay like a discarded toy for a few minutes, getting her senses back together, then sat up, trying to shove the memory of the last few minutes aside.

God. The things she'd said. *May I call you Auntie now?* Her only comfort was that Hester must have known that she was obedient, because otherwise she would never have said she approved of the wedding.

She rubbed her temples. The pressure in her chest had been growing the entire time she was obedient, and she let it out in a sharp teakettle shriek, grateful that Alice was not around to hear. Her maid likely hadn't expected her back so soon after dinner, and that was fine. Better than fine. God only knew how rude her mother would have been in Cordelia's voice. She'd been imperious enough to the maid that she'd ordered the hot compress from.

She was exhausted. Being obedient left her feeling wrung out, muscles aching from stretching just the wrong way and holding positions just a moment too long. She went to the water closet, then shrugged out of her gown and hung it up. Not as neatly as Alice would have done, perhaps, but hopefully it wouldn't wrinkle. Then she crawled under the blankets and pulled the curtains and gazed blankly into the darkness overhead.

*Mother did it. She convinced the Squire to marry her. She won.
Does that mean we lost?*

With Penelope Green dead, it was hard to feel otherwise. Evangeline would turn out Willard the butler and anyone else she didn't like. Hester would have to move away. And once she had what she wanted, how long would the Squire live? What if she killed him, too, to get all his money?

She's not married yet, Cordelia told herself. *There's still a little time.* It was considered borderline dishonorable for a man to break an engagement without a compelling reason, but if they could find some proof that Evangeline was a sorcerer and a murderer, that would surely be sufficiently scandalous. After all, if women's reputations could be compromised by spending ten minutes with the wrong man, surely spending ten minutes forcing someone off a balcony would be considered even worse.

Surely.

Probably.

She'd ask Hester in the morning.

. . . anybody there . . . ?

It was the smallest whisper of a thought and Cordelia would never have noticed it except that she had no reason to think such a thing.

She rolled over in bed. Had she dozed off? Maybe it was just a symptom of that, the random thoughts that drifted through your brain when you were half-asleep.

. . . hello? . . . are you listening? . . .

Cordelia opened her eyes. The banked firelight was just visible as a pale line between the dark swaths of the bedcurtains. The air in the bedroom was still. She couldn't hear breathing.

. . . please, can you hear me? . . .

The words dropped into Cordelia's brain fully formed, without any of the swirling pre-echoes that accompanied actual thinking. Was someone whispering to her? She sat up in bed. "Is someone there?"

. . . Cordelia? Is that you? . . .

Good god, was there someone under the bed? Cordelia froze. Every childhood dream of monsters under the bed came roaring back into her ears. She stopped breathing.

. . . are you still there?

Instinct took over. Cordelia snatched the edge of the blanket and dragged it over her head, curling into the smallest ball that she could. If there were monsters, they couldn't get her through the blankets. Those were the rules.

. . . Cordelia . . . ?

Go away, she thought, yelling the words inside her own skull. *Go away, go away, GO AWAY!*

It worked. There were no more whispers. In the morning, Cordelia had almost forgotten that they'd been there in the first place.

CHAPTER 21

"I'm sorry," Hester said. "I'm sorry I couldn't do anything."

Cordelia looked up, startled. They'd been sitting in the parlor together, not saying much, and it hadn't occurred to her that Hester was quiet because she was feeling guilty. "There's nothing you could have done, though."

"I know," said Hester. "But I'm still sorry. That must be . . ." She rubbed her hand over her face. "I can't imagine."

Cordelia nodded. That was true. She probably couldn't imagine. But at least she knew that it wasn't Cordelia talking when her mother made her obedient, and that felt important.

She was trying to figure out how to express that when the door opened. Both Hester and Cordelia looked up, suddenly wary, like two mice watching a hawk's shadow pass overhead. But instead of Evangeline, it was a familiar face, though unexpectedly haggard.

"You must forgive me for coming to you in all my dust," said Lord Evermore. There were dark circles under his eyes and a thin layer of road grime across his clothes. He pulled off his riding gloves, slapping them once against his leg, and tossed them on a side table.

"I would forgive you anything, now that you've come back," said Hester, unexpectedly emphatic. Evermore blinked at her, his lips parting, and to Cordelia's surprise, Hester flushed and looked away.

"At any rate," said Evermore, after a moment, "I felt that it was important to speak to you both." He shut the door and drew away.

"Willard tells me that there has been quite an upset in my absence."

Hester held up a hand. "Yes. But I can't quite deal with that right now. What have you learned?"

Evermore was silent for a moment. "You were right," he said finally, studying Cordelia with a half frown. "I don't know how you knew, but you were right."

"You'd better begin at the beginning," said Hester. "You found Parker, I take it?"

"Yes." He slumped and rubbed his hand over his face. "Not an easy job, let me tell you. The wardens have been fending off strings of gawkers and alienists and weren't inclined to let another one in. I had to claim to be paying for his lawyer before they'd let me in to see him, so thank you for that, Hester. Now I will have a reputation for bankrolling murderers, which I imagine will serve me wonderfully during the social season."

The ghost of a smile crossed Hester's lips, despite everything. "I wouldn't have asked if it wasn't important."

Richard nodded. "I believe you. And if I hadn't, I would have after I talked to Parker. He's quite sane, as far as anyone can tell, but if you ask why he did it, he gets very agitated. He says he didn't want to, but he can't—or won't—tell anyone why. The wardens told me that if they press too hard, he starts choking, as if he's trying to talk but can't. Eventually he blacks out. They warned me specifically against asking, for just that reason."

Hester nodded to Cordelia. "She did something, then."

"She must have."

Richard glanced between them. "Would you care to explain to me, then?"

"After," said Hester, leaning forward. If they tried to explaining everything all at once, it would become a hopeless muddle. "Finish your story first. What did you learn?"

"I asked him if he knew Lady Evangeline, and he began choking almost at once. I thought the wardens were going to throw me out. Fortunately I backed off and managed to calm him down a little. So then I asked about the carriage." Evermore shook his head slowly. "It was the damnedest thing—beg pardon—"

"I think we're a little past curses by now," said Hester, fighting the urge to roll her eyes. "I'll swear a blue streak later if you like."

"Yes, well. As I said, it was the damnedest thing. He could talk about that. He seized on it. Telling me about his cabriolet and where he bought it and that it was stolen. *She* took it, he said. He couldn't say who she was. It was like he was fighting to get words out." He turned to Cordelia, his eyes cool and full of questions. "*Her,* he said. With the white horse."

"And now," said Lord Evermore, "will you explain what the devil is going on? I left a murder behind me and I've come back to a wedding, it seems. Is this revelation going to stop that? Because I will tell you, Hester, that Parker's a slender reed to hang your hopes on. I don't think he's long for this world. If he lasts long enough for them to hang him, I'd be surprised."

Cordelia winced. "Lord Evermore," she said, holding up a hand. "Before that . . . I have to ask . . . do you know if anyone survived? Any of his . . ." She had to stop and swallow. "His daughters, I mean."

Evermore cocked his head, still watching her thoughtfully. She wanted to shrink away from that gaze, but she squared her shoulders. *You can't stop your mother if you flinch every time someone looks at you. And he's not angry at you.*

"I don't know all of them," Evermore admitted. "I can find out, if it's important. But his two youngest daughters survived, I know that much. Their governess shoved them out the window onto the roof. She was badly injured herself, but seems to have survived."

Ellen was the youngest. Cordelia felt the hard knot in her chest loosen, just a little. Ellen was still alive.

She didn't know how to feel. She wanted to get up and dance around the room or scream or burst into tears. Even though the dead were still dead and it probably shouldn't matter whether she knew them or not, it clearly *did* matter. Very much. She picked up her cup and took a sip, trying, like many before her, to drown her emotions with tea.

"I promised you an explanation," Hester said. She tugged a bell-pull, and a moment later the butler appeared in the doorway, tall and thin as a well-dressed stork. "Willard, can you be certain we aren't disturbed for a bit?"

"I shall see to it personally," he said gravely.

"You're a prince among men."

"I aspire only to be a prince among butlers, my lady." It sounded almost like a joke, but it was delivered so deadpan that Cordelia couldn't be sure until she heard Hester laugh.

The explanation was, of necessity, long and convoluted, even though Hester did most of it. Evermore was particularly appalled by being made obedient, and Cordelia had to explain it at great length. "And you can't move by yourself? At all? Bloody *hell*."

"And there we are," said Hester. "And while I was dithering and sending you off to get proof, she convinced my brother to marry her."

Evermore rubbed his face. "How do we stop the wedding?"

"I don't think we do."

Cordelia stared at Hester. So did Evermore. "What? You're suggesting we just let Samuel march to the altar with this—this—"

"Sorcerer," said Hester. "Yes. Because we have no proof, except Cordelia's word and Mr. Parker's condition. Would you believe that, if you were in love with her?"

He slumped back in his chair and raked his hands through his hair. "I'm not sure if I should believe it *now*. It sounds like a fairy tale." His breath came out in a long whoosh. "If it's true, though, going to Samuel would only tip our hand to Lady Evangeline."

"Precisely. And you've seen what she does when she feels thwarted. It's vital that we don't confront her until we have some way to stop her."

"The old stories say water, wine, and salt—" Evermore began.

"And could you have gotten that down Penelope's throat in the moment?"

". . . Shit," said Evermore, and didn't apologize for his language that time.

Cordelia stared into her empty teacup, thinking of all the ways that Hester and Lord Evermore could die at her mother's hands. *She could make Hester obedient and make her run down the stairs without her cane. It would look like an ordinary fall. Or she could make Lord Evermore strangle her, or something equally horrific.* "If she finds out, it will be very bad."

Evermore looked to Hester. "Do you have something else in mind, then?"

"I do," said Hester slowly, "but it means I must beg a very great favor of you."

"Anything," he said. Looking at him, Cordelia was struck by the thought that he truly meant it.

"I require you to make an offer of marriage."

Evermore blinked at her a few times, and then his face went oddly gentle. He reached out and took Hester's hand with a tenderness that Cordelia felt embarrassed to witness, as if she had looked on something private.

"The offer has always been open," he said. "Always."

It was Hester's turn to be startled. "No," she said, dropping his hand. "No, I didn't mean—oh hang it all, Dick, I need you to marry my young friend here."

There was a brief silence. Something flashed across Lord Evermore's face before he turned to look at Cordelia. Cordelia gulped. He seemed nice enough, and he believed that Evangeline was a sorceress, which were all good points, but he was so *old*.

Marry him? Really? His hair wasn't completely white, it was true, but also he currently had an expression very much like a man who has been hit with a board, although whether that was due to his advanced years or the conversation, it was hard to know.

The hit-with-a-board look smoothed out and was replaced with a questioning smile. "Hester," said Richard, "I am certain that your young friend has many redeeming qualities, but I have not yet stooped to robbing the nursery."

"I don't mean you *really* marry her," snapped Hester. "*Obviously.* You just have to offer for her. And . . . err . . ." She leaned on her cane. "Well, possibly you might actually have to walk down the aisle together. It depends on the timing, you understand. But we can get it annulled later. It will be fine."

Richard looked from Hester to Cordelia. His eyes crinkled up as he smiled at her. "I see that we are both entrapped in one of Hester's schemes. Do you know what is going on?"

She shook her head.

"Oh good. I hate to be the only one in the dark. Very well, Hester, explain to us why you require me to offer for Miss Cordelia here."

Hester folded her hands together. "All right. Let's start at the beginning. Cordelia, what has been your mother's goal this entire time?"

"To have me marry a rich man," said Cordelia promptly. "She's been talking about it as long as I can remember."

Hester leveled a finger at her. "Precisely. And you said that she chose to marry my brother in order to accomplish that goal."

Cordelia nodded. Richard cleared his throat. "Forgive me," he said, when both women looked at him, "but I didn't quite follow that. How does marrying Samuel get her closer?"

Hester tilted her head to one side. "Richard, for a very smart man, you can be surprisingly ignorant. To marry a rich man requires funds. You must bring your prospective bride to the attention of your quarry. In most cases, that will mean a season in town, with all the balls and assemblies and parties and so forth. And for that, you must have gowns and hats and day-dresses and tickets to the theater and all of those things require money."

"Ah."

She folded her arms. "The problem with being rich is that you simply have no idea how expensive it is to be poor."

"Yes, Hester," said Richard meekly.

"Selling Mr. Parker's carriage let us pay for the dresses, I think," said Cordelia. "At least a few."

"But you'd still need a place to stay, and someone to introduce you to the assemblies and so forth." Hester waved her hand. "In that sense, Doo—Evangeline has been extremely clever. My brother and I were perfectly placed to accomplish her goals."

"I don't know," said Richard. "If she were truly that clever, she wouldn't have gone up against you in the first place."

Hester poked him in the shin with her cane. "Flattery will get you nowhere. Practice flattering Cordelia instead. You're supposed to make this convincing."

He raised his eyebrows. "Ah . . . Cordelia, that's a very charming frock."

"Thank you?" She tried to remember how to respond to compliments, but none of her mother's haphazard lectures came to mind. All she could think of was Penelope Green, who had deflected insults and compliments with such self-deprecating grace. "I—ah—it was all the dressmaker. I just stood there and held my arms up."

Hester laughed. "Good answer." Cordelia smiled with relief, though she suspected that her mother wouldn't have liked it much.

"At any rate," Hester continued, pulling the conversation back to more serious channels, "we know that Evangeline wants Cordelia to marry a rich man. We know that she will kill to get that. But we don't know why."

"If I may venture a guess," Richard said, "it's probably for the money."

"That's my guess as well. We just don't know what she'll do when she gets it. Does she want money for some specific purpose, or is a wealthy lifestyle her only goal?"

"So I'm the stalking horse, then? You marry me off to Cordelia and see what she does next?"

"It's that, or we hope that Cordelia goes on the marriage market and finds a decent wealthy man who doesn't laugh off the prospect of sorcery."

Richard nodded slowly. "Given what I know of my peers, we might as well hunt a unicorn. Very well." He extended a hand to Cordelia. "Does this meet your approval, Miss Cordelia? I vow on my soul that I shall not take advantage of my position in any way."

Take advantage of his position? Cordelia wondered if this was somehow related to compromising positions. Still, Hester clearly trusted Richard, and it wasn't as if Cordelia had any better plans. "I don't mind," she said. "We're not really getting married, after all."

"No, indeed. I shall make certain that there are definite grounds for annulment." He gave Hester a wry look. "Though you realize that will destroy my reputation utterly."

Hester snorted. "More the fool if anyone believes it."

"Oh, they will. It's the sort of juicy gossip everyone loves. And I have been single far too long besides." He leaned against the back of Hester's chair. "I don't suppose that I could convince you to come and minister to me in my extremity?"

To Cordelia's astonishment, a flush began to creep up Hester's neck and into her face. "I . . . I might at that."

Richard clearly hadn't expected that response. He pushed away from the chair and stood up very straight. "Well!" he said, and cleared his throat. "We can discuss this later, then. Meanwhile, I would like to point out one small flaw in your plan."

"Oh?"

"Evangeline might kill me. Otherwise she has to be content with taking possession of whatever money I funnel to my new wife."

Cold prickled Cordelia's spine at the thought. "I wish I thought she wouldn't, but . . ." She could picture it all too easily. Being made obedient. Picking up a knife and plunging it into her new husband's throat. She wrung the edge of her shawl with nervous fingers.

Hester was already nodding. "I'd thought of that, yes."

"Oh, well, so long as my death is an acceptable contingency . . ."

She swatted his shins with her cane again. "No, you silly man. But your estate is mostly entailed and if you die, it goes to your heirs. She'd be a fool to kill you off before Cordelia's had at least one child."

The image of stabbing Richard was immediately overwhelmed by the image of being a mother. Cordelia's mouth fell open. She'd never even considered it. She knew how things worked, more or less, and that people married in order to have babies, but somehow *getting married* had always been an entirely separate goal in her head.

The very notion was appalling. *I've never even held a baby. What would I do with one? I can do dishes and clean rooms and ride a horse if the horse doesn't mind, but caring for babies seems like it would be something else entirely.*

"So that should give us some breathing room," said Hester. "And really, Richard, would you prefer that we drag some innocent soul into the line of fire?"

"No, no. Please, let me throw myself into the breach for you. After all, if I die, then society won't go around gossiping that I'm impotent."

Impotent? Cordelia wasn't sure how they'd gotten there. She made a mental note to ask Hester later.

"*At any rate,*" said Hester, giving him a glare, "it will buy us a little time to work out what she wants. And she'll be away on her honeymoon, so we'll have a perfect excuse for the three of us to be seen together without causing a scandal. I shall be Cordelia's chaperone, and of course, as her fiancé, you will have every reason to call upon us regularly."

"Very well, you've convinced me." Lord Evermore gave Cordelia a wry smile. "I suppose while we are pretending to be engaged, Hester will be putting the next stage of her devious plan into action. Do you think she'll tell us what it is, or just drop it on our heads like a flowerpot?"

Cordelia found that she could laugh, and pushed all thoughts of babies and parenting to one side. She wasn't really getting married. "*Is* there a devious plan?"

"Well," Hester said, "I hope there will be." She thumped the book at her side. "I've been reading up on sorcery. Our library's not worth much, though, so I'm hoping that I'll find something worthwhile in a better one. Surely someone in the city has studied this more closely . . ."

Lord Evermore rubbed his chin. "There's bound to be something in my library. The problem would be finding it. My grandfather collected rare books the way that some men collect butterflies. Alas, his passion for books did not extend to a passion for cataloguing them."

"This may all end with us digging through the library and hoping for the best," Hester said.

"If it does, it does." Evermore nodded to Cordelia. "Well, it appears that you and I have our marching orders. I shall speak to the Squire directly."

It sounded like a dismissal, and Cordelia's mind was such a whirl that she was grateful for the excuse. "Yes," she said, getting to her feet. She curtsied to both of them and hurried toward her room, hoping that she could read enough of *The Ladies' Book of Etiquette* to know what to do before the offer arrived.

"Clever," said Richard, as the door clicked shut behind Cordelia. "Not kind, but clever."

Hester swallowed. She'd seen the flash of anger across his face earlier, and watched as he had very deliberately set it aside so as not to frighten Cordelia, but she'd suspected that it was still there.

"I'm sorry," she said. "I didn't mean to make you think that I was asking you to propose to *me*."

He shook his head. "No," he said quietly. "I should have known better. You've made it abundantly clear that marriage to me would be a poor second to the life you want."

"Richard . . ." His name felt as if she were hacking it out with a dull blade. *Ten years, and you thought you'd really given him up? Ten years and you thought you could beg him to come to your rescue and not have it tear your heart out?*

She could have endured that, perhaps, but not the guilt of having torn his heart out in return.

"I'm sorry," she said hoarsely. "It was never you that I didn't want."

He shoved his hands in his pockets and went to the window, staring out. The shadows had grown under the trees and dusk was being dragged down into dark. "You've arranged everything so neatly. Your old friend gets a bride and your young friend gets a husband. Very tidy."

"It's not like that!" Her voice was too loud and she slapped her hand over her mouth, angry with herself, but he didn't turn away from the window. "I don't mean for you to really go through with it. I told you that."

"You know that I would do anything for you." She hated how bleak his voice sounded when he said it. It wasn't a promise, just a statement of fact. A fact that she had taken shameless advantage of. "Of course I'll do this too, if that's what you want."

"You understand why, though?" Hester rubbed her hands over her face. "You believe us, don't you? About what that woman is. I know it sounds like a fairy tale." *He* has *to believe us. Otherwise . . . what? He thinks I'm lying or deluded, but he's doing it anyway because I'm the one asking him?*

The force of his loyalty was a sudden weight on her chest, pressing down, and she did not know how much she could bear.

"Yesterday I wouldn't have believed it," he said, still staring out at the trees. "But after I spoke with Parker . . . yes. All right. It makes more sense of what I saw than anything else. The way he choked when he tried to talk about her . . ." He turned back, and even through the rush of relief, it struck Hester that the lines of his face were much deeper than she had ever realized.

Richard, old? How could that happen? It was a few lines of silver, nothing more. He can't be this old. It must just be exhaustion from a hard ride, that's all.

"I didn't want to say how bad it was in front of the girl," he admitted. "It was terrible. He was biting his own lips and tongue as he tried to get the words out. I've never seen anything like it." He rocked on the balls of his feet. "And yes, perhaps I would rather believe in sorcery of that caliber than that a man would murder most of his family with an axe for no apparent reason, or that Penelope would stab her maid and then throw herself over a balcony."

Hester exhaled with slow relief. "Good. I'm glad." She gave him a wan smile. "I wasn't looking forward to trying to convince you."

"Have you told anyone else?"

She shook her head. "Imogene knows that something's going on. I imagine I'll have to tell her soon. But you're the only two I'd trust."

His smile was pained, but he reached out and took her hand again. "I'm sorry for yelling," he said. "Just . . . next time warn me before you're about to marry me off to someone else."

"It's my fault, and believe me, I hope I'll never have to ask you to do this again."

"I wouldn't mind one more time," he said, lifting her hand to his lips. "If it was the right woman."

He rose and took his leave. "I suppose I should go wash the dust off and congratulate Samuel. What a day this has been . . ."

Hester nodded, trying to pretend that she couldn't still feel the warmth of his breath against her skin.

CHAPTER 22

Hester had settled into the library with three shawls and a tea tray, feeling rather like a burrowing rodent in her den. *One of the big chunky ones that settle in for the winter. A woodchuck or a groundhog, perhaps. Unless those are the same thing.* She couldn't remember, if she ever knew. Normally she would have looked it up, since she was already in the library, but she had bigger problems than rodent nomenclature.

She needed to know how to stop a sorcerer.

Sadly, the family library had a number of books on architecture, a few on etiquette, and a positive treasure trove related to horse breeding, but possessed a very limited selection of books on sorcery. There were several religious texts, none of which had offered anything useful, beyond decrying it as frivolous at best and sinful at worst. There was an old book of fairy tales, which at least took sorcery seriously, but had no good solutions. Evangeline was not likely to hold still long enough for anyone to push her into an oven, and Hester had her doubts that nailing the woman's shadow to the floor would rob her of her powers.

Even if it did, I'd need nails of meteoric iron. Where in blazes do you get meteoric iron these days? I can't even get embroidery floss that's dyed the same color twice.

She'd eventually found herself with the only two books in the library that might help her. One claimed to be *A True Accounte of Divers Remarkable Sorceryes and Devilreys of This New Lande,* by an author with more adjectives than facts at his disposal. The other was an elderly almanac.

Divers Remarkable Sorceryes spent a great deal of time telling the reader how brave the author was for having written it, as he could now expect reprisals from the Authores of Such Devilreys, who would "come down with Great Wrath upon him" for attempting to "make suche a Distillation of the Truth from the Cloudy Liquors of Rumor and Fancye." (Hester was beginning to think that readers of the book were even braver.)

She was almost ready to set the book aside out of sheer exhaustion when the author launched into a lament about so few of his countrymen believing in the "Great Flood of Devilreys that now Surround us" and how "such as was Common Knowledge in days past is now Treated as the Base Ramblings of Superstitione and Rumore." (*Where is he getting all of these e's?* Hester wondered. *Did they simply have more of them lying around back then?*) He blamed it on the work of devils, who he thought had taken great pains to hide their presence and to present sorcery as little better than "the Actes of a Charlatan and Mountebank," but then tossed off, in passing, a passage from a letter that he had received from a scholar who suggested that sorcerers were much like panthers and would not tolerate one another in their territories. "And thus the Stronger take pains to defeat the Weaker, but ignore the Weakest as a Man ignores the Buzzing of the Midges, and thus the Strongest are few and the Weakest many, and Those that a Man might encounter are always the Weakest and seem Laughable and far from doing True Harm, while the Strongest walk Unseen and work great Mischief and Devilreys without Detection."

Hester set the book down and took a sip of tea. It had gone stone cold by now, but she barely noticed.

Like panthers, each with their own territories. She tried to imagine Doom tolerating a rival and felt a stab of grief. *She wouldn't even tolerate Penelope, and that rivalry was mostly in her head. If another sorcerer appeared, I can easily believe that she'd fight to the death.*

It was easy to believe, too, that she might ignore someone that she considered weaker or beneath her contempt. *She ignores me, after all.*

Hester stared down into the cold tea. Suppose that the unnamed scholar was right. Suppose that over time, the powerful had killed off the middling, leaving only those with just enough talent to cheat at cards and disguise a nag as a racehorse. Of course people would start to think that sorcery was just a silly bit of illusion.

And how does it work, anyway? No one seems to know.

Divers Remarkable Sorceryes offered at least three competing theories, including deals with the devil, alignment of "Celestial Bodies of Great Wickedness," and, peculiarly, that sorcery was a birth defect akin to a calf being born with two heads, only less visible to the naked eye.

Would that be a talent some people are born with, then, like perfect pitch or being able to roll their tongue? Is it hereditary, passed from father to son and mother to . . .

. . . daughter?

Hester set the teacup down with nerveless fingers. Was Cordelia a sorcerer too? Did she possess whatever strange talent her mother did?

A log fell in the fireplace and a large crackle startled Hester into a snort. *All these stray e's must be going to my head. If Cordelia was a sorcerer, she wouldn't be letting her mother drive her around like a puppet.* If Hester tried very hard, she could concoct a scenario where Cordelia attempted to enlist her help to depose a stronger sorcerer—her own mother, in this case—but the image of such a cold mastermind fell down immediately when placed beside reality.

No, if Cordelia had any such talent, she either wasn't using it or didn't know that it existed. Perhaps, like perfect pitch, such a talent required training to come to its full potential, and of course Evangeline would never train a potential rival. Or perhaps it had simply skipped a generation. Hester had bred enough geese over the years to know that even the most carefully chosen parents could produce a gosling that took after neither of them. She'd once had two positively elegant parents throw a confused little beast who fell over whenever he tried to run. Hester had been absurdly fond of the little creature and hadn't had the heart to cull him.

The door opened. Hester looked up and saw that Willard had entered the room, which immediately struck her as unusual because Willard could practically ghost through doors. If she'd actually heard the door open, it was only because he meant her to.

She set the teacup aside, puzzled, and he met her eyes with an open sympathy that immediately set her on guard. "Tom . . . ?"

He cleared his throat. "Your brother to see you, madam," he said, which was also completely unnecessary. Willard never announced family. They weren't that kind of household.

Samuel came in behind him, looking unusually grave. That itself was even more ominous. *Has something gone wrong? Did Doom make up some story about me?*

"Wanted to see you, Henny," her brother said, dropping down in the chair next to her. He hadn't called her Henny in years. He didn't meet her eyes, and Hester's alarm grew, even as Willard slipped out of the room as silently as a shadow.

"Is everything all right? Is someone hurt?"

"No, no. Nothing like that! Wouldn't worry two pins about telling you if someone was. You've always kept your head through things like that. No nerves at all, that's my Henny. Why, I remember the time you helped sew up that gash on Blaze's off leg when the old stablemaster was laid up with gout! Cool as a cat, you were, and him fit to kick down the stall the minute we let him."

"Then what is it?" asked Hester, trying to stem the flow of brotherly reminiscence.

He took a deep breath. "It's Richard," he said. "He asked my permission to court young Miss Cordelia."

Hester felt herself sag with relief. *Oh thank heavens. That's all it is.*

"I suppose you are going to be her guardian," she said. "It's only right to ask you."

Samuel leaned forward and took her hands. "Henny," he said kindly. "I know you've always had a soft spot for him. And honestly, I was always surprised he didn't come up to scratch—well, never mind all that."

"We're good friends," said Hester. "That's all. I never expected more." *Liar.*

Her brother's eyes finally met hers and she was struck suddenly by how lucky she was to have him. A little shallow, perhaps, but he'd always stood by her.

"I haven't said yes or no yet," he said. "I almost told him no, but I wanted to talk to you. If you're still holding a torch for him, by god, I'll send him away with a flea in his ear, no matter how good a match it is."

"Oh good heavens, don't do that. It *is* a good match. He's wealthy and well-connected, and he needs to wed. Most men his age have an heir and a spare by now. And he'll be kind to Cordelia. You know he will."

Samuel nodded slowly. "I wouldn't have thought twice if it wasn't Evermore. She won't do better. Though Eva's talked about having a season in town for her, and I don't want to disappoint her."

"She could still have her season," said Hester, who privately thought that Cordelia would rather gnaw her own arm off than go to balls and assemblies and parties in town. "An engagement announcement would keep all the more obnoxious sorts at arm's length, though. If you like, I'll even go along to chaperone her." Inspiration struck her suddenly. "In fact, while you're off on your honeymoon, why don't Cordelia and I go into town and see about opening up the old town house? It's bound to be in a dreadful state, and since you haven't given me an enormous wedding to plan, the very least I can do is see about getting it in a presentable state."

The Squire's mustaches moved over his smile. "That's a marvelous plan, Henny. Would never have thought of it myself. In truth,

I was worried about leaving you and the chit here all alone while we went gallivanting off on a honeymoon, but that will make all right as rain."

Unspoken between them was the knowledge that the town house would give Hester somewhere to stay if his new wife did not wish for Hester to share the same roof.

He squeezed her hands again, then let them drop. "You've solved two problems at a go, m'dear. Thank you. I'll go tell Richard."

"And I'll make plans."

He was nearly to the door before she spoke again. "Samuel?"

"Eh?"

"Thank you for asking me. You didn't have to."

"Course I did." He put a hand on the worn wallpaper and leaned against it. "You're my sister, Henny. Never going to forget that, you know."

Her smile faded as he left, and she looked down at the book beside her. *He deserves better than Doom. I'll find a way to get you free, Samuel. Somehow. Even if it means slogging through this incomprehensible mess of a book.*

It was shortly after breakfast the next day when Evangeline rushed into Hester's solar with her hands outstretched. "Cordelia, you naughty child, why did you never *tell* me?"

Cordelia promptly stabbed herself in the finger with the embroidery needle and yanked it out with a wince. "I . . . uh, I . . ." She looked instinctively to Hester for help, wondering what she'd done wrong. *It must be something dreadful, Mother never comes up here. But she won't do anything to me in front of Hester and Lady Strauss, will she?*

Hester tugged the bellpull for the maid. "Why hello, Evangeline. Let's have a little more tea, shall we?" Lady Strauss continued laying out cards in one of her endless games of solitaire.

Evangeline ignored them both, crossing the floor to the couch and grabbing Cordelia's hands. Cordelia nearly stabbed herself again and hurriedly dropped the embroidery to the floor. The floss would get in a terrible tangle, but she could sort it out later.

"Cordelia, Lord Evermore has *offered* for you!"

Imogene dropped her deck. Cards scattered across the floor. Cordelia blinked up at her mother, still unsure if she was in trouble or not. She'd known it was going to happen, of course, and Hester had assured her that her mother would be thrilled, but now that the moment was actually upon her . . . "That's good, right?"

"Good?" Evangeline threw her arms around Cordelia. "It's wonderful! More than I ever dared dream! You shall be so wealthy and well-placed as Lady Evermore, and since he is such a close friend of the family, we shall see each other so very often. But why did you not tell me that he was courting you?"

"I . . . uh . . . I didn't . . . he wasn't . . ." Cordelia appealed frantically to Hester with her eyes.

"I doubt Cordelia really knew," said Hester mildly, fishing one of Lady Strauss's cards out of the sugar bowl. "Richard isn't one of these fellows that goes in for flowery talk. I imagine his interest was fixed early, but he'd never dream of leading a young lady on until he could speak to her parents and get their approval for the match."

Lady Strauss made a noise somewhere between a croak and a splutter. Hester leaned over and pounded her between the shoulder blades. "Sorry," Lady Strauss gargled. "Frog in my throat."

"If that's the case," said Evangeline, ignoring Lady Strauss and her frog, "then I quite understand. How marvelous!" She released Cordelia and clapped her hands together. "You've done very well." She beamed with maternal pride and Cordelia smiled weakly and began trying to untangle her embroidery floss.

CHAPTER 23

The wedding of Squire Samuel Chatham and Lady Evangeline was to take place in the village chapel, two and a half weeks hence. Hester arranged the date and calmed the priest, who was beside himself with delight. "The Squire, marrying!" he said, at least five times. "And he wants me to perform the ceremony? Me?"

"He'll have no one else," said Hester, with more tact than truth. "And nowhere else would fit half so well." She wasn't sure if the priest really looked about fifteen, or if she had just reached a point where everyone under thirty looked that way. Certainly he seemed too young to have taken holy orders. Nevertheless, she sent him on his way in a haze of gratified astonishment, then sagged back into her chair in the parlor and wondered if ten in the morning was too early to take a nap.

Her next visitor, however, shocked her completely awake. Evangeline opened the door, saw her, and made a beeline for the settee across from her, her lips curving in a smile.

Hester's nerves screamed. She sat up in her chair and said, "Oh, good morning! I was just speaking to the priest who will be performing the ceremony."

"It is the ceremony that I wanted to talk to you about," said Doom, sitting down. Her smile was charming and open and her eyes were the cloudy blue of a snake about to shed its skin.

It occurred to Hester that there was no one else in the room and that she might be in terrible danger. *I'm a fool. An utter fool. What's*

*to stop her from taking control of me the way she did Penelope? She
could make me throw myself down the stairs and it would look like an
accident and who would ever know?*

She reached for her teacup to hide the tremor in her hands.
It would be foolish of Doom to do something like that. Samuel
would have to go into formal mourning and it would look very
strange if he married so soon afterward. Hester was nearly sure
that he wouldn't do that.

There was a great deal more space in that *nearly* than she liked.

"I meant what I said earlier." Doom leaned forward. "I want a
very small, quiet ceremony. You understand, don't you? You know
how people gossip, and what with . . . everything . . ."

She trailed off delicately. Hester was impressed that she managed to pack a sorcerous double murder into a single word. "Oh
yes. Of course."

"It wouldn't bother *me,*" Doom said. "I'm in love with Samuel,
and I don't care who knows it." She hitched herself to the edge of
the seat and gave Hester a firm, friendly look. Her expression and
tone were perfect. Hester wondered how often it worked on people.
Surely some of them could see those snake-scale eyes?

"It's Cordelia I worry about."

"Cordelia?" Hester's puzzlement was genuine. "What about her?"

"Gossip," said Doom. "She's such a sensitive girl. If she were
to overhear people talking cruelly about us, I fear it would quite
crush her."

Hester thought of Cordelia's eyes when she had been made obedient, and took refuge in babbling. "She is very sensitive, it's true.
But such a clever girl. Why, she's learning embroidery as fast as I
can teach her! And so sweet. Why, I was saying to Imogene just
the other day that if I had a daughter, I would be simply delighted
if she were like Cordelia."

Doom broke into the flow of words. "You understand, then,
that I want to protect her. So a small wedding. No second cousins
a dozen times removed. Why, I should be very happy to have only

our friends here attend. I feel quite as close to Lady Strauss as if we had known each other for years, and I am certain that she feels the same."

If you were on fire, Imogene would send for brandy to pour over you. "Oh, I'm sure you're right. Dear Lady Strauss! We were at school together, you know."

"Yes, she's mentioned it. I wish that some of my school friends could come, but I fear we all fell quite out of touch." Doom's lips turned down and a line of sorrow formed between her eyebrows. Hester found herself grudgingly admiring the craftsmanship involved in the expression. "I sometimes think that I should have sent Cordelia to a girls' school, but she is so sensitive, and you know how cruel girls can be when they sense weakness."

It pained Hester to agree with Doom, but she nodded. "You're not wrong there."

Cordelia's mother flung an arm across the back of the settee and turned her head aside. "It is part of why I accepted Lord Evermore's offer for her," she said. "I was so afraid of Cordelia's season in town. Her beauty does not always shine in social settings. His offer seemed a godsend."

"She can still have a little bit of a season. I promised Samuel I'd take her around a bit, just to acquire a little bit of polish. But there's none better than Evermore."

"Will he be good to her? He seems so kind, but you know him so much better than I do."

"He's as good a man as I've ever known," said Hester stoutly. "And I'm not just saying that because he's a friend of the family."

"It seems a wonder he never married before."

Hester shrugged uncomfortably. *Does she know? Samuel might have told her that we were involved once. Is she twisting the knife deliberately, or genuinely seeking information?* "You know how men are. They get to enjoy being bachelors and put things off and suddenly they're pushing fifty and don't have an heir. I've been nagging Evermore to get married for years now. He could have had his pick of young ladies for the past decade, too." She leaned forward herself, feeling a sudden mischief take her, since it was obvious that Doom didn't plan to kill her just this instant. "You'll have to prepare yourself, too. Every marriage-minded mama in the city will be wishing you to the devil for having landed Evermore for *your* daughter."

Evangeline pushed her hair back and laughed. Hester suspected that it was the first genuine laugh that she'd ever heard from the woman. She would have preferred if it had been a witchy cackle or a rising howl, instead of a perfectly normal, rather earthy laugh. "I look forward to it," she said, and Hester knew that for once, Doom was speaking the exact truth.

For Cordelia, the days leading up to the wedding were mostly peaceful. Her mother had what she wanted and was focused entirely on the Squire. The only difficult stretches were when Evangeline remembered that her daughter existed and was engaged to Lord Evermore, whereupon she would sweep in and insist that the couple spend time together, carefully supervised by Evangeline herself.

This morning, she had decided that Cordelia needed to go out riding with Evermore. Cordelia bowed to the inevitable and put on her riding habit.

"That creature again?" Evangeline said, raising an eyebrow as Minnow was led to the mounting block. "You should take Falada."

"I like Minnow," Cordelia said quietly. "She's very sweet."

Her mother's lips thinned, but Evermore emerged from the stable at that moment, so she turned to him with a laugh and said, "I trust that when she is in your care, you shall see her better mounted, my lord!"

Evermore smiled warmly. "The best horse is one that pleases the rider," he said. "My master of horse shall certainly endeavor to find her one that pleases her as well."

It had taken a week of such comments, but Cordelia had come to admire Evermore's technique. His statements were agreeable, correct, and sounded as if they were promising a great deal more than they were. She wasn't entirely certain if her mother was taken in by them, or if she simply didn't want to argue and risk the engagement. "For there is nothing that puts a prospective husband off like a designing mother-in-law," Evangeline had informed her daughter shortly after the engagement was announced. "So you shall tell him that I am easygoing and would not dream of interfering in his business. Is that clear?"

"Yes, Mother."

("Well," Hester had said later, when Cordelia reported this, "no one would accuse her of having a sense of irony, anyway.")

Evermore and Cordelia rode out together, and yes, it probably looked absurd that she was on the short little pony and he was on a tall, elegant mare. Certainly it made conversation difficult, unless she wanted to crane her neck. She didn't mind that much. She still did not quite know what to say to Evermore, unless they were discussing Evangeline's sorcery, and that would hardly be wise in front of the groom.

"Holding up well?" Evermore asked, leaning down. "I know I've had to travel back to my estate regularly, but it seems like your mother can't decide whether to throw us together or keep us as far apart as possible."

"It's because she expects me to say something to ruin the engagement," Cordelia explained. "If you talk to me too much, you'll probably realize that you don't want to marry me."

Evermore started to say something, stopped, started again, and then gave her a wry look. "I am caught between gallantry and reality."

She had spent enough time with him at that point that she could laugh. "It's all right. I don't want to marry you either."

"Yes, but I am certain that some nice young man will be delighted to marry you someday."

Cordelia shook her head, bemused. She had spent her life carried along by her mother's plans that she would marry a rich man, but now that she was actually this close—even fictitiously—it seemed increasingly absurd. Not merely the rich man, but the whole concept. Meeting someone a few times, a few days apart, and then they would go to a church and after that they *lived* together? Forever?

No, it was ridiculous. Nevertheless, it was a lovely day to be outside. Grass rustled around them, dappled with bright coins of sunlight, and birds sang, none of which were willowy frog-warblers. The memory brought a lump to her throat.

Cordelia? Is that you?

Cordelia's fingers tightened convulsively on Minnow's reins. It was the same whisper that she'd heard a week ago, but much, much stronger.

Can you hear me?

She was losing her mind. She'd always wondered what that was like. She just had expected it to happen when she was obedient, not right this minute, riding in the sunlight, with the birds singing around her.

Another thought occurred to her then, somehow worse than the first. What if it was her mother?

Evangeline hated secrecy. Cordelia had no doubts that she would have reached into Cordelia's head and laid her thoughts out like a row of Lady Strauss's playing cards, if only she had the power.

What if she had finally learned how to do just that? What if she'd found the way to break open the last closed door, the one inside Cordelia's skull?

The sound that burst out of her set Minnow snorting and side-stepping. Cordelia fumbled with the reins.

"Cordelia?" Evermore's voice seemed to come from a long distance away.

Stop, stop! I didn't mean to scare you! Am I hurting you? The words were loud and frantic and for some reason Cordelia smelled cinnamon, which made no sense at all.

Can you hear me at all?

Her mother would never have apologized. A wave of relief rushed over her. Perhaps she was simply possessed. Cordelia had no experience with demons, but she was certain that they could not be as bad as her mother.

Am I doing this right? Hello? And then, somehow muffled, as if the speaker was muttering to herself, ***Well, isn't this just typical, you're out of the public eye for five minutes and you can't get anyone to listen to you . . .***

"Cordelia? Is something wrong?" Lord Evermore reined in his mare and looked down at her. "You look like you've seen a ghost."

Not seen, Cordelia thought. *Heard.* She recognized the voice. She had sat beside it for hours, playing cards and working on embroidery.

Impossibly, improbably, Penelope Green was speaking to her from beyond the grave.

Somehow or other, Cordelia got back to the stable. She babbled something to Evermore about having been startled, apologized several times, then slid off Minnow and tossed the reins to a waiting groom.

"You're dead!" Cordelia whispered, as soon as she was far enough away from Lord Evermore to be certain that she wasn't being heard.

Yes, I'd gathered that.

It was almost like having a song stuck in your head. Words ran through, and they weren't *your* words, but still, you couldn't stop them happening. Cordelia gulped. "Are you a *ghost?*"

I suppose I must be. It's not at all what I expected. I know that I was a lamentably frivolous person in life, but someone might have warned me that death was so complicated. The peppery smell of watercress engulfed her. Cordelia wiped at her nose, wondering whether this was something to do with Mrs. Green's voice or if something else was going on as well. *Please, let there not be something else.* She didn't think she could handle a third thing, not on top of her mother and a ghost.

At least as manifestations went, watercress seemed pretty benign. Cordelia had heard of ghosts slamming doors and throwing furniture.

I would never do anything so rude. Although I expect the poor things were just frustrated. Do you know that I've been trying to get someone to notice me for days?

Cordelia rushed back into the house and yanked open the first door she could see, which led to a cloakroom. She pulled the door shut and stood in near darkness, surrounded by shelves and hangers and a line of boots with dried mud congealed on the toes. "*How* are you a ghost?"

No idea. I don't know how ghosts work. If an angel was supposed to show up and explain things to me, they're awfully late. The smell of watercress increased and Cordelia wiped her nose.

"How are you talking to me?"

Damned if I know. It's very dark here, but there are all these blobs of light. You're one of the blobs, but you . . . I don't know . . . you're a little clearer. You stick out more. So I took hold of the blob and sort of focused, and then I could hear you, a little.

Cordelia looked around, half expecting to see the ghostly form of Penelope Green hovering behind her. All she saw was more shelves, some with oilcloth raincoats on them. "What do I do? Do you want to be laid to rest? Because I think you already were . . ."

How long has it been? Did they do something with my body?

"Nearly two weeks."

. . . !!

The door opened. One of the kitchen boys froze with his mouth open, staring at her. Cordelia stared back. "Um," she said.

"Uh . . . uh . . . Milady?" He made a clumsy bow, still clutching the doorknob. "Err, does milady . . . err . . ." He looked at the door, clearly unsure whether or not to close it and let her go back to what she was doing or to offer to help her out of the closet.

"I'm sorry," said Cordelia. The inside of her head was silent again, except for her own thoughts. "I—uh—was looking for something. It's not here."

He nodded as if this was a perfectly reasonable explanation and stepped back. "My Da says it's always in the last place you look," he offered.

"That is very wise," said Cordelia, and swept past him, hoping that she didn't look as big a fool as she felt.

CHAPTER 24

She decided not to tell Hester. On some level, she knew that she probably should, but a coldly practical part pointed out that Hester and Evermore were acting almost entirely on her word that Evangeline was a sorcerer. Yes, poor Mr. Parker had helped, but according to Evermore, he was completely emotionally broken. Layering "By the way, a dead woman has been talking to me" would be asking rather a lot, as if she had told a lie and now had to tell another, even bigger one to top it, like some of the younger children at school.

Sorcery was real. Nobody denied that it existed. Ghosts, on the other hand, were things that had maybe haunted a house at some point in the very distant past, or that someone's brother's cousin's friend had possibly seen, except that it had been dark and he'd been drinking and maybe it had actually been a coatrack. Many people didn't believe in them at all. If someone came in and said, "By the way, I'm hearing a voice in my head," ghosts were not the first thing that leapt to mind.

Maybe it isn't a ghost. Maybe it's another sorcerer. A very clever one who's figured out how to talk in your head.

Cordelia stared into the distance, fork suspended in midair over her dining tray. She could have done without having that thought.

It definitely wasn't her mother, though. She was certain of that. Her mother wouldn't have bothered with anything so bizarre, and she would never have impersonated Penelope Green, even if she could have. *It's too twisty. Mother's never twisty. She just makes people do what she wants them to do. Getting the Squire to notice her breasts is as subtle as she gets.*

She couldn't actually think of a good reason why a sorcerer would want to impersonate Penelope Green. It didn't make any sense.

That she'd finally cracked under the guilt . . . that, unfortunately, made sense. Rather too much sense, in fact.

She finished her meal in a pensive mood, and went to bed early, before her mother could find her and scold her for having broken off the ride with Lord Evermore so quickly.

"Right," said Imogene Strauss, pushing open the door to Hester's solar. "No one else here? Good." She locked the door and then shoved an end table under the knob for good measure.

"Are we planning something criminal?" asked Hester, setting down her embroidery. "I think I can drive the horses if we need a fast getaway, but don't ask me to run."

"Very funny. I could have left ages ago when my husband and Jacob went home, but instead I have been as patient as a . . . a damned patient thing for days. I didn't strangle Richard when he announced that he wanted to marry that poor child, because you obviously knew about it in advance. I have been following your lead, which means I haven't dumped a bottle of red wine over that frighteningly smug woman, and I haven't grabbed Samuel by the collar and demanded to know what the hell he's thinking." She folded her arms and glared down her nose. "And now you're going to tell me why I haven't done any of those things."

"Incredible restraint, clearly."

Imogene made a warning sound in her throat, rather like a goose seeing a stranger get too close to her nest. Hester gave up. It would be a relief to finally tell Imogene. She just wished that she'd had more proof to back her up.

Lady Strauss could conceal her emotions far better than Richard.

Hester relayed her tale, wishing that she had some idea what the other woman was thinking. *Do you believe me? Do you think the laudanum has finally caught up with me? Do you think I'm deluded or lying or telling the exact truth?*

When she'd finished, Imogene said, "Huh."

"That's it?"

"I'm still thinking. It's a lot to take in." She broke out the ubiquitous deck of cards and shuffled savagely, cut the cards several times, flipped one over—the seven of spades—then shuffled them all back together again.

"I should have told you sooner."

"You damn well should have."

"It's just . . . it all sounds so absurd."

"It *sounds* dangerous." Imogene looked up from the cards, clearly frustrated. "And you expected Richard to protect you from that woman?"

Hester bristled. "You think he wouldn't?"

"I think Evangeline'll run rings around him," said Imogene frankly. "He's decent and honorable and you're dealing with a woman with the morals of a rabid fox."

Hester's lips thinned as she considered this. "You're not wrong," she admitted. "But she's a sorcerer. None of us can fight that. I haven't found anything that can help us, and believe me, I've been looking." She'd been through *Divers Remarkable Sorceryes* twice and had learned a great deal about the author's pet theory that sorcerers were descendants of the Nephilim, "got by Fallen Angels upon the Brides of Humankind," but nothing at all about how to keep a sorcerer from controlling your body.

The almanac, meanwhile, had a good dozen suggestions on how to tell if livestock had been "glamoried," none of which applied to humans, and suggested rosemary as a charm against sorcery. Hester, in the spirit of experimentation, had ordered a rosemary-encrusted lamb dish for dinner, then watched glumly as Evangeline put away her plateful and pronounced it a culinary triumph.

"It's got less to do with sorcery and more to do with ruthlessness, if you ask me." Imogene swept her cards up again. "Do you really think that she wouldn't have murdered Penelope if she couldn't use magic?"

Hester opened her mouth, blinked, and closed it again.

"Mm-hmm. Oh, perhaps she'd have found a way to send Penelope home in disgrace, though I doubt it. Penelope was never very good at being disgraced. I suspect we'd have had much the same scene in the end, with Evangeline screaming her head off and Penelope over the balcony with a knife in her hand. Perhaps less dramatic, and poor Ruth might have been left out of it, but something similar." When Hester continued to stare at her, Imogene rolled her eyes. "Come now, surely you see the genius of it? It takes out her rival and makes her the victim all at once. Every overprotective male bone in Samuel's body is roused to protect her. She weeps, she clings, oh my dear Sam, I only feel safe in your arms . . ." Imogene pressed the back of her hand to her forehead and swooned dramatically across the couch.

"I had seen that much," said Hester dryly. "I just hadn't considered that she might try it without magic, that's all."

"She is a ruthless social climber willing to commit murder. Magic is simply expanding what she's capable of, that's all." Imogene tapped the cards together to line the sides up. "I have no doubt that I've played cards with more than one sorcerer in my day. The difference is that none of the others were cheats."

"You really think sorcerers are that common?"

Imogene raised her eyebrows. "What did that book of yours say—that the powerful ones kill off the average ones and leave the weak ones so people hold them in contempt?"

"Something like that, yes."

"Then I think that if I were a sorcerer, I would make sure no one ever found out about it. The *best* that could happen is that I'd be shunned from polite society. The worst is that a stranger would casually murder me. And if I had kids, and it got passed down? I'd make sure they knew it, too."

Hester let out a low whistle. "I hadn't thought of that."

"Neither will Richard. I love you both like family, but you're not sufficiently devious."

"All right," said Hester. "You've convinced me. What do you propose we do differently, then?"

Imogene pulled the end table away from the doorknob. "Keep planning the wedding and acting the fool. I'm going to go talk to Richard about ways to foil a ruthless social climber."

They gathered in the parlor that night after dinner. Imogene had been more than usually wry at dinner and had a gleam in her eyes that Hester knew all too well, although she usually saw it across the card table.

"Evangeline," Imogene purred, sitting down across from Doom, "you simply *must* tell me all about your honeymoon! Hester's been so busy with making certain that the wedding breakfast goes off without a hitch that she hasn't told me simply a *thing* about it."

Half expecting a snub, Hester was surprised when Doom broke into an enthusiastic description of their plans to spend three weeks on the the north coast. "It's been years since I was there," she said wistfully, "and I would like to see it again. I know that they say you should never try to go home again, but the sea and the sky can't really change, can they?"

I believe she might actually be sincere. How very odd.

Richard had been standing by the fireplace, listening, and suddenly clapped his hands together. "I have just had the most splendid idea!" he said. "It is a long drive to the harbor, is it not?"

The Squire made the sort of manly mumble that a certain type of gentleman makes when the answer is most definitely *yes,* but admitting it would require that they also admit to feeling physical discomfort. Richard waved this off. "I know it doesn't bother you, Samuel, but your lady wife would doubtless prefer not to arrive at the ship feeling like she's been dragged through a hedge. Why don't we all go to my estate? It's far closer to the harbor, and you can stay the night there and leave fresh in the morning." He smiled politely at Cordelia. "And Miss Cordelia can see the great pile that she shall be mistress of, and I shall hope that it does not terrify her into crying off."

Cordelia looked startled, which was fine, because Cordelia always looked startled. Hester was more interested in Doom's response. The woman's eyes had narrowed when Richard mentioned crying off, but they smoothed out and gained a flash of avarice. And Imogene . . . Imogene looked like a cat that had placed an order for canary au gratin. *So this is her idea, then?*

"That's a fine idea," Hester said. "Oh no, I don't mean Cordelia crying off, of course, certainly not!" She did her best hen-witted chuckle, and was gratified to see poorly hidden contempt cross Doom's features. "But now the servants can go ahead to the town house and pull the dust covers off so that we are not coming home to a house that looks positively *abandoned*." She leaned out and tapped Cordelia's wrist. "You must know, my dear, that a house that stands empty for any length of time gets the most dreadful *air* to it. Why, you positively feel like a ghost there to *haunt* the place!"

Richard watched this performance with a polite expression, but his eyes danced. *He is going to tease me unmercifully the next chance he gets . . . and truth be told, I think I might be looking forward to it.* As dire as the circumstances were, Hester felt more alive than she had in years. *We have taken control of the situation. We have a plan.*

And you have Richard beside you again.

Shut up, she told herself.

Cordelia had gone rather pale, possibly at the mention of ghosts, but took a deep breath and said, in a voice that almost didn't squeak, "I should like that very much, Lord Evermore," and then shrank back into her chair as if the effort had exhausted her. Hester wondered how much of that was performance and how much was simply the difficulty of keeping up an act in front of her mother.

The Squire glanced at his new bride-to-be, who smiled. "That is a very kind offer, Lord Evermore," she said.

"Then it's settled," said Richard. "I'll send my man back to make the arrangements."

"Good of you," said the Squire, clapping him on the shoulder. "Fine thought. Haven't been out to the Evermore estate in years, have I? Is Old Bernard still in the stable?"

"He claims he's retired, but everyone knows better."

"Wonderful, wonderful. I remember when we went out for grouse . . ." He coughed, his mustache twitching. "Not that we'll have time for hunting, of course, not just overnight. Though they do have some marvelous hunts up north, as I recall. Just the territory for elk. Might look into one or two while Eva's shopping."

Doom laughed. "I shall try not to spend all my time at the shops, dearest."

"No, no. Mustn't skip them on my account." He patted her arm. "I know how you girls can get."

Hester judged the distance to her brother's ankle and regrettably decided that she couldn't quite ding him in the shins with her cane.

"I'm sure that in three weeks you'll have time for at least one hunt," said Doom caressingly.

And let's just hope that three weeks is also enough time for us to find a way to stop a sorcerer.

CHAPTER 25

"Miss?"

"Yes, Alice?" Cordelia turned away from the window. It was dark and there was nothing much to see except the black-on-slightly-less-black cutouts of trees.

Alice chewed on her lower lip, unaccustomedly serious. "You're going to be marrying Lord Evermore, then."

No, I'm not, she wanted to say, but couldn't. "He's offered for me, yes."

The maid nodded. "I don't mean to speak out of turn," she said, "but it struck me that you might not know. When you go to live with him, it's expected that you take your lady's maid with you, if you have one."

My lady's maid? But I don't have . . . oh. "You mean, you? Do you want to come with me?"

"If you'll have me, I'd be glad of it." Alice paused, her eyes grave. "I don't much feel like staying here after the Squire marries, you understand."

"No." Cordelia looked back out into the dark. "No, I don't blame you." She would have liked to take Alice with her. At least she might have saved somebody that way. *We're going to the town house first, Hester said. If Alice comes with me, she'll be safe for a bit. Maybe I can ask Lord Evermore to hire her.* "I'd love to bring you with me. What do I have to do to make that happen?"

"I'll speak the housekeeper," said Alice, "and she'll come ask you. Then you just have to tell her." She took Cordelia's hands. "Thank you."

"No, thank *you*." Cordelia dredged up a smile, trying to think of what Penelope would have said. "You could have been free of me, but now you'll have to keep putting up with my ignorance." *And the locked doors. And the way I sleep in the closet sometimes.*

Alice laughed. "I'll go tell Mrs. Bell at once." She squeezed Cordelia's hands, then hurried out.

Cordelia went back to staring out the window. Was there something out there? She thought she saw a light in the trees for a moment. Falada, pacing around the house again? She shuddered.

Cordelia?

It wasn't quite as shocking the second time, but Cordelia still jumped sideways and nearly crashed into an end table. She grabbed the curtains to keep from falling over, heard a warning creak of fabric, and let go immediately before she tore one by accident.

"Penelope?" she whispered.

Yes. Me again. I didn't mean to startle you.

"What happened last time? You just stopped talking."

Sorry, Penelope said. *What I'm doing is sort of like focusing my eyes, and they get tired. Then it slips and I can't always get the focus back. I didn't mean to stop talking to you, but I was startled and it slipped.*

"It's okay," Cordelia whispered. "How are you doing?"

Mustn't complain. Others have it worse and so forth.

"Do they? You're a *ghost*."

Other ghosts have it worse, I'm sure . . . Actually, no, I'm not sure. I haven't seen any other ghosts. But I can talk to you and I don't have any aches and pains anymore, and no bills coming due, so I'm bound to be doing better than someone out there.

"That's good? I think?" Cordelia heard the door open, realized that Alice might be coming back, and rushed to the water closet, where at least she wouldn't be disturbed.

I was thinking about what you asked about how I became a ghost, and I think it's because I died wrong.

Cordelia winced. "I'm sorry. My mother . . ."

Yes, I know. It's not your fault.

"But she's my—"

My mother was a dreadful woman and it had nothing to do with me either. Now please, I can't focus for too long without getting tired.

Cordelia nodded, and then it occurred to her to ask: "Can you see when I nod?"

Not see, exactly, but I felt that you agreed? It's complicated. None of my adjectives are right at all.

At any rate, when that dreadful woman did whatever she did to me, it felt like I was being pushed down in my own body. I took the knife she held out to me, but I wasn't the one in control of it.

"I know what that's like."

I thought you might. I didn't like it, I can tell you that. And then she wanted me to attack Evermore! Well, I wasn't having that. I pushed back, as hard as I could. I don't think she liked that. We went back and forth for a little while and then she changed what she was doing. Instead of pushing me down, she pushed . . . I don't know. Sideways? Maybe? Directions are a bit odd now too. But instead of being down in my own body, I was off to one side of it. I could see over my own shoulder. And then she walked my body off the balcony.

"I'm sorry," whispered Cordelia again.

It's only dying. Cordelia felt something like a shrug ripple through her skull. It was a very odd sensation, and accompanied by the smell of black licorice. *It's not even the third most awful thing that's ever happened to me.*

"Worse than dying?"

I took a ship across the ocean for my honeymoon and spent two weeks hanging over the edge of the rail, vomiting if I so much as thought about food. At least this was over very quickly. But never mind that. After I was dead, something happened inside my chest. Not a physical thing. Something else.

It was awkward holding a conversation while in the water closet. Even though she wasn't using the facilities, it felt somehow wrong. "Like what?" she whispered, hoping that Penelope wouldn't pick up on her embarrassment.

I can't really explain it. A wave of cinnamon-scented frustration engulfed Cordelia. *I can't even remember it very well. It was like a door opening, but also like something being sucked through a tube? No, that's not right at all. I'm sorry. I feel like I should remember.*

"You'd had a bit of a shock," said Cordelia.

Penelope's ghost laughed, bringing with it the smell of lavender. *A small one, yes. Whatever it was, I think that should have pulled my soul through it, but I was still outside and looking over my own shoulder, so it didn't. And then by the time I figured out what was going on, it was too late. I wasn't really attached to my body anymore, and everything started to get very dim. Even my body just looked like a coal burning down. Some blobs came to pick it up, but I couldn't tell what they were at the time. And everything was so dim, I couldn't tell where the building was, or which way I was facing, or even what up or down was.*

It sounded terrifying. Cordelia had not been particularly eager to die, but this was worse than she had expected. *Maybe it's only like that if you're a ghost. Maybe the thing that she couldn't describe takes care of people who are still in their bodies when they die.*

I think it was the horse that saved me, Penelope said musingly.

"The *horse*?"

The thing that's pretending to be a horse. I'm pretty sure it isn't one, though. It looks like a horse to me, and all the real horses just look like bigger blobs. I don't know what it really is, but it's much brighter than anything else. I didn't like it at all, but everything was so dark and the horse was shining like anything, so I followed it. I stayed well back, so I'm not sure if it knew I was there. Eventually it led me back here. Everything got a little brighter and there were more blobs around. When I focused on one of the blobs, it turned out to be one of the stablehands. That's how I figured out what was happening.

"Falada," said Cordelia. "He's my mother's familiar."

Familiar? Like a sorcerer's—oh, I see. Yes, of course, that makes sense, doesn't it? She'd have to be. Huh.

Well, that's interesting. I always thought I'd probably be killed by someone's jealous lover, but I rather expected them to use a gun.

"We're trying to stop her," Cordelia promised. "Hester and I. And Lord Evermore."

That's good. Someone should probably avenge me. That seems like the polite thing to do.

"Errr." Penelope seemed awfully blasé about the whole thing. "Aren't you angry?"

I probably should be, shouldn't I? Proper murdered ghosts always go shrieking and wailing about, or enchanting harps that shriek their killer's name aloud or something like that. But it seems like so much work. And I've always been a very lazy person, you know.

Cordelia smothered a laugh.

There you go. I've always said that a sense of humor can carry you through anything. Apparently I was more correct than I knew. There was a brief, indescribable sensation inside Cordelia's skull, like a person drumming their fingers thoughtfully, except that it seemed to be happening against the back of her eyeballs. *Really, though, we must stop her. We can't just let her go on killing people. Is there some way that I can help?*

"Uh . . ." Cordelia hesitated. Was there? A ghostly spy seemed like an incredibly useful thing, but if Penelope only saw things as blobs . . .

She sticks out the same way you do. Still a blob, but a three-dimensional one. I saw her riding the horse-thing, but I didn't put two and two together.

"Did you just read my mind?"

Did I? I'm sorry, that was very rude of me. You must have thought it rather loudly.

"Do you think you could read *her* mind?"

I suppose I could try. Not when that horse is around, though. I'm pretty sure it could see me if I went traipsing around in front of it.

And not right now, I'm . . . oh blast, it's slipping again . . .

Cordelia had a brief sense of garbled speech fading away, and then the inside of her skull was silent except for her own thoughts.

When she looked out the window again, she saw a pale shape trotting past, and knew that Falada was once again on his appointed rounds.

CHAPTER 26

The day of the wedding dawned warm and overcast, and was not attended by thunderstorms or earthquakes or cyclones, despite Hester's opinion on the matter.

"So difficult to get good cyclones at this time of year," murmured Imogene, sliding down the church pew with Hester.

"It might have made an effort."

"The ceremony hasn't started yet."

Their conversation was interrupted by the priest, who hurried up to tell Lady Hester how very gratified he was to see her, how honored he was that Squire Chatham had chosen their little chapel, how lovely the flowers looked, how exceedingly honored he was, and how much happiness he wished for the bride and groom. Hester smiled warmly and told him that it was well-deserved, that she knew her brother was grateful that the priest had managed to arrange the wedding so quickly, and that they would not forget his kindness. The priest pressed her hand, gasped something incoherent, and had to hurry behind the altar to regain his composure.

"Has he been like this the whole time?" Imogene asked.

"Very nearly. Poor boy."

"He barely looks any older than Jacob. I can't imagine calling him Father and pouring out my sins."

"Fortunately I haven't been to confession in a very long time."

Imogene clucked her tongue. "I shudder to think of the state of your soul."

"I'm sure it's no worse than yours."

"I go to confession whenever the guilt gets to be too much."

"And how often is that?"

"It hasn't happened yet, but you never know. Our dear Father Reynard lives in hope, anyway."

The few guests filled the rest of the pews. Cordelia sat in the row ahead of them. Her hair was pinned up neatly and her neck looked as fragile as a flower stem. Richard sat down beside her, as befitted a fiancé, though he winked at Hester over her head.

Hester's brother wore a new suit, with a deep blue waistcoat. He stood by the altar looking desperately uncomfortable, and Hester entertained a brief hope that he might be having second thoughts. *Not that Samuel would abandon a bride at the altar. He'd sooner sell his best hunter for dog food.*

She still hadn't quite worked out how she was going to disentangle Samuel. Once they were wed, there was no reason Doom couldn't actively bespell him. Hester's only hope was that they would find a way to break her power and prove her crimes sufficiently for the Squire to cast her aside.

Imogene's suggestion was rather more practical. "Let's just kill her," she had suggested, "dump the body somewhere, and never tell anyone about it."

"Can we actually do that?" Cordelia had asked.

"No," said Richard.

"I don't see why not," said Imogene.

"No one is killing *anyone*," Hester said firmly.

"Thank you," said Richard.

". . . At least not until we've figured out how to keep her from doing something horrible and magical that takes us all with her."

Richard, who was fundamentally an honorable man, folded his arms and tried not to look completely appalled. "I was not expecting this house party to involve quite so much premeditated murder," he muttered.

"If the alternative is having my brother end up like Parker, I'll premeditate all kinds of murders," Hester told him, "with a song in my heart."

"Fair enough."

"You wouldn't be complaining if she was a man," muttered Imogene.

"If she was a man, I'd challenge her to a duel and be done with the matter."

"She'd make you obedient," said Cordelia softly, "and make you miss. Or shoot yourself instead." Which had ended the discussion completely, so far as that went.

The church doors opened and Doom entered. Her gown was a deep ivory color that flattered her skin and brought out warm highlights in her chestnut hair. Samuel turned to look at her and his eyes bugged a little. *So much for second thoughts.*

The ceremony itself was swift. The priest wisely opted not to preach a sermon, and he only stumbled over the ritual words a little. Bride and groom each took a sip from the cup of wine, accepted the brittle wafer of salt, and washed it down with water from the second cup.

Cordelia had told her repeatedly that the Squire wasn't bespelled, and that her mother wasn't using glamours on her appearance. Hester hadn't doubted her, but she'd still held out a slim hope that *something* would happen—that Samuel would suddenly leap back and demand to know what was happening, or that an illusion would break and Doom would turn out to be a gnarled old crone with donkey ears or something equally heartening.

But nothing did happen, except that the priest said "I pronounce you man and wife!" and Samuel planted a smacking kiss on Doom's lips and sealed the bargain.

I see them!

Cordelia nearly jumped out of her skin when the ghost spoke to her in the middle of the wedding. She didn't yelp, but it was a near thing. Evermore glanced at her, brow furrowed in concern, and she shook her head.

I can see everyone! Maybe it's the church—the holy ground—I don't know! You're not just blobs anymore. There's Hester and Imogene and the Squire and—

Penelope's voice cut off abruptly, almost as startling as its arrival. Cordelia waited all through the ceremony, but she didn't speak again, and there was no way to whisper a question without someone noticing.

When the bride and groom had left the chapel and the rest of the guests began to file out, she paused as if to admire a flower arrangement, and whispered "Penelope?" behind her hand.

No response.

Did Mother notice her somehow? If she could see everyone more clearly, did that mean that other people could see her more clearly? She stopped talking right after she mentioned the Squire, and Mother was right beside him.

Did Mother do something to her? Or did the water, wine, and salt banish her? She's a ghost, and ghosts aren't supposed to like water or salt or holy ground . . . although I'm not sure how they feel about wine . . .

Cordelia mulled those questions over all through the return to the estate and the interminably long wedding breakfast. Everyone even remotely associated with Chatham House came to wish the couple well and help themselves to free food. Evangeline smiled and glittered through the entire meal, thanking everyone and curling her hands around the Squire's elbow every few minutes.

It was a very different Evangeline who came to Cordelia's rooms after breakfast. Alice said "Excuse me, ma'am—" but the door was already open and Evangeline pushed past her without a glance.

"Leave us," she instructed the maid. Alice looked at Cordelia, who was busy packing her trunks. Cordelia nodded hurriedly. There was nothing Alice could do to help, and now that her mother was lady of the manor, there was no limit to what cruelties she could get away with.

"Well," said Evangeline, stretching. "At least that's over with." She took a step forward, her eyes hardening. "Now. Is there something you want to tell me, dear?"

Uh-oh. That was a bad sign. Cordelia tried desperately to think of some infraction she might have committed. *Other than, you know, conspiring with her enemies.* "Con-congratulations?" she hazarded.

Her mother's fingers closed over her chin. Cordelia felt the scrape of long nails against her throat as she swallowed. *That wasn't it. It's something else. But what?* There were too many possibilities. Her mother had always been infuriated by things that Cordelia never suspected.

"In the chapel . . ." said Evangeline, in a crooning singsong that made Cordelia's skin go clammy with sweat.

The chapel. She did *see Penelope there.* Fear for the poor lost ghost warred with relief that the plot against Evangeline had not been discovered. At least it gave her a direction to point her lies. "I-I-I felt something. Er, thought I felt something. I wasn't sure. Was there actually something there?"

A puzzled line formed between her mother's eyebrows. "What did you feel?"

"I . . ." Was there anything she could say that wouldn't get Penelope in trouble? Then again, she was already dead, so how much more trouble could there be? "I don't know," Cordelia said. "I thought I heard someone talking?"

Evangeline gave her chin a quick little shake, like a terrier with a rat. "What did they say?"

"I couldn't make it out. It was a long way away, or maybe it wasn't, but it felt like it was—" Cordelia knew that she was making no sense, but ignorance was almost always safer where her mother was concerned. "And it was cold? Maybe? But not like real cold?" The line between her mother's eyes slowly faded and relief flooded Cordelia's veins. "I'm sorry," she finished. "I don't know how to explain it any better than that."

Evangeline's eyes bored into hers. Those long nails scraped across her jaw. "So it wasn't you who tried to pull the cup from my hands."

"*What?*" Her astonishment must have been so clearly unfeigned that Evangeline dropped her. "How could I—I was nowhere *near*—"

Her mother gave a short huff of laughter. "No, of course not. Never mind."

She turned away. Cordelia licked dry lips. "But there was something there? I wasn't imagining it?"

Evangeline moved with the speed of a striking snake, spinning around, one hand raised. She was almost to the door and nowhere near Cordelia, but the motion was so startling that Cordelia squeaked with alarm.

In the next instant, the world seemed to leap around her. Her ears rang as if she'd been standing too near a gunshot, and her heart stuttered in her chest, then came back with a rapid thud. Cordelia pressed a hand to it, gasping. There wasn't enough air in her lungs, in the room, possibly in the world.

"Huh," her mother said. "You didn't try to dodge that at all, did you?"

"Dodge . . ." She managed to drag in a breath. It was hard to think over the ringing in her ears. "Dodge . . . what? What . . . happened?"

"Now don't be cross with me," Evangeline said, taking her shoulder and leading her to a chair. "I had to *check*."

Cordelia knew that she only sounded so petulant when she'd done something. It was magic of some kind, then. *She hit me? With magic?*

She hit me just to see if I'd get out of the way?

"You'll be fine," Evangeline said, avoiding Cordelia's stunned gaze. "It was only a tap. I had to be sure. Go finish packing. Tomorrow we'll see this manor that your fiancé thinks so highly of."

And with that, she got up and left the room before Cordelia's ears had stopped ringing.

In the end, Alice took most of the clothes out of the suitcase and repacked them in a rather more efficient manner, while Cordelia stood around feeling useless. Her ears were no longer ringing, but when she moved her head too quickly in any direction, it throbbed and black spots danced across her vision.

She pled lack of hunger after the enormous wedding breakfast and dined in her room. Even then, she couldn't bring herself to eat more than a few bites. Food seemed like a bizarre habit. You used your teeth to gnaw off a hunk of something and then tried to force it down your throat with the back of your tongue, while dry bits stuck to the roof of your mouth. *Whose idea was this? This is absurd.*

Alice took the tray away after she had mangled the pastries into crumbs. "Not feeling quite the thing?"

"Not really. It's good food! Please tell the cook it was! I just can't seem to . . . to quite *believe* in eating right now." Which sounded silly, so she tried to explain, and eventually found herself saying, very earnestly, "Why do tongues even *exist*?," and gave up.

One corner of Alice's mouth crooked up during her recitation. "I'll make sure Cook doesn't feel like it's a reflection on her."

"Thank you."

The maid slowed as she neared the door. "Ah . . . forgive me, miss, but . . . are you all right? Your mother came in here earlier, and I know that sometimes that takes you hard."

I believe she hit me with some kind of magic spell, just to see if I could dodge it. This would have been much worse than asking why tongues existed, so Cordelia shook her head and said, "I'll be fine after a night's sleep. And she's leaving for her honeymoon soon."

Alice nodded and slipped out of the room.

Cordelia sighed and poured a cup of water out from the pitcher.

She had barely taken the first sip when Penelope's voice exploded into her head.

What did you just do!?

Cordelia dropped the cup with a yelp. The handle broke off when it hit the floor, and she yelped again.

"Cordelia!" The door banged open as Alice rushed in. "Are you all right, miss?"

Sorry, sorry! The scent of watercress filled the air with eye-watering strength. Cordelia wiped her eyes frantically.

"Did you cut yourself? Sit down here and let me look."

"No, no, I'm fine. I just . . ." *Tell her a ghost yelled at you. That will go over wonderfully.* ". . . uh, the mug slipped. I'm sorry! I didn't mean to break it. Maybe we can glue it back?"

"I'm sure someone can," said Alice, more reassuring than truthful. "Let me fetch a dustpan, and careful where you step."

When she was gone, Cordelia whispered, "Penelope? What happened to you? Are you okay?"

Insomuch as I'm still dead, not exactly. Other than that, I'm fine.

"Errr . . . well, yes. You broke off so fast earlier, I was afraid something had happened to you."

Cinnamon air swirled around her. **My own stupidity, I'm afraid. I could see actual objects. I haven't been able to see those since I died.**

"What were they?"

The altar. And on top of it, the water, wine, and salt. They were real. As solid as anything. The priest picked up the water and I tried to pull it out of his hand, just to see if I could actually touch it.

And then Evangeline took the cup and her hand went through me.

Cordelia inhaled sharply. That must be what her mother had felt, and for some reason she thought *Cordelia* had tried to pull the cup from her hands. Which made no sense at all. "She felt you."

Oh, I know. I heard her say "Now, what are you?" as clearly as you talking to me. So I ran. Everything went to blobs as soon as I left the edge of the churchyard, but I didn't dare get close to her again.

Cordelia couldn't blame her. Left to her own devices, she would never get close to her mother again.

It was very odd about the water, wine, and salt, though. When they drank the wine, it was like . . . oh blast, I don't have a word for it! It rang like a bell, but I'm not sure if it was really a sound. And then the salt rang too, when they ate it, and the two made a harmony together, and then the water. I was running away then, but I could hear it behind me, all three of them together ringing so loud that it drowned out everything.

Maybe that's why I got away, because she couldn't see me through the ringing.

"That sounds like magic," said Cordelia. "Or maybe the opposite of magic. Maybe that's why they break spells together?"

Maybe. I don't think I would have wanted to stay there, even if Evangeline hadn't seen me. It felt like it might have drowned me out, too.

Alice came back in and hastily swept up the shards of crockery. "Are you sure you're all right?"

"I'm fine. Just . . . um . . . tired, I guess." Cordelia tried to smile.

Alice paused, still holding the dustpan. "It won't be so bad, going to Evermore House, miss. No one in service has any complaints of him."

Cordelia was sure her face looked as blank as her mind felt. "Err . . . good?"

"If you were worried about that, I mean."

"Oh."

They stared at each other for a moment over the broken cup; then Alice curtsied—*how can she do that so well when she's carrying a dustpan? I must get her to teach me*—and left, shutting the door behind her.

Alone again? Good. What were you doing, just now? When I yelled?

"Having a drink of water?"

Do it again, if you would.

Puzzled, Cordelia scooped up a palmful of water and sipped.

There! Yes! It happened again!

"What happened?"

The water. When you drank it, it rang, like it did in the church. Not as loud, but a little bit. And I could see it.

Do you have any salt?

"There's probably a saltcellar in the breakfast room." Cordelia wasn't looking forward to sneaking down there, past Alice, to try and find one, and wine, of course, was out of the question. "Wait, though. You should know that we're leaving tomorrow. Going to Lord Evermore's estate."

You are? A mournful drift of cinnamon filled the room. *That's so far away.*

"Are you still going to be able to talk to me?"

I don't know. It gets very dark when I get too far from living people. Like a night with no stars and no moon. I've gone to the edge of the estate a few times, but I'm afraid that if I go too far, I'll get turned around and never find my way back.

"Don't do that! I'm sure I'll be back here . . . err . . . eventually. When we find out how to stop my mother. Maybe we can find a way then."

Maybe. Although ghosts are supposed to haunt the place they died, aren't they? Maybe I can't leave here at all.

"I'm sorry."

She sensed a gathering, a determined cheer. *Don't fret about me. What's the worst that can happen? I'm already dead.*

"I won't forget you're here," Cordelia promised.

Of course you won't. I am . . . I was . . . Penelope Green. Some people may have hated me, but nobody ever forgot me.

CHAPTER 27

It took three coaches to travel to Lord Evermore's estate. Privately Hester thought that they could have done with two, but the Squire insisted on packing up multiple guns, in case of hunting, and Doom had an entire trousseau that half filled the baggage coach by itself.

Hester rode in the first coach with Imogene and Cordelia. "For you cannot possibly restore the town house without me," said Imogene, in Doom's hearing. "I won't hear of it."

"I wouldn't think of trying," Hester assured her. She was prepared to defend this, if the Squire asked, but he didn't. Possibly he was pleased at the propriety of another chaperone for his new daughter-in-law. More likely he simply didn't think of it at all.

Hester had been dreading the long ride in close quarters with Doom, but the woman chose to ride alongside Richard and the Squire, on the tall white horse with its pale green eyes. Hester hadn't been this close to the creature before, but looking into its pale eyes, she could readily believe that it wasn't entirely canny.

Still, it was a long, bruising ride, even so. The coach was old and not as well sprung as it could be. Her knee ached and she stretched it out as best she could, but there were limits to what she could do without kicking one of her companions. *I shouldn't complain. Poor Mary is riding in the servants' coach, and that's a regular bone-rattler. She'll need a hot poultice more than I will, by the time we get in.* Imogene tucked her chin against her chest and fell asleep with an ease that Hester envied. Cordelia simply stared out the window, watching the landscape pass. She had a distracted look, as if there was something on her mind.

Hester snorted at her own thoughts. *Yes, what could she possibly have on her mind, other than a fake engagement, a murder, and a sorceress for a mother?*

Eventually the coach halted. Hester looked out the window but saw only dense trees.

"Ladies," said Richard, as the driver opened the door, "you'll want to ride for this last bit. The carriage lane is full of potholes, and we can't repair it until it dries out for the summer. Your luggage will be carried up by wagon."

Hester was relieved to see that the horses brought up included several patient-looking ponies. Mounting with her knee was always unpleasant, and the taller the beast the worse it got.

Richard helped her up and then did the same for Cordelia, on a similar pony. Doom looked slightly irked by his choice, but she had the sense not to complain.

The path for the horses snaked through the woods that circled Evermore's house. Even on an overcast day like today, it blazed with green, as the new growth of spring erupted around them. Water dripped between the leaves, and insects hummed through the air.

"It's like a jungle," said Cordelia wonderingly, looking around her. The path was lined with ferns, and the enormous leaves of catalpa blotted out the sun.

"My grandfather's head gardener was a genius," said Evermore. "We have spent the last two generations simply trying to keep up what he created. Fortunately, I am told he left detailed notes—ah, here we are. Evermore House, in all its glory."

Hester had visited any number of times, but the sudden revelation of Evermore House after the thick wood still delighted her. The junglelike wood suddenly broke into low, lush ferns, bordering a broad lawn that rolled downward, with the manor house squarely in the center. It was barely half the size of Chatham House, but built entirely of tan stone, with two round towers reflected in a small lake. Where the Squire's manor had multiple wings, Evermore House was all one piece and generations of descendants had, quite sensibly, avoided sticking on extra architectural bits. This had required the addition of a number of outbuildings, but preserved the overall impression that one had just encountered a fairy castle dropped into the middle of the countryside.

So far as Hester was concerned, however, the best feature of the property was even now emerging from the lake, waddling rapidly toward them and honking loudly.

"Geese, milord?" said Evangeline, trying to sound haughty and amused, though the effect was somewhat ruined by the large number of geese that immediately swarmed around Falada's feet, some of them hissing like serpents.

"I'm allergic to dogs," said Richard. "Nevertheless, I must have something to raise an alarm if prowlers come calling. And they lay quite impressive eggs."

"Historically geese are wards against misfortune and evil magic," said Hester mildly.

"No one believes that old wives' tale anymore, surely," said Evangeline sharply.

"No, of course not, my dear," said the Squire hastily, shooting Hester a look.

"Merely an old story," agreed Richard pleasantly. "I suspect they may dislike your horse. I've never had a white horse here, now that I think of it. Perhaps they think he's a swan."

The white horse pawed the ground. The geese drew back to give him an inch or two, then immediately regrouped, hissing.

"They look very healthy," said Hester happily. "And that is a very fine gander there, and that one looks fit to grow up the same. Oh dear . . . no, that one over there needs to be culled, I expect. He's awfully short. Now how did you turn out like that, my lad?"

"You may take up all discussion of goose breeding with my master of fowl," said Richard.

"You have a master of fowl?" Doom sounded incredulous, then apparently caught herself and flashed Richard a smile. "Very sensible, of course. I can see they would require a dedicated . . . err . . . hand."

"He is mostly the second gardener," Richard admitted, "but as he is the primary keeper of the geese, we call him the master of fowl. Hester, I am not letting you get off that horse and take out that gander right now, so stop looking like that."

Hester harrumphed. Cordelia was clearly fighting back laughter. Imogene didn't even try to fight it back.

At the door of the manor, they slid off their horses—in Hester's case, a sturdy groom stepped forward to assist her, to her mild chagrin—and the doors of Evermore House opened before them.

Cordelia loved Evermore House immediately.

Despite its imposing appearance, the interior was very plain. The walls were covered with whitewash instead of wallpaper, and the floor was made of ancient oak planks, dark stained and rock-hard with age. Her bedroom lay in one of the towers and had a window seat that overlooked the grounds. The light from the window rippled off the coverlet in the way that only very expensive silk can ripple, but the rag rug on the floor was much like the one that had adorned the floor of Cordelia's bedroom in Little Haw, only cleaner and (apparently) rather newer.

This room doesn't make me feel like someone's poor relation, even though I am. Not that anyone at Chatham House ever tried to make me feel that way, but everything was so . . . so carelessly wealthy.

It reminded her of Penelope's lecture on style, and why she had refused to wear ruffles and saved a great deal of money and dignity in the process. This was a house that refused ruffles.

The bed had spindle posts, turned into elaborate knobbly pillars. Cordelia ran her hand up one, delighted by the way the shapes bulged out and tucked back in again.

"Don't rub the bed like that, dear, it looks vulgar." Her mother sailed in, looked around the room, and made a small huffing sound. "I see that you'll have your hands full redecorating this place. It looks like a convent."

"I rather like it," said Cordelia quietly.

"Don't be absurd. Evermore can afford not to live like a peasant. I'll be here to assist you, though, so you needn't worry." She went to the window seat and looked down. "The grounds, at least, are quite elegant, except for those wretched geese. I thought they were going to pursue him clear into the stables."

"Can they tell he's a familiar?"

"It seems likely. I can't say that I ever bothered spending much time among waterfowl, so perhaps they're all like that, though. Dreadful things. You'll have them turned into feather beds, naturally."

"Yes, Mother."

"Such a lot of work to be done. Still, we shall make a start on it as soon as I return." She sat down on the bed and patted the mattress beside her. Cordelia sat obediently.

Just get through the rest of the day. She's leaving in the morning. Leaving for weeks and weeks. *You can get through today.*

"Now," her mother said, "it is vital to remember, while I am gone, that you are still unmarried. Do you understand me? You must not allow *anyone* to place you in a compromising position and jeopardize your engagement."

"I'll be careful."

"That includes your fiancé."

Cordelia blinked at her, puzzled. How could her fiancé compromise her? He was already supposed to marry her, wasn't he?

Evangeline sighed. "Some men have a tendency to . . . ah . . . wish to anticipate the wedding. You must be on guard for such things! If word got out, it could damage your reputation terribly. Under no circumstances are you to allow yourself to be alone with Evermore, do you hear me? Go nowhere unless you have a suitable chaperone."

Her expression must have been suitably appalled, because her mother nodded, clearly satisfied. "I see you understand."

"I . . . think . . . so?"

"Good. It is only three weeks. And that is the only thing that you need to worry about." She rose to her feet, patting Cordelia's head absently, like a dog. Cordelia was surprised at the flash of rage she felt, but she squelched it immediately. *Just get through today.*

"Don't fret," her mother said cheerfully. "You'll be fine without me. It's not that long. And of course you won't be alone."

"Of course, Lady Hester and Lady Strauss will be here . . ."

"Those two!" Evangeline rolled her eyes. "Useless, both of them. No, I mean that I'm leaving you Falada."

Get through breakfast, Hester told herself. *Get through breakfast and they'll go off on the honeymoon. You just have to get through breakfast without going across the table and throttling Doom or beating your brother around the head and shoulders while screaming "Don't you see what's going on!?"*

But of course he didn't see. Samuel was the one person at the table who had no idea what was going on, which was probably why he seemed oblivious to any tensions taking place over the poached eggs.

"Such wholesome food," Evangeline said. "Lord Evermore, your cook has done wonders."

"Err . . . yes . . ." Richard said, looking over at the sideboard, which contained eggs, toast, bacon, and fresh asparagus, none of which had required any great culinary inspiration to prepare.

"And it is so charming to see the estate that my dear Cordelia will be mistress of! I am so sorry that we must rush off so quickly."

"Well, I am certain that when you return, Cordelia herself will be able to give you a tour," said Richard, while Cordelia turned a dull crimson and stared at her toast.

Imogene started to say something, but Hester had been watching her like a hawk and poked her smartly in the shin as soon as her mouth opened. Imogene turned it into a cough.

"You didn't have to smack me with your cane," she muttered, once the dreadful breakfast had come to a close and Evangeline had gone to make certain that all her trunks had been brought down.

"I absolutely did. I recognized that look."

"What look?"

"The I'm-about-to-say-something-extremely-clever look."

Her friend scowled, but didn't argue. "It *was* clever."

"Yes, and this is not the time to be clever, or have you forgotten what we're dealing with?"

Imogene muttered something else, but sufficiently under her breath that Hester didn't catch it.

"Everything in order?" asked the Squire, glancing at his pocket watch as Doom came traipsing down the stairs.

"Perfectly. Thank you *so* for your hospitality, Lord Evermore." She turned to Cordelia. "Come give me a kiss and mind your manners while I am gone."

"Yes, Mother," said Cordelia, kissing her dutifully on the cheek. The girl turned to the Squire. "I hope to see you back soon, sir."

"Mmm? Oh, yes, yes, quite." Samuel patted her arm in a distracted fashion. "Back before you know it."

Hester was surprised by a sudden rush of affection for her brother. Loud, satisfied, and oblivious as he often was, she loved him very much, and she was sending him off with the proverbial viper in his bosom. *And other, rather lower bits, if we're being honest. Dammit, Samuel. She* won't *kill you, it would be* foolish *to kill you, both she and Cordelia would have to go into mourning for a year and she wants Cordelia safely married off first, but I still feel like I'm abandoning you.*

She hugged him tightly. "Here now, old girl," he said, looking surprised. "Only going to be gone a few weeks. Not like we're sailing to the old country, or dropping off the face of the earth."

"I know," she said, stepping back. "Just . . . err . . . be happy."

"Happiest man in the world," he assured her, glancing at his watch again. "Blast, is everything ready? Why do these things take so long . . . ?"

The carriage was announced to be ready and waiting at the edge of the estate. Cordelia and Hester stood on the step and waved as the Squire and his doom rode away, down the road and into the gap in the trees.

Long after the last sign had vanished, Hester leaned on the doorframe. "Well," she said, and exhaled. "They're gone."

Cordelia wiped at her eyes. "I don't know why I'm crying," she said. "I'm relieved, really."

"That's probably why you're crying. Come on." Hester turned. "Let's go take a look at this library of Richard's, and see what we can see."

CHAPTER 28

"Look," said Evermore, "there's a reason I describe it as a collection and not as a library. Granddad wanted to *own* the books. Catalogue and display were someone else's problem."

They stood in what was likely the largest room in Evermore House. Acres of oak flooring stretched out before them, mostly obscured by stacks and piles and boxes of books. Knee-high stacks braced up waist-high stacks that leaned precariously against stacks towering over Cordelia's head. The room held more books than Cordelia had ever seen in her life, from tiny palm-sized books of hours to enormous folios bound in calfskin, and where normally Cordelia would have been enthralled by the prospect of so many books to read, the idea of trying to locate one single piece of relevant information was daunting.

"Mother of God," said Imogene. "Was this a ballroom?"

"It was. We don't have many balls. Grandfather took it over for his collection."

"This isn't even a collection," said Hester, gazing at the precarious stacks. "This is a hoard. Did your grandfather sleep on them like a dragon, too?"

"Certainly not while my grandmother was alive. I won't swear about after. Being a widower didn't agree with him." He ran a hand through his hair. "Come to think of it, about half of these arrived in the year after she died."

"Grief takes people in odd ways," said Imogene, lighting another lamp. "Though compulsive book-buying isn't one I've heard of before."

There were several long tables, all piled with books, and a number of chairs that someone had arranged in a semblance of a reading nook. (The chairs had also been overrun with books.) There were also bookcases pressed against the walls, though they had long since given up any hope of holding the collection and now appeared more like bulwarks that had fallen to the enemy.

Cordelia picked up a book and opened it cautiously. It was dry and clean and thankfully didn't rain silverfish. "They seem to be in good condition, at least?"

"The staff takes very good care of the room, and we employ two highly skilled mousers." He leaned over and wiggled his fingers, and a small tuxedo cat ambled from behind the desk. "Here's one now, in fact."

The cat accepted tribute in the form of head skritches, then strolled away, twining once around Hester's ankles, and out the door.

"So what do we do?" asked Cordelia, looking down at her book. "Everyone grab a book, start reading, and hope to find something about stopping sorcery?"

"Seems like it." Richard moved a stack of books aside and pulled a chair close to the window for Hester, then drew his own up alongside. "Lady Hester . . . would you care to share a stack?"

"Scandalous," said Imogene, plopping down onto a couch. "Someone ring for tea. I expect we're going to be here for a while."

By midafternoon, they had achieved exactly nothing.

"The problem is that too many things *could* be useful," said Imogene bitterly. "I thought, 'Oh, this book of herbal remedies can't possibly help,' but then it occurred to me that one of the herbs might actually be used to break spells, and I had to fish it back out of the discard pile and skim through it."

"And?" Richard looked up from his book. "Were any of the herbs useful?"

"If you've got scrofula or an upset stomach, I can probably whip something up. For magic, though, no luck."

Cordelia slumped back against the sofa. Her stack had gone down by four books, but like Imogene, she hated to set a book aside that might be useful. She was currently halfway through a book of folktales, and everything had begun to blur together into a morass of lost princesses, feckless soldiers, evil wizards, and dogs made of bones.

"At this rate, Evangeline will die of old age before we find a solution," said Hester.

A delicate cough sounded in the doorway. "Perhaps I might be of service, madam?"

Hester sat up. "*Willard?*"

Everyone turned. Cordelia felt her spine trying to straighten, because sure enough, Willard the butler stood just inside the library door. She immediately felt underdressed.

"What are you doing here?" asked Hester. "Is something wrong at home?"

The butler shook his head. "I fear I do not know. Shortly before leaving for her honeymoon, the new Lady Chatham informed me that my services would no longer be necessary."

"She *what?*" Hester half rose from her chair, her face going chalk white with rage. "How dare she? She can't do that to my friends in *my* hou—"

She stopped. Her teeth closed in the middle of the word with an audible click.

For the first time, Cordelia saw an emotion cross the unflappable butler's face, as sorrow and pity filled his eyes.

"Oh," said Hester, much more quietly. "Oh. I suppose it's not my house any longer, is it? She's the mistress of the place now, and I am there on sufferance." She wiped her hand across her face, then waved Richard away as he moved toward her. "Don't worry about me. Tom's the one who's out of a job."

"Indeed," said Willard. "I thought perhaps I would come here and ask if you were planning to set up your own household, and if there might be an opening there."

"But Jack . . ." Hester put her hand to her mouth. "You and he have an understanding."

Willard inclined his head. "It has made things more difficult, yes."

"Has he quit?"

"I have convinced him to wait. There are not so many jobs available for a stablemaster who comes from outside, instead of being promoted."

Richard cleared his throat. "I suspect that we can sort something out," he said. "I can't possibly replace my butler—I'm sorry—"

"Lord Evermore," said Willard, with cool dignity, "I should not consider it a kindness to put another out of his longtime job on my account."

Richard's mouth crooked up at the corner. "You're right, and I apologize."

"Nevertheless," said Willard, "it seems to me that you have a task where, perhaps, my organizational skills may help." His gaze swept the library. "And since I am no longer an employee, at the moment, perhaps, Lady Hester, you will finally deign to explain to me what *exactly* is going on?"

Tom Willard took the explanation about sorcery far more matter-of-factly than any of the rest of them had. He did not argue. He did not even express doubt. He simply nodded. "Very well. The immediate path is clear, then."

"You believe us?" asked Cordelia meekly.

He turned toward her, still tall and imposing, like a great heron sighting a fish. Then he smiled at her and Cordelia nearly fell off her chair. "It is not my place to believe or disbelieve," he said. "You all believe it, and therefore we shall act as if it is true. If it turns out that you have all been misled—well, then we shall deal with that when it comes." He turned back to the library ahead and brushed his hands together. "Now. What is needed here is triage."

"Triage?" asked Cordelia, who wasn't entirely sure what the word meant.

"Triage," said Willard firmly. He pointed. "Any book that is most definitely useless goes there. Any book that might possibly have something useful goes here. Any book that looks as if it is exactly what we need, put on the table here and Lady Hester shall start reading it at once."

"Why does she get to do the reading?" asked Imogene.

"Because I read fast and my knee hurts too much to carry books back and forth."

". . . Fair enough."

Willard tapped a finger on the table. "I would bring in more servants, but I fear that the gossip would become unmanageable in short order. I understand why you attempted to keep it quiet at Chatham House." He nodded to Hester.

"Did we succeed?"

"Admirably, yes. All of us belowstairs knew that there was a conspiracy of some sort, of course, but the assumption was that you were to elope with Lord Evermore and perhaps take Cordelia with you, out of reach of her mother."

Hester blushed. "But . . ."

"Come now," said Willard, in a chiding tone, "do you think that anyone who has known both of you *really* believed that Lord Evermore would marry anyone else?"

Richard grinned like a shark, grabbed Willard's hand, and pumped it enthusiastically. "We will *absolutely* find a post for you," he said.

"As long as my mother believed it," said Cordelia, torn between worry and relief.

"As to that, miss, I cannot say. But I daresay that we will find a way to deal with such a complication." He gazed at the stacks and snapped his fingers. "To work, then. And for the next little while, as I am in no one's employ, I believe that you may all call me Tom."

CHAPTER 29

Cordelia worked harder in the next seven days than she could ever remember working in her life. Her eyes ached from focusing and her mind ached from trying to sort through so much information. Scrubbing the floors and peeling potatoes back home seemed like a fond dream by comparison.

Willard had worked a minor miracle sorting the books. They had discarded everything written in a language that no one could read—"For," as Imogene said, "even if it lays out all the solutions in plain text, none of us would be able to tell"—and set aside many books that seemed highly unlikely to be useful.

"If it turns out that the secret was hidden in *A Brief Treatise on the History of Potatoes,* I shall be very cross," Hester said.

"You may blame me," Willard told her, "and I shall retire and take up potato farming to make up for it."

Nevertheless, this still left a daunting pile of texts before them, many of which were densely written or printed in the old black-letter style that seemed to swim on the page in front of Cordelia's eyes.

Worse than the eyestrain was the fear that she would miss something vital. She would often find herself halfway down a page with no memory of what she had just read, and would be forced to start again. So far it had only ever been about crop rotation or pigeon keeping or artesian wells, but she dreaded the possibility that she might mindlessly turn the page on a footnote that would be the solution to their problems.

There was this much to be grateful for, though: she was not afraid. Her mother was far away, and would be for many days. She no longer cared if she grabbed the wrong fork at dinner, because everyone was eating dinner on a tray in the library with a book in their hand. She did not have time to feel guilty about Ellen's father, and she did not worry that Imogene or Hester would hate her, because all of them were tired and alternated between snappish and giddy with exhaustion and one chased the other, usually with a mumbled "Sorry. You know," and everyone forgave everyone else because they were too busy to do otherwise.

Once, briefly, she wondered how Penelope's ghost was faring. She was skimming a book of old plays, full of magic and high tragedy, and a ghost appeared to denounce her murderer. *I hope she's okay,* Cordelia thought, turning the page. *I hope she found someone else to talk to.* And then the act ended and a pair of comedic nursemaids came on stage and Cordelia skimmed fifty more pages and everyone died but not of sorcery, so she shut the book and stopped thinking about it.

"I think I've got something here," said Imogene, on the afternoon of the eighth day. "Maybe?" She hefted the tome in her hands, the sunlight streaming through the windows behind her and outlining her in golden light, like a saint's halo. The others set down their books and came to see.

"*On Reagents, Their Uses, and the Alchemical Work That May Be Done with Them,*" Richard read from the binding.

"It's not going to outsell the latest serial novel," Imogene said, "but it has a ritual in it for 'the breaking of sorcerous powers.'" She looked at them over the top of her glasses. "And it uses water, wine, and salt."

"How can we be sure it'll work on Evangeline?" Hester asked, after they had all read the ritual in the book several times. "If it's just another version of what they do in church, that won't help."

"It's a lot more involved than church," Richard said. "We have to draw sigils. And a circle inside a triangle. It says it takes four people. One to use each reagent, and one to chant the words."

"Not to mention how we're going to get her to just stand in a circle while we chant at her," Imogene added. "I don't like the woman, but I don't think she's daft enough to just stand there." She scowled down at the book. "But if we could, this sounds like it might work. It doesn't just break a spell, it says it 'renders the gold of sorcery into base human metal.'"

Cordelia leaned over Imogene's shoulder and read the paragraph underneath, which told of how the ritual had been used on "one who delighted in sorcerous wickedness" and how "forever after, he had not the smallest gift of such." "That sounds good," she said. "If she couldn't do magic anymore, that would be enough, wouldn't it?"

The four adults exchanged looks, which Cordelia could see, even if she couldn't quite decipher them. She straightened, annoyed. "You can tell me. There's not much p-point in sheltering me now."

"You're right," said Hester. "In answer to your question—well, she could probably still get up to a lot of mischief."

"But it would be ordinary mischief," said Imogene, her eyes sparkling with interest, "and we've more than enough experience with that. It's only the magic that makes her impossible." She tapped the book. "In fact, once she's no longer a sorcerer, we could probably just kill her."

"*Imogene,*" said Hester.

"What? You can't tell me that it wouldn't be a great deal easier all around."

Evermore gave Cordelia an apologetic glance and murmured something about not allowing that, which Cordelia found both sweet and largely misguided. "My m-mother's a monster," she said. She rubbed her face. Guilt tried to raise its head—*how dare you even consider such a thing!?*—and she stomped it down hard. "If there was some way to . . . to put her somewhere where she could never hurt anyone ever again, then I would. But I don't think there is, is there?" She didn't wait for an answer. "We can't just let her keep going, just because we don't want to kill her. It's not fair to anyone else she might hurt."

"We need to break the magic first," said Hester. "If she's gotten her hooks into my brother somehow, I want that spell broken. 'Great chaos is unleashed when a sorcerer dies,' according to the book I found, and you can't tell me that a woman like that wouldn't have put all manner of things in place to make life unpleasant after she died."

Cordelia winced. What had her mother said once, so many weeks ago? *Even if they did decide to burn me as a witch, they'd get no joy of it.* "I think you're probably right," she said faintly.

"We could probably drug her," said Imogene practically, "and get her into the circle that way. Enough laudanum and she won't care if we drag her into the lawn, the parlor, or the back of beyond. But we still need to test it first."

"I know how we can test it," said Cordelia. "We'll do it on Falada."

Falada still walked the grounds in the evening, just as he had at Chatham House. The difference now was that he never did so alone. The groundskeepers did not whisper about how uncanny he was, because it was hard to look uncanny when you were surrounded by a ring of agitated geese.

They found a window that evening, and watched him glide by, accompanied by his waddling bodyguards. Sometimes he would break into a run to get away from them and the geese would scatter, but they would all immediately take to the air and come down beside him and form a ring again.

Cordelia had to admit that they were not particularly graceful birds, and standing beside Falada's unearthly beauty made them seem even more ungainly. Yet they were fearless and apparently tireless, never allowing Falada to roam the grounds without being watched.

"I take back what I said about the short-legged one," said Hester, gazing out the window into the twilight. "I still wouldn't breed him, but he's remarkably good at corralling a horse."

"We have to draw the circle around that particular horse," said Imogene, looking down at the book. "It's very clear. You can't just lead him into it, you have to actually draw it around him or it won't contain him. It suggests a bag of white chalk. Then the triangle around it, with each of us at one point. Then we invoke the water, wine, and salt—"

"Invoke it *how?*" asked Hester. "I've never invoked anything in my life."

Cordelia remembered the ghost of Penelope saying that the wine in the church had rung when it was drunk, and that the water had done the same when she drank it. "I think you just have to drink it," she said cautiously. "That seems to be enough? Maybe?"

Please don't ask how I know that, because this is complicated enough already.

"Drinking it seems to be enough in a church wedding," Evermore said. "Although perhaps the priest blesses it beforehand. I'm not sure."

Imogene frowned down at the book. "'Let he who invokes the reagent be he who is best suited to the task, water to water, wine to wine, salt to salt. Let him reflect on the reagent that is his: the salt that comes of earth, the water that is borne on the swift stream, and the wine that is made of growing grapes and the art of man. For salt bars the entry of the shadowed ones; water fills the space it is given and washes away that which is impure; and wine binds the space between the seen and unseen, even as it binds the bargains struck between men.'"

"And we're supposed to do this while a horse is tied up in front of us?" Richard asked.

"I know that I reflect best on reagents when a thousand-pound animal is screaming at me," said Hester.

Imogene shrugged. "Look, if it fails, all that happens is that we look silly and Richard's grooms think we've joined a cult."

"You know they used to burn people at the stake for that," said Richard mildly.

"So you have to buy the Archbishop a new church somewhere. You can afford it."

"That's not all that happens," said Cordelia.

"Eh?"

"Falada's her familiar. Even if it fails, she'll know that we did something." She stared out the window, where the bone-white form stood on the grass, surrounded by a ring of watchful geese. Whenever the horse took a step, the ring shifted to keep him in the center. It would have been hilarious if she had not known what Falada truly was.

"How does he communicate with her?" asked Richard. "Do you know? Does she have to come here?"

Cordelia tried to remember every detail of her mother appearing when she had tried to run away on the horse's back. "I don't know. I tried to get away once, and he must have contacted her somehow, because she came after me as soon as I did. But I don't know how much she knows when they're apart." She remembered all the questions she'd asked Ellen. Her mother had never seemed to pick up any of them. Perhaps she had to choose to listen in, or perhaps Falada simply hadn't told her.

"In that case . . ." Hester clasped her hands together. "We'll try the spell, and if it doesn't work, we'll simply have to kill the beast."

Cordelia stared at her. "Kill him?"

"You object?"

"No. Oh, no!" The rage and horror that she had kept under her breastbone since she had learned that Falada was not her friend roared suddenly to life. Kill him. Yes. *Yes.*

"Can you kill a familiar?" asked Richard doubtfully. "Do they die like normal animals?"

Imogene moved to the windowsill, looking down. "Well," she said, "I don't know very much about magic, but I do know that cutting their heads off kills just about anything."

CHAPTER 30

Everyone objected when Cordelia announced that she was going to be the one inside the spell circle.

"It has to be me," she said. "Don't you see?"

"I see that you'll be in the circle with, at best, a deranged stallion and at worst, some kind of demon," said Lord Evermore. "I won't hear of it. I'll say the words."

Cordelia shook her head. "Falada won't hurt me," she said. "I'm the only one he won't hurt. He wouldn't dare. All of Mother's plans hinge on me. Whatever he does, I'm the only one who has any chance of being safe."

Her logic was unassailable, and she knew it. Eventually the others came around, but no one liked it. "Don't worry," said Imogene dryly. "None of us are going to be all that safe. There'll be a line of chalk between us and that same horse, remember?"

Evermore scowled. "I had thought perhaps Willard and I, and one of my men . . ."

"Absolutely not," said Hester. "You can't order someone to do this. And what would you even say? 'You, stand here and invoke wine.' No, it's got to be us. I'll take water."

"I agree with Hester," said Imogene. "And obviously I'll take salt."

"Leaving me with wine, I suppose," said Evermore.

"Lady Hester, are you certain? Your knee—"

She folded her arms. "Tom, someone has to draw the triangle around all of us. I'd much rather stand in one place and have you walking around with the chalk."

Willard and Evermore exchanged looks. "I suppose she's right," muttered Evermore. "As usual."

The former butler inclined his head. "I will do my best. And in this case, at least we will have an extra set of hands when something goes wrong."

No one argued. Cordelia just wished that he'd said *if* instead of *when*.

They did the spell in late evening. "I've asked three men to stay on to help wrangle the beast, and cleared out the rest of the stablehands for the evening," Evermore said. "They'll likely think I'm a monster for doing this to a horse, but at least this way, fewer of them will be around to stop me."

"Would they try to stop you?" asked Cordelia. "You're their lord."

One corner of Evermore's mouth curved up in a humorless smile. "No man in my stables should stand by and watch a horse mistreated, whether by a king or a beggar. Normally they know that their lord has their back. I suppose tonight we find out how much that's been worth."

There were three stablehands waiting for them, and a very old man. Evermore's breath hissed through his teeth. "Dammit," he muttered. "I hoped Bernard wouldn't catch wind of this."

"Your mistake was asking them to keep silent," said Imogene. "That pretty much guaranteed it would be everywhere by nightfall."

The old man was bowlegged and nearly toothless, but his eyes were as sharp as penny nails. "What's this I hear?" He stomped up to Evermore, heedless of the fact that he was a good head shorter. "What are you planning to do to a beast?"

Evermore looked over Bernard's head, into the depths of the stable, then ushered him away. Cordelia suspected that he was trying to get out of Falada's hearing. She couldn't see the familiar, but one of the stalls was a little lighter than the others, as if the shadows had been lit up by something large and bright.

She could just catch snatches of the men's conversation where she stood.

". . . taught you better . . ." Bernard said, in clear disgust.

Evermore's voice was deeper and harder to make out, but she thought it included *Trust me*. Judging by the old man's querulous voice, that was asking a great deal.

She looked over her shoulder, to the entrance of the stables. Willard, Hester, and Imogene all stood just to one side. Since it was going to be difficult keeping Falada still, they'd decided to do the ritual as close to the mouth of the stable as possible. There was a post with an iron ring used for hitching horses, and their plan, such as it was, was to tie Falada to the ring and then draw the circle around him.

Cordelia had a feeling that Falada was not going to cooperate.

He'll know something's going on. Somehow. As soon as we start, he'll know and try to break loose.

The stablehands were there to secure the familiar to the post and hobble him there, but Evermore had told them the truth that Falada could not survive the night. They did not look happy about it. *Well, and why would they be? If you don't know what he is, it looks like Evermore is going to put down a magnificent horse in his prime. One that doesn't even really belong to him.*

"Fine," she heard Bernard growl, stalking back toward them. "I don't know what your father would say, but I'll not stop you. Put those damn ropes away, lads. I'll bring him out myself."

"Bernard . . ." Evermore's protest was more resigned than sharp. Cordelia watched the old man take a halter off the wall and walk toward the stall.

"Is that safe?" she whispered, even though what she meant was *That is most definitely not safe. You should let me do it.*

"Bernard could control the Devil himself if he took the form of a horse."

Cordelia swallowed hard.

"Come on then, beauty," she heard the old man crooning from the stable depths. "I know, it's late. But you've been jumping the door and wandering the place at night, haven't you? Don't think Old Bernard doesn't know. Let's have a bit of a walk before you wander, eh? Here we go, over the ears, there's a good beauty . . ."

Falada emerged from the dark, head high, with the old man holding the halter under his chin. He saw Cordelia and his pale eyes widened just a little.

"Come on, beauty, just a little farther . . ."

They reached the entrance to the stable and Falada stopped. The old man tried to lead him another step, but the familiar's hooves were set.

"Come now, beauty, nothing to be worried about. You've come out plenty of times by yourself, haven't you? Get a good look, nothing frightening . . ."

Falada turned his head, looking over Bernard to where the conspirators waited. His nostrils flared and Cordelia had a sudden panicked feeling that the familiar could smell the wine in the bottle that Willard held and the sack of salt in Imogene's hand.

Maybe he doesn't even need to smell them. Maybe he sees like a ghost and they're more real than everything else.

Falada growled. It was a deep, savage sound, far more suited to a mastiff than a horse. The stablehands all stepped back, and one of them cursed. Evermore stiffened and Imogene said something soft and foul, not quite under her breath.

Only Bernard remained calm. If the noise had startled him, he gave no sign. "Gently there, beauty," he said, his voice as soothing as cool water. "No need to make such a fuss. Just come with Old Bernard and I expect I can find a treat for you, eh?"

He stepped forward with such assurance that it was impossible to believe that any horse wouldn't follow. Everyone held their breath.

Which was why Cordelia heard, so clearly, the rubbery crunching sound as Falada turned his head at an impossibly sharp angle and bit the old man's ear off.

Bernard staggered but did not lose his grip on the halter, which was the only reason that Falada didn't trample him at once. He let out a high-pitched yell and went to one knee, blood pouring in sheets down the side of his face.

Falada bounced on his front hooves and *giggled*.

"Get the ropes on him!" Evermore shouted, but the stablehands were too slow, they were still staring with their jaws slack because horses didn't move like that and they didn't sound like that and in another instant, Bernard was going to lose his grip and the thing that wasn't a horse was going to kill him.

It wasn't courage. Cordelia was clear on that even at the time. Courage was what you did when you were afraid, and as much as she loathed Falada, she did not fear him. She had learned to ride as a toddler, her chubby fingers twined in his mane. He had been her nursemaid. She *hated* him, she hated every deceitful bone in his body, she hated that she had loved him for most of her life, but she was not afraid.

Cordelia flung herself past the too-slow stablehands and threw herself over the old man, shielding his body with her own. Falada snaked his head down to look at her and she grabbed the rope just as Bernard's grip failed, and for a moment everything froze and she was kneeling in the dirt with the old man's head pressed against her shoulder and his blood spreading hot and sticky across her neck and someone yelled her name and Falada growled again but he couldn't hurt her, she knew he couldn't hurt her and Evermore was shouting "Throw the goddamn ropes!" and finally one landed over Falada's head and tightened around his neck.

He squealed loudly, horselike this time, and then his neck came around at that impossible snakelike angle and one of the stablehands was praying loudly and another one said, "That is not a bloody *horse*," in a voice that sounded like a prayer.

Falada grabbed the halter rope just above Cordelia's fingers and yanked it neatly out of her hand. The only rope on him was suddenly the one from the stablehand, and instead of pulling against it, the horse pivoted neatly on his hind hooves, ready to lunge.

Cordelia flung herself forward and threw her arms around the familiar's hind leg.

It was a supremely foolish thing to do with any horse, and even if she hadn't known that, Evermore's shout of "Cordelia, no!" would have warned her, but it worked. Falada froze, and then came down, with incredibly delicacy, not daring to take a step for fear of kicking her. That horrible growling started again, his whole body vibrating as if his rage would shake him apart, but he did not move.

"Cordelia, get away from there!"

"Throw me a rope," Cordelia said hoarsely.

"Cordelia, you'll be killed!"

She wanted to scream. All these adults who were supposed to know how the world worked, who understood things faster and better and knew all the things that Cordelia had never been taught, and *none* of them could figure out what she was doing? She *had* Falada, for the love of god, she had him pinned, why wouldn't they stop screaming at her and *do what she said*?

"*Throw me a rope!*" she screamed, and her voice disturbed her because it sounded very much like her mother's.

A rope landed in the dirt beside her.

Her hands shook. She had to wrap her elbow around Falada's hock and her cheek was against his pale hide, which twitched and jumped under her touch. She got the rope around his leg and tried to knot it, but her hands were slick with sweat.

"Here, lass." Gnarled fingers wrapped around hers. Old Bernard, his face a mask of blood, slumped against her. His breath rasped in his throat but his fingers were quick and sure as he helped her pull the knots tight.

She flung the rope toward Evermore and saw him grab it. He and a stablehand went to the post and pulled the rope tight and

Cordelia wrapped herself around Old Bernard like the lover she was too young to have and the two crawled together out from under the familiar's hooves.

The moment they were free, Falada threw his head back and roared. He reared again and crow-hopped forward, but the instant he gave up any slack on the leg rope, the two men yanked it tight. The familiar stumbled forward, unbalanced, and crashed to his knees.

"Now!" yelled Evermore, and another rope went over Falada's neck, while Willard threw himself into the fray, pulling on the leg rope.

It took all their strength, and Cordelia darting in to pull a rope taut, but the familiar was well and truly bound. A rope ran from his hind leg to his neck. "Aye, that's right," rasped Old Bernard, slumped against the wall, while Hester pressed a cloth to his head. "Kick too hard and you'll break your neck, you bastard." He rolled his head slightly to look at Evermore. "Shouldn't have doubted you, lad. Whatever that thing is, it's only pretending to be a horse."

"And we aim to stop it," said Evermore. He straightened. Sweat dripped off his face despite the cool night air. "Bernard, I want the doctor to be sent for and you in a bed at once. Ladies . . . Tom . . . shall we?"

Falada's lips writhed as Cordelia stepped up to face him. The old man's blood had stained his pale lips. She wound her hands into his mane and leaned in close to him, just as she had a thousand times, ready to whisper her secrets and her frustrations into his ear.

"This is for telling my mother everything, you bastard," she whispered.

It seemed to take an hour for Willard to draw the circle, and then to draw the triangles to hold each of the participants. Falada's lip curled in clear contempt as he watched. Even in the terrible solemnity of the moment, she felt a flash of amusement as Lord

Evermore took the wine bottle and then patted helplessly at his pockets.

"Allow me," said Willard, ever proper, taking out a corkscrew. "And would my lord care to sniff the cork?"

Imogene and Hester barked with laughter. Cordelia recognized the slightly hysterical note and didn't dare start laughing herself.

When Willard finally closed the last triangle, he stepped back. "It is done," he said solemnly.

A goose made a very unmagical honking sound and pale shapes waddled out of the gloom. Cordelia laughed then, a hard, hacking sound, and bent her head.

"Will they break the circle?" asked Imogene warily.

"No," said Hester. "Look. They know what they're doing."

And indeed, the geese had stopped a few yards away, their necks tall, watching. "They're guarding us," said Hester. "That's what the sentinels do when the rest of the flock is feeding."

"I'm glad they're on our side, then," said Evermore. "What now?"

"Now each of us must focus on our reagents," said Imogene. It was too dark to read now, but she clutched the book anyway. The chalk was bright against the darkness of the stableyard, but not so bright as Falada. "And Cordelia recites the words."

"For how long?" asked Hester.

"For as long as it takes."

The words were easy. There were not many, and she had read them so many times that they were practically engraved on the backs of her eyelids. She took a deep breath and recited:

> *By my knowledge and my will*
> *By water, wine, and salt*
> *In the name of Hermes Trismegistus*
> *Let gold return to base metal*
> *Let all that glitters fade away.*

Her voice sounded thin and feeble against the darkness, and against the terrible light in Falada's eyes. Surely it was the depth of foolishness to think that mere words and the contents of a pantry could affect something like Falada. Surely this was merely playacting and the chalk outlines were the scribblings of some failed alchemist reduced to writing books instead of turning lead into gold.

Then Hester took a sip of water and the world changed.

Cordelia understood immediately what Penelope had meant. It did not ring, but there was no other word for what happened, for the way the air suddenly pulsed like a plucked string, for something that wasn't exactly a sound or a glow or a wash of heat to flow outward, one note that rang on and on, growing louder instead of softer. It rang over her, ignoring the chalk outlines as if they were nothing, pouring out of Hester like a waterfall.

Falada shrieked as the water-note struck him, throwing his head back until it lashed his flanks, no longer even pretending to be a horse. Cordelia realized that she had stopped breathing, which meant she had stopped chanting, and she started again immediately, "By my knowledge and my will . . ."

Imogene was next. The salt-note washed out from her and joined the water-note, the two forming a harmony that was stronger than either. Cordelia could *feel* Imogene and Hester in the harmony, as if she was inside the older women's hearts. She saw Hester's terrible fear of losing herself, whether to love or dependence, and it flowed like water. She tasted Imogene's darkness, the absolute ruthlessness that she kept under lock and key and only allowed to emerge when playing cards, and it tasted like salt on Cordelia's tongue.

If Falada had been a real horse, his anguish would have cut her to the core. The wooden post creaked as he flung his weight against it, twisting violently. It felt like mercy that his movements were so unnatural. She did not need to pity this pale, lashing thing that seemed to have no bones.

"By water, wine, and salt," she gasped, and waited for the wine-note to join the song.

Lord Evermore lowered the bottle, lips stained red . . . and nothing happened.

No, wait. Is that . . . ? Cordelia strained her senses and caught the faintest vibration, the shadow of a note that should have been rich. She could feel Evermore like the other two, but he was made of earth and stone and the wine-note was being washed away and the inside of his heart was a great hopeless love and she read his loyalty and his courage and that he was a good and decent man but his soul did not taste of wine at all.

Two notes rang against each other, but without their third, they died away finally into silence.

Falada stilled. He lay on the ground, his hind leg suspended in the air by the rope, and his flanks heaved. He closed his eyes, and then the familiar began to laugh.

CHAPTER 31

"It *almost* worked," said Hester.

"But it didn't work," said Imogene.

Cordelia said nothing. The sound of Falada's eerie, whining laughter still rang inside her skull, going on and on, long after they had left the circle. She hunched her shoulders against the memory of the sound.

Willard had dropped his jacket over her as they went inside. The smell of camphor and starch clung to it, but it was warm and Cordelia hadn't realized that she was cold until he did. Then she realized that her gown was torn and dirty and that both her gown and her skin were crusted with drying blood, and then everything began to seem like too much.

She didn't quite swoon, but she had no real memory of coming inside the house, or of entering the parlor, or of anything until a mug of tea was thrust into her hands. She wrapped her fingers around it and let the heat leach into her skin.

Willard and Lord Evermore and the stablehands were still outside. *Killing Falada,* she thought, and then amended it to *Trying to kill Falada.*

"Hang it all," said Hester. "I could *feel* it working. Why didn't it take?"

"Because Richard wasn't the right person," said Imogene. "It's in the damn book, except the author didn't feel obligated to do something useful, like underline it in red ink a few times. *Let he* who invokes the reagent be he who is best suited to the task, water to water, wine to wine, salt to salt."

"That's ridiculous," Hester said. "We're people, not elements. It's not like if you cut me, I'll bleed water. It doesn't make any sense."

Imogene unscrewed her flask and dumped a glug of something into her tea. "It doesn't have to make normal sense, it just has to make magic sense. And it does, sort of. We got two out of the three elements right, but Richard wasn't supposed to be wine. Couldn't you feel it?"

Hester pressed her lips together. "I felt *something*," she admitted. "Everything seemed to vibrate. But then it fell apart."

"I got a bit more than that. Cordelia?" Imogene nudged her shoulder. "Did you feel it too?"

Cordelia nodded. "I did," she croaked. Her throat was dry and she took a swallow of tea and nearly burned the roof of her mouth. "It was working, until Lord Evermore joined. And then it felt like the wrong note."

"He had the wine," said Hester obstinately.

Imogene rolled her eyes. "Nobody's saying it was your precious Richard's fault. You or I couldn't have done it either. We needed a different person for that reagent."

Hester grunted. After a minute she said, "Would it work, do you think? If we got someone who was actually like wine, whatever that means?"

"I think it might," said Cordelia. There was a buzzing in her head, but she couldn't quite focus on it. "Whatever we were doing, Falada was scared of it. At least at first."

"That damned horse," muttered Hester. "Or whatever it is."

The parlor door opened. Evermore and Willard came in, both exhausted. "It's dead," Evermore said. "They're burying it now." He paused, looking both triumphant and slightly sheepish. "I don't know if it was necessary, but we burned the head. It seemed . . . wise."

Cordelia felt something in her chest unknot. "Thank you," she whispered. Falada was dead. Relief crashed over her, so deep and sweet that she thought she was probably crying, but she didn't care. He was dead and he would never lie to her again. "*Thank you.*"

She climbed to her feet and stood, swaying slightly. "I think," she said, "that I am very tired."

"You were amazing out there," said Evermore. "You saved Bernard's life. The doctor's with him now. If you hadn't jumped in . . ." He reached out and squeezed her shoulder. "I'm in your debt," he said. "Really and truly in your debt."

Cordelia could not think of any response to that, so she smiled vaguely, and let Willard take her arm and lead her up the stairs. "Alice is waiting for you," he said. "I took the liberty of ordering a bath sent up for you as well."

She squeezed his arm. A few minutes later, Alice opened the door and said, "Mary's *tits,* what happened to you?," and Cordelia heard Willard say something over her head, but she couldn't focus on it. Whatever it was, Alice asked her no more questions.

She must have taken the bath because when she slid into bed, she was distantly aware that her hair was damp, but that was the last thing she knew until morning.

Cordelia? Cordelia, can you hear me?

The voice was loud and insistent and Cordelia was so very tired. The inside of her skull felt tender and raw. She rolled over in bed.

Cordelia! Am I doing this right? Oh blast, maybe I've forgotten how . . .

Her eyes snapped open. She knew that voice. "Penelope?"

Yes! Oh, thank god. I tried to talk to you last night—I think it was last night?—but you couldn't seem to hear me.

The odd buzzing in her skull the night before suddenly made sense. Penelope had been trying to talk to her, and she'd been too exhausted to understand it.

"You came here!" Cordelia whispered. "I thought you were afraid you'd get lost!"

Yes, and with good reason. I did get lost. A cinnamon smell of distress filled Cordelia's sinuses. *I thought I could follow the horse again, if I stayed far back. He shines like anything. But that woman was on his back, and after—Lord, I don't know how long—suddenly there were these strings coming out of her, wrapping around poor Samuel, and it was horrible. I got too close. I was trying to think if I could get the strings off him. But then it was like the church again, and she could see me, and I had to run away.*

"She must have been ensorcelling him," said Cordelia glumly. "Of course she doesn't have to worry now, they're already married, so there won't be more water, wine, and salt."

Seems likely. But once I bolted, I lost sight of the horse. Everything was just darkness, and sometimes little blobs, but they ran away when I came near. Animals, maybe.

I wandered like that for ages. How long has it been?

"A little over a week."

That's not so bad. Penelope laughed. *I was afraid I'd be like one of those people who go to sleep in a fairy hill or under the waves and when they come back out, a hundred years have passed.*

"Did you stumble in here by accident, then?"

No. I saw the . . . the ritual? The water, wine, and salt. It was so much louder than the one at the church. It blazed up like a burning city, and I saw it and went toward it. Another uneasy laugh. *I was afraid to get too close to it, but it didn't work, did it? Something went wrong. One of the notes was missing.*

"The wine-note." Cordelia tried to explain what she'd felt and what Imogene had said. "She thought—we thought—that Lord Evermore wasn't able to do it. He was the wrong sort of person. But we don't know who the right sort is."

Of course he isn't. If you need someone with wine in their soul, he'd be exactly wrong. He's good and decent and reliable and if you told him that fun had been made illegal, he would bow his head and avoid ever having it again.

Cordelia choked on that description. "We need to find someone," she whispered. She could hear Alice moving in the next room, and suspected that she was about to lose her chance to talk privately. "Can you see if anyone here is able to do it? Is that something you can tell?"

I don't know, the ghost admitted. **You all look like blobs to me. I suppose I could wander around and see if any of you are wine-flavored blobs, though.**

"Do that," Cordelia begged, and then the door opened and she had to turn it into a cough so Alice wouldn't think she was talking to someone who wasn't there. She suddenly missed the water closet enormously.

"You're awake!" said Alice happily. "It's nearly noon, miss—not that anyone is expecting you anywhere, not after what you did last night."

What you did last night was a phrase that would strike terror into the heart of stronger mortals than Cordelia. She took a step back. "Last n-night?"

"You saving the old stablemaster!" Alice beamed. "It's all anyone's talking about belowstairs!"

"Um," said Cordelia. "What . . . what are they saying?"

"That horse went mad and went for Old Bernard and tore him up good, and you threw yourself over him until the lads could pull the horse off!" She grinned, the grin of someone whose social currency has shot up remarkably in the last twelve hours. "You're a hero, miss!"

"Oh god no," said Cordelia.

"Oh yes." Alice tackled her scalp with the hairbrush. "And here was me thinking last night that you'd been running through the woods and rolled through the mud. You might've said!"

"It wasn't like that," Cordelia protested. "I knew the horse, that was all. It wasn't . . . I didn't . . ." She pinched the bridge of her nose. "Is Old Bernard all right?"

"Oh, they say he's made out of wire and rawhide. He looks a sight, but Charlotte, who's stepping out with the second groom, she says the doctor stitched him up and as long as he doesn't get lockjaw, he'll just be short an ear."

Lockjaw. Could a familiar transmit lockjaw? Cordelia had no idea. It didn't seem like they should be able to.

By the time she was dressed and had a moment of privacy on the stairs, the ghost no longer answered her whispers. Cordelia went down to breakfast, trying to figure out the best way to explain to the others about Penelope.

"Your dead friend has been talking to me and I'm very sorry I didn't mention it before now" seemed somehow tactless, but she wasn't certain how else to phrase it. *Maybe I could . . . err . . . say that I only now heard her? Then it wouldn't look like I had been hiding it? Because I didn't* mean *to hide it, it was just that I didn't think anyone would believe me, and then everything was very . . . very . . .* She let that thought trail off because she wasn't certain how to describe the last few weeks, even in her head.

Dammit, she hated to lie to her friends. And it was probably just a bad idea. No, she should try to explain, and if they were angry that she hadn't told them sooner (and how could they not be?) she'd bear up to it. She deserved it.

She picked at breakfast. Only Hester and Imogene were down yet, although Willard joined them a moment later. Her stomach churned and she told herself sternly that she would not wait another day, these were her friends and she had already waited too long and dammit, they must *want* to talk to Penelope, of course they would, it was selfish to hold off just because she was scared.

She set down her napkin and opened her mouth and the door to the breakfast room slammed open.

Hester stopped in the middle of buttering a roll as Richard flung open the door. *He never gets that particular crease in his forehead unless there's a problem, and he never slams doors unless it's a big problem.*

"Something wrong?" asked Imogene. "You look like you've just drawn the queen of spades in a game of Bluebeard."

"I think you had better see this for yourself," said Richard. "All of you." He took Hester's arm and helped her to her feet. She might have protested that she could do it herself, but a look at his face made her think that they had bigger problems right now.

He led them around the back of the mews, to the pits where garbage was burned. "This is where they buried Falada," he said grimly. "I saw it myself yesterday morning."

He pointed.

Hester followed the line of his finger. She heard Cordelia make a soft sound of horror, but for a moment, she could not think why. The grave had to be around here somewhere, perhaps beyond that cattle wallow . . .

The presentiment of doom, which had been so quiet since she had acknowledged Lady Evangeline's presence, suddenly poured cold water into the chambers of Hester's heart.

It wasn't a cattle wallow. It had the same look to it, a wreckage of earth churned up by hooves, but far narrower and sloping downward. The far end emerged from freshly disturbed dirt, edged by a semicircle of grass. A few stray feathers lay scattered through the dirt, and Hester didn't need to look closely to know they came from geese.

"Hell and damnation," said Imogene. "He dug himself out."

CHAPTER 32

"He was *dead,*" said Evermore, when they had all retreated indoors. "We cut his head off. I used the axe myself. And then we burned it. His body can't have just dug itself out of the ground."

Cordelia put her face in her hands. "He's not a real horse," she said, through her fingers. Her mind was an empty horror. "He just looked like one."

"He's got no head!" said Imogene. She sounded more outraged than frightened, as if the notion of monsters going around without heads was a terrible social faux pas. "Things don't just walk around without heads!"

"Chickens, sometimes," offered Willard.

"That was not helpful, Tom."

"No, but I've already poured tea, so I'm afraid I've run out of helpful things to do at the moment."

"What if he's even less like a horse than we thought?" asked Hester, into the glum silence that followed. "What if he's like a ghost?"

Cordelia jumped, wondering if Penelope had seen what happened, but heard nothing. She resolved to ask her the next time she spoke.

"You can't cut off a ghost's head," Hester went on. "Or I suppose you could, but it doesn't do anything, because they're not using their head to think with. They're a spirit. All the thinking bits happen . . . I don't know, somewhere else. Another plane of existence."

"He was rock solid, though," said Evermore. "It wasn't a ghost that bit off Old Bernard's ear."

"But familiars are tame demons, aren't they? Or tame spirits, anyway." Hester rose to her feet, patting absently at her pockets. "Where's that book . . . I must have left it in my room . . . not that the author knew either. Familiars can touch things and move things in the real world, but that doesn't mean they follow the same rules as the rest of us."

"He doesn't have to eat," said Cordelia. "He can, I mean. I think he did when he was pretending to be a horse. But he doesn't have to."

Imogene yanked out a deck and began dealing cards so rapidly that several spun across the table and had to be rescued by Willard. "I feel like there's a big difference between not having to eat, and being able to gallivant around without a head!"

"*Is* he gallivanting?" asked Willard. "Has anyone seen him?"

"We'll know soon enough," said Hester, making her way to the door. "The geese will tell us."

It was a little after sunset. Hester sat on the little patio that led into the garden from her rooms. She was quite certain that the room that she had been given was not actually a bedroom, but a former parlor with the furniture moved out and a bed moved in. There were no stairs between it and the main floor, though, and only three down from the patio to the garden. Her knee was grateful for Richard's kindness. Her pride wasn't sure how to feel.

A single candle on the table was no longer enough light to read by, but Hester had stopped reading. She rubbed her eyes wearily. The books were exhausting to read. Sometimes, for a few minutes, she could pry some sense out of them, but then it would all fall apart into nonsense about immortality and homunculi and magnetic fields. The foolishness of it seemed to actually steal meaning from the other parts, until she was no longer sure that there was anything there at all.

Maybe I'm deluding myself that I understand any of it. Probably you have to be an alchemist or a member of a secret society or a scholar of ridiculous texts.

She stared broodingly across the low stone wall at the patio's edge. Only a narrow band of rosebushes separated her from the lawn, and across the lawn, the almost tropical lushness of trees. Normally she loved the woods that bordered Evermore House, but now they seemed oppressively secretive. Their green depths might conceal anything. Even a horse risen from the dead.

She reached for her wineglass. The glass door behind her opened. She didn't turn her head, hoping that it was Richard, suspecting by the lightness of the tread that it was not.

"I am right," said Imogene, "and I can prove it." She dropped a book on the table. "Prepare to be dazzled."

Hester stifled a sigh. It didn't surprise her that Imogene had managed to keep her focus. Being right was the one thing that she loved more than winning at cards.

"Very well," she said. "Dazzle me."

"I found a chart of alchemical correspondences. It's like the bodily humors, I think, only they've made it infinitely more complicated." She opened a book and shoved it across the table. "Look. It breaks down how they defined people as water, wine, salt, or . . . well, there's a lot of them, I'm afraid."

Hester picked up the book, realized she couldn't read it in the gloom, and was reaching for the candle when she froze.

There was a light in the woods.

"Imogene," she said, her own voice very calm in her ears, "look over there."

Imogene turned her head, just as the distant honking and hissing of agitated geese reached them.

Falada was coming through the trees.

"Oh no," said Imogene. "No, no, no." She rose to her feet, knocking over the chair.

Without a head to anchor the eye, the horse's outline had gone dreadful and alien, like a half-crushed spider scrabbling across the grass. The remains of his neck flopped limp and bloodless. Hester stood, frozen in horror, as the dead familiar scurried toward them.

She might have sat there until he actually reached the stone wall, petrified like a rabbit under a hawk's shadow, if not for the geese.

The flock landed heavily on the grass, led by the short-legged gander. Falada veered, trying to avoid them, but they struck at his legs, hissing and flapping. Suddenly he reared up, striking out, that bloodless neck flapping horribly, and the unmusical squawk of a goose in pain cut through the night.

It freed Hester from her paralysis. How *dare* this monster attack one of her geese?! She shoved herself upright, grabbing at her cane, as the flock scattered and the familiar came on, moving almost sideways, like a crab.

"What are you doing?!" Imogene snarled, grabbing her shoulder. "Get inside! It'll kill you!"

"The geese—"

"Can fly! *You can't!*"

Very much struck by this logic, Hester hobbled toward the door. Imogene snatched the book from the table and followed. They slammed the door behind them, and Imogene grabbed for the chest of drawers. "Mary! *Mary!*"

Hester's maid appeared in the doorway. "Eh? What's all the commotion?"

"Take the other end of this and help me bar the door," snapped

Imogene, getting a grip on the dresser. "I don't trust the glass to hold."

"Hold against *what*?"

"Mad horse," said Imogene shortly.

Mary's expression indicated that she thought the horse wasn't the only thing that had gone mad, but she grabbed the other end of the dresser and helped Imogene drag it. Hester grabbed the bell-pull and yanked on it until the servants' rooms must have sounded like a church belfry.

Crash! Glass shattered as something—*"something" my ass, you know what it is*—hit the door. Jagged silver rained down and the dresser was knocked back several inches. Mary screamed, as much in shock as fear. Imogene snatched up an ornamental vase and flung it in the direction of the door. Her aim was terrible and it smashed against the wall, leaving a dent and a second spray of shards.

Hester abandoned the bellpull and grabbed a chair, shoving it toward the broken glass door. Imogene hefted the second vase of the pair. On the patio, geese hissed and screamed and something thumped hard against the stones.

Then silence.

After a long, long moment, broken only by the surly mutterings of geese, Imogene lowered her vase. "Is it gone?" she whispered.

"What the hell is going on?" Mary demanded.

And finally, finally, someone answered the bell.

"Get Richard," Hester gasped to the shocked footman who burst into the room. "Tell him it's come back."

Cordelia lay in bed, her mind stuffed full of horrors. Falada wasn't dead. Or rather, he was dead, but it hadn't stopped him. He had dragged himself out of the earth and God only knew where it would end.

Can Mother raise the dead? Or is it because he's something else?

A spirit, like Hester said. She closed her eyes. *Please, god, let it be because he's a spirit. Because if Mother can make the dead walk . . .*

She could hear Evangeline's voice saying *I made you, just like I made Falada* and imagined being dead but still obedient, her body still walking and talking and simpering. Would she know? Would she still be trapped inside, screaming, while her mother wielded her dead flesh like a puppet?

Cordelia shuddered.

By the time that Lord Evermore had organized any kind of response, Falada had vanished into the woods again. Cordelia had thought to offer her help—not that she knew where he was going, but at least he wouldn't hurt her. She had seen Evermore holding Hester tightly, though, and Hester looked so gray and worried, and for once wasn't pushing him away, so Cordelia slunk off, unwilling to interrupt them.

The whole house was locked down. The doors were barred, the windows bolted, and no one was allowed outside. The word put around was rabies, even though no one had ever heard of a rabid horse attacking people. It was easier than trying to explain the truth.

Sleep seemed impossible, and when it finally came, there was no relief from the dread that crawled along her spine and soaked her skin with sweat. Instead she dreamed of a blackened horse skull looking down at her, its mouth opening and closing in a mockery of speech.

Hello, Cordelia, said Falada silently.

The surface of the skull was charred and pitted, and as she watched, bits of ash flaked off and tumbled away, leaving discolored bone beneath.

If only your mother could see you now, the skull said.

No, no, it's not real, this is a nightmare, he doesn't talk, he never *talked—*

Not to you. Your mother and I talk all the time. More ash flaked away and the jaw gaped open in a horrible approximation of a smile. I tell her everything, remember?

Shut up, shut up! Cordelia tried to put her hands over her ears but it didn't help because the skull was talking without sound, just as Penelope did, except that Penelope's voice was different—

Is it? asked the skull. Are you sure? Perhaps I'm the one who's been talking to you all this time. The jaw gaped wider, the long row of molars rising from charred gums. You know that you always tell me all your secrets in the end.

"*Shut up!*" screamed Cordelia, sitting up in bed.

"Miss?!" The door to her room was flung open, and she heard Alice blunder through, run into a piece of furniture, and curse. "Miss, what's wrong?"

She took a shuddering breath. Hands came out of the dark as Alice found her and gripped her shoulders. "You're having a night terror," she said, practical as ever.

"It was a dream," rasped Cordelia. "It was just a dream. It wasn't real."

"That's right. Do you need some tea?"

Cordelia took another breath and let it out. Her hands were cold with sweat where they gripped Alice's. "No," she said. "No, I'm . . . I'm fine. It wasn't real. I just needed to wake up, that's all."

"No wonder you're having nightmares, with monsters gadding about in the woods," said Alice. "Everybody belowstairs is in a tizzy about it."

"Oh dear. What are they saying?"

The maid snorted. "All sorts of nonsense. That the lord killed it and now it's a ghost horse back for vengeance, or that it's got the hydrophobia and Old Bernard's next." She rolled her eyes. "And one of the scullery boys says he saw it and it's got eight hooves and no head, like a big old spider. I don't believe a word of it."

"No, of course not," said Cordelia faintly.

"Do you want me to stay up with you, miss?"

She was tempted to say yes. If she was talking to Alice then she wasn't thinking about the skull's words. *It isn't true. It was a dream. He's not Penelope. That's just the nightmare talking.* But Alice had to get up very early, and it wasn't fair to keep her here half the night, just because the last few days had spilled over into Cordelia's nightmares.

"It's all right," she said instead. "It's over now. Thank you."

After Alice had left, she lay in bed, curled on her side, listening to her heart thudding in her chest, like the hooves of a running horse.

"I have good news and bad news," said Hester, when they had gathered together in the library the next morning.

"Please, god, give me some good news," said Richard. He had dark circles under his eyes that hadn't been there a week ago. Hester wanted to smooth them away. Unfortunately her news wasn't likely to do that.

"Imogene and I have gone through all the texts we can find, and we finally determined how they . . . err . . . *type* the individuals." She glanced at Imogene and added, "Imogene was right, I was wrong."

"Damn straight."

"So now we actually understand who is water, who is wine, who is salt."

"And who's a dozen other things," Imogene put in. "The alchemists recognize a vast number of elements, including fire, air, quicksilver, iron, stone, wood, sulfur, gold, lead, and tin. Fortunately for our purposes, there's some overlap. In theory, someone who was quicksilver could perform the wine part, and someone who was stone could perform the salt part."

"There's a chart of cross-potencies," said Hester. "It looks like utter balderdash, mind you, but here we are. It looks like we just got lucky getting two of three right."

Richard rubbed his forehead. "I don't pretend to understand, but I haven't understood any of this so far. So we can find someone to do the wine part, then?"

Hester and Imogene exchanged a look. "That's the bad news. Apparently nobody bothered to write down *how* you tell which is which."

Richard put his head in his hands and moaned.

"We're working on it."

"Something attacked one of the storage sheds last night," he said, straightening.

"Attacked?" Hester saw Cordelia sit up, suddenly alert. "How do you attack a shed?"

"As far as I can tell, they broke down the door with some kind of dull instrument. A mallet, say. Or hooves."

Cordelia's face blanched to the color of wet bone. "Was anything damaged?" she whispered.

"The contents were smashed. Jars broken, sacks slashed open. It was mostly gardening equipment, but it was thoroughly trampled." Richard's lips pressed together in a grim line.

"Falada," said Cordelia.

"Falada."

They sat in dead silence for a few moments. Willard shook his head. "Is there any way to find where he goes to ground during the day?"

"I've got the head gamekeeper looking. He knows these woods better than anyone. I'm hoping that perhaps it sleeps during the day—although why an undying headless horse has to sleep, I'll be damned if I know."

"We'll keep looking," Hester promised.

"I'll start sorting books looking for anything about alchemy," Cordelia offered.

"Please do." Richard sighed. "I have too many responsibilities today, but I'll join you when I can."

They put their heads down to work. Willard brought sandwiches, and Hester scoured books that seemed to be written half in some other language, trying to make sense of any of it. *"Arsenic is the most transformational of all metals, excepting only Quicksilver, and thus is it*

called the Swan, for just as the Cygnet becomes the Swan, so does Ar-
senic transform itself between the crystalline and the metallic" . . . *holy*
mother of God, what does this have to do with anything?

She leaned her head back against the back of the chair and
closed her eyes, wishing that the past two months had never happened. *Back when my largest concern was running out of the proper
color of embroidery floss. How lucky I was, and didn't even realize it.*

"I found something," said Imogene. "Sort of."

"That's good!" She opened her eyes.

"It requires access to a birth chart, aqua regia, a magnetic field,
and about two ounces of platinum. Also it takes thirty days."

The sigh that echoed through the library came from Willard,
but Hester rather felt it spoke for them all.

"Trial and error would work better," she said. "Have someone
stand in the circle and try to invoke the wine. I imagine we could
go pretty quickly that way."

Willard cleared his throat. "May I point out that forcibly involv-
ing those belowstairs in something that the Church would very
much frown upon is neither kind or wise?"

"I know," said Hester glumly. "I know."

Richard didn't return to the library until late that evening, and
when he did, he brought news that the head gamekeeper had been
found trampled to death at the edge of the woods.

CHAPTER 33

Sheets rustled as Cordelia slipped out of bed. She'd waited until the house fell quiet, and then she waited for what felt like hours until she'd gathered her courage to get up.

I have to do this. Falada killed someone. He's got to be stopped, and I'm the only one he won't hurt.

I think.

She shoved her feet into her boots. Surely the same rules that applied when you were alive applied when you were dead. Deadish. Dead-like.

Regardless, I have to try. I didn't try to stop Mother, and Penelope died. Falada's already killed the gamekeeper. I have to stop him, before he kills anyone else.

The floorboards creaked as she moved. She winced, trying to avoid the squeakiest bits, but every time she stepped aside, it seemed to wake an even louder squeak. Was it this bad during the day? *It must be. It's not as if someone comes in and tunes the floor at night. I just don't notice it when I'm not trying to be stealthy.*

She eased the door open and was just congratulating herself on shutting it with an almost noiseless click when Alice said "Miss?" and frightened her out of her skin.

"Don't try to stop me!" Cordelia said, which was exactly the wrong thing to say if she had any hope of brazening her way through the encounter.

Alice's eyebrows climbed toward the ceiling. "Stop you doing what, miss?"

"Um . . ."

Alice surveyed her charge's hastily donned clothes and put her hands on her hips. "Are you running away?"

"What? No!"

"If you're going to meet a man, if you'll forgive me saying so, you should probably look a lot happier about it."

Cordelia's mouth fell open. That thought hadn't even occurred to her. She didn't know what to do with it. "I'm . . . I wouldn't . . . I . . . I don't even know any . . ."

Alice leaned against the doorframe. "You could order me out of the way," she said gently.

"I could? Um." Cordelia swallowed. The pressure in her chest had built so high that she wanted to scream a little, but that would *not* be stealthy. She rubbed her sternum. "Could you . . . err . . . pretend you didn't see me? Please? It's important."

"All right," said Alice.

"Thank you."

"If you tell me where you're going."

Cordelia groaned. Alice put a kind hand on her arm. "Miss, sneaking out at night won't help your reputation one bit. If you're being blackmailed or if some fellow's asked you for a meeting, you just tell me and I'll help you sort it."

"It's nothing like that," said Cordelia. "It's . . . oh hell." She rubbed her forehead. "It's the horse," she said. "The one that's out there. I'm hoping to get it away from here. It knows me. It won't hurt me." She looked up into Alice's frankly skeptical expression. "It's my mother's horse."

"Ohhh . . ." Understanding dawned on Alice's face. "Oh, I see." She gnawed her lower lip, clearly torn, then nodded to herself. "All right. Pull up your hood. We'll take the servants' stair."

Cordelia's mouth fell open again.

"No one will notice you," said Alice. "If you go out the front door, everybody will notice. Come on."

She led Cordelia down the hall, to a narrow door set unobtrusively in the wall. It led down an equally narrow set of steps, and though the walls had clearly been whitewashed recently, they were covered in scratches and dark smudges from heavy use.

Halfway down, they passed one of the footmen, who was yawning. "You're up late," he said to Alice.

"So're you," she replied, while Cordelia huddled in her shadow.

"Ah, well. We're all at sixes and sevens, trying to chase down this monster horse in the woods." He scowled. "Tell the truth, I didn't half believe in it until I saw what happened to Gamekeeper Ross. Don't you be going outside alone. That thing's a killer."

"Hadn't planned to," said Alice. Cordelia tried not to look horribly guilty. She flattened against the wall to let him pass and he winked at her, which only made things worse.

Alice led them through the darkened kitchen. The fire was banked down to coals and cast an orange glow across the floor. "Be glad it's not a baking day," she murmured over her shoulder. "Someone'd be in to start the bread rising before long."

The kitchen led onto the kitchen garden, with its high stone walls to shelter the plants. At the gate, Alice stopped. "You sure it's safe to go alone?" she asked.

"Safer for me than it would be for anyone else," Cordelia said, which was true.

"Mmm." The older girl gnawed on a fingernail. "Thinking maybe I should go with you, for all that."

"No!" Cordelia bit back panic. The space in her chest was so full that any moment she would start shrieking like a steam kettle just to relieve the pressure. "You'll be in terrible danger. He won't hurt me, but he doesn't know you at all."

Alice sighed. "All right." Cordelia nearly wilted with relief when she added, "If you're not back by first light, though, I'm telling Lady Hester. So don't be gone long."

"I won't," promised Cordelia fervently, even though she had no idea how long it would take to get Falada away. For all she knew, she'd have to ride him clear to Little Haw, or worse, to the north where her mother was. Still, none of that mattered as long as she got the familiar away from anyone he could hurt. "At least, I'll try not to. And Alice . . ." She darted forward and hugged the other girl. "Thank you."

Before Alice could react, Cordelia opened the gate and slipped through it, into the night.

She'd worried that it would be hard to find Falada. It seemed like it was easy for him to vanish when people went looking. But either she was lucky or he was looking for her, because she was barely halfway to the tree line when she saw the glowing shape coming toward her.

"Oh god," she said, involuntarily, and bit the side of her hand to keep from yelling.

She almost didn't recognize him. She had known him her entire life, and would have sworn that she could identify him from a single hoof glimpsed under a stall door. But he moved wrong now, all his grace lost, his stride gone scrabbling and uneven. She didn't know if it was because his balance had changed, without the mass of his head, or if the severed neck muscles no longer flexed with each stride, but he was no longer a thing she understood.

Of course it's him, she thought, high and hysterical. *It's not like there could be* two *headless white horses walking the grounds.*

He galloped toward her and she flinched back and closed her eyes. She could hear his hooves on the ground and the crackle of twigs and her own breath going in and out like a bellows.

The geese were still watching him, she realized, hearing a low noise in the distance. Apparently they had learned not to get too close. Falada was no longer pretending to be polite. Now he meant to kill.

The noises stopped. She cracked her eyes open, and there he was, standing in front of her. She could see directly into the wound that gaped bloodlessly open at eye level. A single vertebra sprouted from the stump, splintered and broken from the axe wound.

He could not look at her any longer, but she still felt the weight of his regard bearing down on her, full of duty and mockery and rage.

"You have to stop," Cordelia said. Her voice sounded very small and thin in her own ears. "It's me you want. You have to stop hurting people."

Falada danced in place for a moment, side to side, then slowly extended one front leg. The other curled up and he bowed to her, a mockingly theatrical gesture, the meaning clear.

"Oh no," breathed Cordelia. "Oh no, no."

He stayed bowed before her, waiting. She swallowed around the lump in her throat. "Is that the deal, then? I get on your back and you take me away?"

He could no longer nod, but his whole body shuddered up and down.

You have to do it. It's the only way.

She bit the side of her hand again and muffled a scream with it. It relieved the pressure a little, like lancing a wound, but no more.

"All right," she whispered. "All right." She wiped her hands on her skirt. "We'll go, then."

She hated the ease with which she mounted. Years of muscle memory could not be so easily forgotten. She hiked up her skirts and flung herself up onto the familiar's back and for an instant, it was all exactly as it used to be.

Falada rose to his feet and turned deeper into the woods, taking off at a lurching gallop. Her balance started to slip and she grabbed instinctively for his mane. One hand caught hair. The other gripped a rucked flap of skin and then her fingers were plunging into something cold and sticky and she looked down and she had grabbed the edge of his wound and this time there was no muffling her scream.

Ohgodohgodohgod

She started to slide sideways, but Falada had always been pre-ternaturally sensitive and he moved with her, keeping her upright.

Then he was off again, his muscles heaving but his ribs unnaturally still. *Of course, he isn't breathing,* she thought, and then wondered if he had only ever been pretending to breathe.

Leaves slapped her face as he wound through the trees. A normal horse running through the woods could have injured its rider any number of ways—scraped her off on a tree trunk or run her into a low-hanging branch, say. Falada could not hurt her, but he clearly had no orders about making her uncomfortable. A twig landed like a lash across her cheek and she could not even see in the darkness to duck.

Her first instinct was to flatten herself along the horse's neck, but that did not bear thinking about. She gripped what was left of his mane with one hand and kept the other in front of her face. All her bravado about leading Falada away from Evermore House was exposed as foolishness. She was not leading him anywhere. *I have no reins. And where would I put a bit and bridle, even if I did?*

Did he ever really need to obey me, or was he just pretending all along?

No. She took a deep breath and fixed her gaze straight ahead. *No, I can't think like that. The important thing is that we're going away, so he won't hurt any more people.*

It lasted hours. It lasted years. On some level, Cordelia knew that it could not have been that long, for it was still full dark. Falada broke from the trees, into countryside she did not know, and when she looked up, the moon was still high overhead, a thin crescent smile sharp enough to draw blood.

On another, more fundamental level, it was eternity. She could not feel her feet. Her back throbbed from sitting upright without benefit of saddle or stirrups. Her fingers were numb with cold and at least once she looked down and saw that she was gripping the edge of Falada's open wound again and all she could feel was vague disgust.

This is nothing, she thought dully. *This will go on for days, maybe weeks. However long it takes us to reach my mother in the north. I wonder if he'll let me off to sleep, or wait until I collapse?*

They met no other people. Presumably Falada was avoiding them. She saw houses in the distance sometimes, clustered in little villages, but no people. *And what would I do if I saw one? Call for help?*

A dog came out of some unseen farmstead and began barking at them, high and panicky. Falada swerved toward it and it tucked tail and ran. Cordelia envied it bitterly for having a hole somewhere to hide.

The moon was most of the way down the sky when Falada swerved into another little copse of trees. Cordelia bowed her head against the onslaught of leaves, and then it stopped.

The familiar stood still under her. The world seemed to rock and sway in her head, but it too stopped moving.

Is he letting me rest? Cordelia thought, feeling a gratitude so piteous and nauseating that she moaned in protest.

A moment later, the flaccid stump of neck in front of her shuddered, as if he sought to turn his head.

"Cordelia," her mother said, from the shadows. "I might have known."

CHAPTER 34

"What a busy little bee you've been," her mother said. Her tone was light and her smile was amused and her eyes were as frozen as a glacier's heart. Cordelia recognized that combination. It had never been directed at her before.

"You're supposed to be up north," she said. She had thought that she was too exhausted to feel anything, but it seemed that terror was quite an effective antidote after all. "How . . . how are you . . . ?"

"Silly child. Did you think I wouldn't come as soon as I felt the spells on Falada start to break?" Evangeline shook her head. She pointed to the ground and snapped her fingers. "Down."

As if I'm that dog that ran away, thought Cordelia, sliding off Falada's back. Her mother's scent reached her nose, sharp and dry and green. Her legs buckled immediately and she fell to her hands and knees in last year's leaves. *Which I might as well be, for all the courage I'm showing.*

And what good would courage do you? she answered herself. *Particularly now?*

"Those damnable ships don't leave when you want them to," her mother said musingly. "Tides are the same, no matter how willing the captain is to please." She scowled at Falada, running a fingertip along the ragged edge of the wound. "Stupid beast, letting them do this to you. I'll have to build you a whole new body now. *Ugh.*"

Cordelia found that it was easier to simply stay on the ground. She fell over on her side.

A boot nudged her ribs. "As for you . . ." Her mother's lips compressed into a flat line, even as her voice stayed light and conversational. "I suppose you thought you could strip a few spells off him, replace them, and take him from me? Make him your familiar instead?"

Cordelia blinked at her mother in astonishment. "W-what . . . ?"

"It wouldn't have worked. The spells that go into a familiar are layered like an onion. You're luckier than you know." She laughed. "It's why I didn't let him anywhere near the church when we had the wedding. Even if it only took off the outer layers, it would have been inconvenient. Mind you, the layer for obedience to *me* is right at the center. If you'd gotten that far, he wouldn't be answerable to anyone at all. If you were *very* lucky, you might have gone too far and unsummoned him completely, but more likely he'd simply kill everyone. Of course, he wouldn't have looked much like a horse by then, so who knows what people would think had happened?"

Cordelia licked cracked lips. "He . . . he already killed someone . . ."

"Only one? My, you *have* been lucky, then." She slapped the familiar's flank. "Not lucky enough, though. I don't suppose it was the Squire's fool sister?"

Cordelia shook her head silently.

"Right. Up you get." She made a gesture and suddenly Cordelia was being pressed down, down into herself, and her body was rising and bracing her back against a tree trunk. *Obedient,* she thought, and wished that she could pass out.

Her mother bent down and began to rummage through a pack on the ground. "Now, let's see what that groom left in here . . . ah, here we go. Just the thing." She turned toward Cordelia, holding a penknife in one hand. "Now, then. You're going to tell me exactly what you were doing, and more importantly, who you told. Do you understand?"

Cordelia stared at the little knife in her mother's hand and thought, *What? Is she going to stab me?*

The obedience lapsed and she sagged against the tree. "I said, do you understand?"

I can't tell her anything. I won't. She can't read minds. "I haven't told anyone," she croaked. "It was all me. I wouldn't tell anyone."

Her mother sighed, looking disappointed. "*Try* not to be stupid, will you, dear? For me? Obviously you had help. You couldn't chop off a chicken's head, let alone Falada's. And he's already told me that there were more of you."

Cordelia gulped, her mind a blank. "I . . . I . . ."

"I can see we'll have to do this the hard way. *Really,* Cordelia."

Obedience gripped her again. She pushed herself back up. One hand went down, grabbed the edge of her skirt and lifted.

"Outer thigh, I think," her mother said, handing her the knife. "Your future husband won't see the scar until the wedding night, and it'll be too late by then."

She can't mean . . . she can't possibly mean . . .

Her obedient body rucked up handfuls of fabric, exposing her left leg. Her own hand set the blade against the skin a few inches from the knee.

"This hurts me more than it hurts you," her mother said, and then Cordelia felt the cold edge of the knife enter her skin.

She couldn't scream. That was the worst of it, somehow. If she could have screamed then she could have wedged the scream in between herself and the pain, but her body didn't scream, not even when the knife slipped, not even when she began sawing mindlessly away at her own flesh, cutting off a shallow triangle of skin and leaving a bloody flap that hurt and hurt and went on hurting, even after the obedience dropped and she dropped the knife and then fell over on her side, clutching her leg, and had no strength left to scream with.

"Tell me," said her mother, standing over her. "Tell me who knows."

Cordelia whimpered, curling in a tight ball around the pain, trying to contain it. There was nothing in the whole world except the pain and the choking smell of wormwood.

Fingers snapped next to her ear. "Cordelia," her mother said. "I don't want to have to get your attention again."

"It . . . it was . . . Lord Evermore," Cordelia gasped. She hated herself for saying it, but she needed to say *something* and it had been his estate, after all. She could hardly think through the pain.

Her mother groaned and ran a hand through her dark hair. "You had to spoil the engagement, too? *Really?*"

"I didn't . . . I . . ." Cordelia tried to think of something that her mother would believe. The pain made it hard to think. "He . . . he and . . . he . . . I . . ."

"Don't tell me you fell in love with him!"

The words were like a gift from heaven. The lie opened up in front of her and Cordelia plunged inside. "You were right," she whispered. If she pressed hard on the wound, it hurt a little less. "It's not like anything else I've ever felt. Being in love."

"Oh Cordelia." To her astonishment, her mother sat down next to her. "I tried to warn you. It's amazing, isn't it? But it doesn't last. And you do terribly foolish things when you're in love. And then you have to clean up the mess." She sighed, patting Cordelia on the shoulder. "I was certainly that way with your father."

"My f-father . . . ?" The words seemed as if they should be important, but Cordelia didn't have the energy to spare to care.

Evangeline sighed. "You're hardly the first to make a fool of themselves for a man, believe me. I was young and I thought he'd have to marry me. But he never even considered it, just sent me away to the country and sent me money to keep me quiet. I held out hope for far too long, but I was so very much in love."

A week ago, I would have cared so much about this. And now I can't make myself care at all. Cordelia made a choked sound that would have been shocked laughter if there wasn't so much pain in the way.

"By the time I finally realized that he was never going to marry me, you were toddling around and clinging to Falada's tail." Her mother shook her head. "I almost killed you, too. It's so impossible to marry up with a brat in tow. And were you ever grateful?"

". . . sorry . . ." whispered Cordelia, who had known her role in this play for a long time.

"I know." Evangeline stroked her hair. "And anyway, it will all come right, you'll see. You weren't a sorcerer and I realized that you could marry where I couldn't. Real money, not just sad little nobles like the Squire. I know it hurts now, but it'll be better this way. You'll see. Being wealthy is much better than being in love. If you'd ever been *really* poor, you'd know that." She squared her shoulders. "Now, who else knows?"

Cordelia swallowed. "He . . . he ordered the servants to help. It was in a book in his library. They didn't know what was going on, they just did what he said. Except the head gamekeeper." *He's safely dead, she can't do anything to him.* "Ev . . . Richard . . . told him. So he could help draw the circles. Then Falada killed him, and Richard chopped his head off." She began to cry, which didn't take any effort at all. "I didn't . . . I'm sorry . . ."

"I know you are," her mother said kindly. Evangeline picked up the penknife and tapped the hilt against her lower lip. "Now, are you sure you're telling me everything? Do you need another reminder?"

Cordelia cringed, desperately trying to think of something to distract her mother without getting someone else hurt. "Lady Imogene found the book," she said. "But she didn't believe it. She said it was nonsense." She closed her eyes, trying not to look at the knife. "She doesn't believe in sorcery, not really. And Lady Hester said that it's only good for cheating people buying livestock."

Her mother snorted. "Well, she's in for a surprise."

"W . . . what? What are you going to do?"

Evangeline put the knife away and relief poured over Cordelia like water. She felt like the worst kind of traitor. *I just sold out Lord Evermore and now it sounds like Hester too even though I was trying not to and I shouldn't have but it hurt so much . . .* Hot tears slid down her cheeks.

"Well, obviously Evermore must be dealt with. It's a shame, that's all. Such a good match. Still, the Squire says that he and that fool sister of his used to be in love, so it'll make perfect sense when she stabs him out of jealousy." Her mother sighed, shaking her head, and reached down to pull Cordelia to her feet. "And that way no one will expect a full year of mourning for a murderess. Yes, I think that'll work. Come on. Up, up. Time to deal with this before it gets too far out of hand."

Hester woke because someone was pounding on the door.

Her first thought was that no one ever pounded on her door. Mary would have gone after them with a tea tray if they tried. Maybe the house was on fire?

Her second thought was that Mary was still recuperating from her earlier encounter with Falada, had taken nerve pills and gone to bed. This did not rule out the house being on fire, but did explain why the pounding was going on.

Her third thought, as she swam toward consciousness, was that she wasn't wearing a stitch of clothing and Richard was curled up around her, snoring gently against the back of her neck.

Hester stared wide-eyed into the dark. She hadn't meant for that to happen. Come to think of it, she didn't think he'd meant for it to happen either. He had come to her room last night, hastily relocated to a small guest bedroom with more stairs but fewer glass doors, and asked if all was to her comfort.

"What, other than the monster terrorizing the grounds?" she asked dryly. "It's fine, of course. I'm hardly going to complain about the accommodations under the circumstances."

"Practical of you," he said, leaning against one of the tall bed-posts. "I'm sorry this has happened."

"Don't be ridiculous." She set aside the book that she'd been trying, and failing, to read. "I'm the one who brought all this to your doorstep. It's my fault you've lost a good man."

He frowned at her. "Nothing of the sort. I was the one who failed to keep my people safe." His shoulders slumped and he no longer looked the least bit boyish.

"Against a monster."

"Against anything. What good is it, to be a lord, if you can't protect the people who rely on you?"

His voice cracked on the last word, and Hester started to get up, knee be damned, and then he closed the distance between them and dropped down at her feet, pressing his forehead against her leg.

"Richard . . ." She ran her fingers through his hair, guilty and heartbroken. *This* is *my fault, even if he'd never blame me. I called him in to help me.*

And then, a colder little voice, one that sounded a bit like her grandmother and a bit like Imogene, said, *What utter tripe. The fault belongs to Doom and always has. It's her monster that's gone on a killing spree. If she hadn't murdered Penelope and ensnared Samuel, none of this would have happened at all.*

Richard turned his head to look up at her. He was not a man who wept easily, but there was a suspicious redness to his eyes. "I could have lost you yesterday," he whispered. "I keep thinking of that. You could have died before I even knew you were in danger."

"But I didn't," said Hester. She stroked back the silver at his temples. Poor Evermore. He was no one's image of a warrior. He liked books on culverts and had strong opinions about crop rotations. He spent his life mostly trying to make things a little better for the people who depended on him, and for fifty years, that had required nothing more than listening closely to their problems and hiring good people to implement solutions.

"But I couldn't protect you. Hell, I couldn't even help Bernard." His laugh was more of a croak. "I couldn't hold up my end of the ritual. What *good* am I?"

She pulled him up and wrapped her arms around him, sinking her face into the crook of his neck and smelling starch and after-shave. "I'm here," she said, because that was the only thing she could think of to say. "I'm safe."

When he started to argue—because of course he started to argue—she kissed him.

They were both ten years older. Hester turned out the lamp and was glad of the darkness to hide another decade's hard use. Richard didn't seem to mind. She wished that she could look at him without being looked at in return, but that would have involved more conversation and what they both needed right now was comfort, not to go around the old arguments again.

And it was comfortable. Quick and somewhat furtive, of necessity, but familiar. Her body hadn't forgotten anything in the past decade. Neither, it seemed, had his.

The real prize came afterward, when he held her tightly, and she heard his breathing slowly even out and his grip relax as he slept. She told herself that she'd stay awake. It wouldn't do to be caught abed with another woman's fiancé, for God's sake, even a fake and temporary one. People would notice. There would be gossip.

She told herself this very firmly, and then fell immediately into the deepest sleep she'd had in ten years.

The pounding on the door that had woken her was growing in intensity. "Ma'am!" someone called through the door. "Lady Hester! Are you there?"

Alice? Cordelia's maid?

Hester sat up. Her movement woke Richard, who "Whuzzh? Huh?," and then his eyes snapped open.

Hester put a finger to her lips, then called, "Alice? Is that you?"

"Yes, ma'am! Please, open the door!"

Richard, with unexpected athleticism, rolled off the bed and under it. Hester grabbed a dressing gown and went to the door, opening it a crack. "Good heavens, Alice, what time is it?" A thought penetrated the fog of sleep. "Is Cordelia ill?"

"She's gone," said Alice. "Off to stop Falada by herself." The maid's face was grim. "And it's nearly dawn, and she isn't back yet."

"Shit," said Hester, with feeling. "Get out from under there, Richard. It doesn't matter now."

CHAPTER 35

Returning to Evermore's estate seemed to take less time, or per-haps Cordelia simply slept through it. She couldn't believe that anyone in that much pain could sleep, let alone on horseback, but she was simply done in. Evangeline rode before her, so all she had to do was wrap her arms around her mother's waist and rest her head between her mother's shoulder blades. It wasn't good sleep, but it was better than being conscious.

Dozing like that woke a memory of being very young, too young to sleep apart. She remembered the feel of the sheets and the lumps of the down pillow, but mostly she remembered the smell of her mother's skin.

The same smell was in her nostrils when she lifted her head, thinking that she'd heard someone call her name. They were in the woods again and it was dark, but Falada did not let leaves slap Evangeline in the face. He picked his way to the edge of the wood and Cordelia saw a streak of light across the edge of the sky, yel-lowish as a fading bruise. Below them, lanterns moved across the lawn and the garden, swinging in the hands that carried them.

"Good," her mother murmured. "They're making this easy for us."

Cordelia was about to ask how when she heard her name again, thinly, being shouted in the distance. *"Cordelia . . . ? Are you there . . . ?"*

"Down you get," her mother said, sliding off Falada herself.

"That's Evermore nearest us. Now call his name, and make it convincing."

"I . . . uh . . ." Cordelia wondered what would happen if she screamed "Run away!"

He wouldn't listen. No one ever listens when you shout something like that. They just come running to see what you've done to yourself.

Her mother narrowed her eyes. Cordelia gulped. "Richard!" she shouted, hoping that using his first name would tip him off that something was wrong. "Richard, I'm here!"

The bobbing lantern turned their way. *"Cordelia!? Is that you?"*

Cordelia closed her eyes. *Here it is, the only brave thing I'll ever do . . .* "Don't come any closer!" she shouted. *"Mother's here—"*

Her mouth snapped shut so quickly that she bit her tongue. Blood filled her mouth and she couldn't spit it out. Couldn't do anything at all, but stand there, tasting copper and salt.

"I'm not surprised," her mother said. "Disappointed, but not surprised." She shook her head and clucked her tongue. "Really, Cordelia. You might have at least thought this through." She took out the penknife and pressed it into Cordelia's palm. "We'll discuss your behavior later."

Cordelia's body turned and stumbled toward Evermore. The wound on her leg cracked open and she could feel it leaking down her calf. "I'm so sorry," she called, her voice much too giddy. "I didn't mean to make everyone worry. I think I must have been sleepwalking. I've had the most dreadful nightmare."

Evermore halted and set down the lantern. His gaze flicked past her, to the edge of the woods. "Ah," he said.

Can he see Falada? Did he hear me warning him?

"I feel terrible for putting everyone through so much trouble," her voice prattled on. She felt her fingers clench on the knife.

And then—

Cordelia?

Penelope! She screamed the name inside her head, hoping that it was loud enough to hear. *Can you hear me? You have to warn Evermore! I've got a knife and Mother's in control of my body and she's going to stab him!*

I hear you, but I can't warn Evermore. He can't hear me. There's all these things on you, like ropes. Is that the spell?

It must be! Can you do something?

I don't know. I'm not sure I can—oh shit, she's right there, she'll see me—

Cordelia's mind echoed with a scream she couldn't voice. *No! Penelope, don't run away! You have to stop me!*

Her body drew closer to Evermore. He turned his head and called "I found her!" to someone closer to the house, then turned back to her. "You're sure you're all right?"

"Of course," she said, smiling. Surely blood had to be leaking out of her mouth. Surely he must *see* that something was wrong. "It was just a nightmare." She took another step forward.

Cinnamon flooded her sinuses. **I'm trying to grab the ropes but they're like glue. You have to fight it!**

Fight it? How did you fight something like this?

I fought back! She wanted me to stab him too and I wouldn't! You can too!

Evermore's eyebrows drew down and his mouth opened in surprise, but it was too little, too late.

Fight it! Penelope screamed in her head. **Fight back! It's your body, not hers!**

But it is *hers,* Cordelia thought miserably, lifting the knife. *She made it. She made me just like she made Falada, and she's used my body whenever it was convenient. I've only been allowed to have it because she lets me.*

You are not Falada!

Each word struck her like a blow, directly in the chest, where all her fear and hope and terror lived.

She was not Falada.

Falada had been her creature and when Cordelia had trusted

him, he had gleefully betrayed that trust. But Hester and Imogene and Penelope had trusted Cordelia, and she had not betrayed them.

Even when her mother had gripped her chin and stared in her eyes and demanded truth, she had not betrayed her friends.

I am not Falada.

I am not her creature.

I do not belong to her.

The knife rose and Cordelia felt her muscles straining under her mother's hand, eager to plunge it into Evermore's throat. She knew that she could not turn it completely, but she threw every ounce of strength she had into lifting *too* far, too fast, and when it snapped forward, she turned her wrist.

Even that motion felt as if she had set her shoulder to a mountain, but the knife missed his throat. Instead the blade skidded upward. Too slow, Evermore threw up a hand. The tip tore a line across Evermore's cheekbone and into his hair before he knocked it aside.

Blood poured down his face in a sudden torrent, just as it had from Old Bernard's. He grabbed her wrists—*Oh sure,* now *you do it, now that I've already stabbed you*—and stared at her, blinking red out of his eyes. "Why?" he asked, sounding not so much mortally injured as baffled.

"Because it's not *her,* you idiot!" Hester shouted, stomping across the lawn. "It's her mother controlling her! I told you—oh dear god, Richard, your *face!*"

I'm sorry! I'm sorry! I did the best I could! Cordelia's body stood motionless, not fighting the grip at all.

I know you did. I saw you.

"Damn it all," her mother said from the edge of the wood. Her tone was mild and slightly exasperated. "I suppose if you want something done right, you have to do it yourself."

Hester had been waiting with Imogene on the stone patio—the same one, ironically, where they had been sitting when Falada attacked. Imogene had convinced her, barely, that she would be better off leaving the search to people with functional knees, but she didn't have to like it.

The moment that she heard Cordelia call Richard's name, though, she snatched up her cane and bolted. Imogene had gone in to get tea, and a moment later she heard her friend calling after her, but she was already hobbling as quickly as she could toward Richard.

That isn't Cordelia. Cordelia never calls you anything but Lord Evermore.

She cast around desperately for another search party, but there were none nearby. Most of them had concentrated on the back of the property, near where the gamekeeper had been found. *Blast. Hold on, Richard, the cavalry is coming as fast as it can . . .*

She arrived just in time to see Cordelia slap at him and to see him grab her wrists in turn. It wasn't until she drew abreast of him that she realized it hadn't been a mere slap.

Dear god, there was so much blood. She yanked off her shawl and pressed it against the side of his face, trying to stem the flow.

And then the voice of Doom tolled across the grass like a bell.

"I suppose now that you're both here, it'll be easier," she said. "Hester, I'll need you to stab Lord Evermore."

Hester spat the filthiest word she knew in Doom's direction.

Evangeline rolled her eyes and thrust out her hand, and Hester's world turned the color of pain.

It came from everywhere, burrowing into her skin like shards of glass. It was a sea of agony, and she was drowning in it. She went to one knee, clutching her cane to keep from falling full length on the ground. She did not scream—she had always been too proud, even now that she had so little left to be proud of—but her breath went out in a long hiss and it was gruelingly hard to draw the next one.

"Meddling old spinster," said Evangeline, turning away. She frowned at Cordelia. "Is this who you want to replace me with? These useless old women? This is how you repay me, for all that I've done for you?"

Cordelia could not have replied, even if she wanted to. Her jaws were locked tight, and her muscles shook with strain, but under that, she felt triumph.

For an instant, when her mother had turned and thrown magic at Hester, the obedience had slipped. Not completely, not enough for her to run away, but just enough for her to open her fingers, sending the knife clattering into the ground. In her head, Penelope crowed with delight.

Evermore dropped Cordelia's wrists. She doubted he'd even realized that she'd dropped the knife. "*Hester!* Hester, love—" He grabbed for the kneeling woman's shoulders, missed, and crumpled to the ground as Evangeline flung a hand at him.

The honking of outraged geese suddenly filled the air. A heavy body landed on the grass, then another, both birds hissing in rage but not quite daring to approach.

"Ughh," Evangeline muttered, massaging her temples. "*Why* does nothing ever go smoothly? Cordelia, finish the job."

Cordelia's body marched toward the downed pair, lifted a fist— and stabbed down with knifeless fingers, hitting Evermore's shoulder blade.

Evangeline let out a short scream of frustrated rage, like a hawk that had struck for prey and missed. "*Really!?*"

She's trying to do too much! Penelope said, her mental voice breathless with excitement. **She did something to both of them, but it's like she's running out of ropes. There's fewer on you now, too.**

Cordelia tried to fight back against the obedience and actually managed to take two steps away from Evermore. Her mother snarled and the obedience tightened on her again. "Where is that damn knife?"

Of course, Cordelia thought, almost dreamily. *If she wants to make it look as if Hester stabbed Evermore, she can't just have Falada trample them.*

I'd rather no one got stabbed or trampled. I have decided that

the fashion this season is for being flung off balconies, thank you very much.

Evangeline froze abruptly. "What is that?" she hissed. "Is that *you,* Cordelia?" She spun in a circle. "Something's here. I feel you. Are you another sorcerer?"

I think she finally noticed me.

Cordelia flung herself against the bonds of obedience again. Her mother shook her head like a horse trying to rid itself of a fly. "What—how—no, I killed you, I know I killed you—"

Something moved behind Evangeline. Cordelia jerked her chin up an inch, trying to see.

"You think a little pain is going to stop me?" rasped Hester, and brought her cane down on the back of Cordelia's mother's head.

Cordelia's muscles went slack as the obedience broke. She managed to keep from falling on either her mother or Hester, but only just.

"You hurt?" asked Hester gruffly.

"Yes," said Cordelia honestly, "but it doesn't matter. We have to get out of here now. Before—"

Falada erupted from the trees, accompanied by the screams of geese. Cordelia spun around, saw the headless horse charging her, knocking birds out of the way like matchsticks. From the corner of her eye, she saw Hester lift her cane, standing over Evermore like a protective bird herself.

This is it, Cordelia thought. *He tramples everyone but Mother and me. She might have had something fancy planned, framing Hester for murder, but it's just going to be hooves.*

She stepped in front of Hester and Evermore, wondering how long she could keep them safe.

And then a voice, familiar but deathly cold, said, "Horse, I know you understand me. Stop where you are, or I cut her throat."

Between one stride and the next, Falada stopped. His hooves

tore great gouts out of the turf and his hindquarters dropped nearly to the ground. Geese shouted and honked, rising to their feet. The short-legged gander was up immediately, hissing like a cobra.

Lady Strauss crouched over the unconscious form of Evangeline, holding a large pair of scissors to her throat. Cordelia recognized it absently as the one from Hester's embroidery basket. Imogene's breath was coming in ragged pants and her hair had come out of its bun and fallen into her eyes, but the scissors didn't waver. "That's right," she said to Falada. "Back up. Everyone else is too damn decent, but I'll kill her with a glad heart. Back up."

Falada retreated, step by step, to the edge of the woods.

"What happened?" asked Evermore groggily. Hester wiped at the blood on his face and made an unhappy sound.

"Evangeline took over Cordelia and stabbed you, then hit you with . . . I don't know what that was. Very unpleasant, if it was anything like mine." Her voice dropped. "Now she's unconscious, Imogene's got a knife to her neck, and we're trying to figure out what to do next."

"Why don't we just kill her now?" asked Imogene. "We'll throw her in a well and say she never arrived here at all." She looked from face to face. "If you're all too squeamish, I'm certainly not."

"Because we don't know what kind of spells she's got on my brother now!" Hester snapped. "Believe me, I'd put a knife across her throat myself if I knew I could do it safely. But I don't want my brother turning out like Parker, and if that means her magic has to be broken before we kill her, that's what we're going to do!"

"I believe we shall have to do the ritual again," said Willard. He looked immaculate despite the hour, and despite having sprinted across the lawn toward them. Alice, beside him, was staring round-eyed at everyone. "I suggest we do it as soon as possible, in fact. *Before* the lady wakes up."

"We don't have anyone to stand as wine," said Richard. He clutched Hester's shawl to the side of his face, the cloth already turning scarlet. "We can't do it unless someone can be wine."

They looked at each other helplessly, and then Penelope said, *I can.*

"It'll kill you!" protested Cordelia. "You said it felt like you were being washed away!"

It can't kill me, I'm already dead. Maybe it'll just send me where I'm supposed to be.

"But—"

Look, I never did anything noble while I was alive. I was vain and shallow and exceedingly lazy. I might as well take one last stab at it.

"Cordelia?" said Hester. "Who are you talking to?"

Oh hell. "Penelope's ghost," said Cordelia. She held up a hand. "I know. I *know.* It's . . . look, I wanted to tell you but then I thought she hadn't followed us and we were so busy looking through the books and then she *was* here but then Falada dug himself up and there's . . . there's been a lot going on . . ." She trailed off, aware of how weak that sounded.

"I'd like to yell," said Imogene, "but this hardly seems like the time, does it?" She grimaced. "Willard, can you take the scissors? My hand is getting a cramp."

"Certainly, Lady Strauss."

"And promise you'll kill her. No gallantry, now."

"Madam." He frowned at her. "I am a *butler.* Do you truly believe that I do not know how to dispatch a houseguest if required?"

Imogene grinned, looking shockingly feral. "I always liked you, Willard. Now, as for ghosts . . ." She shook out her hand, turning to Cordelia. "Are you sure it's really Penelope?"

Cordelia listened for a moment, then said, "Uh . . . she says to remind you of what she told you on your wedding night about the—"

"*Right,*" said Imogene hastily.

Tell them, said Penelope. *I can do it.*

Please.

Cordelia swallowed. "She says she can do the wine part of the ritual."

"Do it soon," said Willard. "I believe Lady Evangeline's starting to come around."

"Already?" Imogene bared her teeth. "Hit her again."

"It might kill her."

Imogene looked ready to argue. Willard frowned, then closed his hand over Evangeline's throat. His lips moved as if he was counting to himself. When he reached twenty, he released his hold and Evangeline sagged, her face flushing bright red.

"You have some very unusual skills," Lord Evermore observed, slightly muffled by the bloody shawl.

"As I said, I am a butler. Now, may I suggest that you perform this ritual immediately?" asked Willard. "I do not know how long I can prolong her unconsciousness without causing serious damage."

"But we can't perform it," said Imogene. "We don't have the circle and the symbols and the triangles and all that."

She doesn't need it. They don't do anything. They aren't real. No more than any other drawing, anyway. And the church didn't have them.

"But we don't have a church either!" said Imogene, when Cordelia relayed this. "We need holy ground. That's how it *works.*"

"No." Cordelia pinched the bridge of her nose. "No, it's not. You said it yourself, ages ago. You said that maybe holy ground was only holy because people believe in it."

Imogene's angular face drew into sharper lines as she frowned. "I suppose I might have said that, but—"

"The lines don't do anything." Cordelia waved her hands, trying to get the words out. "They're just there to make you believe they do something. You believe in it the way you believe in holy ground, because they're all twisty and impressive, but that's all they do. I didn't feel them do anything and Penelope didn't feel it and Falada laughed when he saw us drawing them!"

"So we need to find a church?" said Hester.

"*No!*" It was so clear to her but she didn't know how to make them understand. "You just have to believe this is holy ground! Right here! Or magic or consecrated, whatever you want, just believe it!"

They all stared at her as if she'd lost her mind. "Penelope says I'm right," she said weakly, quailing under the weight of all those looks.

"We can't all just believe something on command," said Imogene.

"The hell we can't!" Hester snapped. She wheeled on Imogene. "You've seen sorcery and a dead horse walking and you felt the magic when we did it earlier, and *this* is where you draw the line? That *this* ground isn't holy enough?"

Imogene swallowed. "Well," she said. "When you put it like that, I guess . . ."

"You all believed my mother was a lady," said Cordelia. "There was no proof of any of it. You just believed it and you introduced her to other people that way and that made it true. It's all the same!"

Hester nodded. "Alice, bring us water."

"But miss, I don't have a bucket or—"

"Soak your skirt in the lake. We don't need much, but we don't have time. *Run.*"

Alice sprinted.

"We also don't have any wine," said Imogene. "Do we have time to get it?"

Evangeline mumbled something, her eyelids fluttering.

"No," Willard said.

"Don't you tell me you don't have a flask of brandy on you, Imogene," Hester said. "I've known you too long."

"Brandy isn't—no, wait, I suppose it is wine, isn't it? Wine that's, err, gotten ambition." Imogene laughed, half-incredulous. "It'll do." She handed it to Cordelia.

"Can you see this?" Cordelia asked the air above her, dumping brandy into her palm.

I can't—no, wait! Yes! There! I can see it!

"Cor . . . del . . . ?" Her mother shifted. Willard tightened his hold.

"I suggest that you do not move, madam," he said.

"My . . . head . . ."

Cackling alerted them to Falada shifting position again. "Don't do it, horse," called Imogene.

"Salt," muttered Hester. "Salt, salt, how do we . . ."

"Don't worry about that," said Imogene, with another feral grin. "We're all full of it."

"What?"

Alice returned, holding a bundle of sodden fabric. Her undershift, Cordelia thought. She dropped it into Hester's hands with a wet splat.

Cordelia passed the flask to Alice. "Pour this into your hands," she said. "A little at a time. And don't drop it."

Alice met her eyes, and Cordelia was struck by the memory of the older girl saying "It will be all right."

It will, she thought. *But only if we can make it so. Right here, right now.*

She drew a deep breath and began to speak.

> *By my knowledge and my will*
> *By water, wine, and salt . . .*

Hester squeezed water from the cloth into her mouth, and the water-note rang out, loud and clear, filling the space around them.

> *In the name of Hermes Trismegistus . . .*

Crimson bloomed on Imogene's face as she bit savagely into her own lower lip. Cordelia remembered the taste of salt in her own mouth. Would it be right? Was it enough for alchemy?

Apparently it was, or perhaps more than the sigils was based on belief. The salt-note came in, thin at first, but gaining strength, echoing off the water-note, the two of them a harmony that grew louder, calling for the third.

Let gold return to base metal . . .

She waited for the wine-note in hope and dread. Perhaps a ghost couldn't do it. Perhaps brandywine wasn't enough. Perhaps Penelope had thought better of things and fled.

And then Alice jerked, as if someone had grabbed her outstretched hand, and the wine-note flooded the air around them, so loud and so strong that it drowned out not just sounds but smells and colors and the feeling of the grass under Cordelia's knees.

Let all that glitters fade away . . .

Water, wine, and salt came together in a harmony that spiraled outward and became a whirlwind. Cordelia could feel that wind pulling at her, stripping away things that she hadn't known were there, as if it sought to refine her down to her very essence, or possibly just down to bone.

"No," said a small voice in the center of the maelstrom. Her mother, struggling to lift her head. Willard was a shadow behind her, his knife hand slack as he battled to keep his own footing in the storm.

"By my knowledge and my will," Cordelia repeated. "By water, wine, and salt."

"*No!*" Evangeline thrust out her hands toward her daughter. Her voice was a harsh croak. "Stop! He's too close! You're going to unmake it all!"

"In the name of Hermes Trismegistus—"

"I won't be able to hold him!"

"Let gold return to base metal—"

Her mother lunged. Willard grabbed for her shoulders, too late. Evangeline's eyes blazed the blue of the hottest part of the flame and she flung herself at Cordelia, reaching for her daughter in a parody of an embrace.

It didn't hurt. Nothing hurt. That must have been the wind, drowning out pain as effectively as everything else.

Cordelia wrapped her arms around her mother. She could smell that scent again, her mother's skin, unforgettable. Perhaps she was very small again. Perhaps the wind had washed away the last fourteen years and they could start again.

It was a pleasant thought. She held it for a moment, then let it tumble away into the roaring of the whirlwind. Not even alchemy could change the past.

"*He'll kill us,*" Evangeline wailed.

Cordelia turned her head so that her lips were close to her mother's ear, and whispered, "Let all that glitters fade away."

In the last instant before the wind tore away consciousness as well, she heard a voice say, **Tell everyone goodbye.**

CHAPTER 36

"Easy," Richard said. "Easy, love."

Hester opened her eyes to the face she loved most in the world, which was, frankly, a horror. The knife had opened up his cheek, and if there hadn't been so much blood, she expected that she'd be looking at his molars. But his eyes were still familiar, brown and deep-set and full of concern, and she clutched at his arm and let him help her to her feet.

For once, her knee wasn't the thing that hurt most. It was her throat. She'd sung the water-note somehow—or something like singing—exhaled it, maybe, or had it pulled out of her. While it had been happening, she hadn't felt it, but the instant the strange wind dropped, she felt as if she'd drunk boiling lye. She rubbed her neck, not that it did any good. *God, if only I could grab the inside of my neck . . .*

She noticed that Imogene was doing the same. Cordelia and her mother had been knocked flat by the wind—if it had been a wind—and Willard was crawling toward them.

"I guess it worked," Richard said.

Hester rasped out a laugh, which only hurt worse. Yes. It had worked. She'd felt it work. She'd felt the wind lashing out, stripping away magic in great ragged sheets and sending it flying like shingles in a hurricane.

Willard got Cordelia to her feet. Evangeline was still lying crumpled in the grass, but not like a corpse. Hester could see her ribs moving as she breathed.

And what are we supposed to do with her now? Maybe Imogene was right, maybe we should kill her and dump her down a well—

The geese screamed. Richard spun around, dragging Hester with him, and she had a confused impression of the flock scattering, feathers erupting as they fled, not fighting but shrieking in absolute terror as they went.

Then she saw it.

Him.

Falada.

No longer a horse at all, but something else. He still glowed the same too-bright white, and his eyes were still green, but there were too many eyes and his legs had too many joints and his rib cage had cracked apart and the rib bones jutted up like teeth set in a jaw and then a tongue licked across them, rubbing lovingly across the points.

Richard laughed, the short, disbelieving laugh of a man witnessing the impossible.

Falada laughed back.

Evangeline sat up.

The familiar ran toward them. His leg joints rippled like a centipede and if Hester had had any time to think, she would have been sick, but it was all happening so fast. Now Falada was becoming strangely transparent, his skin turning to milky glass, and she could see the shadows of viscera inside, pulsing.

Evangeline thrust her arm out in front of her, the same gesture she had made at Hester. Falada did not miss a step. "NO!" the former sorcerer shouted. "Go back! I command you! I banish you! *I—*"

Bones crunched as Falada struck her. Hester twitched in Richard's grip. The sound was so loud and so wet and it kept happening because Falada did not stop. He was *dancing* on top of the dead woman now, his hooves—if they were still hooves—hammering her into the dirt, as if determined not just to kill her but to bury her forever.

At last, he stopped. The dawn light streamed through him, casting strange, bobbing shadows on the grass. He might have been a stained-glass-window monster, the sort that lay brooding and defeated under the sandals of a saint.

The familiar swung from side to side, perhaps looking for his next target. Cordelia hung limply between Willard and Alice. Imogene had, perhaps wisely, gone flat against the ground.

Sickly green eyes locked on Richard and Hester.

There was no fear left in her. The wind had driven it all away. All she felt was a brief pang of regret that she had been such a fool about Richard. She could have spent every night of the last decade in his arms, and instead she'd been afraid of what? That he would stop loving her when she grew old?

Doesn't seem like either of us will get the chance now, does it?

Richard pushed her back, trying to interpose his body between her and Falada. A brave, generous, utterly futile move. She suspected that he knew it as well as she did.

Falada stamped one many-jointed leg. She could see the grass rippling through it, only slightly distorted.

Was the familiar fading somehow? Had Evangeline managed, at the end, to banish him after all? Or was this some kind of further transformation, into a monster made of teeth and crystal?

Please, god, let him not become invisible on top of everything else. None of us will stand a chance.

Falada moved. He *was* fading, Hester was almost sure of it. Parts of him were little more than suggestions of light in the air. But not fast enough.

Richard squeezed her hand fiercely and let it drop. He took a step forward, as if to meet the monster, and put up his fists in a useless schoolboy boxing stance.

"No," Hester croaked through her raw throat. "Don't—*no*—"

Falada charged.

Something honked. Loudly.

The fading familiar shied back as the short-legged gander flew into his face, wings beating madly. They struck the clear-glass legs and passed through them, as if Falada were made of jelly. The monster reared up, striking out with things that might have been mandibles or teeth or tongue. One caught the gander's wing and sent him spinning out of control, to crash in the grass with a grace-less squawk.

Falada turned back and his rib-cage mouth cracked even wider, and he lunged forward, a fraction too late.

His last cry turned to a whisper as daylight poured between his jaws, and the familiar was gone.

One Week Later

"So was that thing a demon, then?" Lord Evermore asked, as they all sat in the parlor together. The windows were open and the air of late spring—or possibly early summer—shone through. Cordelia could hear birds and, distantly, the shouts of the laborers restoring the road to the manor house.

Except for the massive scar down Evermore's face and Hester's new wheeled carry-chair, none of them looked different. Cordelia found that surprising, somehow. She felt about a thousand years old, and had been surprised that the face in her mirror still only looked fourteen.

Alice and Willard had a very brief scuffle over who was going to pour the tea, which Alice won, because butlers—even butlers officially on holiday—did not pour tea for maids.

"I don't know if Falada was a demon," Cordelia said, when the tea had been passed around. "He might have been. I'm afraid I re-ally don't know very much about sorcery, when you get right down to it. Moth . . . Evangeline . . . never told me much. I think she was afraid I'd try it myself."

"Reasonably so," said Imogene tartly. "If a ghost could see you, that probably means you had some kind of gift."

"It's gone now," Cordelia said. "It went away along with everything else in the ritual." She suspected that Imogene had not quite forgiven her for not telling anyone about Penelope's presence. A week ago, she might have cringed away from the notion. Now she simply sipped her tea. She'd apologized, and there was no way to make amends now. She hoped that Imogene would forgive her someday. She owed the other woman far too much.

"At any rate," Cordelia continued, "she did say that the spells on familiars were layered like an onion. So my guess is that the ritual pulled away the one that kept him looking like a horse, and then the one that made him obedient, and then finally the one that kept him here."

"The last one took its own sweet time taking effect, then," said Hester.

Cordelia frowned into her teacup. "Maybe," she said slowly. "Or maybe Falada was trying to stay here as long as he could, and just ran out of strength." She thought of Penelope trying to communicate with her, and how sometimes she would simply drop out completely, unable to stay in contact.

"For revenge," suggested Imogene. "Well, I can see why he'd want all of us dead, particularly Richard. You *did* chop off his head."

Richard smiled, then winced as his scar pulled a little. "I did."

"What I don't see is why he wanted to kill Evangeline so badly. He was her pet."

"That was why, I think." Cordelia set her teacup down, and was pleased that her hand barely shook at all. "I hated being obedient, but she only did it to me sometimes. Falada was obedient all the time. Maybe not quite the same way, but he was completely under her power. Not even his shape was his own." She shook her head. "I hated him, but I feel sorry for him, too. I think he enjoyed some of the things she had him do, but he always wanted to get away. He just wanted to do as much damage as he could before he went."

Hester grimaced. "I can't feel sorry for him. That thing I saw at the end . . ."

"I was unconscious for that bit," Cordelia admitted.

"Whatever it was, it sure wasn't from around here," said Alice. She shuddered. "I'm never going to stop seeing that thing. Those teeth—or whatever they were—ugh."

Imogene snorted. "I imagine he thought we looked just as horrible, poor devil. Or demon, or whatever he was." She shook her head. "I don't know. I'm going home tomorrow, to sleep in my own bed and listen to my own son talk my ear off about horses."

"And what are you going to tell Lord Strauss?" asked Hester, smiling into her teacup.

"As much as I can without sounding like I'm raving. God knows how much that will be." She shook her head. "Hester, my dear, the next time you throw a house party . . ."

"Leave you out of it?"

"Certainly not. But do invite another card player, will you?" She brandished a card menacingly. "Otherwise I'll insist you play with me, and it won't be for penny stakes this time."

"What troubles me," said Willard, clearing his throat, "is how little we knew about what we were doing. It seems to me that we came extremely close to disaster." He tapped his fingers on the arm of the chair. "I wonder if the world might benefit from an updated monograph on dealing with sorcery?"

"Willard," said Richard warmly, "you are a man after my own heart. I was just toying with the notion myself. Granted, my previous writings have all been on the subject of culvert design, which is perhaps a specialized field, but I do know one or two publishers who might be willing to print up such a monograph, if you and I were to write one."

The butler considered this. "Well," he said. "As it seems that I have been rehired at Chatham House—and the Squire was clearly puzzled as to why I left at all—I do not know how much time I will have to devote to such an endeavor. Nevertheless, I might be able to make a start." He lifted his teacup. "I am, after all, on holiday."

"Is there room for another here?" asked Evermore, later that day, joining Hester on the patio. She was sitting in her new carry-chair, experimenting with how far she could move herself. She still required someone to push the chair any great distance, which galled her, but she could manage to get around a room, slowly. And there was no denying that her knee hurt less.

"By all means." She waved to the other chair. "Though I'd keep hold of your glass. I keep ramming into the table on accident."

"The doctor assures me that this is the very latest and most maneuverable model."

"Possibly, but that doesn't mean it corners very well." She huffed. "Perhaps I'll get a very small pony and hitch it to the front."

"Your entrance to the assemblies in town would be *extremely* dramatic."

"Assemblies. Lord." She rubbed her forehead. "It seems so unreal, after everything we've been through, that we might go and stand around and drink weak punch and watch people being cutting to each other. What's the point?"

"What was *ever* the point?"

Hester grunted. On the lawn, the geese waddled past, led by the short-legged gander. His wing had been broken and despite bandaging, he was unlikely to fly again, but that did not seem to bother him much. She'd already seen him mount a much taller lady, who seemed quite pleased with the attention.

I suppose the bloodline will simply have to endure being shorter. If anyone asks, I will tell them that I am breeding for heroism.

"I had a question for you," said Evermore finally.

Hester felt a knot of tension build under her breastbone. Something about the way he asked seemed important.

Is he going to ask me to marry him again? After everything?

What will I say if he does?

She suspected that Samuel had seen it coming. When she had spoken to him last, shortly after the hurried funeral, he had implied as much.

"Odd sort of thing," Samuel had said. "That horse of hers! Who'd have thought it? Such a well-mannered beast, and then to turn on her like that."

"I know."

"Never a word about it, and then what should she do but get a flash of women's intuition or some such and demand we come home by the next ship. And then she went haring off to Evermore's without telling me, and look what happens."

Hester stroked his cheek. "Are you sure you're all right?"

"Oh, well." Her brother made a *hrrrmph* sound and looked away. His eyes were a little too bright, but that was all. "Whole thing seems like a dream now. A few beautiful months, and now I'm right back here, same as I always was." He shoved his hands in his pockets. "Feels like it would hurt more if we'd had longer together. Now it's just like she left at the end of the season. I miss her, but nothing's changed here. Does that sound very bad of me?"

"I think it sounds very sensible."

"Bah. You've always been the sensible one, Henny." He smoothed down his mustache. "And you needn't worry I won't do my duty by the girl. She's a shy little thing, but she's my stepdaughter now, and I'll see that there's a dowry settled on her that won't shame anyone. Since it seems like Evermore won't be coming up to scratch after all." He gave her a sly look. "Or am I wrong?"

The version of the story that had spread was that Evermore had been wounded protecting Hester from the maddened horse that had killed Lady Evangeline.

Not that the wound was *that* significant. Hester studied the side of Richard's face. The edges had only just started to heal, and it would certainly be a raw pink slash, but his eyes looked just as they always had, and who would notice a scar on anyone with eyes like that?

Richard raised an eyebrow at her, tilting his head. "Admiring my war wound? I'm told women find such things irresistible."

"If you're going to ask me to marry you again, in hopes that I'm overcome with pity because of your injury . . ." Hester began.

"Perish the thought. No, I've finally learned my lesson." He lifted his hands. "It may take a decade, but even my thick skull will eventually yield."

"Good," said Hester, telling herself that she did not feel the tiniest stab of disappointment.

"Actually, it was about Cordelia."

"You can't possibly still mean to marry her."

"Heaven forfend! She's a child." He shook his head. "Actually, I was thinking about adopting her."

Hester blinked. Several times. "Adopt," she said.

"Well, her stepfather is bound to be distraught for some time, isn't he? As an old family friend, how could I fail to step in? And I do owe her a debt for saving my life from that mad horse that everyone saw rampaging about the place."

"I suppose that's true," said Hester.

"Of course, you'd hardly want a girl to grow up alone in a bachelor's house. She might learn all sorts of bad habits."

"That's *definitely* true."

"Do you know, I thought that her aunt might make a fine chaperone?" asked Richard musingly. "Assuming she'd be willing to relocate to Evermore House for a few years, of course."

Hester swallowed. Possibilities, sudden and glittering, opened up before her. A way, maybe, to be together, that didn't require her to give everything up.

Hester reached across the table and covered his hand with hers. "I think," she said carefully, "that that could be arranged."

"Who knows?" said Richard. "Perhaps by the time Cordelia's

ready to leave the nest, her aunt might not be thoroughly sick of me."

"Let's not get ahead of ourselves."

"Mmm. Would it be getting too ahead of ourselves for me to kiss the aunt in question, do you think?"

"Well," Hester said, "I think that could probably be arranged too."

The grave of Lady Evangeline Chatham was still raw earth, the headstone hastily erected at the top. The Squire had been unable to decide on garlands, angels, or flowers for the stone, and so had settled on all three, lending a decidedly baroque air to Cordelia's mother's final resting place. Cordelia barely gave it a second glance. She wore mourning black, but she knew who she was really in mourning for.

Her destination was deeper in the city cemetery, in an area less fashionable and thus less expensive. That was fine. Fashion was unimportant. What mattered, after all, was style.

One grave was older, the edges softened by grass. The headstone read simply "Silas Green—Husband" with two dates underneath. The newer one was very new, though in the same sleek, unornamented style. Moss had not yet gained a foothold on it, and the lines were sharply etched.

PENELOPE GREEN
"Tell Everyone I Said Goodbye"

Cordelia laid flowers at the foot of the stone. She was pleased to see that she wasn't the first person to do so. Someone had left a dozen red roses in a fan across the grave, and someone else, not to be outdone, had left a single white rose with a long poem attached to it.

She read the poem. It wasn't very good. *I suppose not much rhymes with Penelope, does it?*

She sat back on her heels and looked at the sky overhead. "I have no idea what I'm doing," she told Penelope. "Hester says she'll hire someone to teach me deportment if I want, but I don't have to. I think I might want to, if only so I'm not constantly worried that I'm doing something people will laugh at."

A cloud drifted overhead, white and puffy, the sort of cloud that no one paints in landscapes for fear of looking trite.

"Hester thinks we might be able to track down who my father was. I don't know if I want to know or not. Lord Evermore's settled some money on Ellen and her sister. I'm going to go see her next week. I don't know if I should tell her what really happened or not." She stared at the distant cloud. "I suppose I'll decide after we've talked. She might like to know it wasn't her father's fault. Or maybe she wouldn't believe any of it. I don't know what to do. I wish I could ask you for advice."

She already knew the answer, though. Cordelia got to her feet, dusting off her skirts. Penelope would tell her that whatever she did, she should do it with style.

"I'll try," she promised. She turned away and wound her way between the graves, to the high wrought-iron gates, where Hester and Lord Evermore were waiting.

Overhead, the cloud drifted on, brighter than any horse's white coat, and cast no shadows in the dazzling summer sky.

ACKNOWLEDGMENTS

Another book down, and another chance to thank all the people who make it possible who aren't me.

Thanks go first and foremost to my friend Deb, aka Sabrina Jeffries, who got me to read my first Regency romance novel, whereupon I became hooked and wound up writing . . . well, this isn't *technically* a Regency, but it's in the same ballpark, right? You should read her books. They have fewer reanimated dead horses.

The Ladies' Book of Etiquette and Manual of Politeness by Florence Hartley is a real book, published in 1860, and I have quoted from it with great abandon. Miss Hartley would doubtless find my personal manners appalling, but nevertheless, I am grateful for both the stuffiness of some of her opinions and the earnest desire for her readers to avoid embarrassment that shines through many of the chapters. "True politeness is the language of a good heart," she wrote, "and those possessing that heart will never, under any circumstances, be rude. They may not enter a crowded saloon gracefully; they may be entirely ignorant of the *forms* of good society; they may be awkward at table, ungrammatical in speech; but they will never be heard speaking so as to wound the feelings of another; they will never be seen making others uncomfortable by seeking solely for their own *personal* convenience; they will always endeavor to set every one around them at ease; they will be self-sacrificing, friendly, unselfish; truly in word and deed, *polite*." I genuinely think she believed what she wrote, and I am grateful to her, even if I have used her words for comic relief more often than not.

Huge thanks, as always, to my editor Lindsey and the crew at Tor for handling all the nitty-gritty bits of publishing while I sit in a room and type. Thanks to my agent, Helen, who makes sure that food gets shoved under the door while I'm typing, and to my husband, Kevin, who opens said door occasionally and waits patiently while I hiss like Gollum and rail against the sun. (This is normal author behavior.)

Finally, for all the people who, by this point in my career, have asked, "What is your whole thing with horses, anyway?" I must say that A) I'm embarrassed that you noticed and B) there was an Incident when I was about twelve years old. I had only ever ridden Girl Scout trail horses and the son of a family friend put me on a horse, on a saddle pad, with a rope bridle and no bit. He doubtless thought this was easy beginner stuff, but he also happened to be an ex-jockey. The horse realized quickly that I had no idea what I was doing, took off at a run (I had never been on a running horse before), the saddle pad slid sideways with me on it, I lost the reins, grabbed the horse's neck, looked up, and saw a rather large tree trunk heading toward my head. That I am typing this is proof that my reflexes are much smarter than I am, because I let go a second or two before the traumatic brain injury with my name on it. I hit the ground, rolled, looked up, and saw the underside of the jockey's horse, who was politely rearing to avoid trampling me. That is not an angle one generally wishes to view a horse from, though it's actually the approaching tree trunk that is really seared into my memory.

(I did, in fact, get back on the horse, but it took forty-five minutes to find a mounting block to do so, because of the lack of stirrups. Also I was sore the next day in a way that, at twelve, I had never experienced in my entire life.)

Years later, I mentioned this story in passing to a professional equestrian person, who was profoundly appalled and uttered a lot of words like "criminal negligence" and "what's his name, I just wanna talk," which did much to soothe my battered soul, since I had spent the intervening thirty-odd years thinking I was just really bad at being on horses. In the meantime, though, I'd written a number of books where riding a horse is hard and painful and causes you to fall off, culminating at last in this one, where riding a horse is hard and painful and also the horse has no head and also it isn't really a horse.

. . . It's possible I'm working through some trauma here. And also I accept that it's misplaced and I should be blaming the guy who put me on the horse. (But in my defense, *A Sorceress Comes to Call* would have been a very different book if Falada was shaped like a weird unshaved former jockey, so I think we gotta accept that one in the name of art.)

Anyway, I promise to try to write a book in the near future where the horse is pleasant and not attempting to murder anyone. Probably. Thanks for bearing with me.

T. Kingfisher
North Carolina, 2023

ABOUT THE AUTHOR

J.R. Blackwell

T. KINGFISHER writes fantasy, horror, and occasional oddities, including *Nettle & Bone, Thornhedge, What Moves the Dead,* and *A House With Good Bones.* Under a pen name, she also writes best-selling children's books. She lives in North Carolina with her husband, cats, and absolutely no horses.